Uncorrected Proof

HEART

TAKES THE STAGE

HEART
TAKES THE STAGE

A HEART OF THE CITY
COLLECTION

BY STEENZ

Andrews McMeel
PUBLISHING®

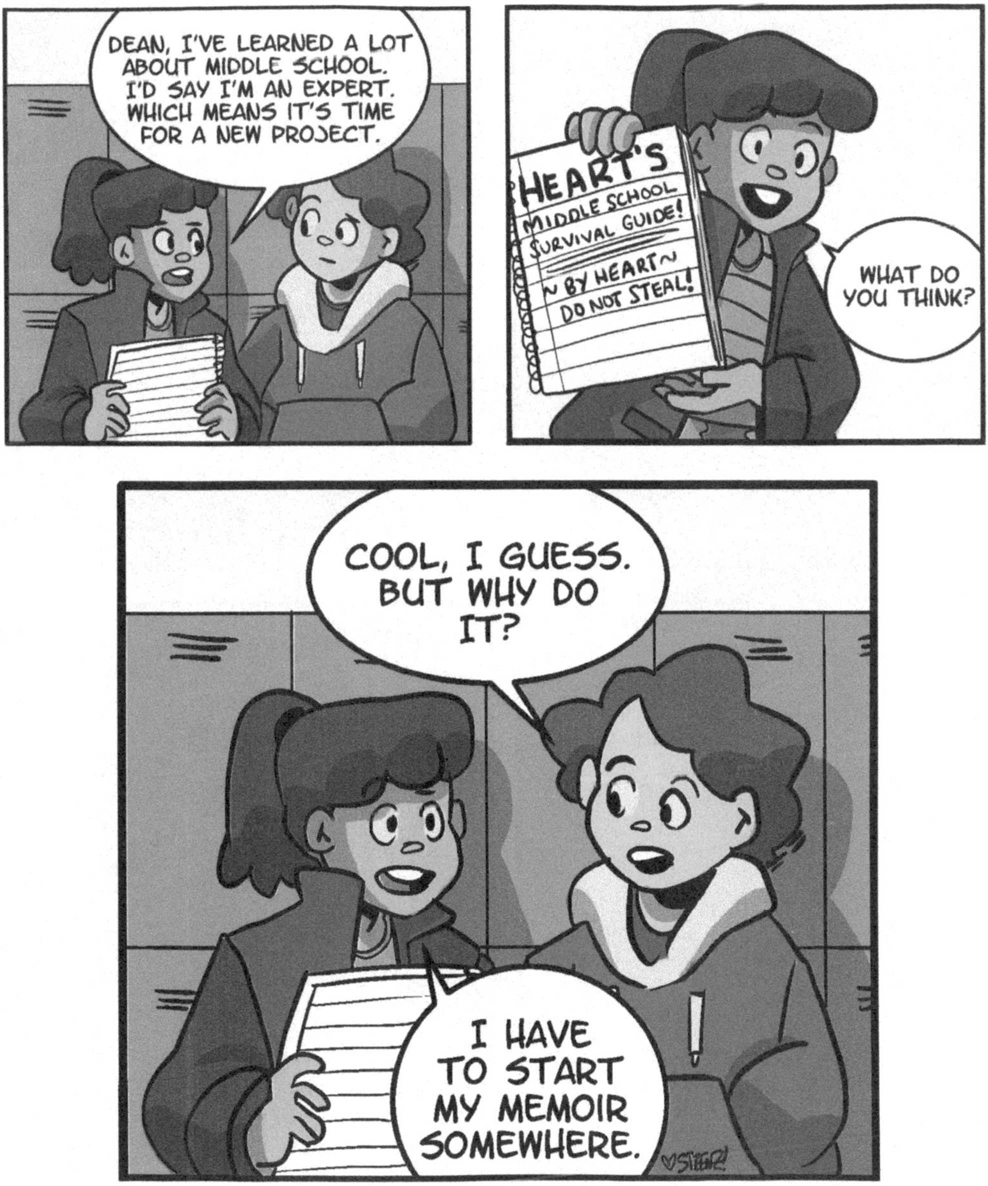
DEAN, I'VE LEARNED A LOT ABOUT MIDDLE SCHOOL. I'D SAY I'M AN EXPERT. WHICH MEANS IT'S TIME FOR A NEW PROJECT.
HEART'S MIDDLE SCHOOL SURVIVAL GUIDE! ~BY HEART~ DO NOT STEAL!
WHAT DO YOU THINK?
COOL, I GUESS. BUT WHY DO IT?
I HAVE TO START MY MEMOIR SOMEWHERE.
STEGER!

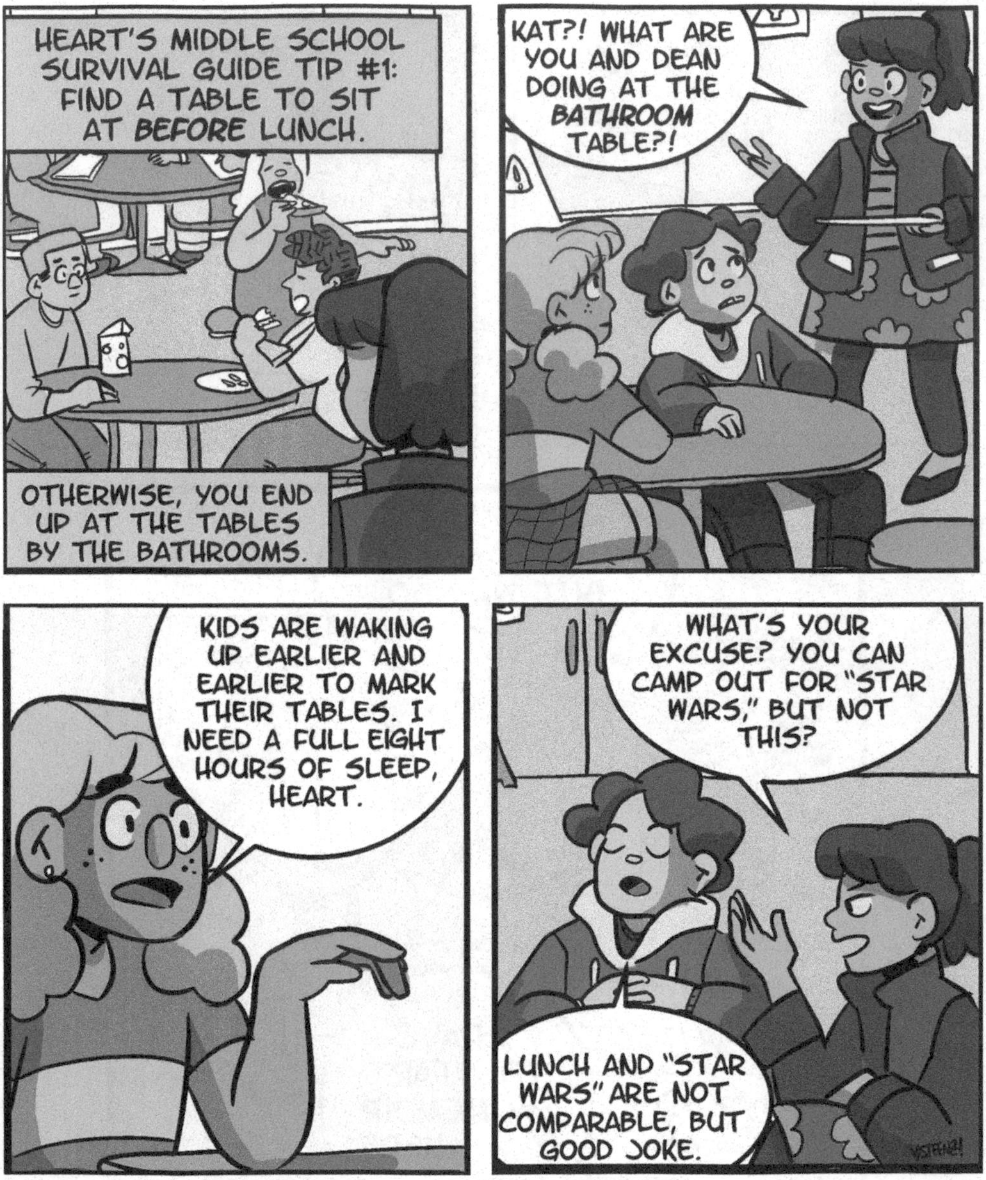
HEART'S MIDDLE SCHOOL SURVIVAL GUIDE TIP #1: FIND A TABLE TO SIT AT BEFORE LUNCH.
OTHERWISE, YOU END UP AT THE TABLES BY THE BATHROOMS.
KAT?! WHAT ARE YOU AND DEAN DOING AT THE BATHROOM TABLE?!
KIDS ARE WAKING UP EARLIER AND EARLIER TO MARK THEIR TABLES. I NEED A FULL EIGHT HOURS OF SLEEP, HEART.
WHAT'S YOUR EXCUSE? YOU CAN CAMP OUT FOR "STAR WARS," BUT NOT THIS?
LUNCH AND "STAR WARS" ARE NOT COMPARABLE, BUT GOOD JOKE.

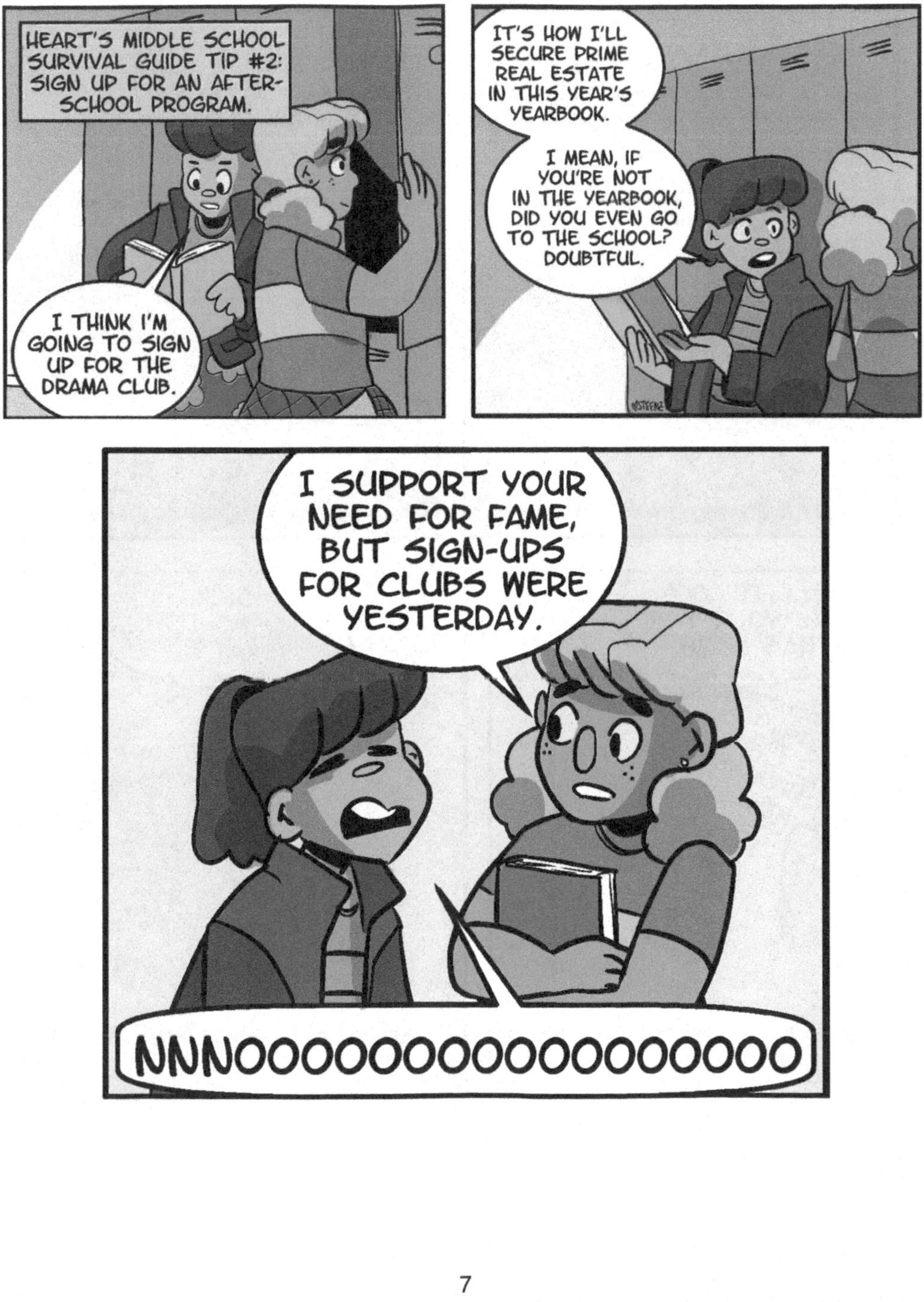
HEART'S MIDDLE SCHOOL SURVIVAL GUIDE TIP #2: SIGN UP FOR AN AFTER-SCHOOL PROGRAM.
I THINK I'M GOING TO SIGN UP FOR THE DRAMA CLUB.
IT'S HOW I'LL SECURE PRIME REAL ESTATE IN THIS YEAR'S YEARBOOK.
I MEAN, IF YOU'RE NOT IN THE YEARBOOK, DID YOU EVEN GO TO THE SCHOOL? DOUBTFUL.
I SUPPORT YOUR NEED FOR FAME, BUT SIGN-UPS FOR CLUBS WERE YESTERDAY.
NNNOOOOOOOOOOOOOOOOOOOO

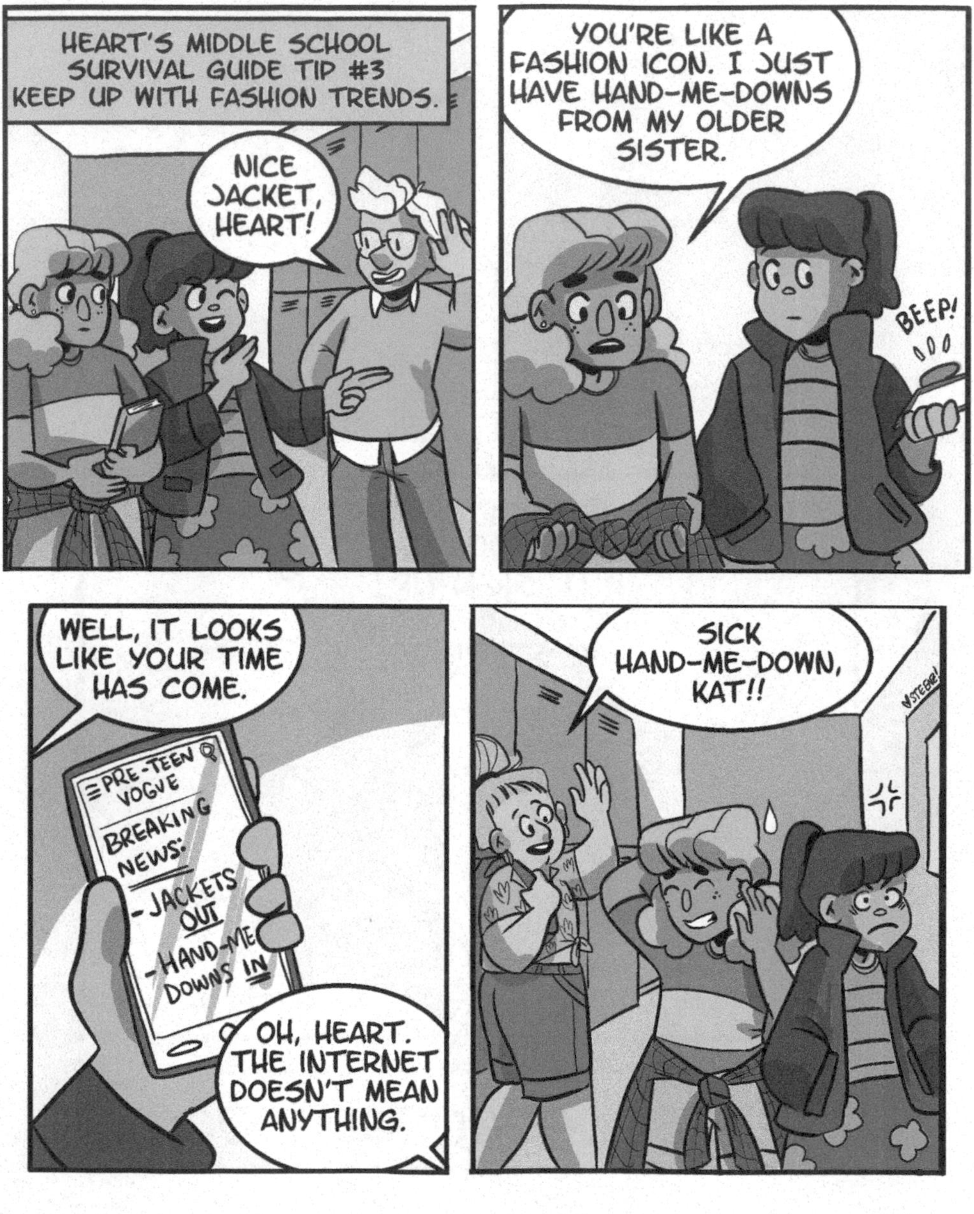
HEART'S MIDDLE SCHOOL SURVIVAL GUIDE TIP #3 KEEP UP WITH FASHION TRENDS.
NICE JACKET, HEART!
YOU'RE LIKE A FASHION ICON. I JUST HAVE HAND-ME-DOWNS FROM MY OLDER SISTER.
BEEP!
WELL, IT LOOKS LIKE YOUR TIME HAS COME.
PRE-TEEN VOGUE
BREAKING NEWS:
- JACKETS OUT
- HAND-ME-DOWNS IN
OH, HEART. THE INTERNET DOESN'T MEAN ANYTHING.
SICK HAND-ME-DOWN, KAT!!

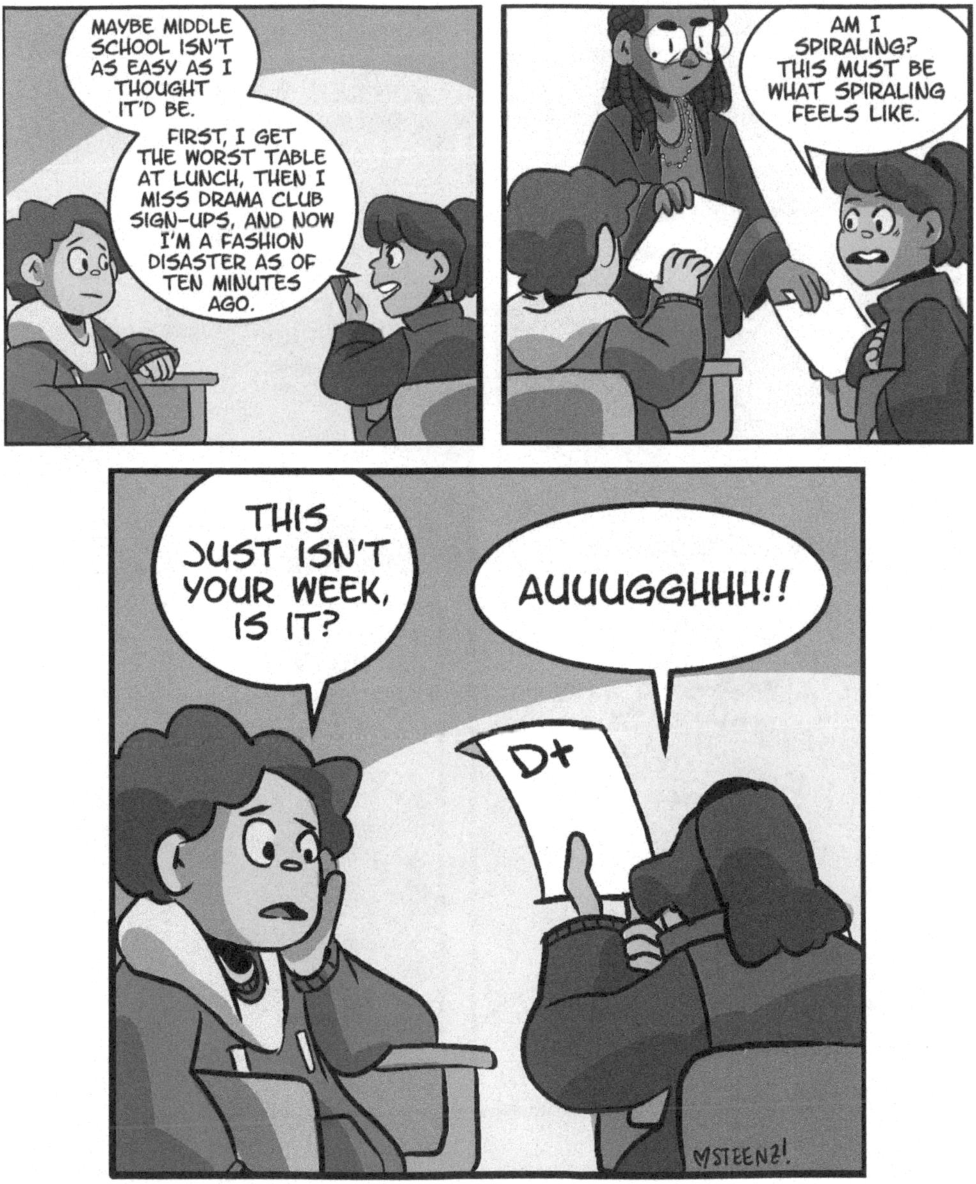
MAYBE MIDDLE SCHOOL ISN'T AS EASY AS I THOUGHT IT'D BE.
FIRST, I GET THE WORST TABLE AT LUNCH, THEN I MISS DRAMA CLUB SIGN-UPS, AND NOW I'M A FASHION DISASTER AS OF TEN MINUTES AGO.
AM I SPIRALING? THIS MUST BE WHAT SPIRALING FEELS LIKE.
THIS JUST ISN'T YOUR WEEK, IS IT?
AUUUGGHHH!!
D+
STEENZ!

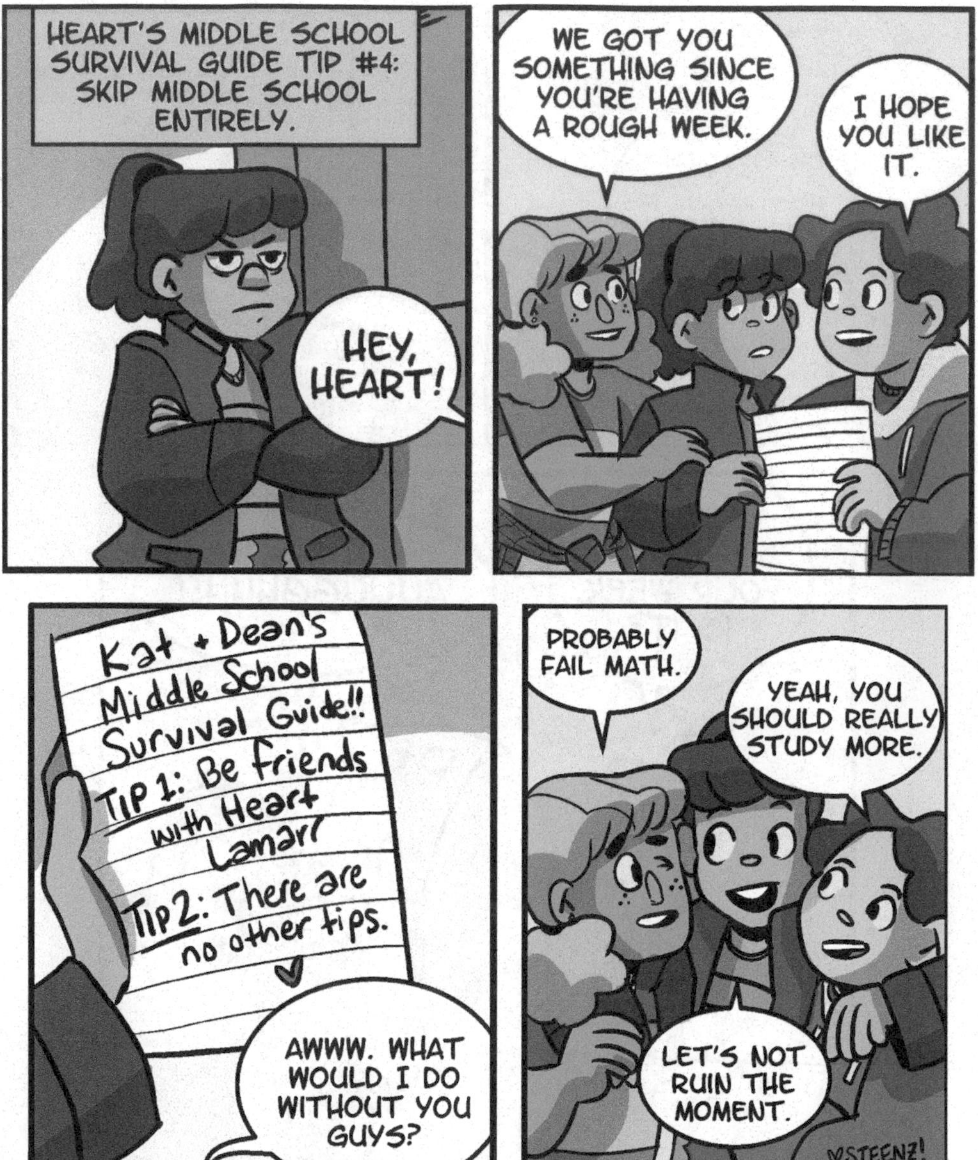
HEART'S MIDDLE SCHOOL SURVIVAL GUIDE TIP #4: SKIP MIDDLE SCHOOL ENTIRELY.
HEY, HEART!
WE GOT YOU SOMETHING SINCE YOU'RE HAVING A ROUGH WEEK.
I HOPE YOU LIKE IT.
Kat + Dean's Middle School Survival Guide!!
Tip 1: Be friends with Heart Lamarr
Tip 2: There are no other tips.
AWWW. WHAT WOULD I DO WITHOUT YOU GUYS?
PROBABLY FAIL MATH.
YEAH, YOU SHOULD REALLY STUDY MORE.
LET'S NOT RUIN THE MOMENT.
♥STEENZ!

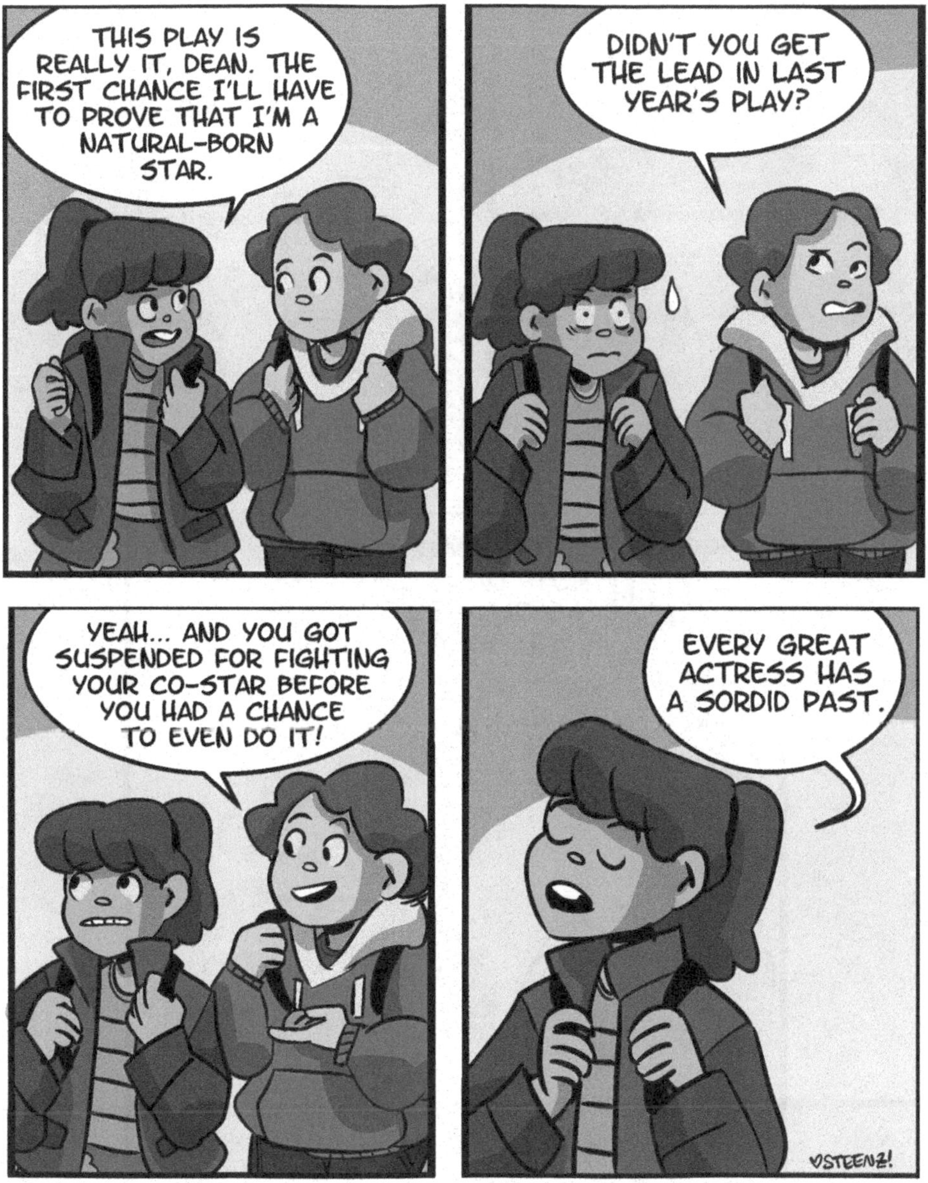
THIS PLAY IS REALLY IT, DEAN. THE FIRST CHANCE I'LL HAVE TO PROVE THAT I'M A NATURAL-BORN STAR.
DIDN'T YOU GET THE LEAD IN LAST YEAR'S PLAY?
YEAH... AND YOU GOT SUSPENDED FOR FIGHTING YOUR CO-STAR BEFORE YOU HAD A CHANCE TO EVEN DO IT!
EVERY GREAT ACTRESS HAS A SORDID PAST.
♡STEENZ!

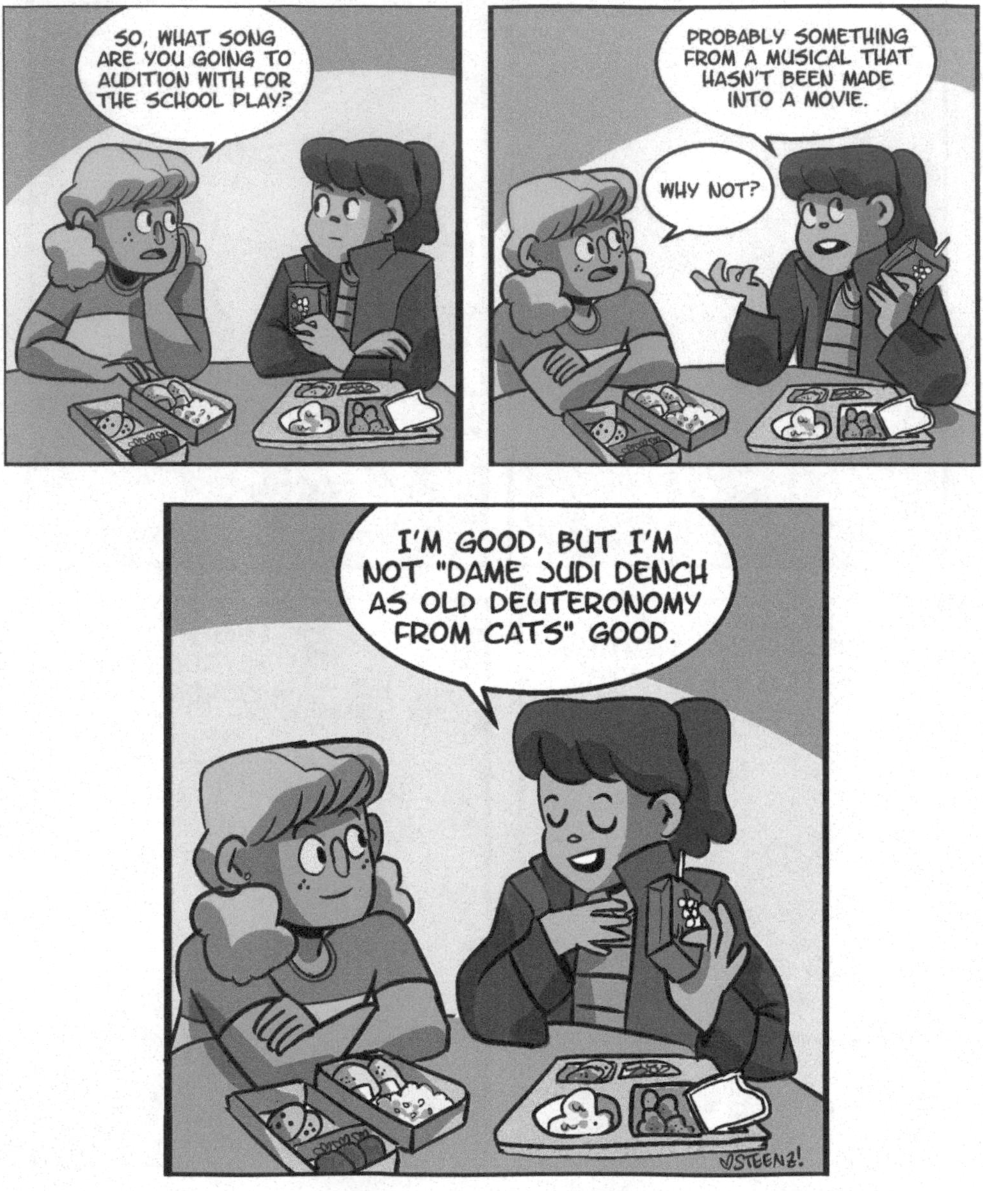
SO, WHAT SONG ARE YOU GOING TO AUDITION WITH FOR THE SCHOOL PLAY?
PROBABLY SOMETHING FROM A MUSICAL THAT HASN'T BEEN MADE INTO A MOVIE.
WHY NOT?
I'M GOOD, BUT I'M NOT "DAME JUDI DENCH AS OLD DEUTERONOMY FROM CATS" GOOD.
STEENZ!

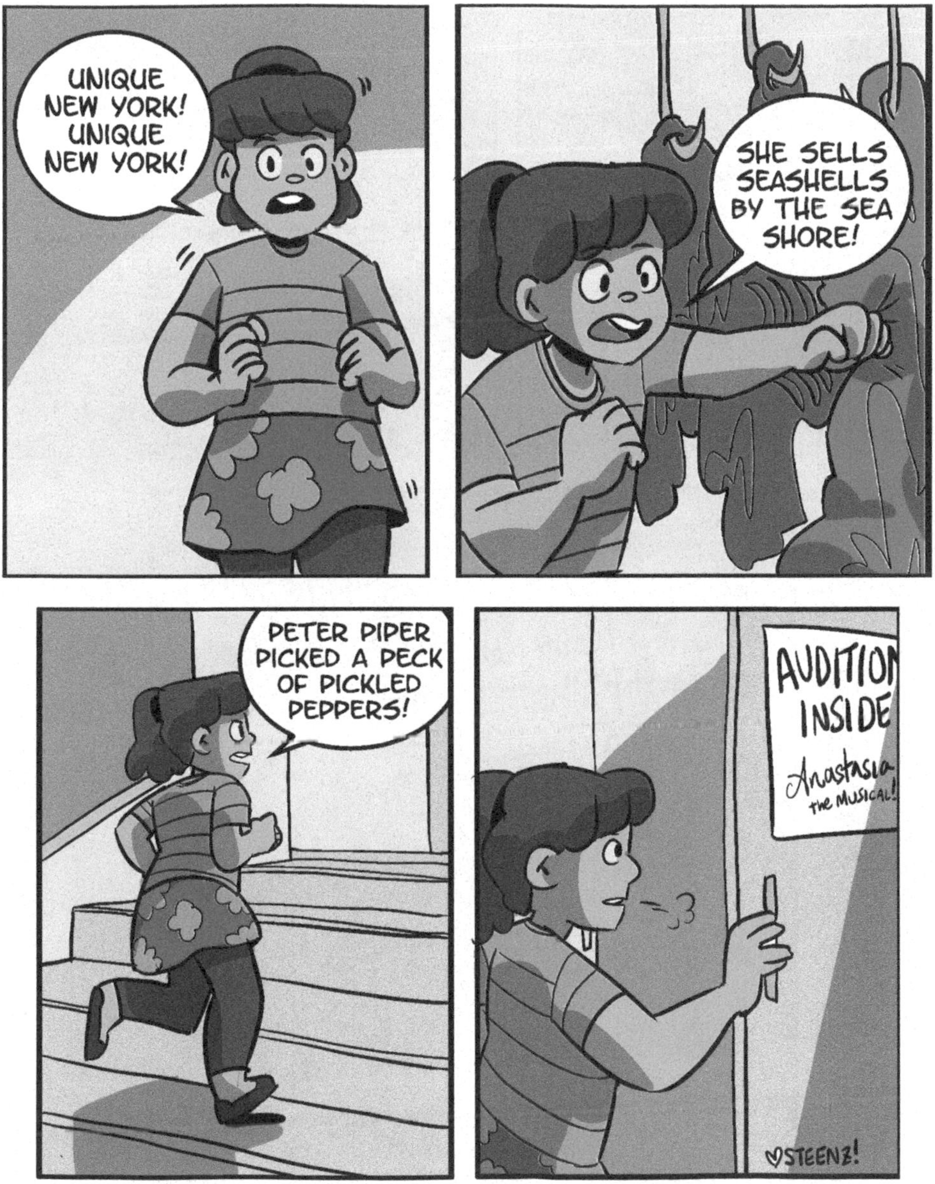
UNIQUE NEW YORK! UNIQUE NEW YORK!
SHE SELLS SEASHELLS BY THE SEA SHORE!
PETER PIPER PICKED A PECK OF PICKLED PEPPERS!
AUDITION INSIDE
Anastasia the MUSICAL!
STEENZ!

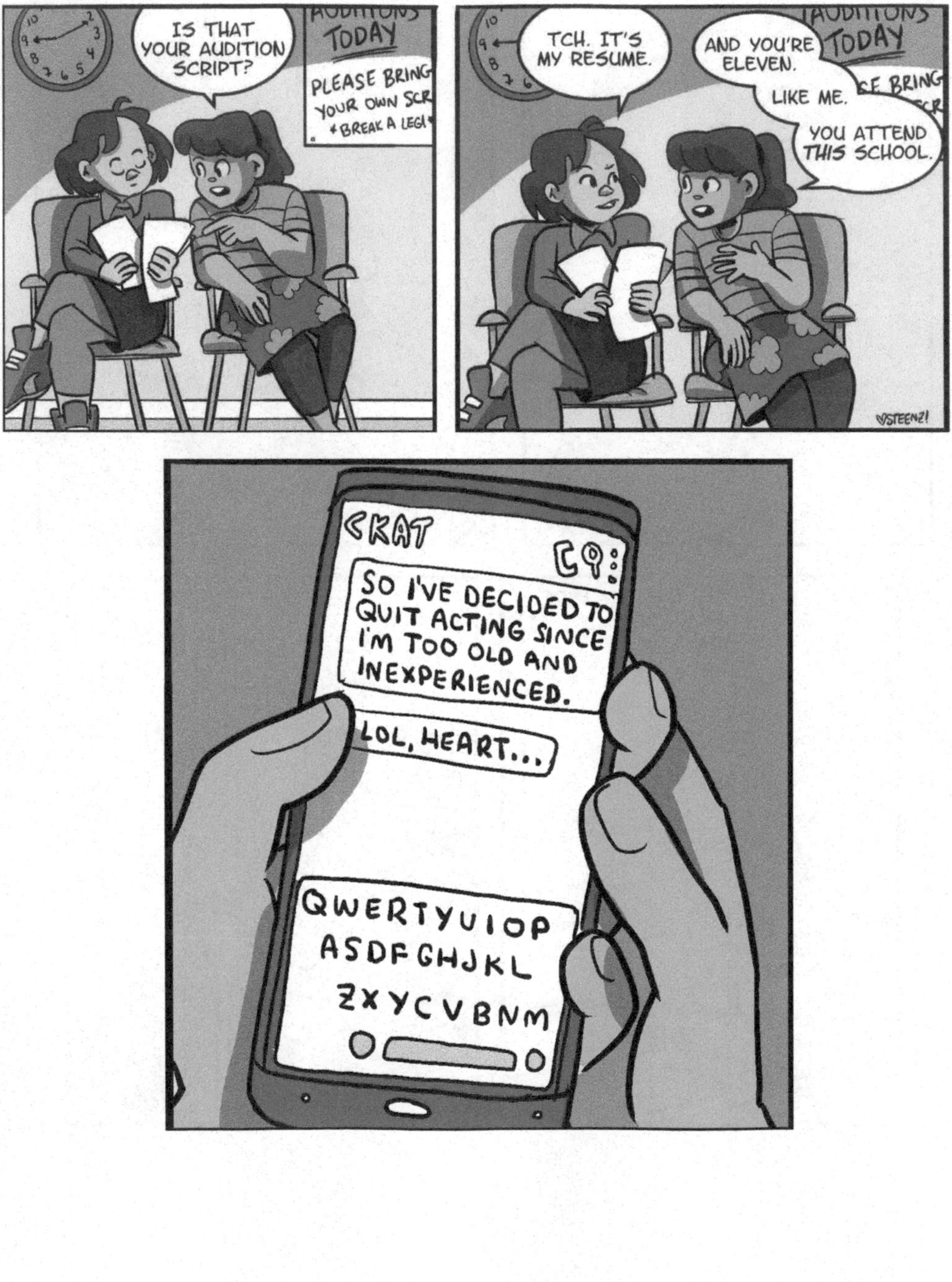
IS THAT YOUR AUDITION SCRIPT?
TODAY
PLEASE BRING
YOUR OWN SCR
BREAK A LEG!
TCH. IT'S MY RESUME.
AND YOU'RE ELEVEN.
LIKE ME.
YOU ATTEND *THIS* SCHOOL.
TODAY
STEENZ!
<KAT
SO I'VE DECIDED TO QUIT ACTING SINCE I'M TOO OLD AND INEXPERIENCED.
LOL, HEART...
QWERTYUIOP
ASDFGHJKL
ZXYCVBNM

THE PERFECT ACCEPTANCE SPEECH. I CAN TOTALLY FIT THIS IN UNDER 45 SECONDS.
STEENZ!

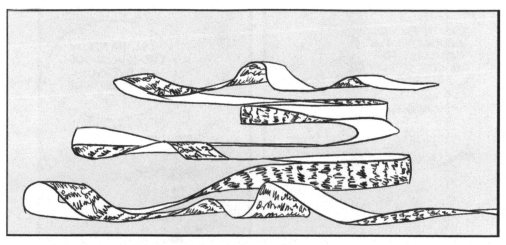

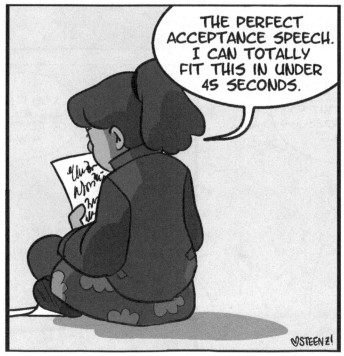

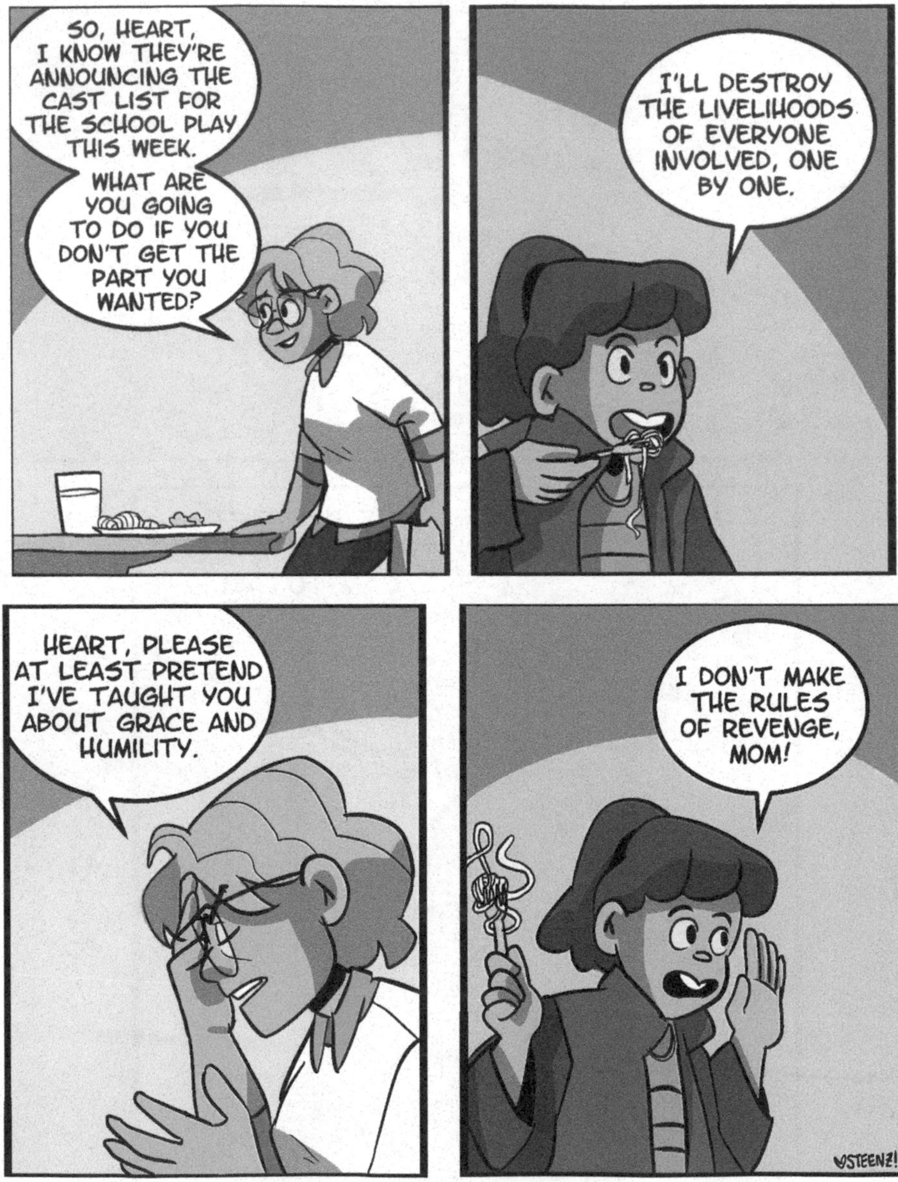
SO, HEART, I KNOW THEY'RE ANNOUNCING THE CAST LIST FOR THE SCHOOL PLAY THIS WEEK.
WHAT ARE YOU GOING TO DO IF YOU DON'T GET THE PART YOU WANTED?
I'LL DESTROY THE LIVELIHOODS OF EVERYONE INVOLVED, ONE BY ONE.
HEART, PLEASE AT LEAST PRETEND I'VE TAUGHT YOU ABOUT GRACE AND HUMILITY.
I DON'T MAKE THE RULES OF REVENGE, MOM!
STEENZ!

I HOPE HEART GOT A GOOD PART IN THE PLAY.
I HOPE SHE GETS THE PART OF A TREE.
I CAN'T HANDLE HER EGO IF SHE GETS A PART WITH LINES.
H-HEY HEART... HOW'D IT GO?
I GOT THE LEAD.
HA HA!
I BET YOU THOUGHT I DIDN'T GET THE PART. IT'S CALLED *ACTING.*
STEENZ!

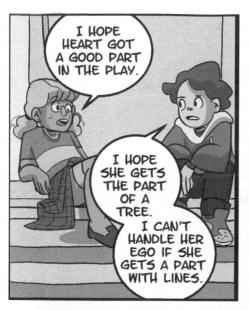

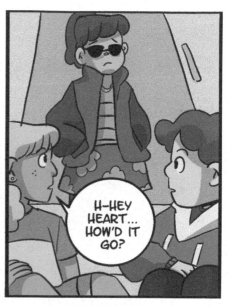

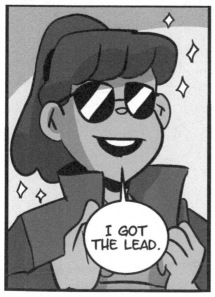

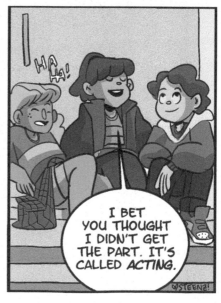

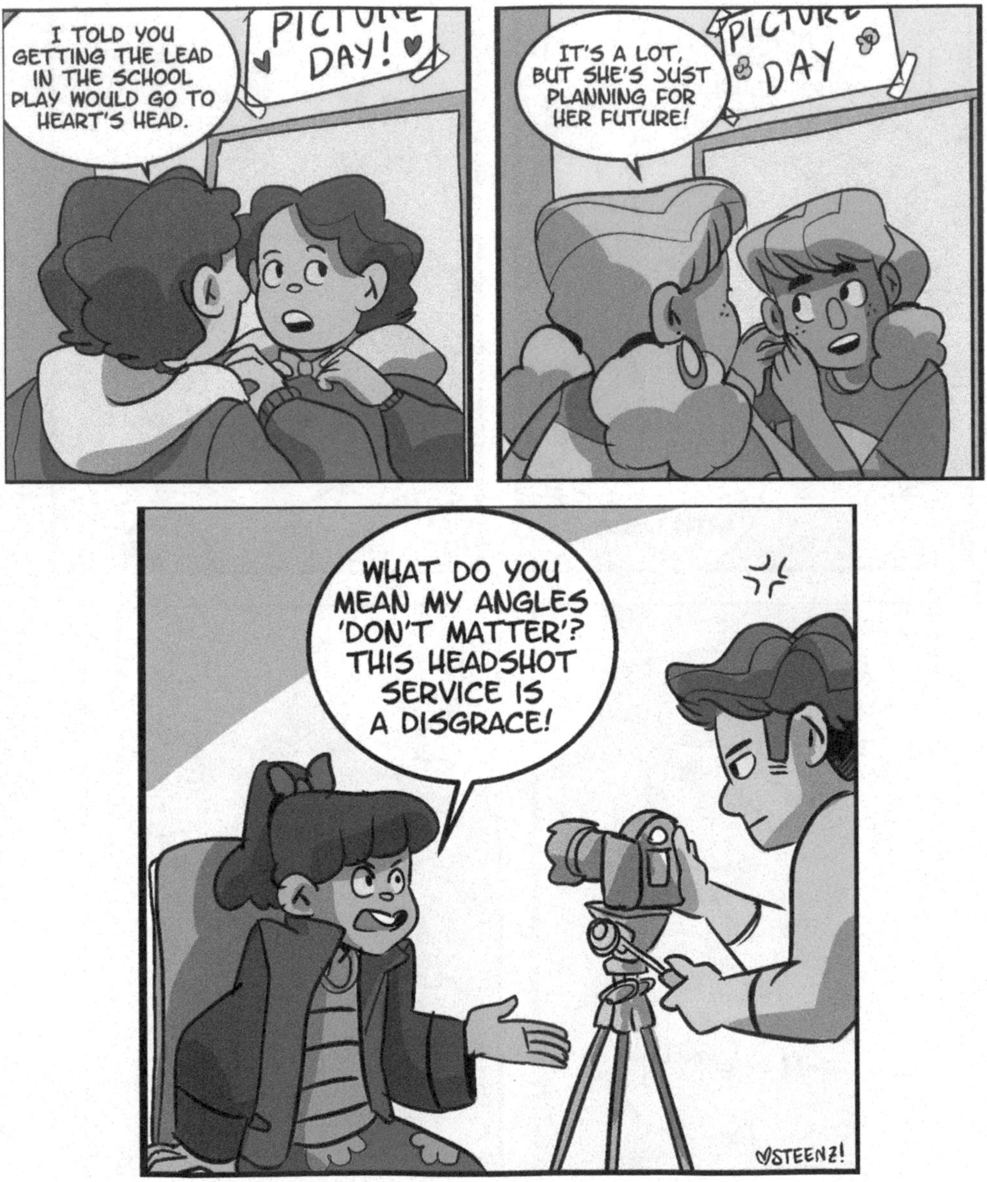
I TOLD YOU GETTING THE LEAD IN THE SCHOOL PLAY WOULD GO TO HEART'S HEAD.
PICTURE DAY!
IT'S A LOT, BUT SHE'S JUST PLANNING FOR HER FUTURE!
PICTURE DAY
WHAT DO YOU MEAN MY ANGLES 'DON'T MATTER'? THIS HEADSHOT SERVICE IS A DISGRACE!
STEENZ!

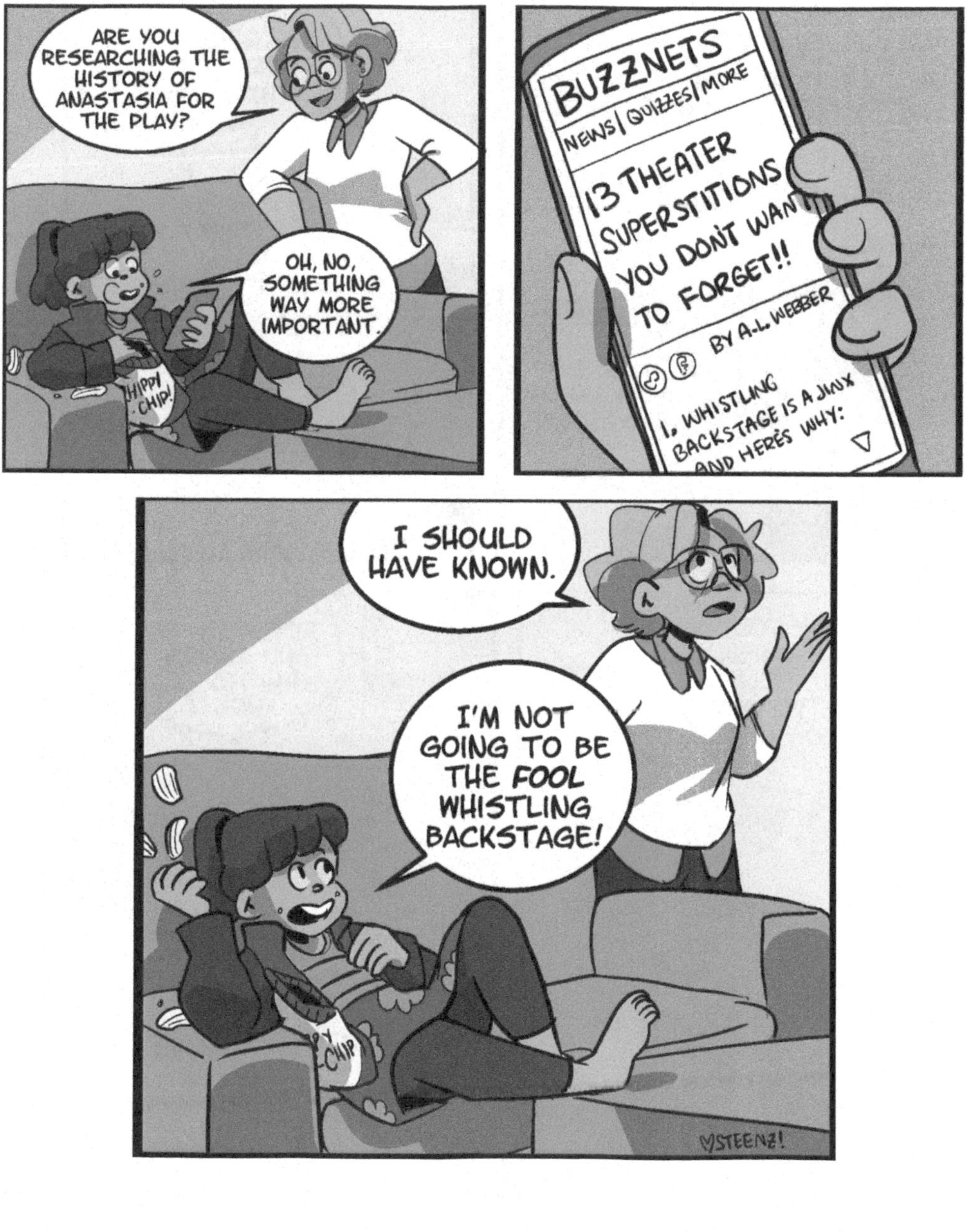
ARE YOU RESEARCHING THE HISTORY OF ANASTASIA FOR THE PLAY?
OH, NO, SOMETHING WAY MORE IMPORTANT.
HIPPY CHIP!
BUZZNETS
NEWS | QUIZZES | MORE
13 THEATER SUPERSTITIONS YOU DON'T WANT TO FORGET!!
BY A.L. WEBBER
1. WHISTLING BACKSTAGE IS A JINX AND HERE'S WHY:
I SHOULD HAVE KNOWN.
I'M NOT GOING TO BE THE FOOL WHISTLING BACKSTAGE!
STEENZ!

DID YOU WANT TO COME OVER AFTER SCHOOL TODAY?
NAH, I'M WORKING ON PLAY STUFF.
BUT REHEARSALS DON'T START UNTIL NEXT WEEK!
THE THEATER IS LIKE A NEW FRIEND, DEAN. I HAVE TO GET TO KNOW HER!
IT'S A STAGE AND CHAIRS! WHAT'S TO KNOW?!

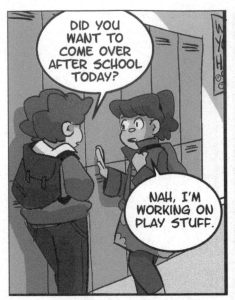

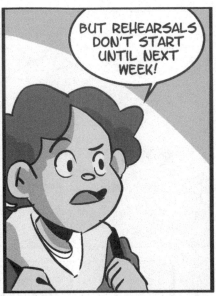

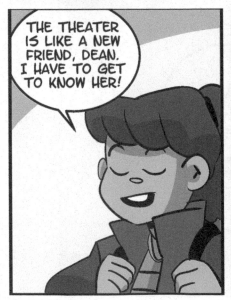

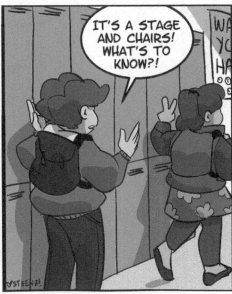

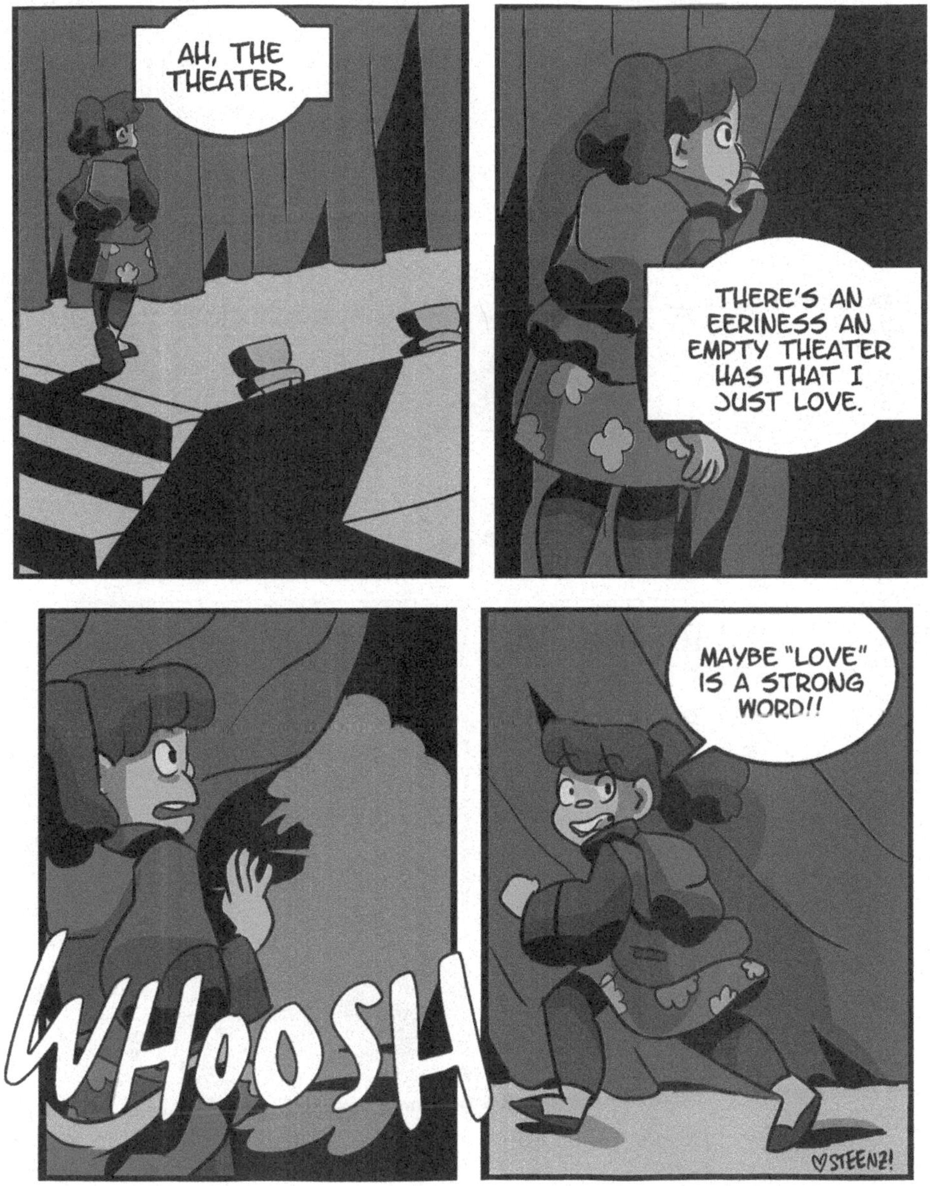
AH, THE THEATER.
THERE'S AN EERINESS AN EMPTY THEATER HAS THAT I JUST LOVE.
WHOOSH
MAYBE "LOVE" IS A STRONG WORD!!
STEENZ!

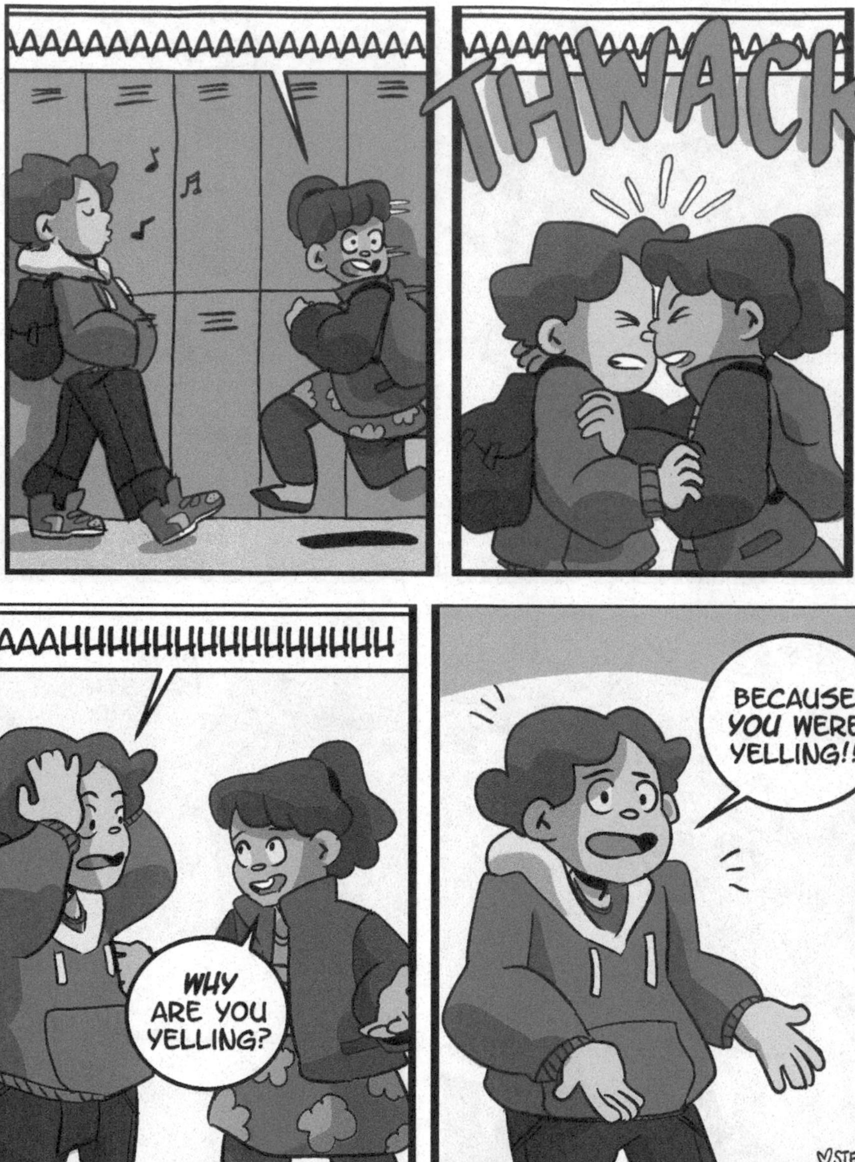
AAAAAAAAAAAAAAAAAAAAAAAA
AAAA
THWACK
AAAAAHHHHHHHHHHHHHHHHH
WHY ARE YOU YELLING?
BECAUSE YOU WERE YELLING!!
STEENZ!

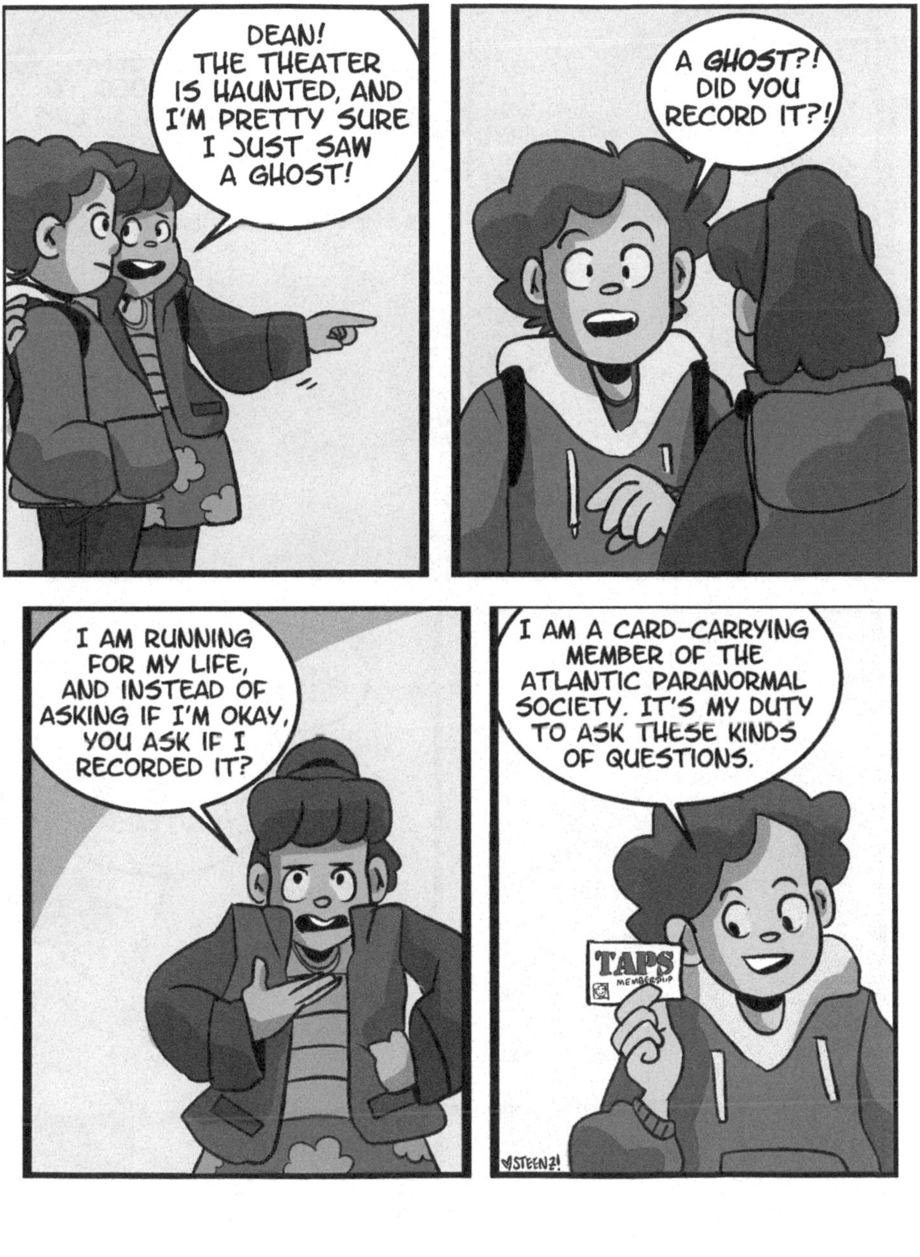
DEAN! THE THEATER IS HAUNTED, AND I'M PRETTY SURE I JUST SAW A GHOST!
A GHOST?! DID YOU RECORD IT?!
I AM RUNNING FOR MY LIFE, AND INSTEAD OF ASKING IF I'M OKAY, YOU ASK IF I RECORDED IT?
I AM A CARD-CARRYING MEMBER OF THE ATLANTIC PARANORMAL SOCIETY. IT'S MY DUTY TO ASK THESE KINDS OF QUESTIONS.
TAPS
MEMBERSHIP
STEENZ!

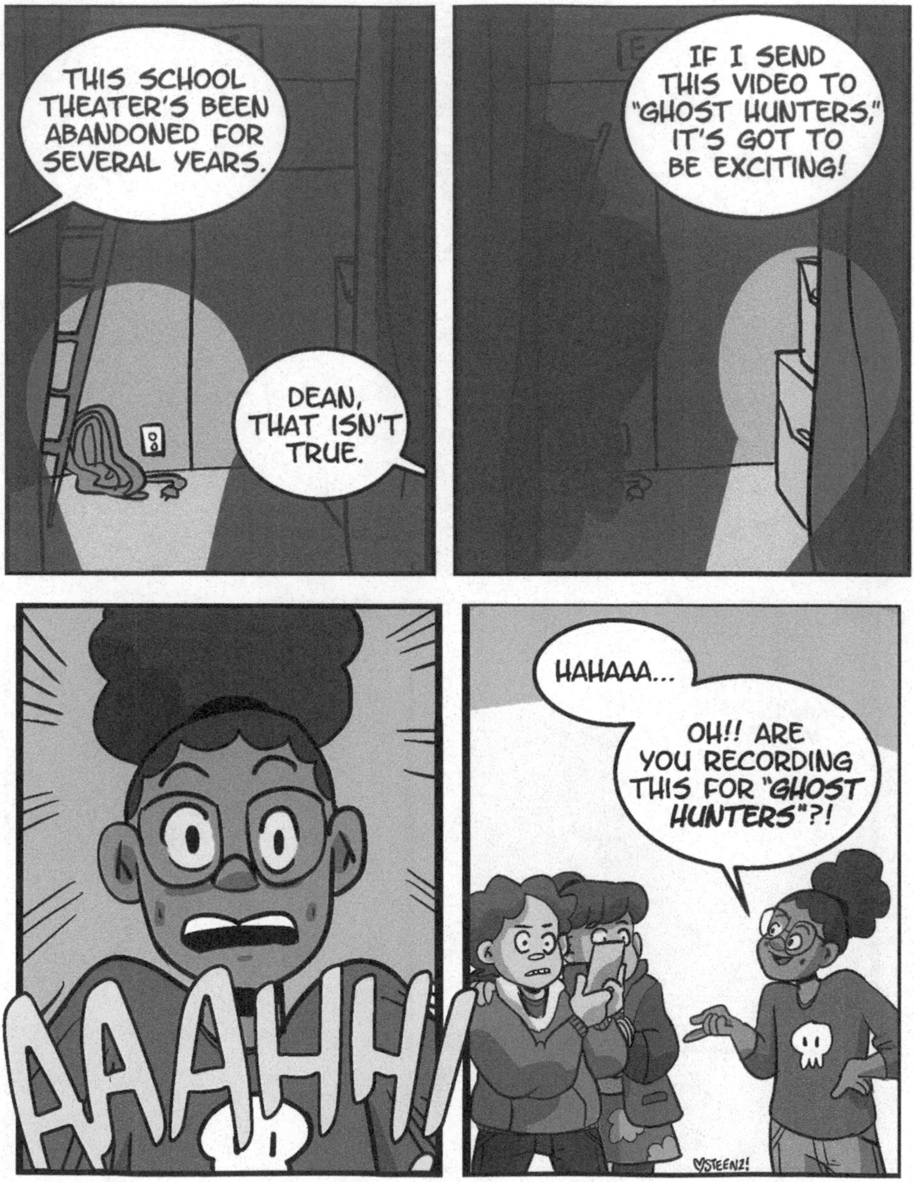
THIS SCHOOL THEATER'S BEEN ABANDONED FOR SEVERAL YEARS.
DEAN, THAT ISN'T TRUE.
IF I SEND THIS VIDEO TO "GHOST HUNTERS," IT'S GOT TO BE EXCITING!
AAAHH!
HAHAAA...
OH!! ARE YOU RECORDING THIS FOR "GHOST HUNTERS"?!
STEENZ!

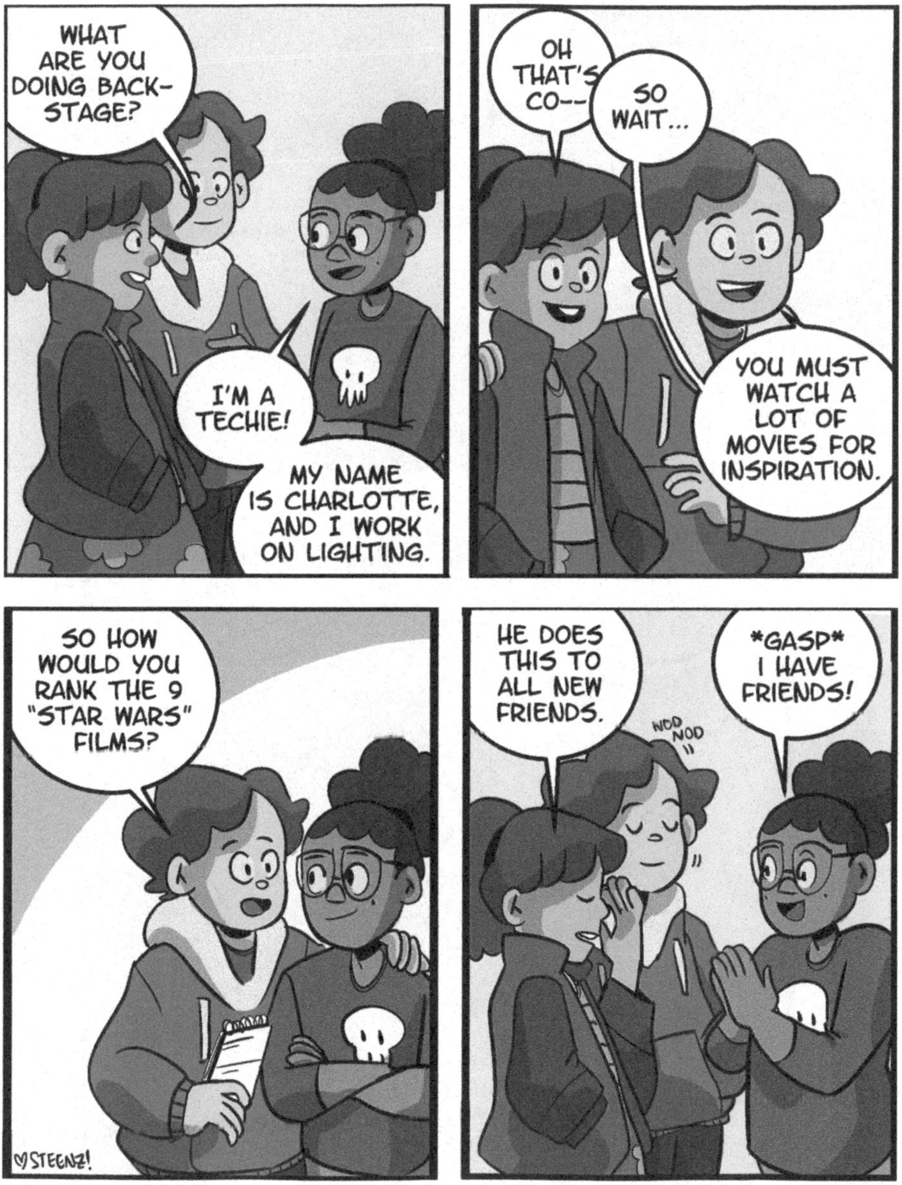
WHAT ARE YOU DOING BACK-STAGE?
I'M A TECHIE!
MY NAME IS CHARLOTTE, AND I WORK ON LIGHTING.
OH THAT'S CO--
SO WAIT...
YOU MUST WATCH A LOT OF MOVIES FOR INSPIRATION.
SO HOW WOULD YOU RANK THE 9 "STAR WARS" FILMS?
STEENZ!
HE DOES THIS TO ALL NEW FRIENDS.
NOD NOD
GASP I HAVE FRIENDS!

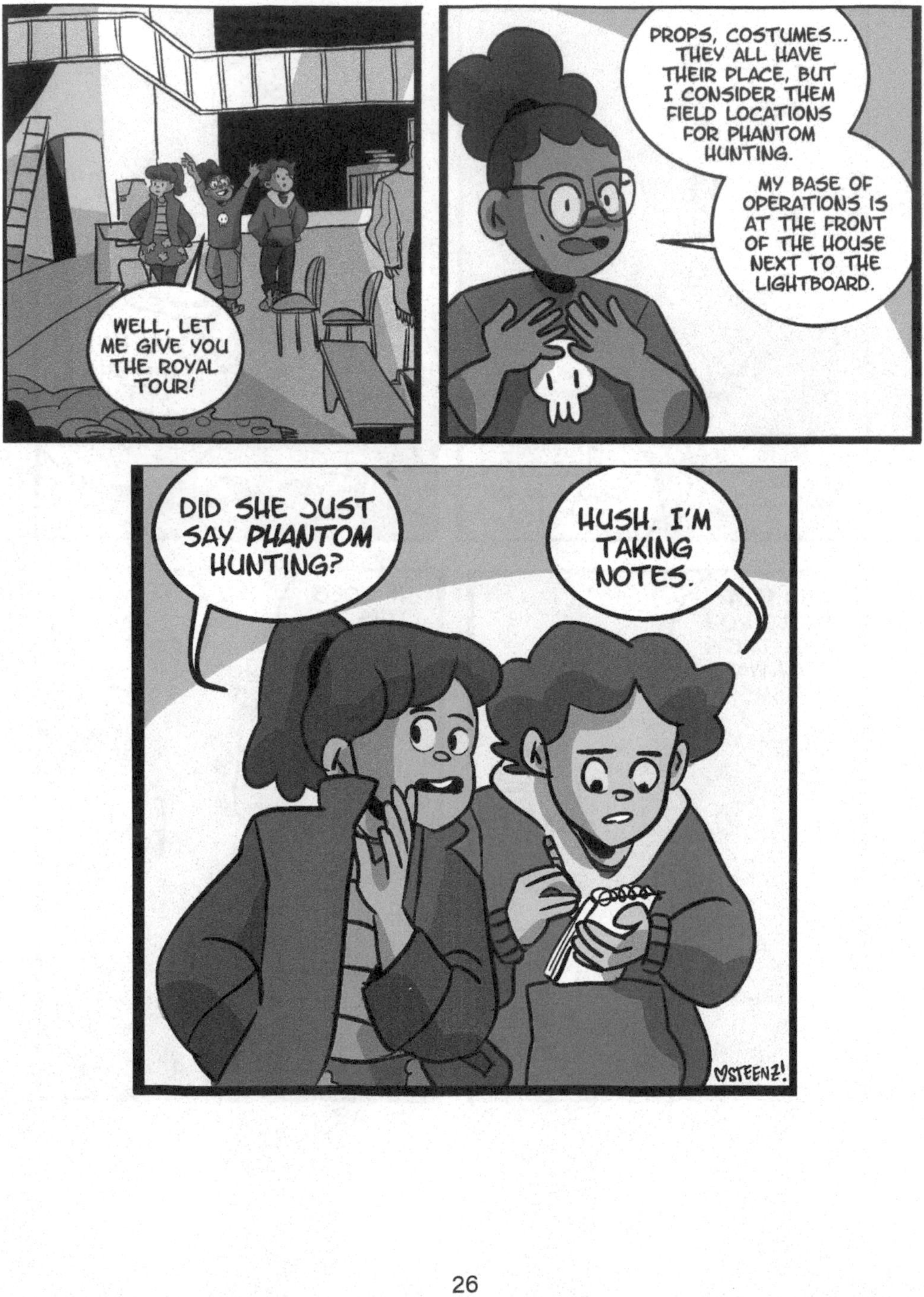
WELL, LET ME GIVE YOU THE ROYAL TOUR!
PROPS, COSTUMES... THEY ALL HAVE THEIR PLACE, BUT I CONSIDER THEM FIELD LOCATIONS FOR PHANTOM HUNTING.
MY BASE OF OPERATIONS IS AT THE FRONT OF THE HOUSE NEXT TO THE LIGHTBOARD.
DID SHE JUST SAY *PHANTOM* HUNTING?
HUSH. I'M TAKING NOTES.
♡STEENZ!

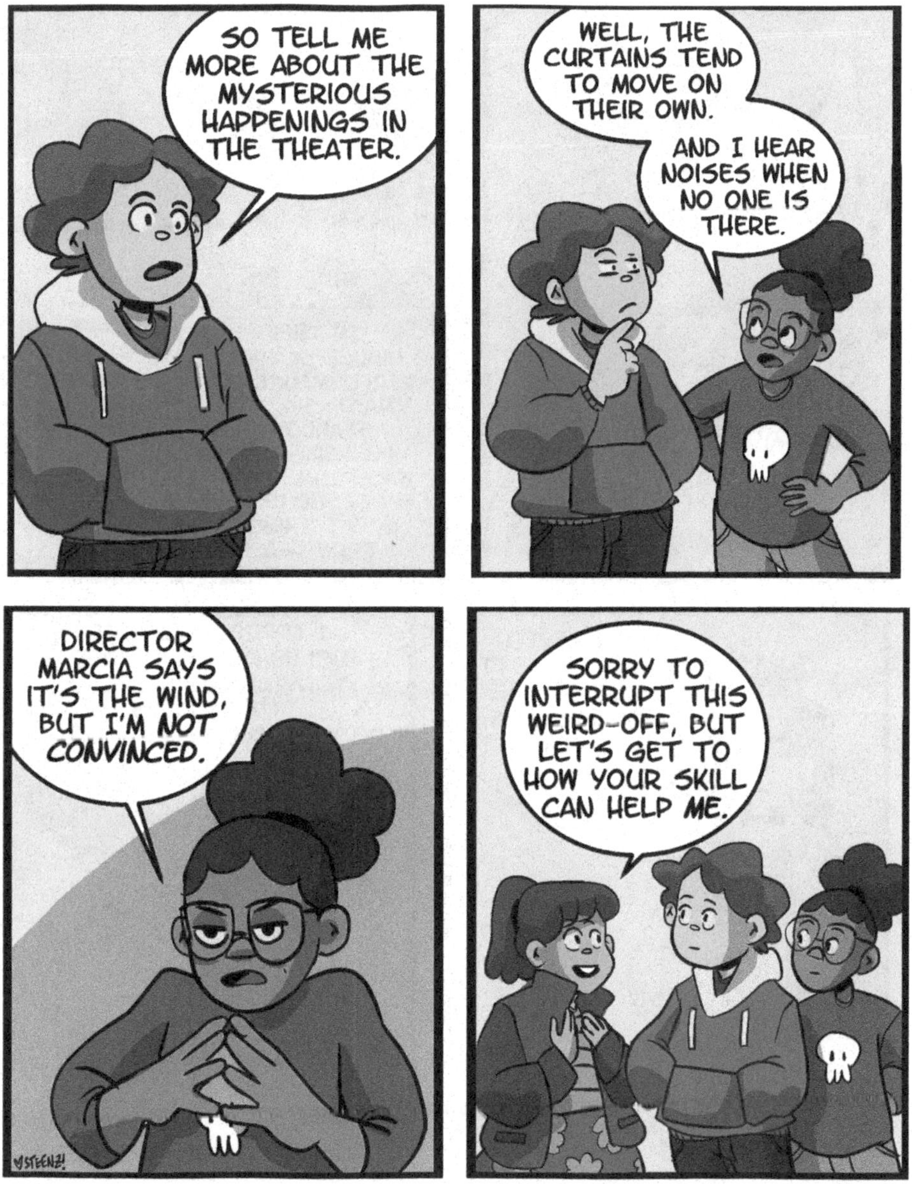
SO TELL ME MORE ABOUT THE MYSTERIOUS HAPPENINGS IN THE THEATER.
WELL, THE CURTAINS TEND TO MOVE ON THEIR OWN.
AND I HEAR NOISES WHEN NO ONE IS THERE.
DIRECTOR MARCIA SAYS IT'S THE WIND, BUT I'M NOT CONVINCED.
STEENZ!
SORRY TO INTERRUPT THIS WEIRD-OFF, BUT LET'S GET TO HOW YOUR SKILL CAN HELP ME.

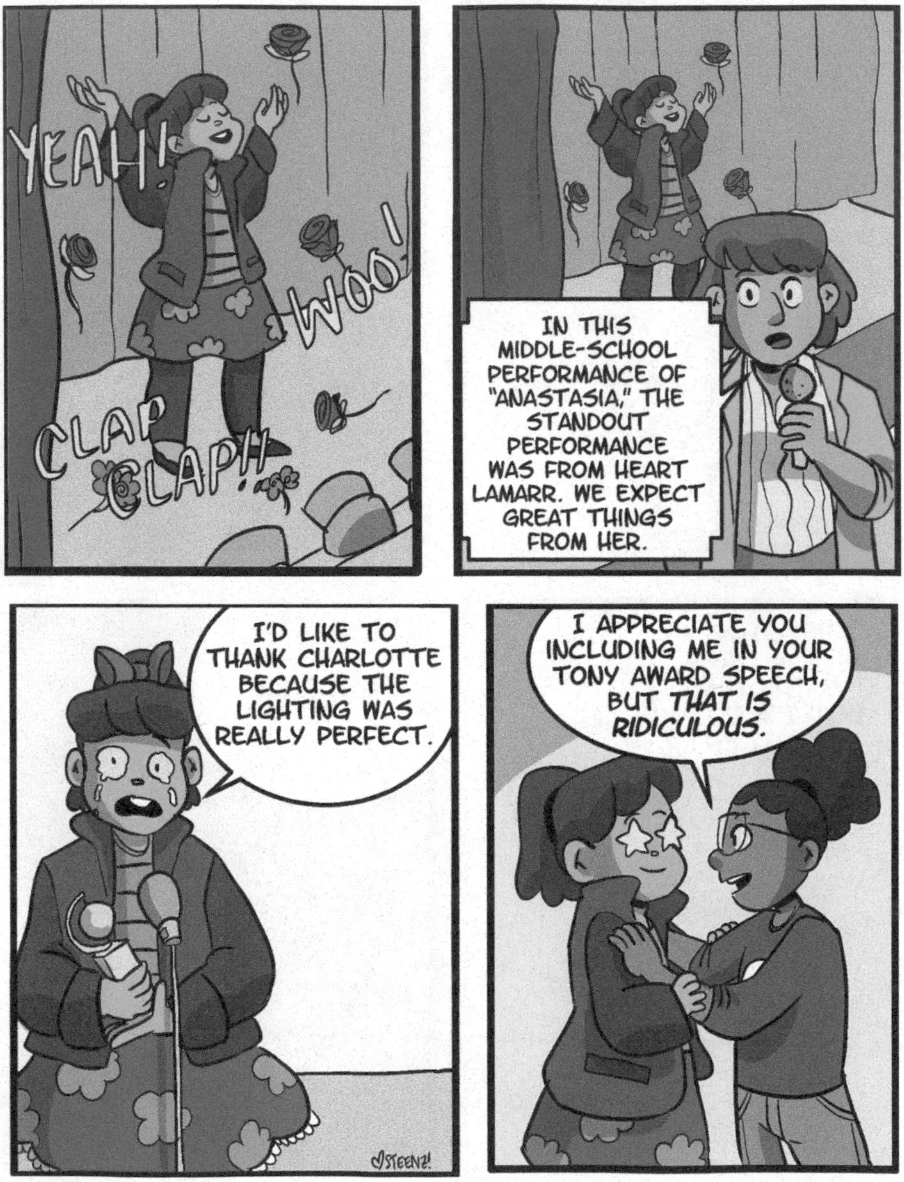
YEAH!
WOO!
CLAP CLAP!!
IN THIS MIDDLE-SCHOOL PERFORMANCE OF "ANASTASIA," THE STANDOUT PERFORMANCE WAS FROM HEART LAMARR. WE EXPECT GREAT THINGS FROM HER.
I'D LIKE TO THANK CHARLOTTE BECAUSE THE LIGHTING WAS REALLY PERFECT.
STEENZ!
I APPRECIATE YOU INCLUDING ME IN YOUR TONY AWARD SPEECH, BUT *THAT IS RIDICULOUS*.

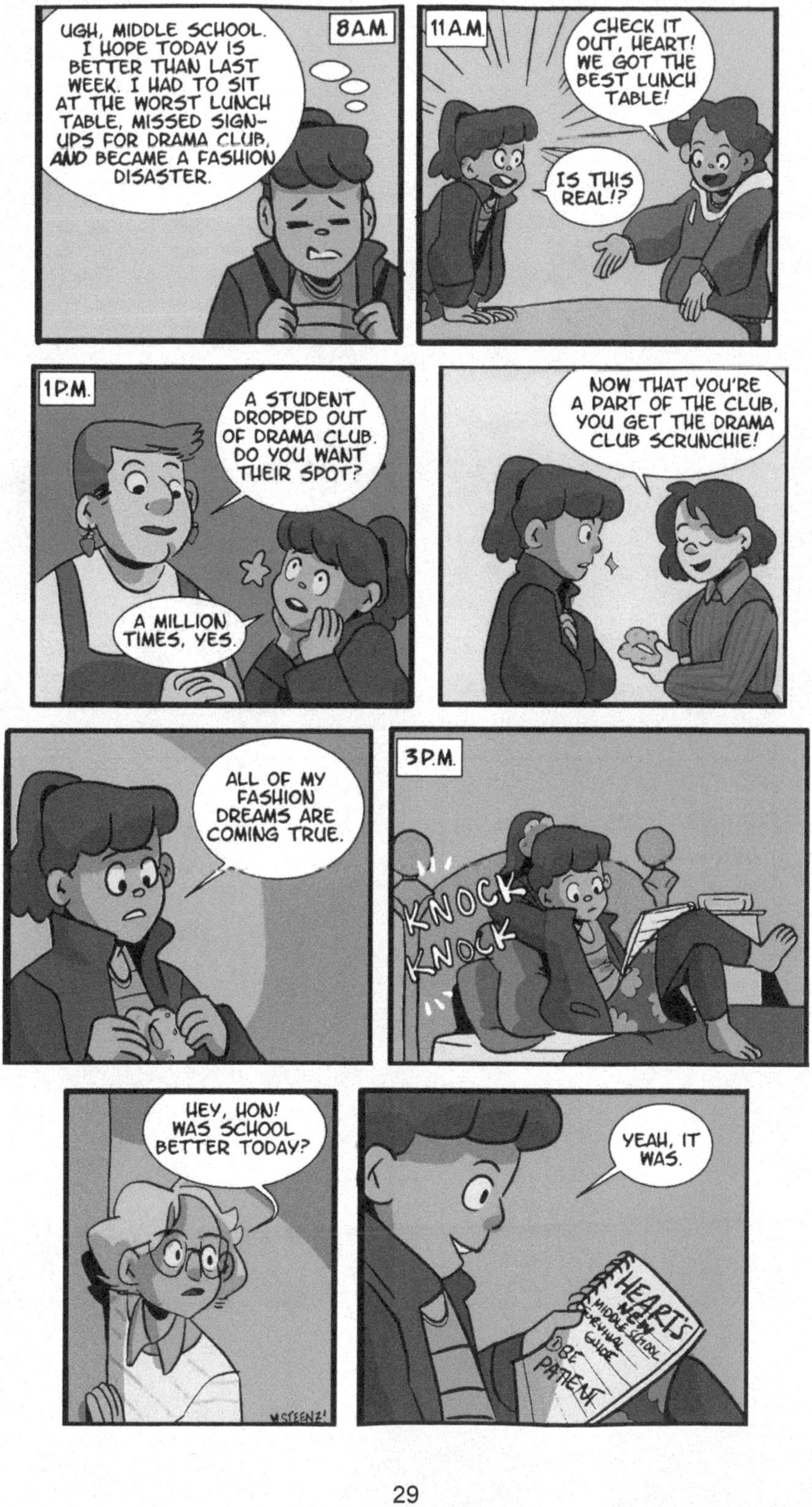
8A.M.
UGH, MIDDLE SCHOOL. I HOPE TODAY IS BETTER THAN LAST WEEK. I HAD TO SIT AT THE WORST LUNCH TABLE, MISSED SIGN-UPS FOR DRAMA CLUB, AND BECAME A FASHION DISASTER.
11A.M.
CHECK IT OUT, HEART! WE GOT THE BEST LUNCH TABLE!
IS THIS REAL!?
1P.M.
A STUDENT DROPPED OUT OF DRAMA CLUB. DO YOU WANT THEIR SPOT?
A MILLION TIMES, YES.
NOW THAT YOU'RE A PART OF THE CLUB, YOU GET THE DRAMA CLUB SCRUNCHIE!
ALL OF MY FASHION DREAMS ARE COMING TRUE.
3P.M.
KNOCK KNOCK
HEY, HON! WAS SCHOOL BETTER TODAY?
M.STEENZ
YEAH, IT WAS.
HEART'S NEW MIDDLE SCHOOL SURVIVAL GUIDE
1) BE PATIENT

H-HEY, GOOD JOB TODAY, DANA.

SURE.

EXIT

COME ON, HEART... "GOOD JOB"? WHAT AM I, HER TEACHER?

OH, HEY CHARLOTTE!

HEY, LET'S EAT LUNCH TOMORROW. I FOUND SOME ARCHIVAL PHOTOS OF "ANASTASIA" FOR YOU!

ARE YOU ACTUALLY TALKING TO HER?

YES? IS THAT BAD?

THERE'S A FOOD CHAIN. AND ACTORS ARE ON TOP. TECHIES ARE NOT.

WHERE DO THEY PLACE? LIKE MID-RANGE?

THE BOTTOM

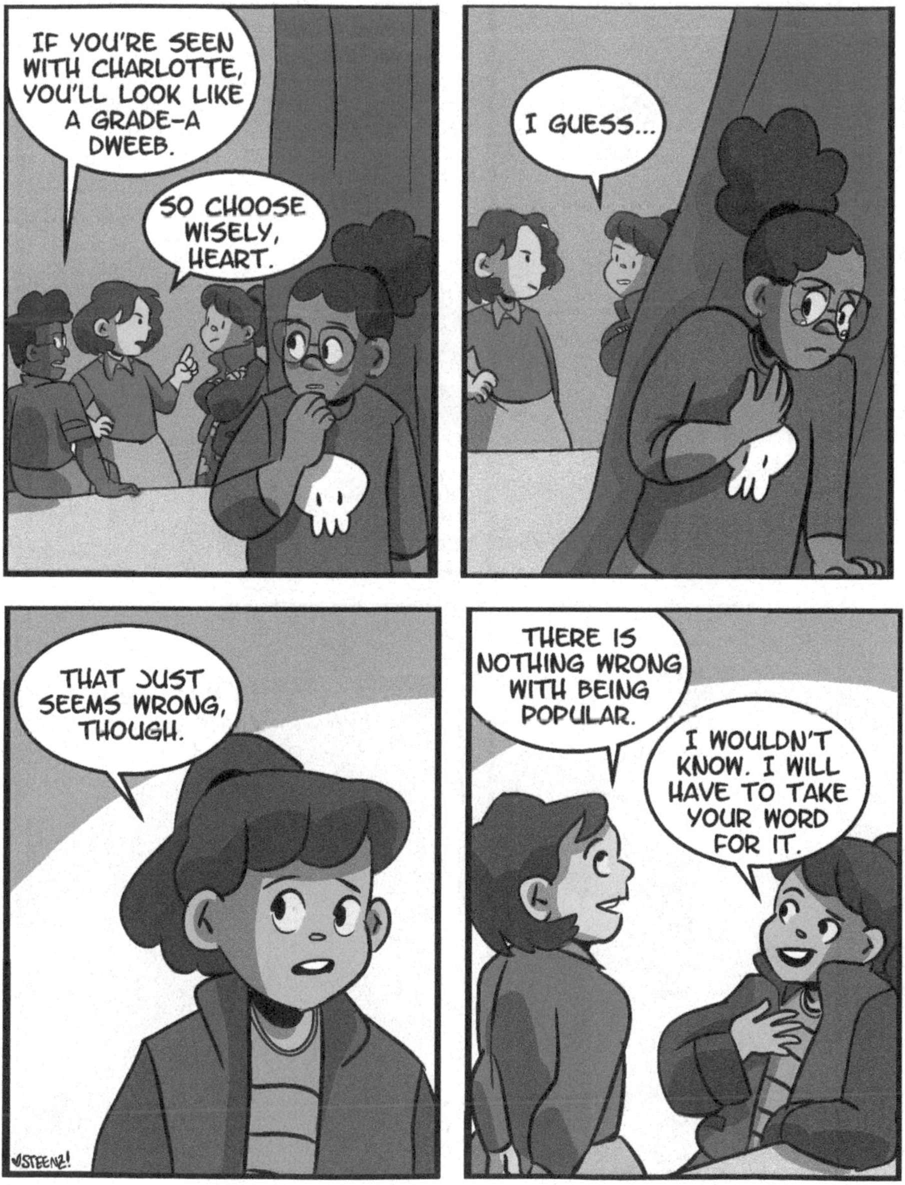
IF YOU'RE SEEN WITH CHARLOTTE, YOU'LL LOOK LIKE A GRADE-A DWEEB.
SO CHOOSE WISELY, HEART.
I GUESS...
THAT JUST SEEMS WRONG, THOUGH.
♥STEENZ!
THERE IS NOTHING WRONG WITH BEING POPULAR.
I WOULDN'T KNOW. I WILL HAVE TO TAKE YOUR WORD FOR IT.

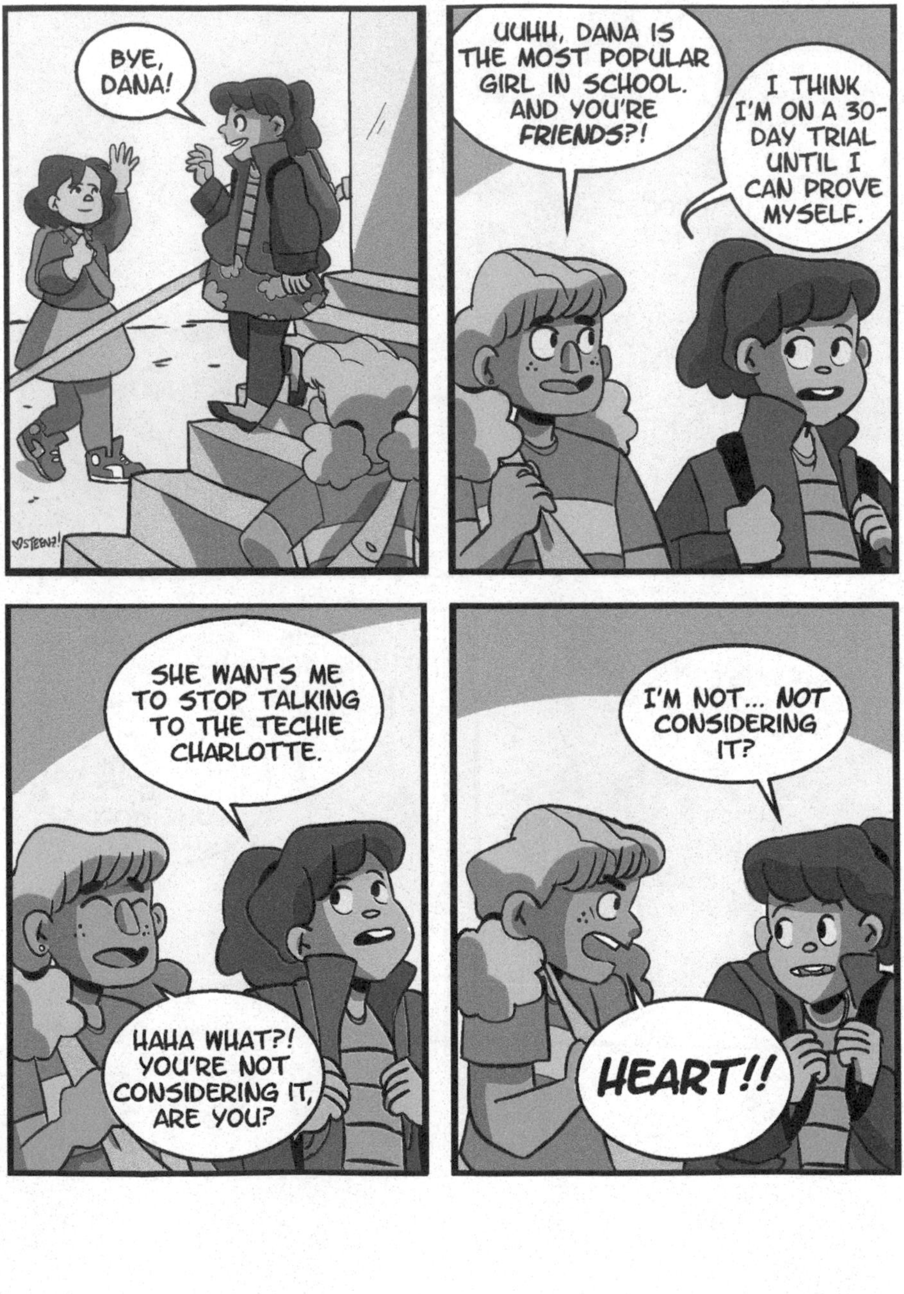
BYE, DANA!
UUHH, DANA IS THE MOST POPULAR GIRL IN SCHOOL. AND YOU'RE FRIENDS?!
I THINK I'M ON A 30-DAY TRIAL UNTIL I CAN PROVE MYSELF.
SHE WANTS ME TO STOP TALKING TO THE TECHIE CHARLOTTE.
HAHA WHAT?! YOU'RE NOT CONSIDERING IT, ARE YOU?
I'M NOT... NOT CONSIDERING IT?
HEART!!

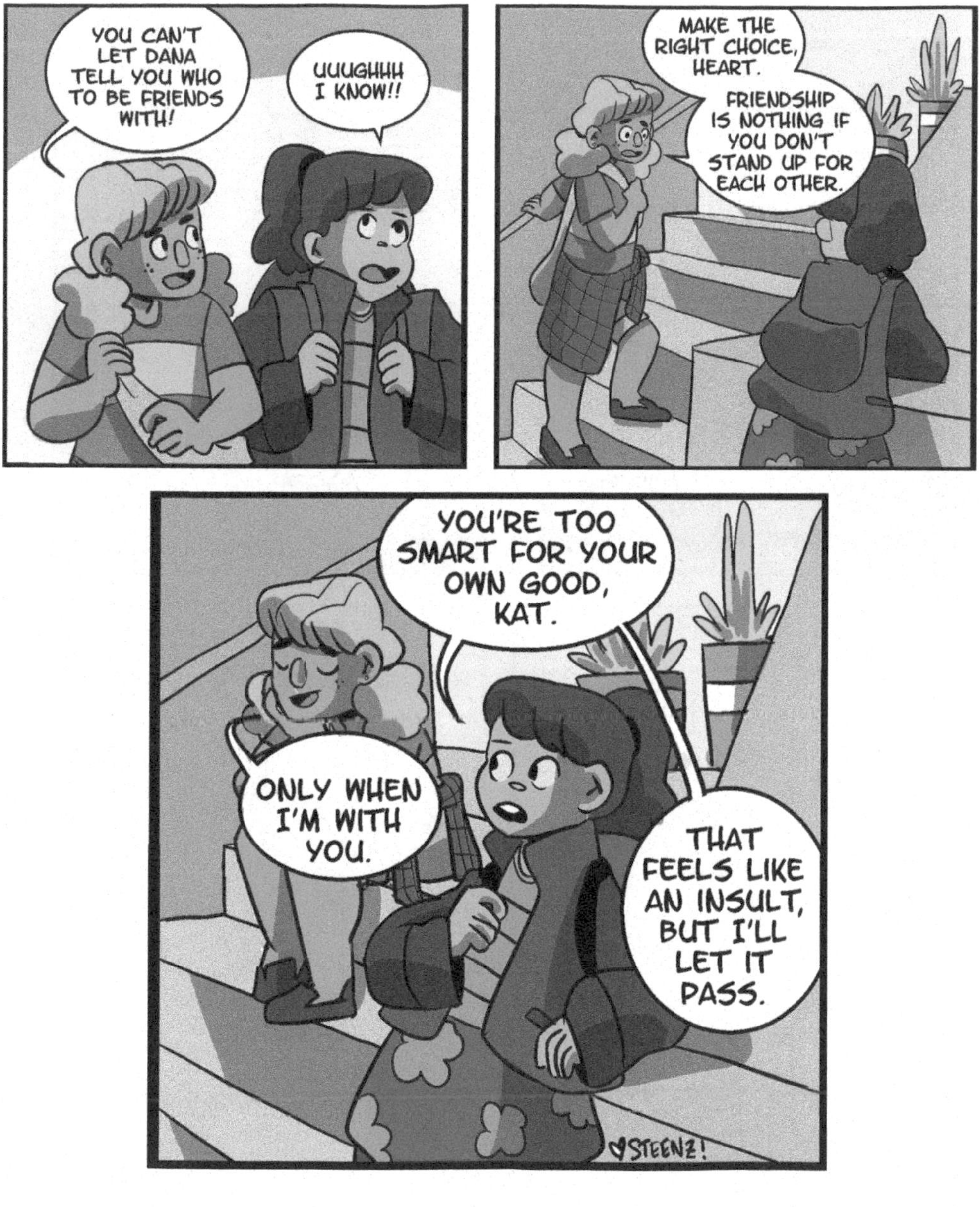
YOU CAN'T LET DANA TELL YOU WHO TO BE FRIENDS WITH!
UUUGHHH I KNOW!!
MAKE THE RIGHT CHOICE, HEART.
FRIENDSHIP IS NOTHING IF YOU DON'T STAND UP FOR EACH OTHER.
YOU'RE TOO SMART FOR YOUR OWN GOOD, KAT.
ONLY WHEN I'M WITH YOU.
THAT FEELS LIKE AN INSULT, BUT I'LL LET IT PASS.
♡STEENZ!

BLURGH. THERE'S NEVER ANYWHERE TO SIT AT LUNCH...
I SHOULD HAVE EATEN IN THE THEATER...
HEY, CHARLOTTE! COME SIT WITH US!
I DON'T NEED YOUR CHARITY SEAT. I CAN SIT WHEREVER I WANT!
BUT, UH... WASTE NOT, WANT NOT, RIGHT? HEH...

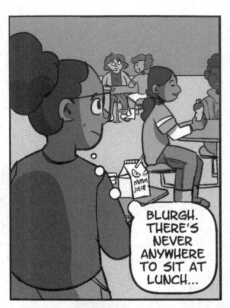

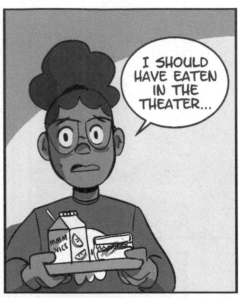

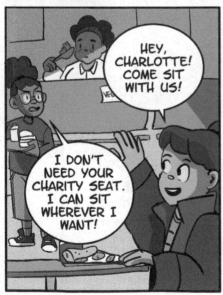

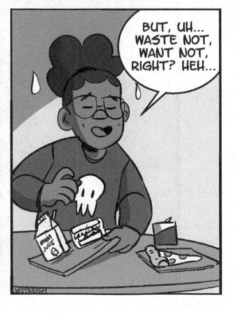

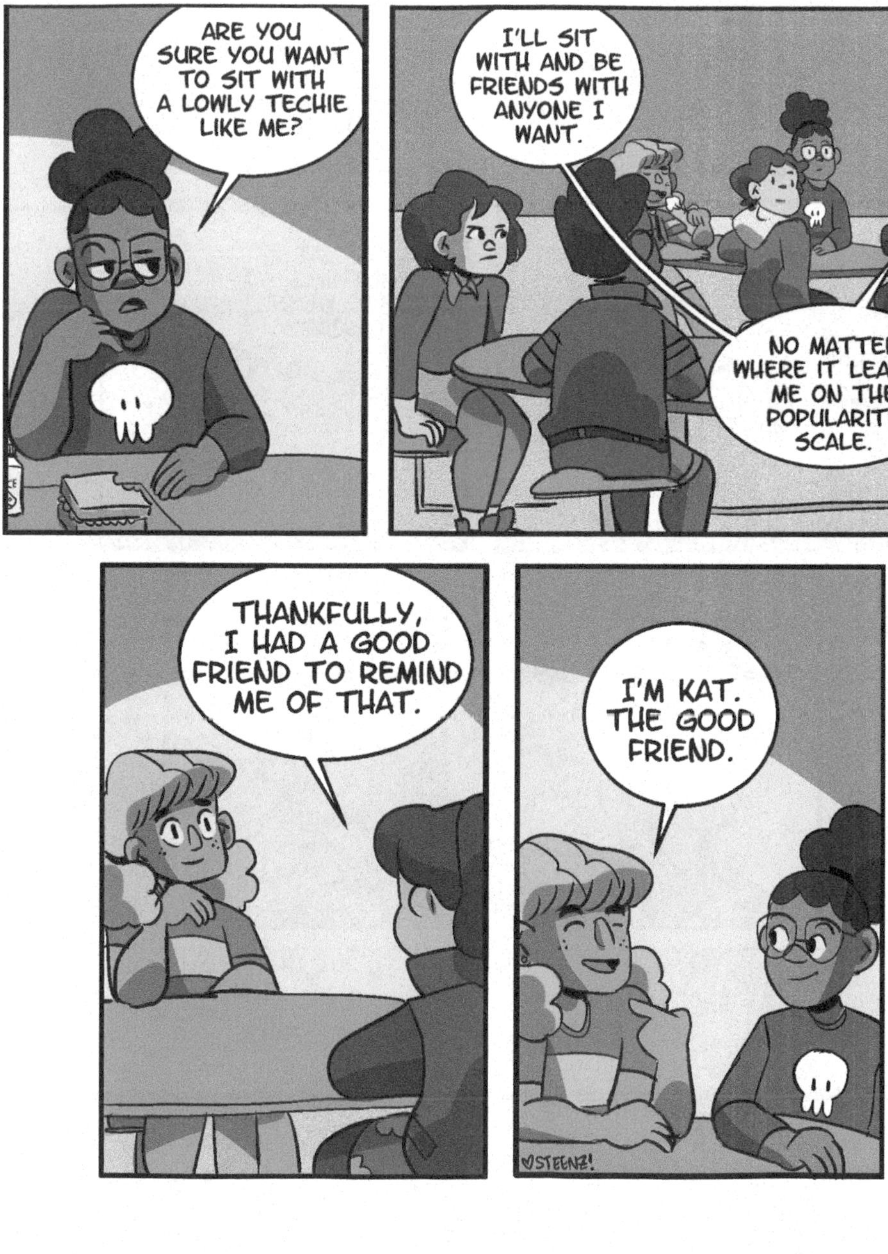
ARE YOU SURE YOU WANT TO SIT WITH A LOWLY TECHIE LIKE ME?
I'LL SIT WITH AND BE FRIENDS WITH ANYONE I WANT.
NO MATTER WHERE IT LEAVES ME ON THE POPULARITY SCALE.
THANKFULLY, I HAD A GOOD FRIEND TO REMIND ME OF THAT.
I'M KAT. THE GOOD FRIEND.
♡STEENZ!

CRONCH
CRONCH
CRONCH
CHIPS
HEART, SHUSH... YOUR CHIPS ARE SO LOUD.
I GET HUNGRY WHEN I READ!
WELL, AT LEAST EAT SOMETHING QUIETER. WE'RE IN A *LIBRARY!*
ALRIGHT, LET'S SEE WHAT I'VE GOT...
HEY! A HONEY BUN!
CRINKLE
CRINKLE
OH MY GOD.
BLAME THE MANUFACTURER, NOT ME!!
STEENZ!

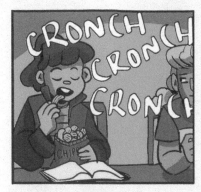

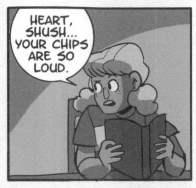

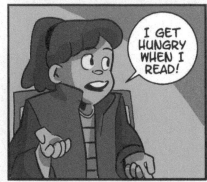

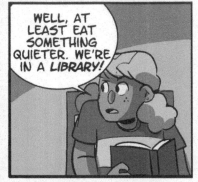

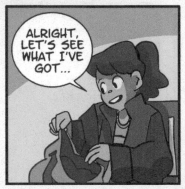

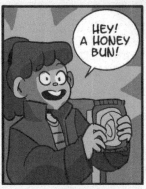

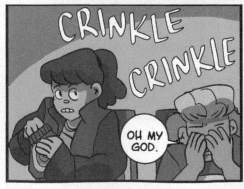

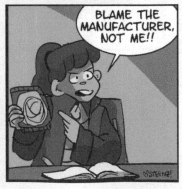

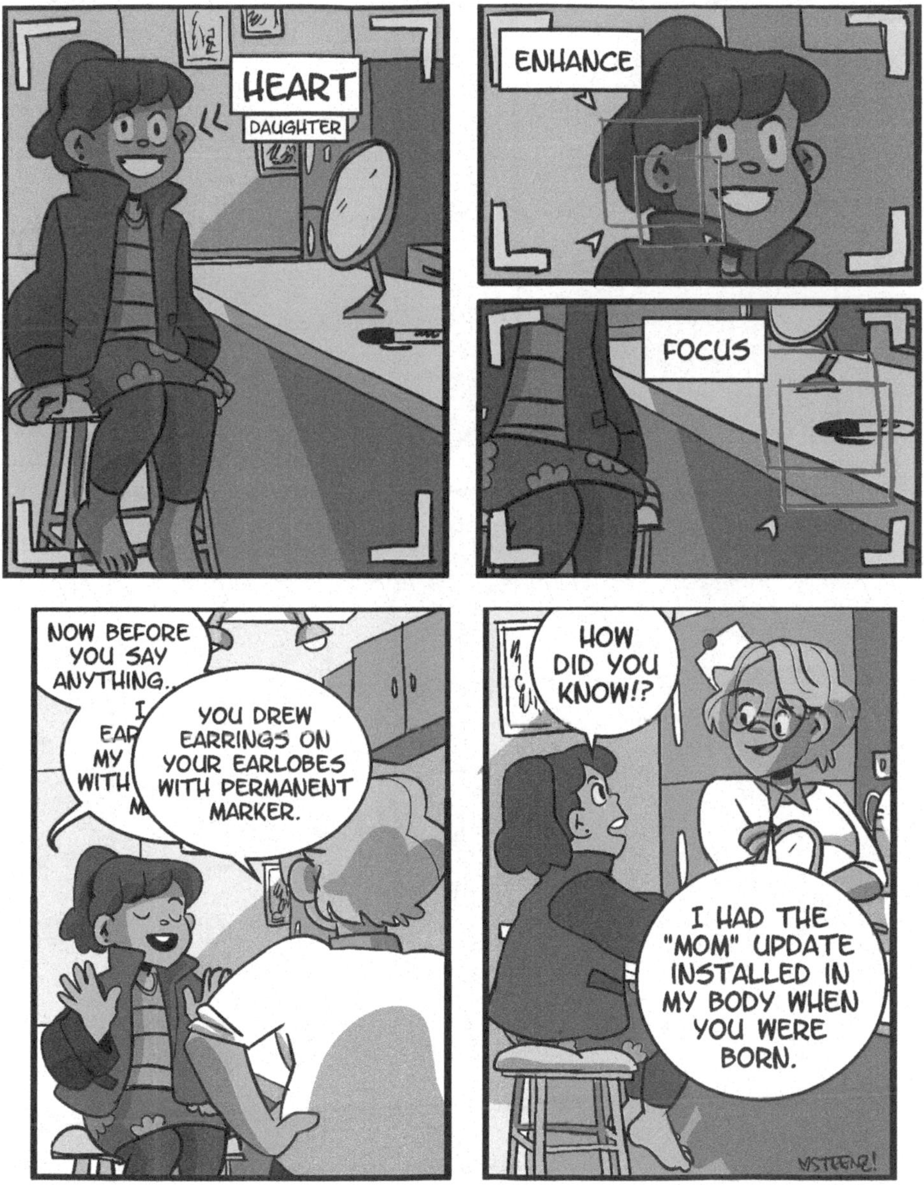
HEART
DAUGHTER
ENHANCE
FOCUS
NOW BEFORE YOU SAY ANYTHING...
YOU DREW EARRINGS ON YOUR EARLOBES WITH PERMANENT MARKER.
HOW DID YOU KNOW!?
I HAD THE "MOM" UPDATE INSTALLED IN MY BODY WHEN YOU WERE BORN.

YOU KNOW, I DIDN'T GET MY EARS PIERCED UNTIL I WAS 13. YOU'RE 11. WHAT'S THE RUSH?
I DON'T WANT YOU IN A NURSING HOME!
EXPLAIN.
OKAY. IF I DON'T GET MY EARS PIERCED, I'LL BE A SOCIAL OUTCAST, WHICH WILL LEAD ME TO QUITTING SCHOOL. I WON'T GET A GOOD JOB, NEVER MOVE OUT, AND WE'LL BE STUCK TOGETHER FOREVER.
SCRUB SCRUB
UNTIL I PUT YOU IN A NURSING HOME.
HMM. YOU'RE ACTUALLY MAKING A GREAT CASE FOR YOURSELF.
♡STEENZ!

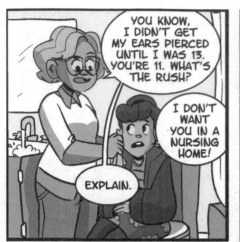

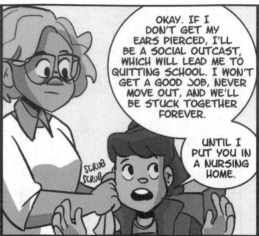

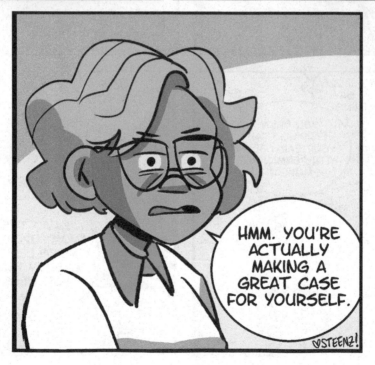

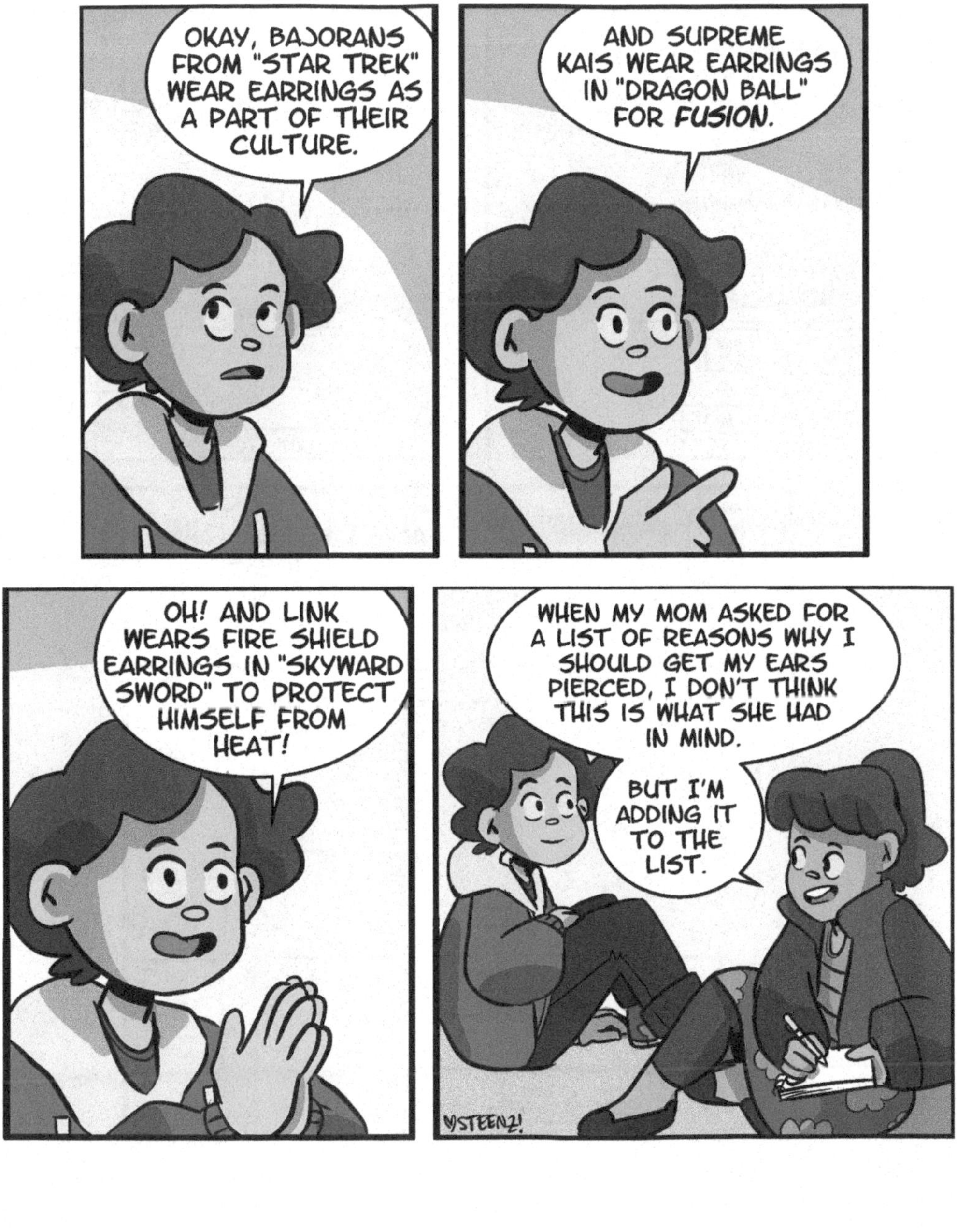
OKAY, BAJORANS FROM "STAR TREK" WEAR EARRINGS AS A PART OF THEIR CULTURE.
AND SUPREME KAIS WEAR EARRINGS IN "DRAGON BALL" FOR *FUSION*.
OH! AND LINK WEARS FIRE SHIELD EARRINGS IN "SKYWARD SWORD" TO PROTECT HIMSELF FROM HEAT!
WHEN MY MOM ASKED FOR A LIST OF REASONS WHY I SHOULD GET MY EARS PIERCED, I DON'T THINK THIS IS WHAT SHE HAD IN MIND.
BUT I'M ADDING IT TO THE LIST.
♡STEENZ!

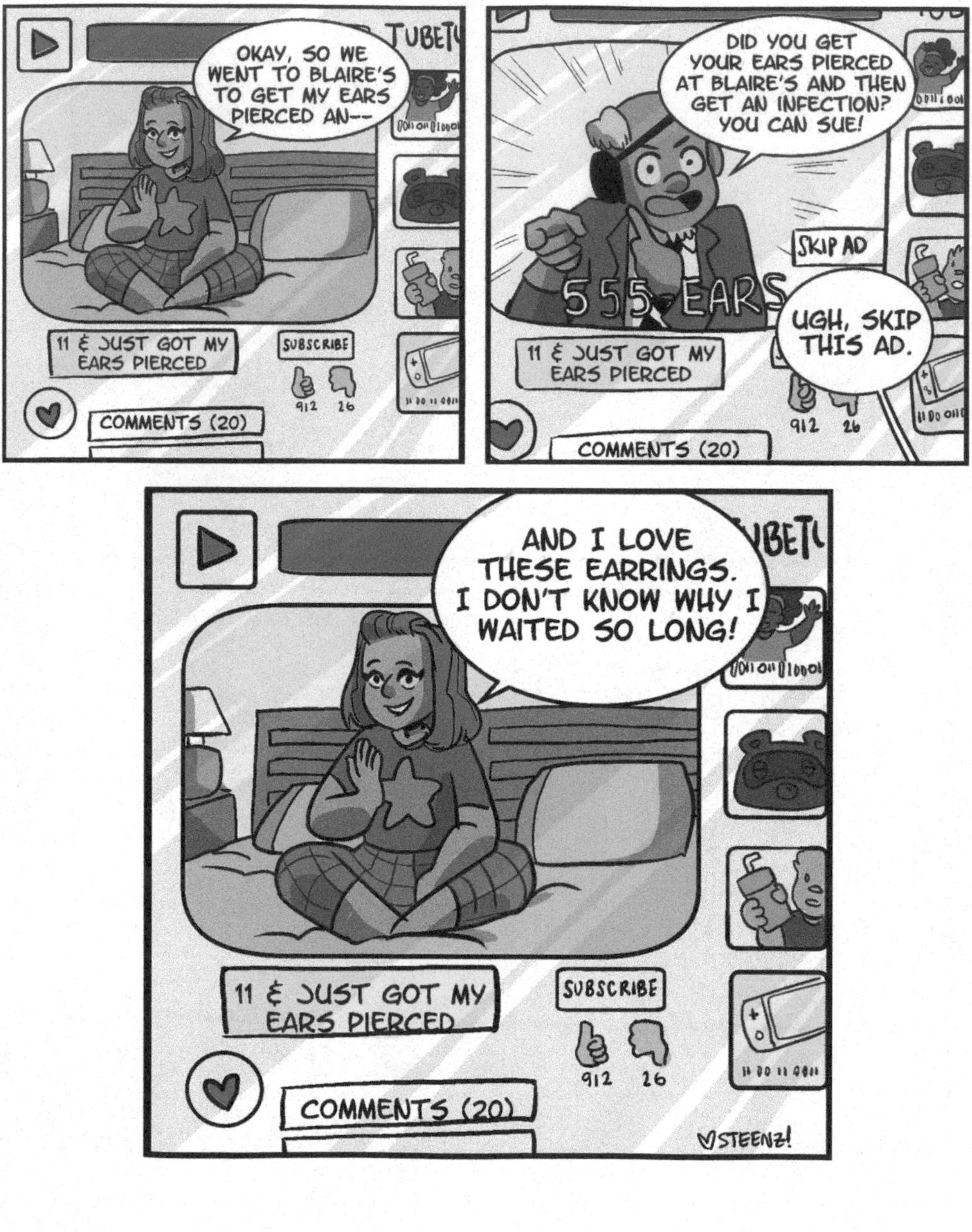
TUBETY
OKAY, SO WE WENT TO BLAIRE'S TO GET MY EARS PIERCED AN--
11 & JUST GOT MY EARS PIERCED
SUBSCRIBE
912 26
COMMENTS (20)
DID YOU GET YOUR EARS PIERCED AT BLAIRE'S AND THEN GET AN INFECTION? YOU CAN SUE!
555-EARS
SKIP AD
UGH, SKIP THIS AD.
11 & JUST GOT MY EARS PIERCED
912 26
COMMENTS (20)
AND I LOVE THESE EARRINGS. I DON'T KNOW WHY I WAITED SO LONG!
11 & JUST GOT MY EARS PIERCED
SUBSCRIBE
912 26
COMMENTS (20)
STEENZ!

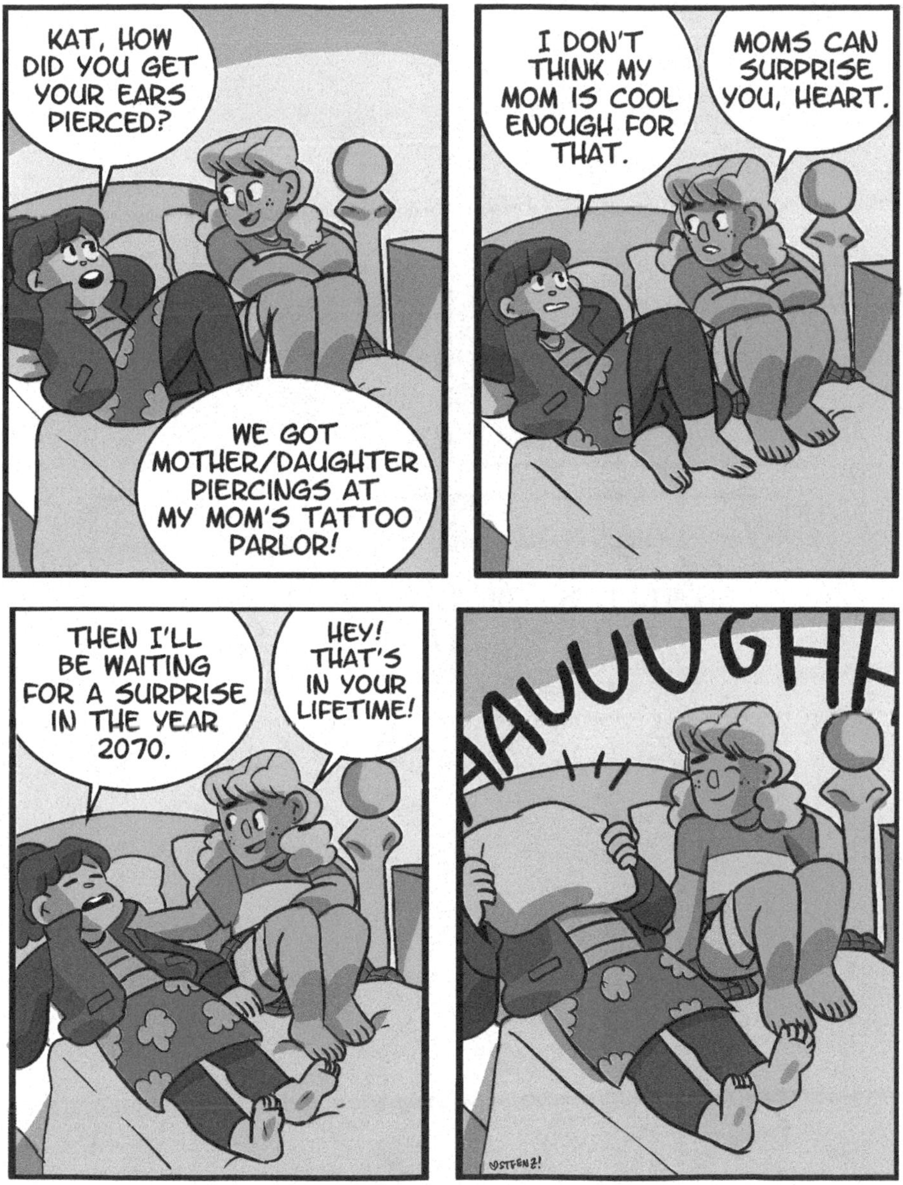
KAT, HOW DID YOU GET YOUR EARS PIERCED?
WE GOT MOTHER/DAUGHTER PIERCINGS AT MY MOM'S TATTOO PARLOR!
I DON'T THINK MY MOM IS COOL ENOUGH FOR THAT.
MOMS CAN SURPRISE YOU, HEART.
THEN I'LL BE WAITING FOR A SURPRISE IN THE YEAR 2070.
HEY! THAT'S IN YOUR LIFETIME!
AAUUUGH!
♡STEENZ!

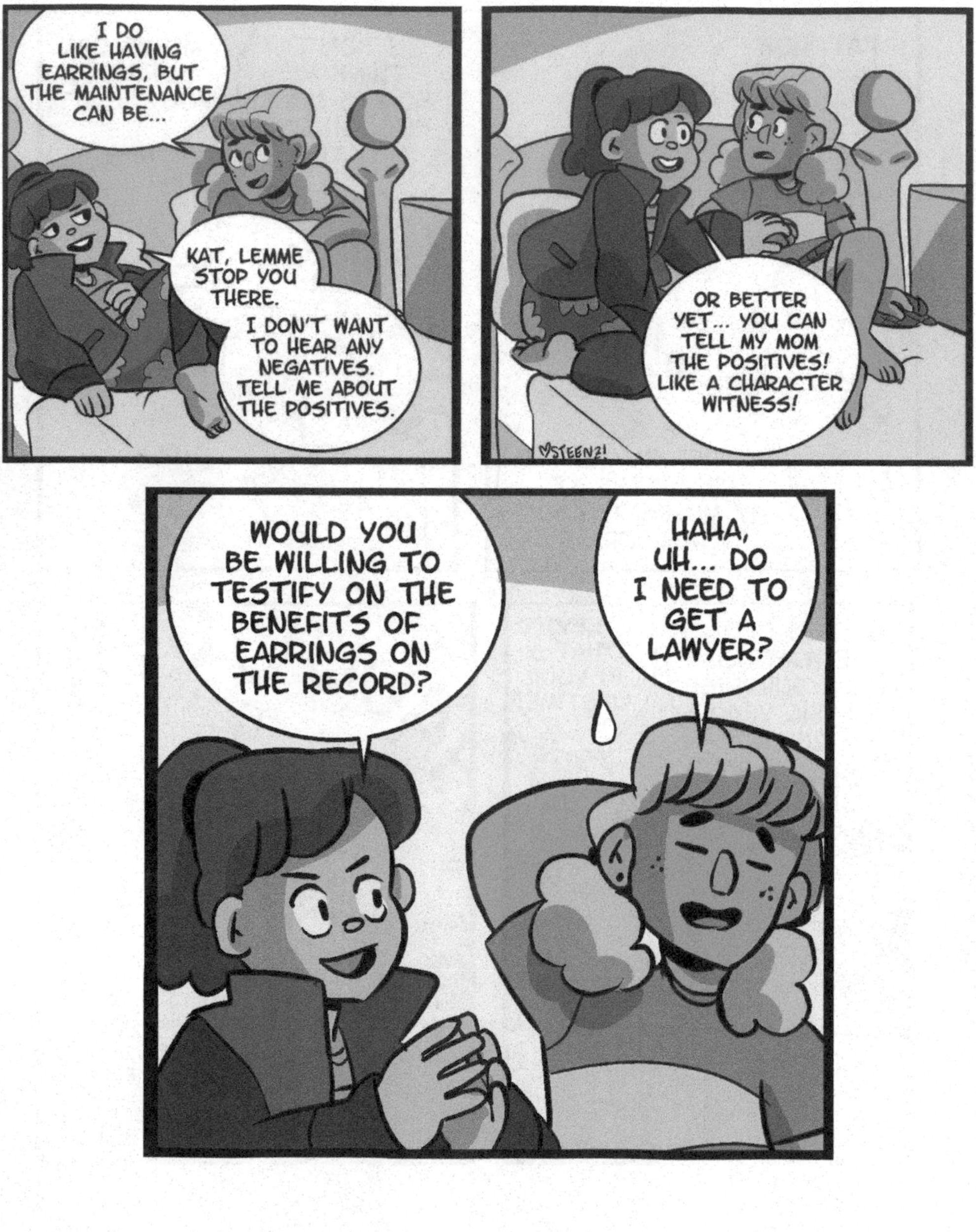
I DO LIKE HAVING EARRINGS, BUT THE MAINTENANCE CAN BE...
KAT, LEMME STOP YOU THERE.
I DON'T WANT TO HEAR ANY NEGATIVES. TELL ME ABOUT THE POSITIVES.
OR BETTER YET... YOU CAN TELL MY MOM THE POSITIVES! LIKE A CHARACTER WITNESS!
STEENZ!
WOULD YOU BE WILLING TO TESTIFY ON THE BENEFITS OF EARRINGS ON THE RECORD?
HAHA, UH... DO I NEED TO GET A LAWYER?

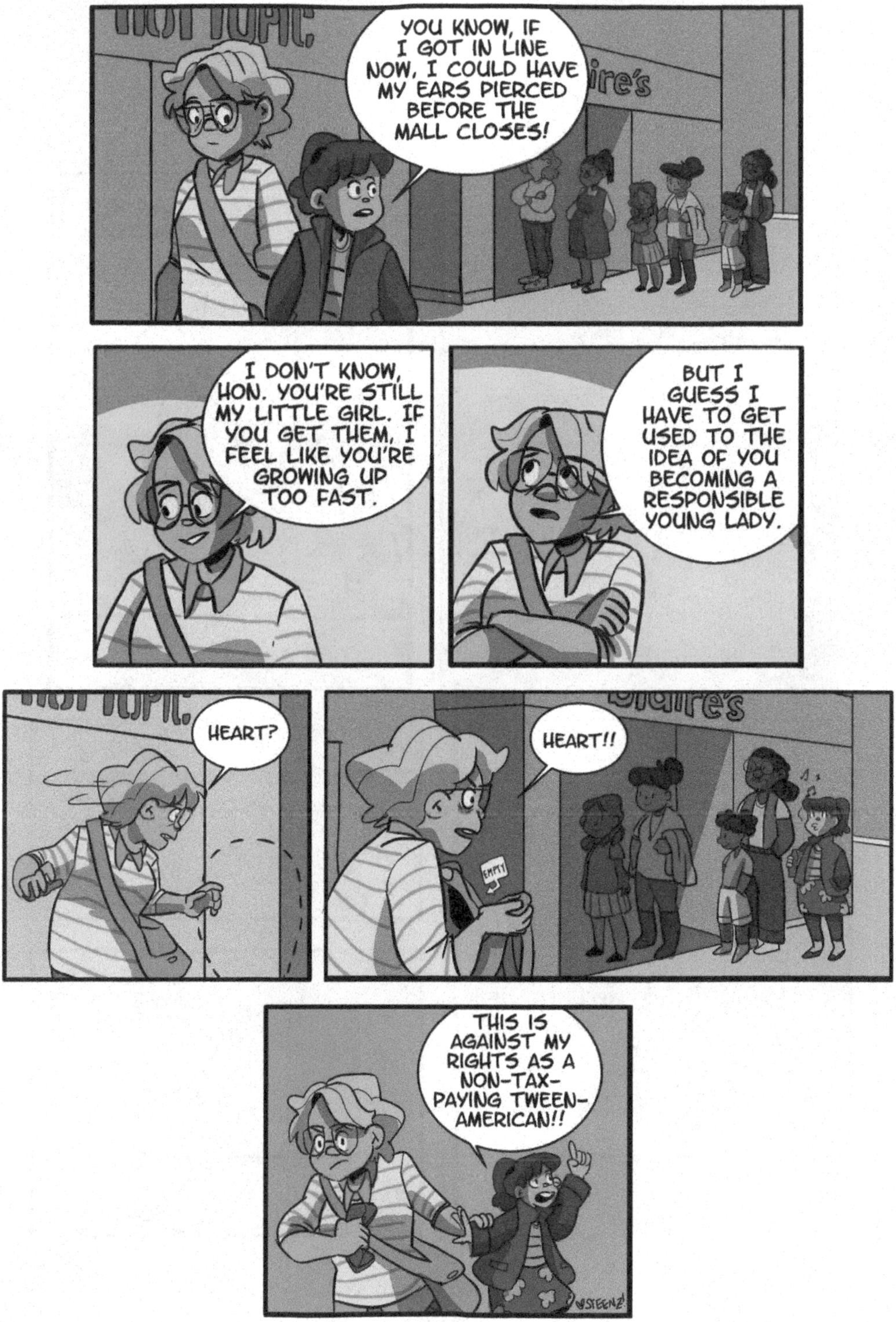
YOU KNOW, IF I GOT IN LINE NOW, I COULD HAVE MY EARS PIERCED BEFORE THE MALL CLOSES!
I DON'T KNOW, HON. YOU'RE STILL MY LITTLE GIRL. IF YOU GET THEM, I FEEL LIKE YOU'RE GROWING UP TOO FAST.
BUT I GUESS I HAVE TO GET USED TO THE IDEA OF YOU BECOMING A RESPONSIBLE YOUNG LADY.
HEART?
HEART!!
EMPTY
THIS IS AGAINST MY RIGHTS AS A NON-TAX-PAYING TWEEN-AMERICAN!!
STEENZ

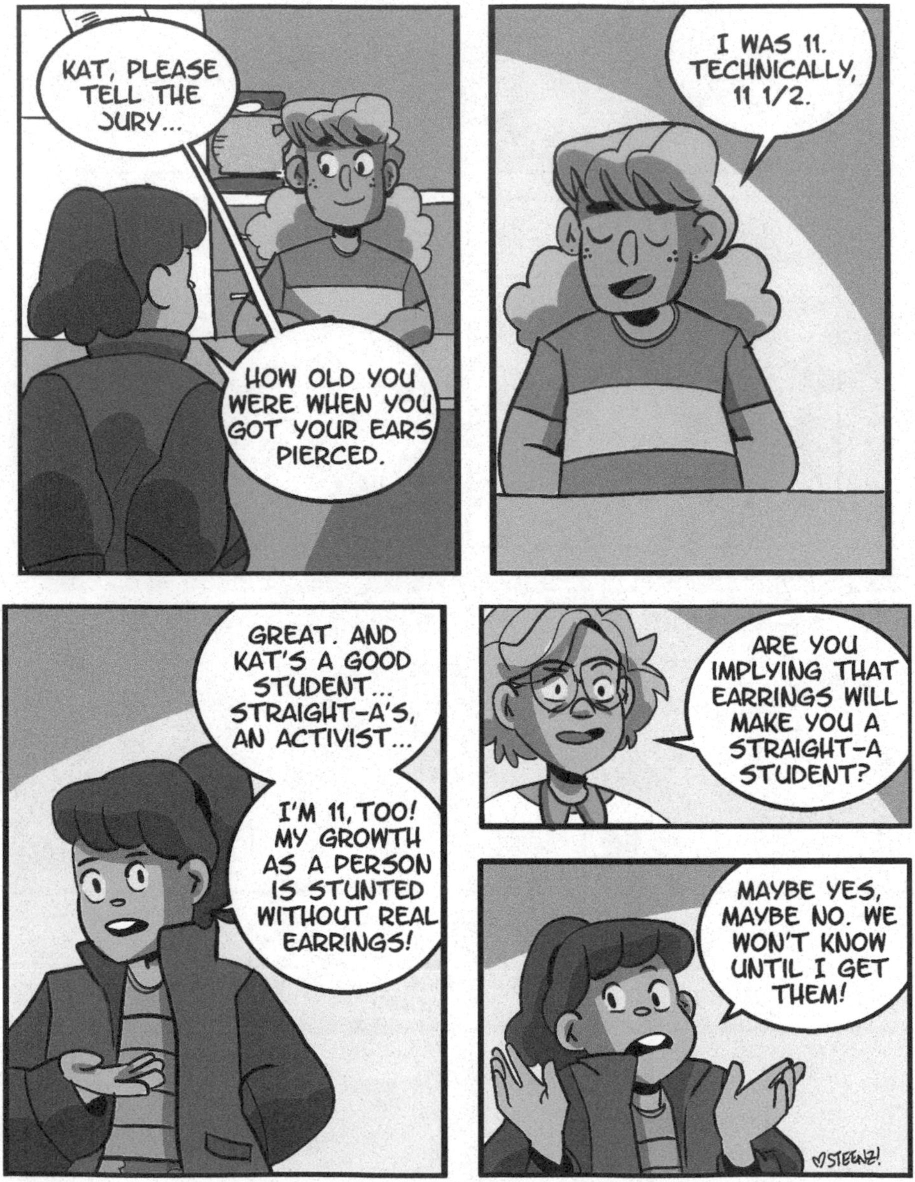
KAT, PLEASE TELL THE JURY...
HOW OLD YOU WERE WHEN YOU GOT YOUR EARS PIERCED.
I WAS 11. TECHNICALLY, 11 1/2.
GREAT. AND KAT'S A GOOD STUDENT... STRAIGHT-A'S, AN ACTIVIST...
I'M 11, TOO! MY GROWTH AS A PERSON IS STUNTED WITHOUT REAL EARRINGS!
ARE YOU IMPLYING THAT EARRINGS WILL MAKE YOU A STRAIGHT-A STUDENT?
MAYBE YES, MAYBE NO. WE WON'T KNOW UNTIL I GET THEM!
STEENZ!

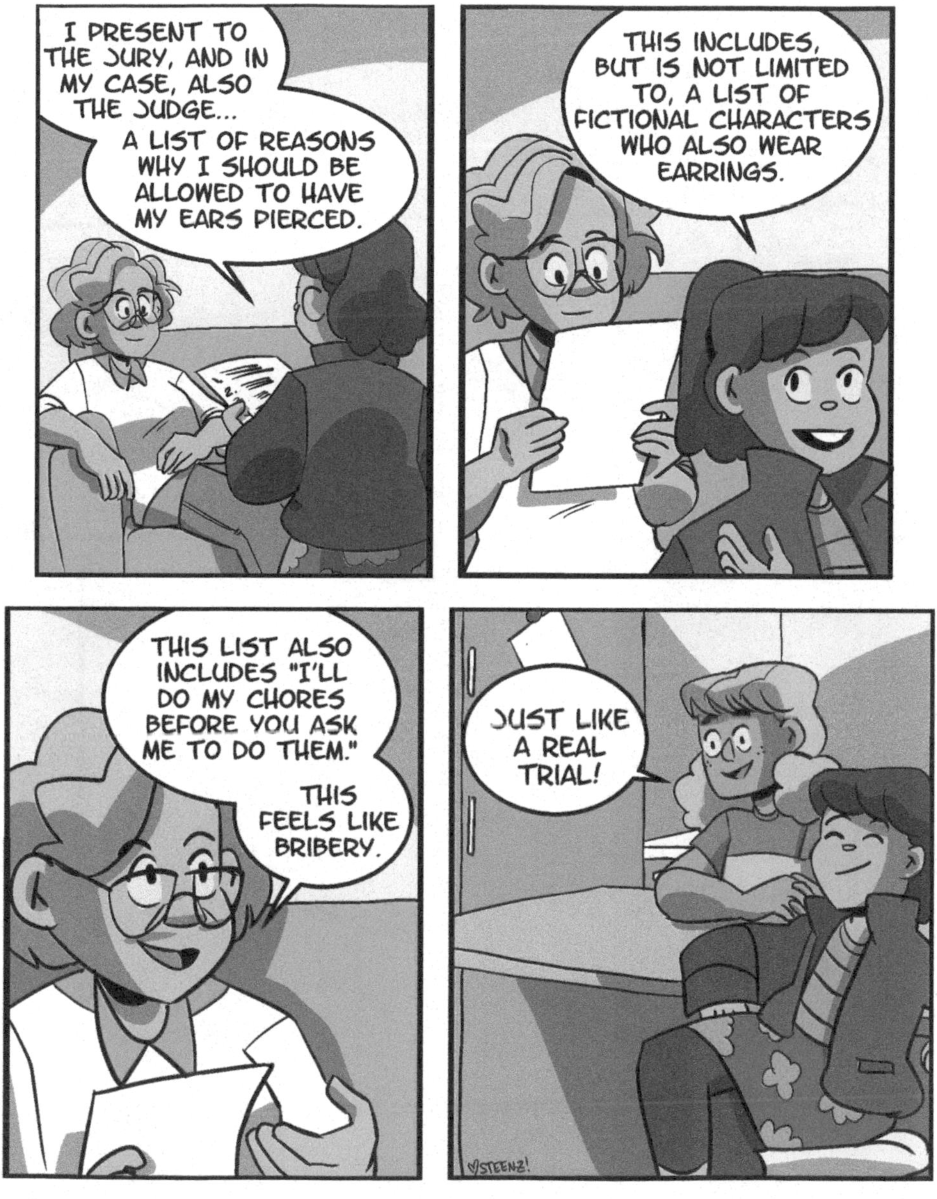
I PRESENT TO THE JURY, AND IN MY CASE, ALSO THE JUDGE...
A LIST OF REASONS WHY I SHOULD BE ALLOWED TO HAVE MY EARS PIERCED.
THIS INCLUDES, BUT IS NOT LIMITED TO, A LIST OF FICTIONAL CHARACTERS WHO ALSO WEAR EARRINGS.
THIS LIST ALSO INCLUDES "I'LL DO MY CHORES BEFORE YOU ASK ME TO DO THEM."
THIS FEELS LIKE BRIBERY.
JUST LIKE A REAL TRIAL!
STEENZ!

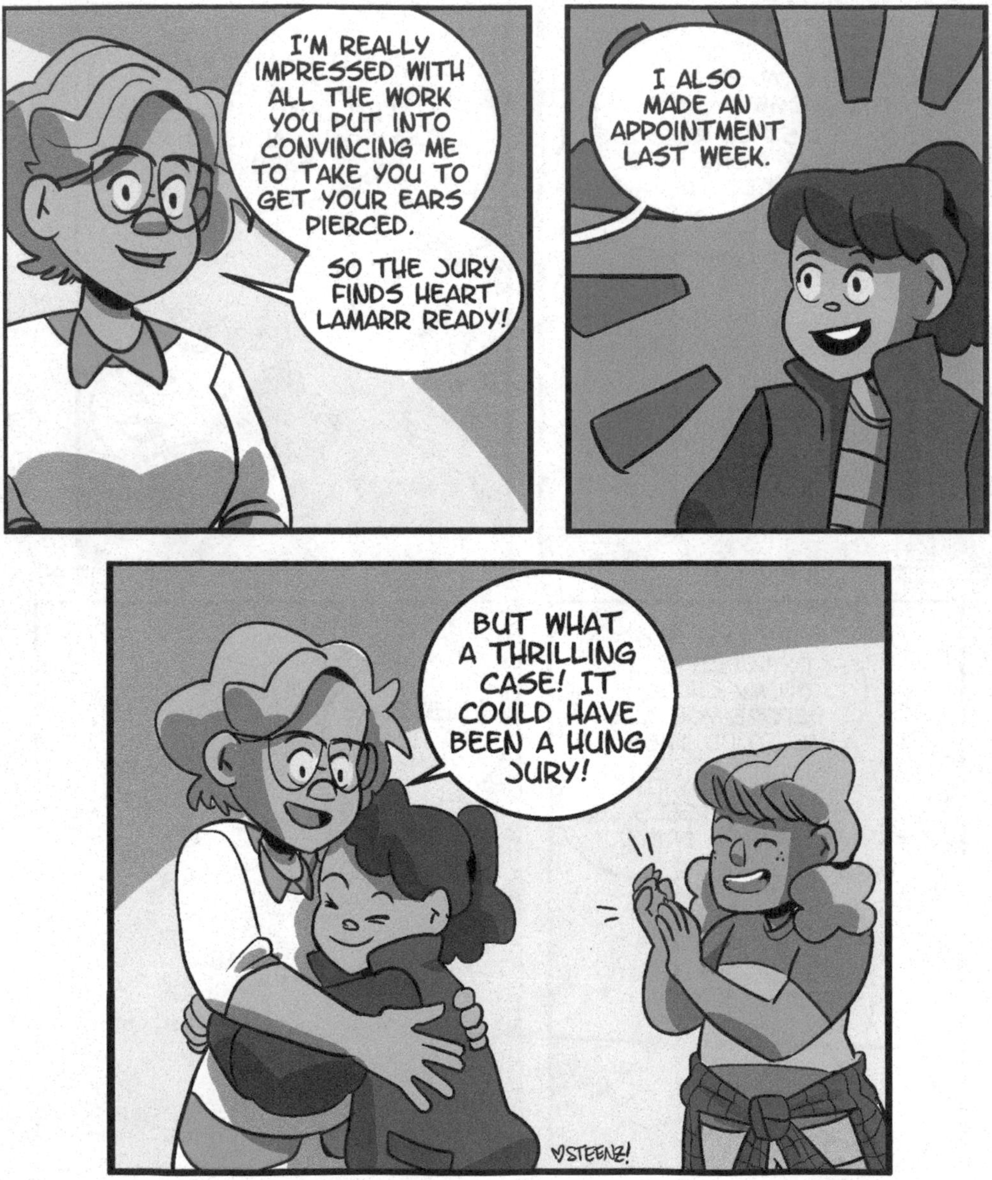
I'M REALLY IMPRESSED WITH ALL THE WORK YOU PUT INTO CONVINCING ME TO TAKE YOU TO GET YOUR EARS PIERCED.
SO THE JURY FINDS HEART LAMARR READY!
I ALSO MADE AN APPOINTMENT LAST WEEK.
BUT WHAT A THRILLING CASE! IT COULD HAVE BEEN A HUNG JURY!
♡STEENZ!

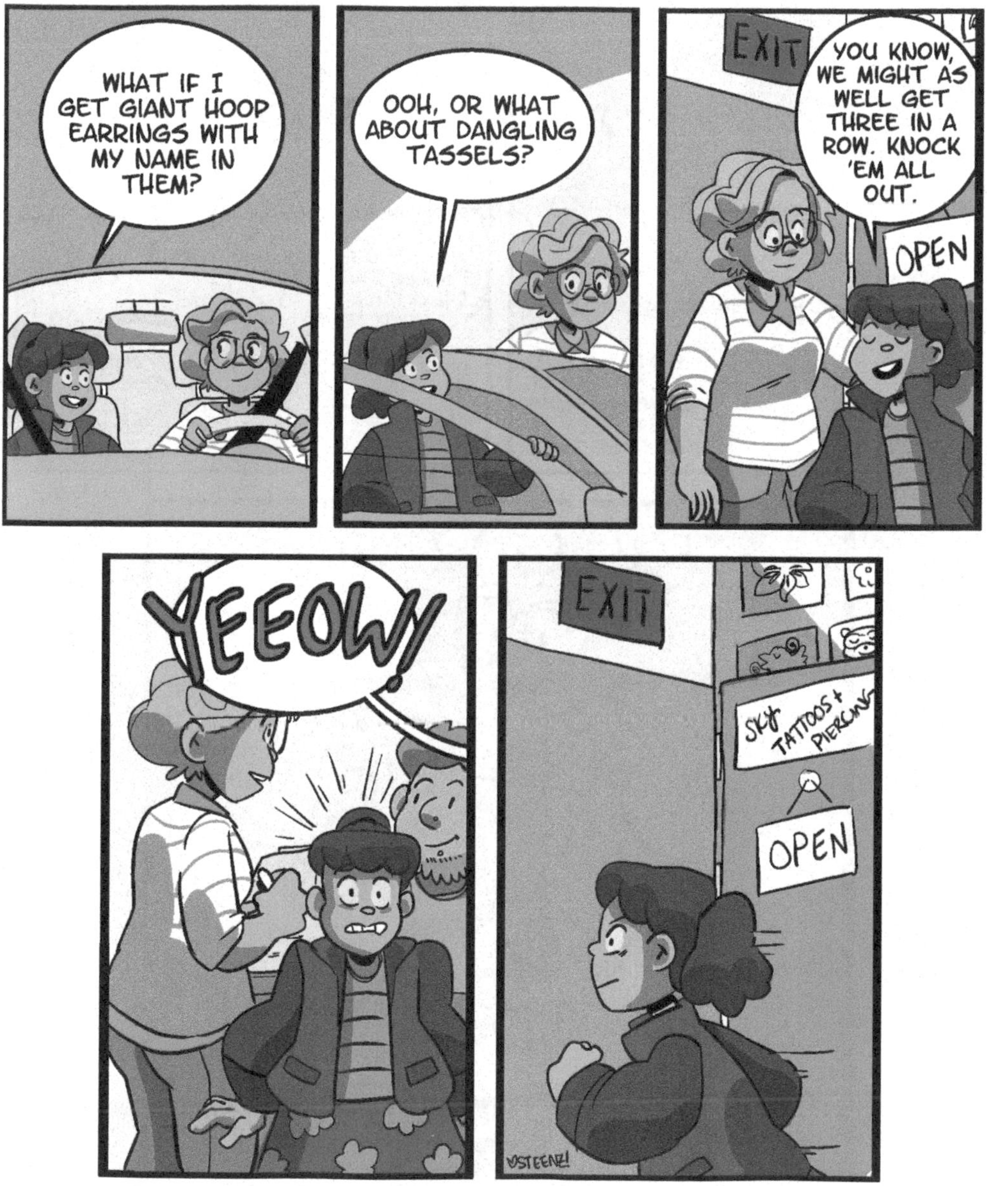
WHAT IF I GET GIANT HOOP EARRINGS WITH MY NAME IN THEM?
OOH, OR WHAT ABOUT DANGLING TASSELS?
EXIT
YOU KNOW, WE MIGHT AS WELL GET THREE IN A ROW. KNOCK 'EM ALL OUT.
OPEN
YEEOW!
EXIT
SKY TATTOOS & PIERCING
OPEN
STEENZ!

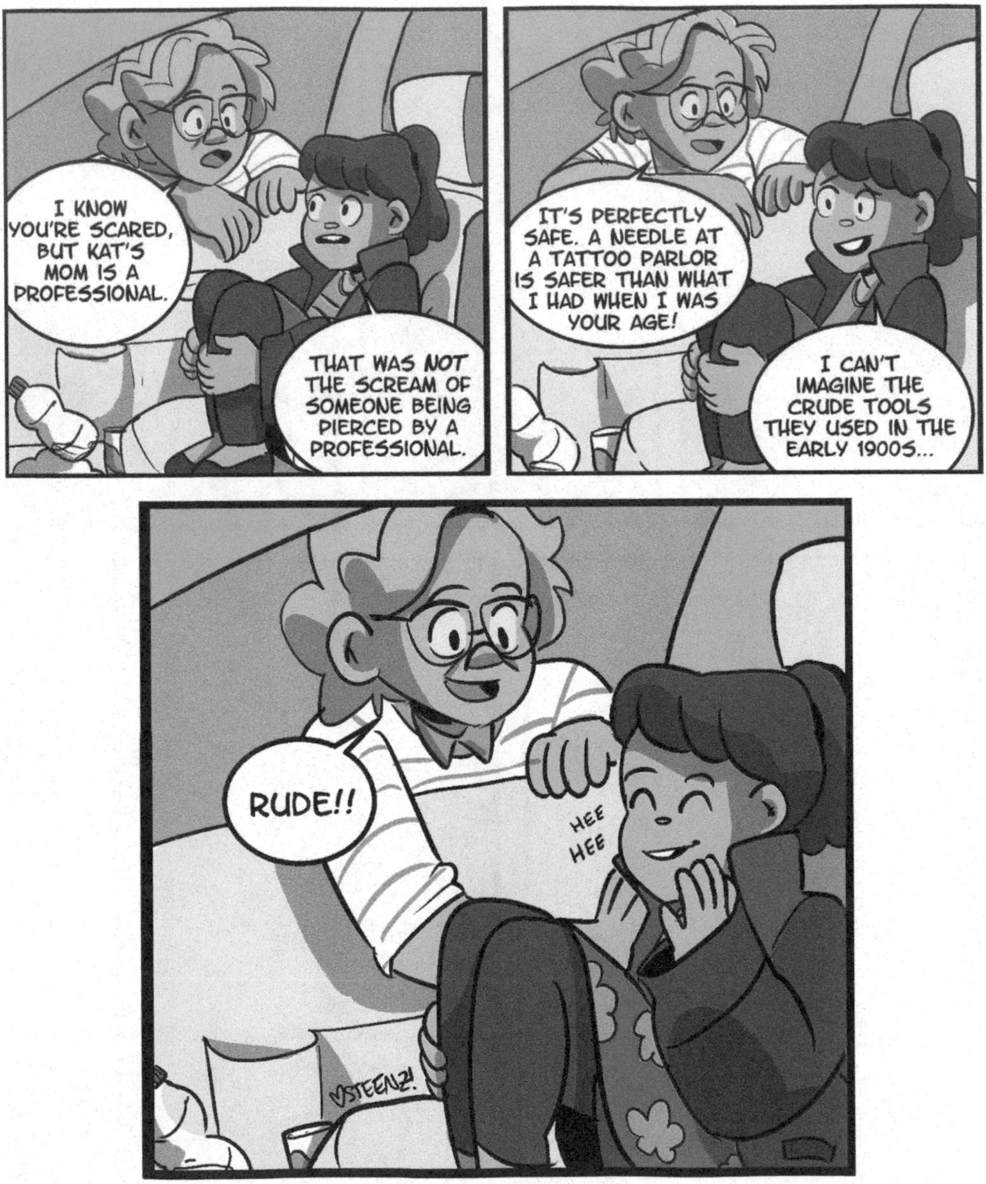
I KNOW YOU'RE SCARED, BUT KAT'S MOM IS A PROFESSIONAL.
THAT WAS NOT THE SCREAM OF SOMEONE BEING PIERCED BY A PROFESSIONAL.
IT'S PERFECTLY SAFE. A NEEDLE AT A TATTOO PARLOR IS SAFER THAN WHAT I HAD WHEN I WAS YOUR AGE!
I CAN'T IMAGINE THE CRUDE TOOLS THEY USED IN THE EARLY 1900S...
RUDE!!
HEE HEE
♡STEENZ!

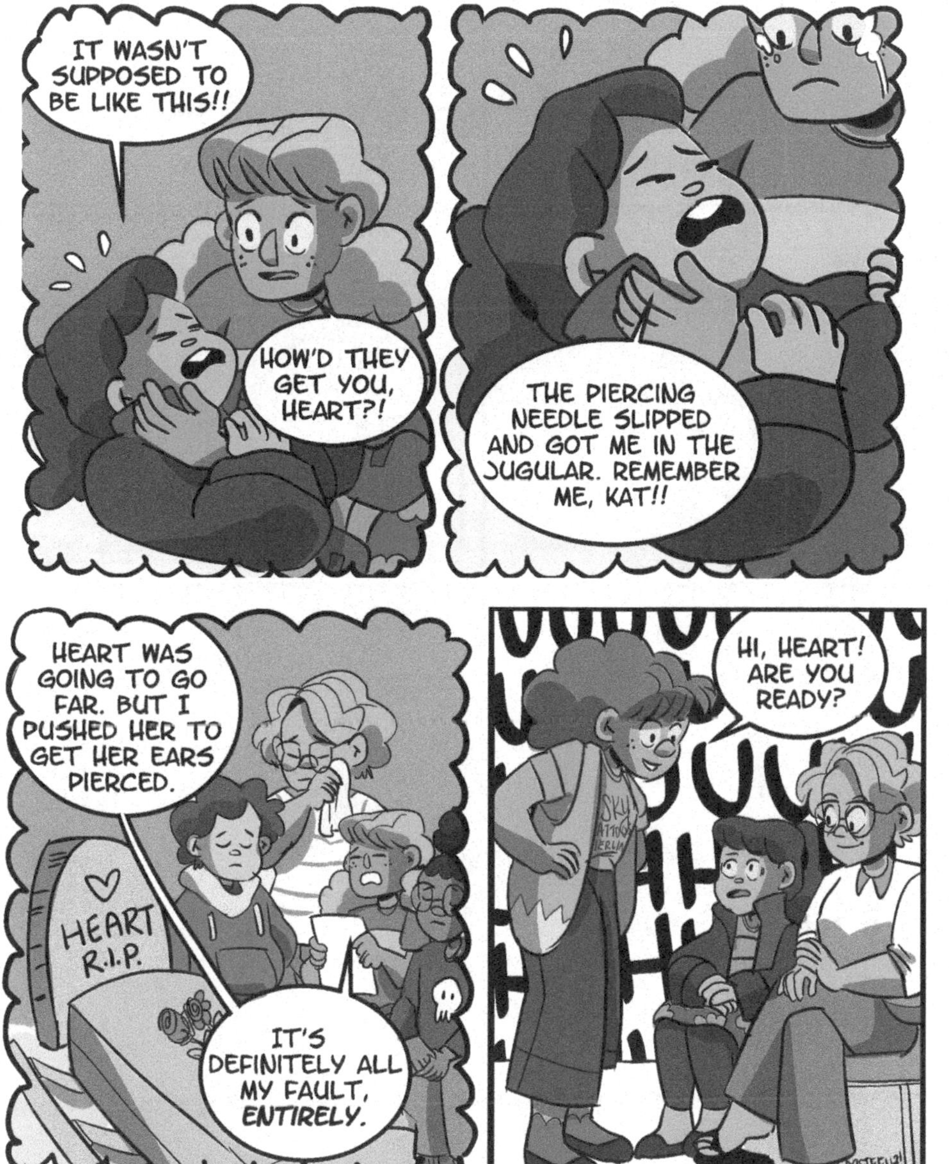
IT WASN'T SUPPOSED TO BE LIKE THIS!!
HOW'D THEY GET YOU, HEART?!
THE PIERCING NEEDLE SLIPPED AND GOT ME IN THE JUGULAR. REMEMBER ME, KAT!!
HEART WAS GOING TO GO FAR. BUT I PUSHED HER TO GET HER EARS PIERCED.
HEART R.I.P.
IT'S DEFINITELY ALL MY FAULT, ENTIRELY.
HI, HEART! ARE YOU READY?

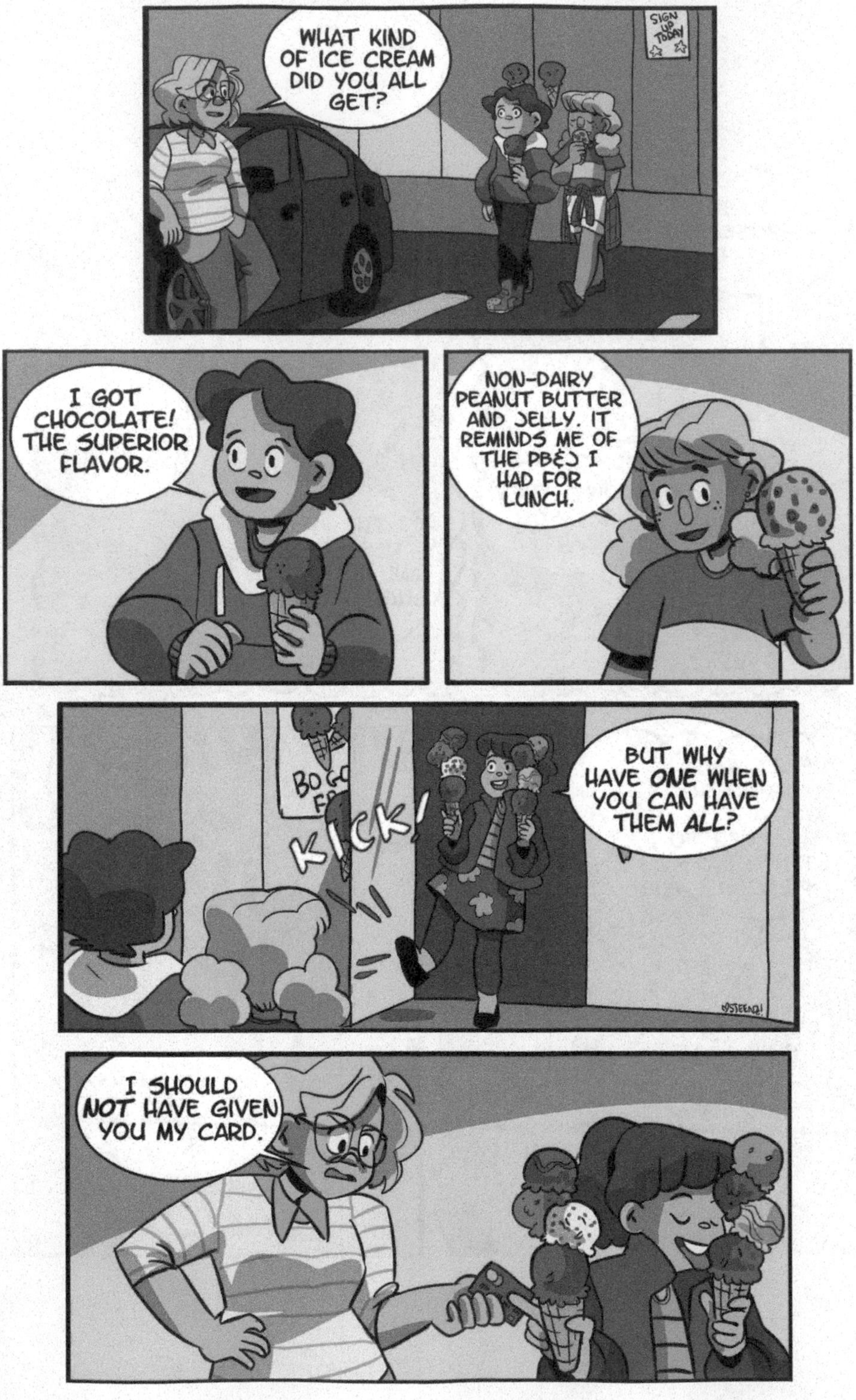
SIGN UP TODAY
WHAT KIND OF ICE CREAM DID YOU ALL GET?
I GOT CHOCOLATE! THE SUPERIOR FLAVOR.
NON-DAIRY PEANUT BUTTER AND JELLY. IT REMINDS ME OF THE PB&J I HAD FOR LUNCH.
KICK!
BUT WHY HAVE ONE WHEN YOU CAN HAVE THEM ALL?
I SHOULD NOT HAVE GIVEN YOU MY CARD.

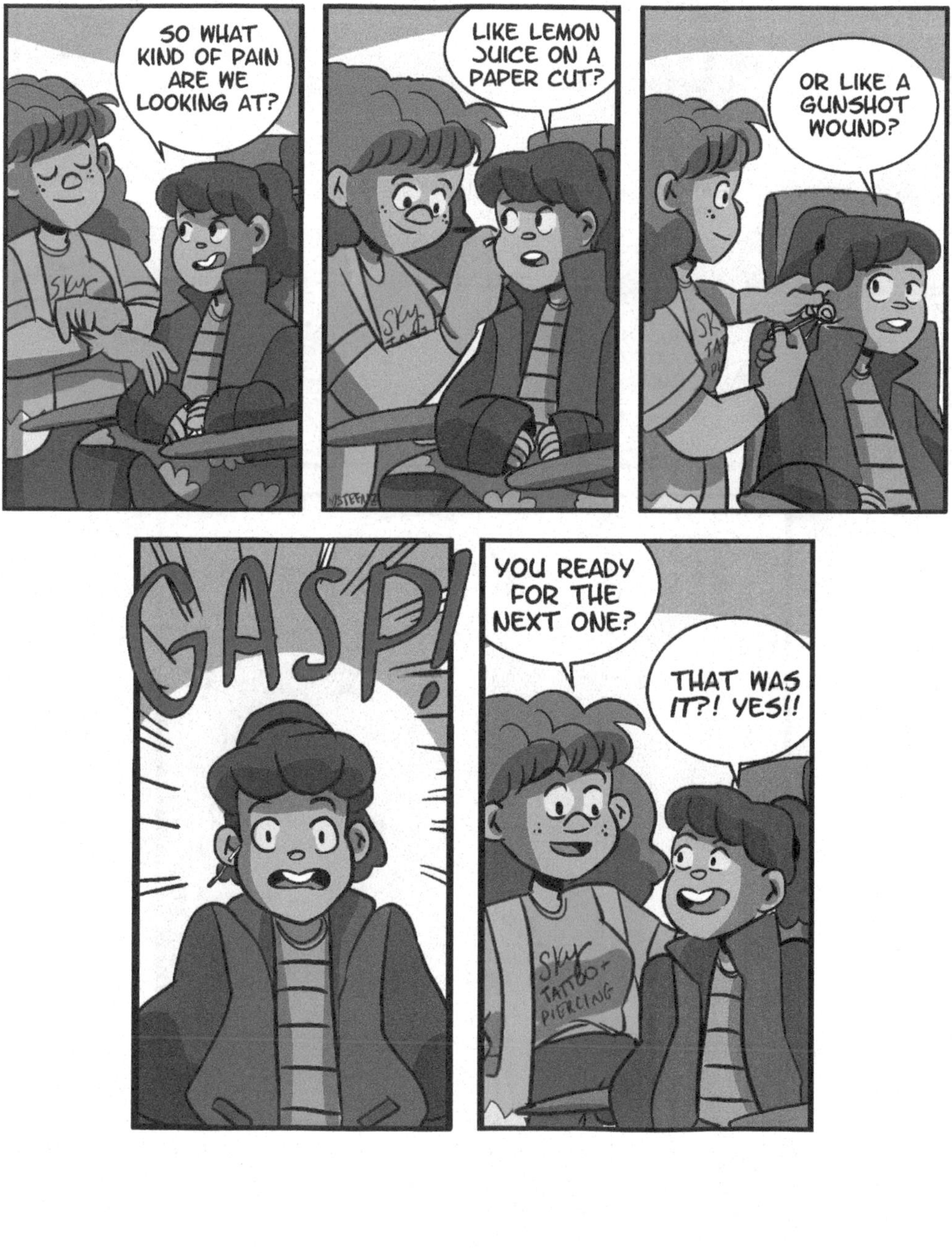
SO WHAT KIND OF PAIN ARE WE LOOKING AT?
LIKE LEMON JUICE ON A PAPER CUT?
OR LIKE A GUNSHOT WOUND?
GASP!
YOU READY FOR THE NEXT ONE?
THAT WAS IT?! YES!!

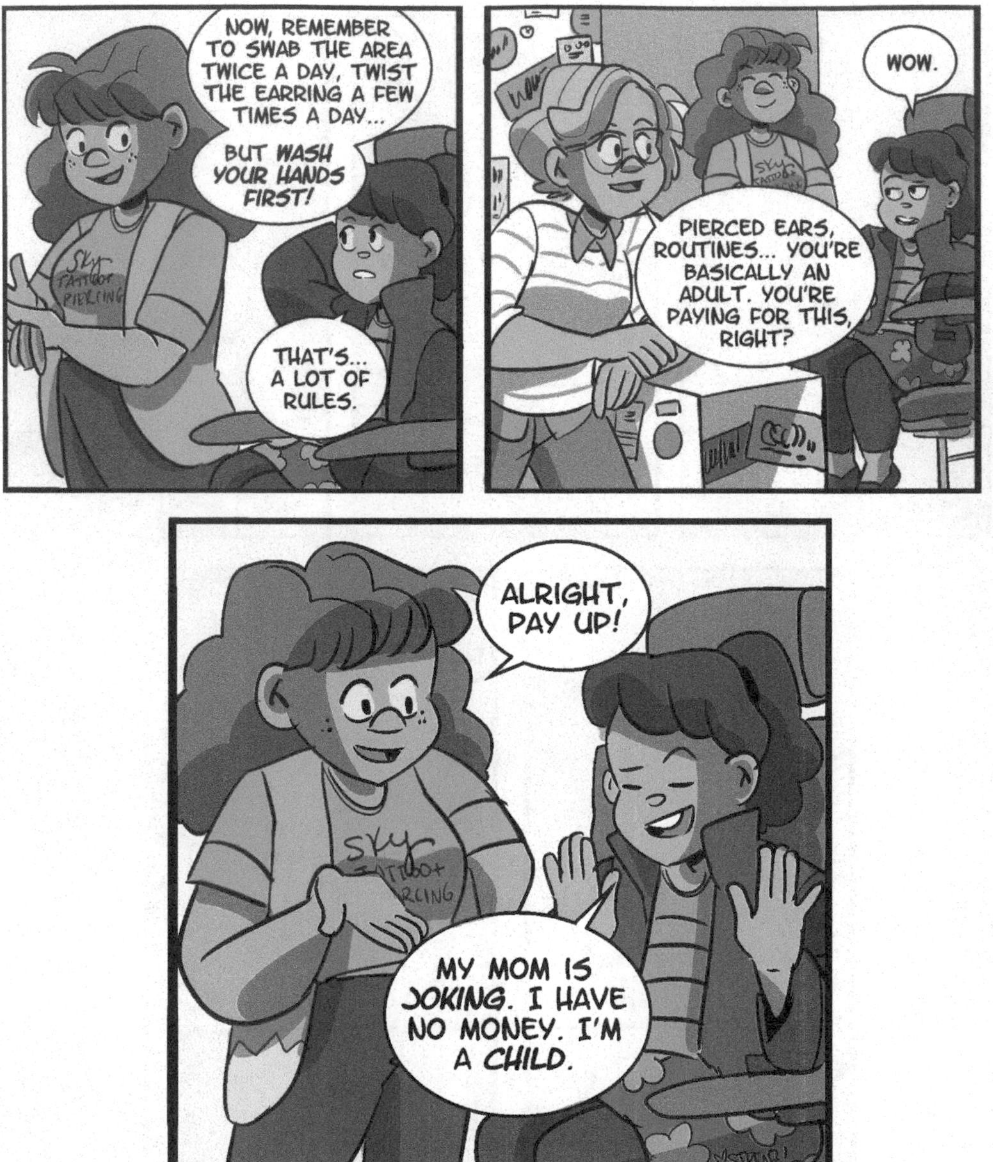
NOW, REMEMBER TO SWAB THE AREA TWICE A DAY, TWIST THE EARRING A FEW TIMES A DAY...
BUT WASH YOUR HANDS FIRST!
THAT'S... A LOT OF RULES.
WOW.
PIERCED EARS, ROUTINES... YOU'RE BASICALLY AN ADULT. YOU'RE PAYING FOR THIS, RIGHT?
ALRIGHT, PAY UP!
MY MOM IS JOKING. I HAVE NO MONEY. I'M A CHILD.

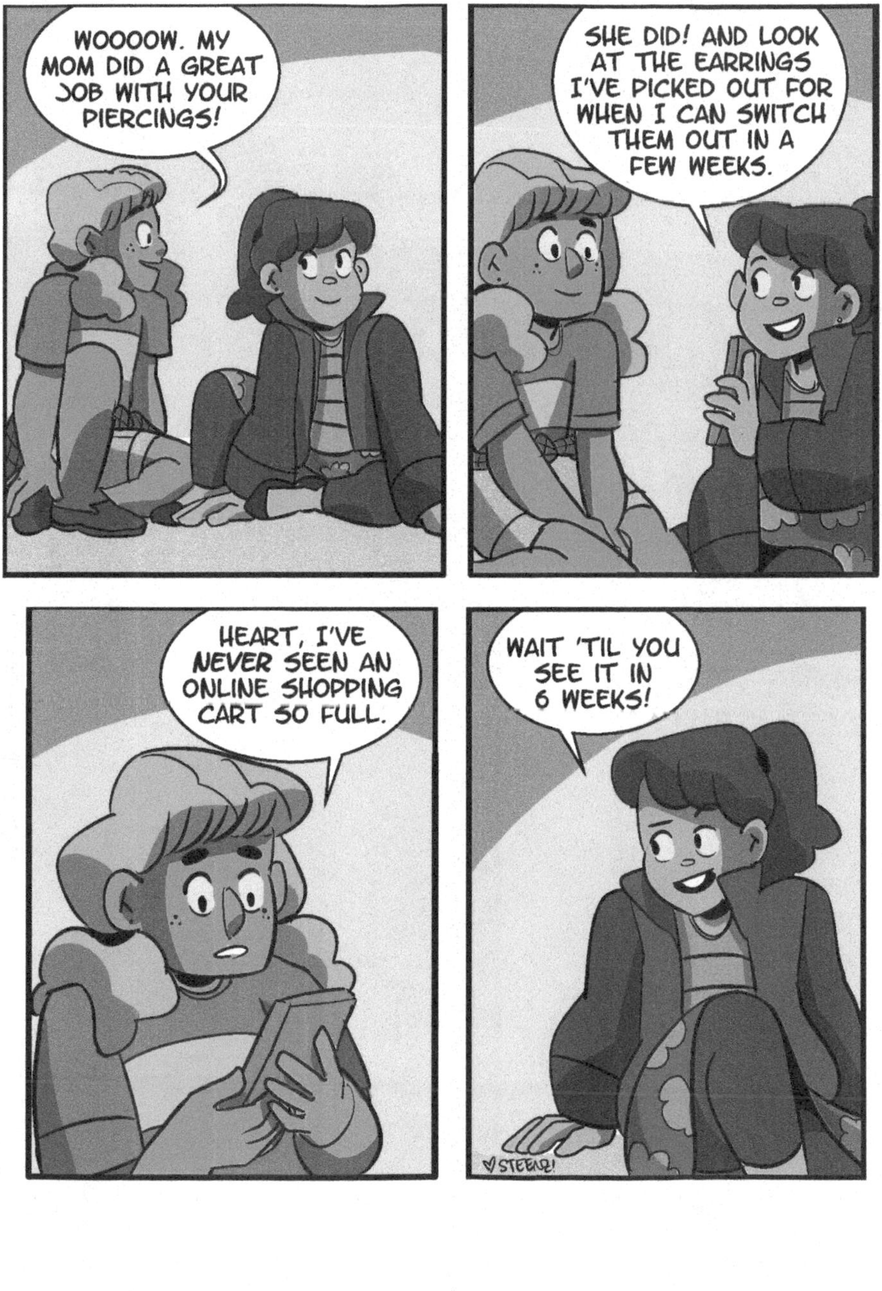
WOOOOW. MY MOM DID A GREAT JOB WITH YOUR PIERCINGS!
SHE DID! AND LOOK AT THE EARRINGS I'VE PICKED OUT FOR WHEN I CAN SWITCH THEM OUT IN A FEW WEEKS.
HEART, I'VE NEVER SEEN AN ONLINE SHOPPING CART SO FULL.
WAIT 'TIL YOU SEE IT IN 6 WEEKS!

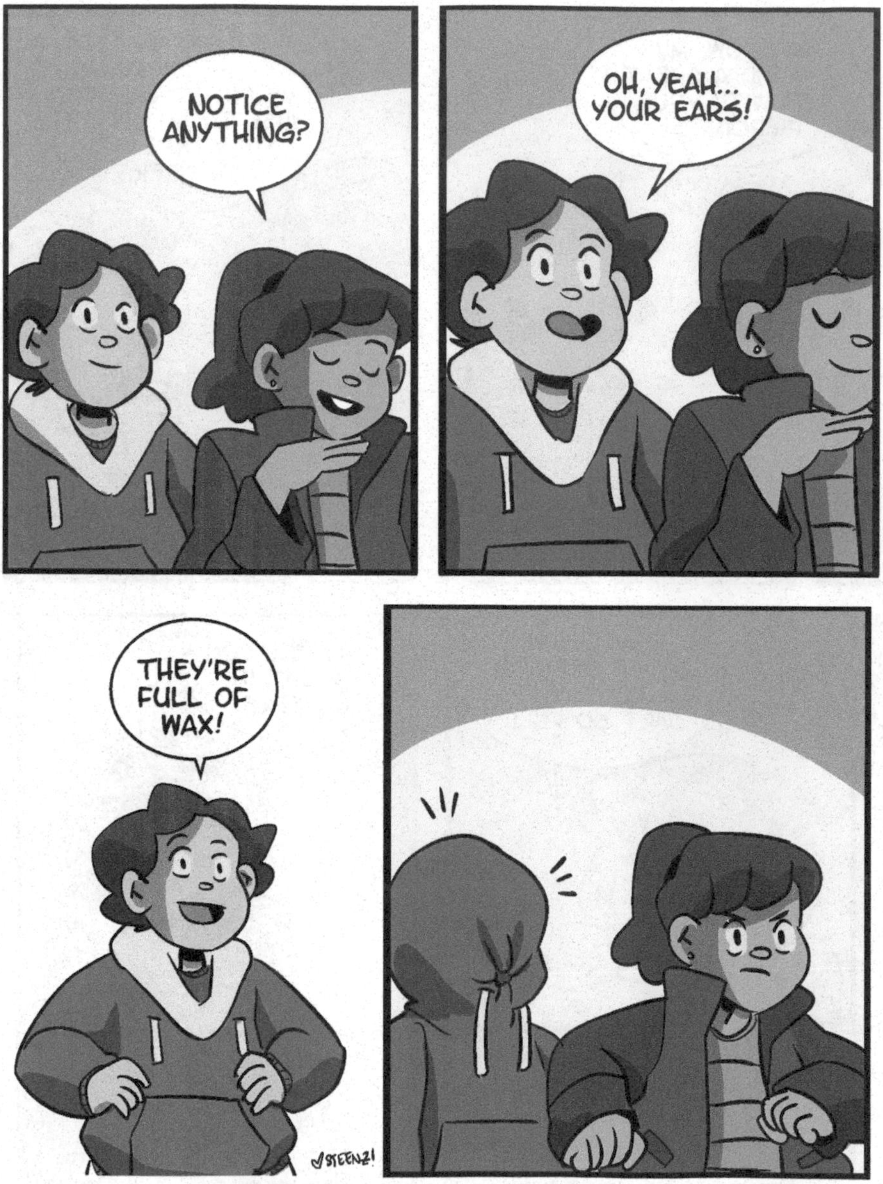
NOTICE ANYTHING?
OH, YEAH... YOUR EARS!
THEY'RE FULL OF WAX!
♡STEENZ!

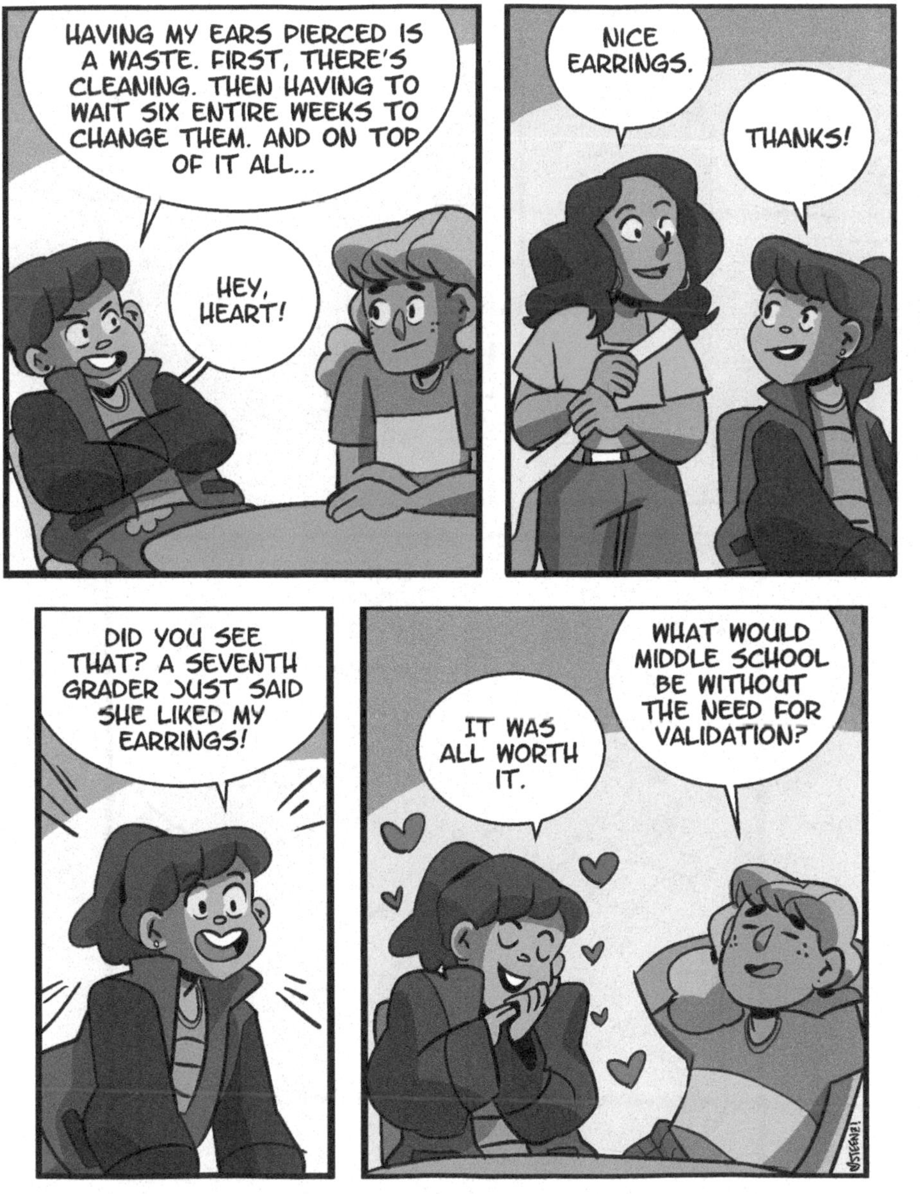
HAVING MY EARS PIERCED IS A WASTE. FIRST, THERE'S CLEANING. THEN HAVING TO WAIT SIX ENTIRE WEEKS TO CHANGE THEM. AND ON TOP OF IT ALL...
HEY, HEART!
NICE EARRINGS.
THANKS!
DID YOU SEE THAT? A SEVENTH GRADER JUST SAID SHE LIKED MY EARRINGS!
IT WAS ALL WORTH IT.
WHAT WOULD MIDDLE SCHOOL BE WITHOUT THE NEED FOR VALIDATION?

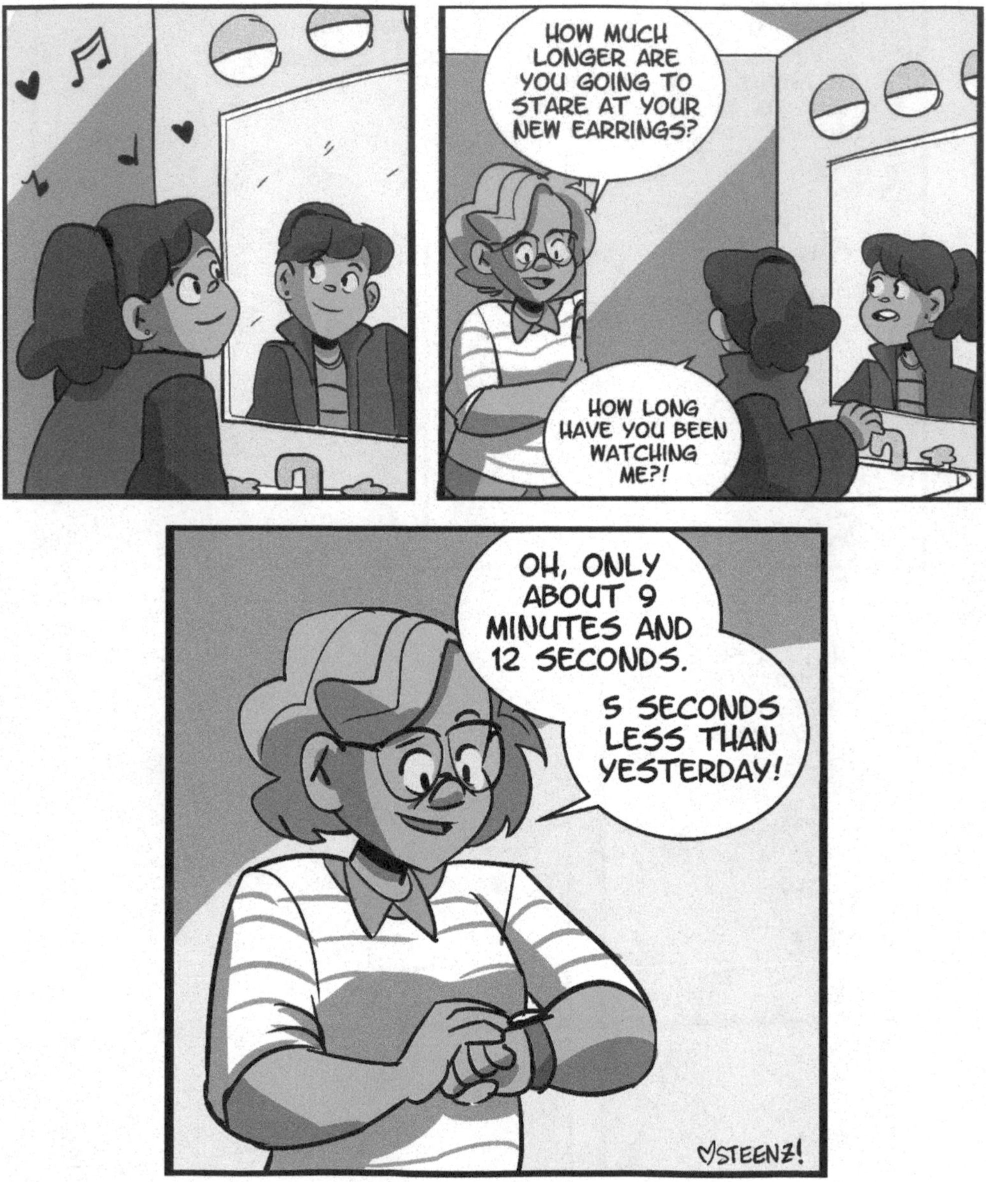
HOW MUCH LONGER ARE YOU GOING TO STARE AT YOUR NEW EARRINGS?
HOW LONG HAVE YOU BEEN WATCHING ME?!
OH, ONLY ABOUT 9 MINUTES AND 12 SECONDS.
5 SECONDS LESS THAN YESTERDAY!
♡STEENZ!

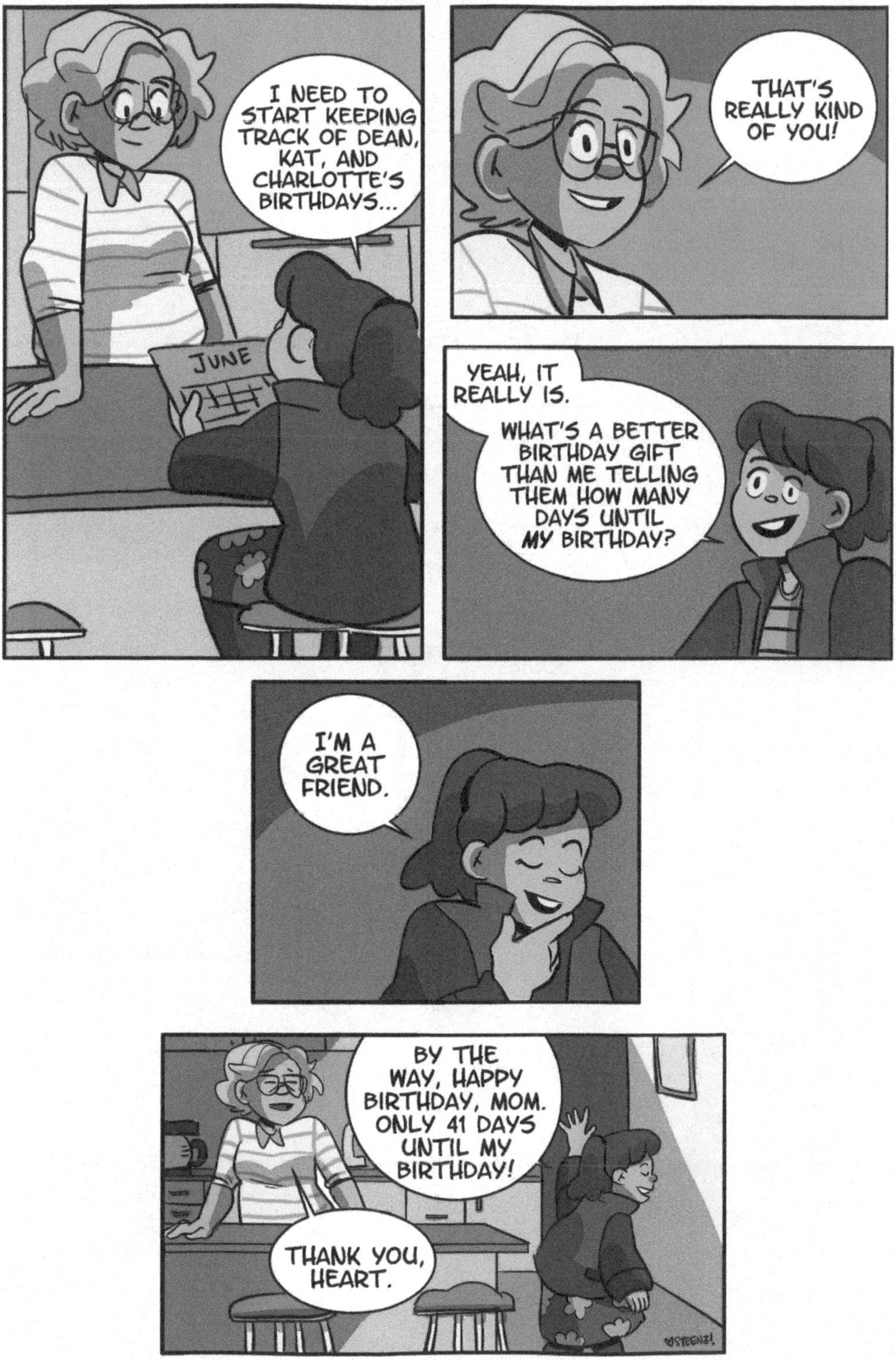
I NEED TO START KEEPING TRACK OF DEAN, KAT, AND CHARLOTTE'S BIRTHDAYS...
JUNE
THAT'S REALLY KIND OF YOU!
YEAH, IT REALLY IS.
WHAT'S A BETTER BIRTHDAY GIFT THAN ME TELLING THEM HOW MANY DAYS UNTIL MY BIRTHDAY?
I'M A GREAT FRIEND.
BY THE WAY, HAPPY BIRTHDAY, MOM. ONLY 41 DAYS UNTIL MY BIRTHDAY!
THANK YOU, HEART.

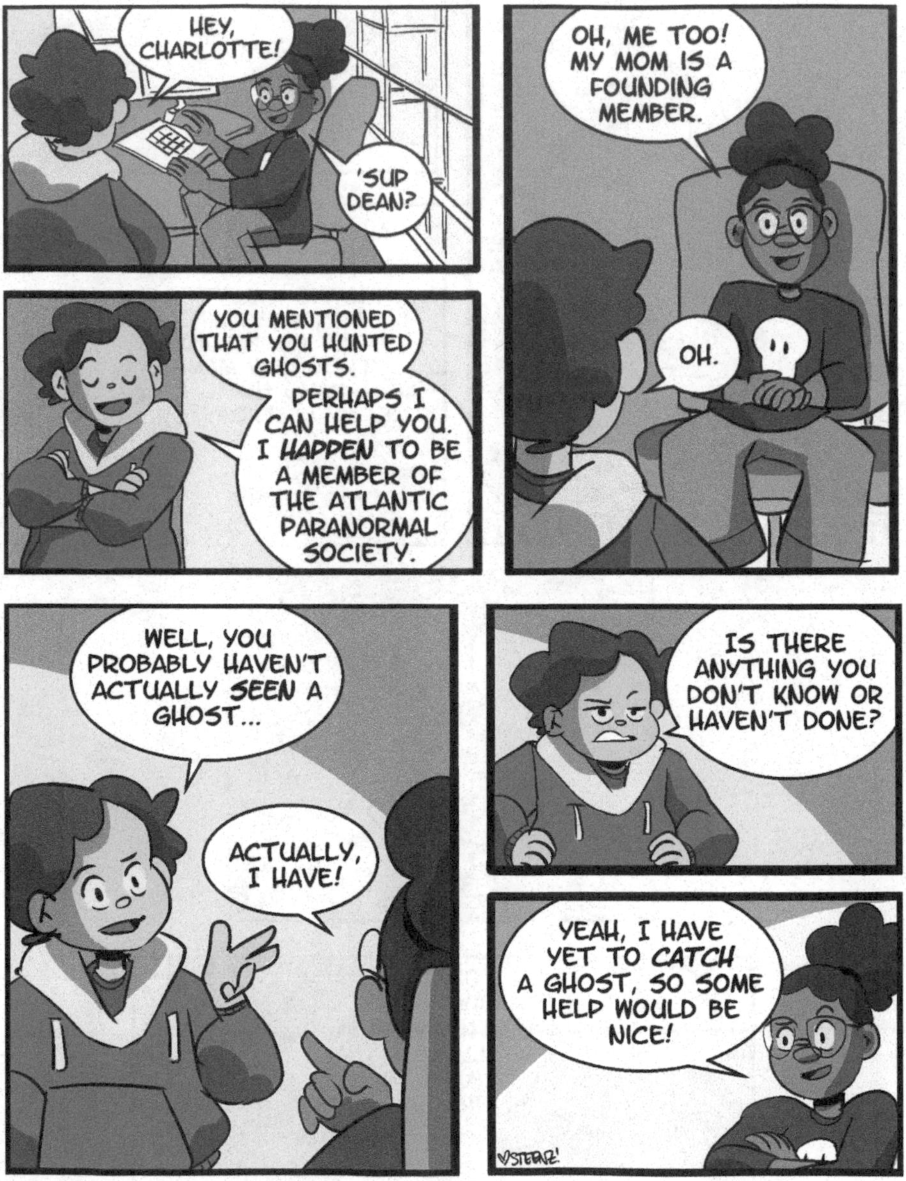
HEY, CHARLOTTE!
'SUP DEAN?
OH, ME TOO! MY MOM IS A FOUNDING MEMBER.
YOU MENTIONED THAT YOU HUNTED GHOSTS.
PERHAPS I CAN HELP YOU. I HAPPEN TO BE A MEMBER OF THE ATLANTIC PARANORMAL SOCIETY.
OH.
WELL, YOU PROBABLY HAVEN'T ACTUALLY SEEN A GHOST...
ACTUALLY, I HAVE!
IS THERE ANYTHING YOU DON'T KNOW OR HAVEN'T DONE?
YEAH, I HAVE YET TO CATCH A GHOST, SO SOME HELP WOULD BE NICE!

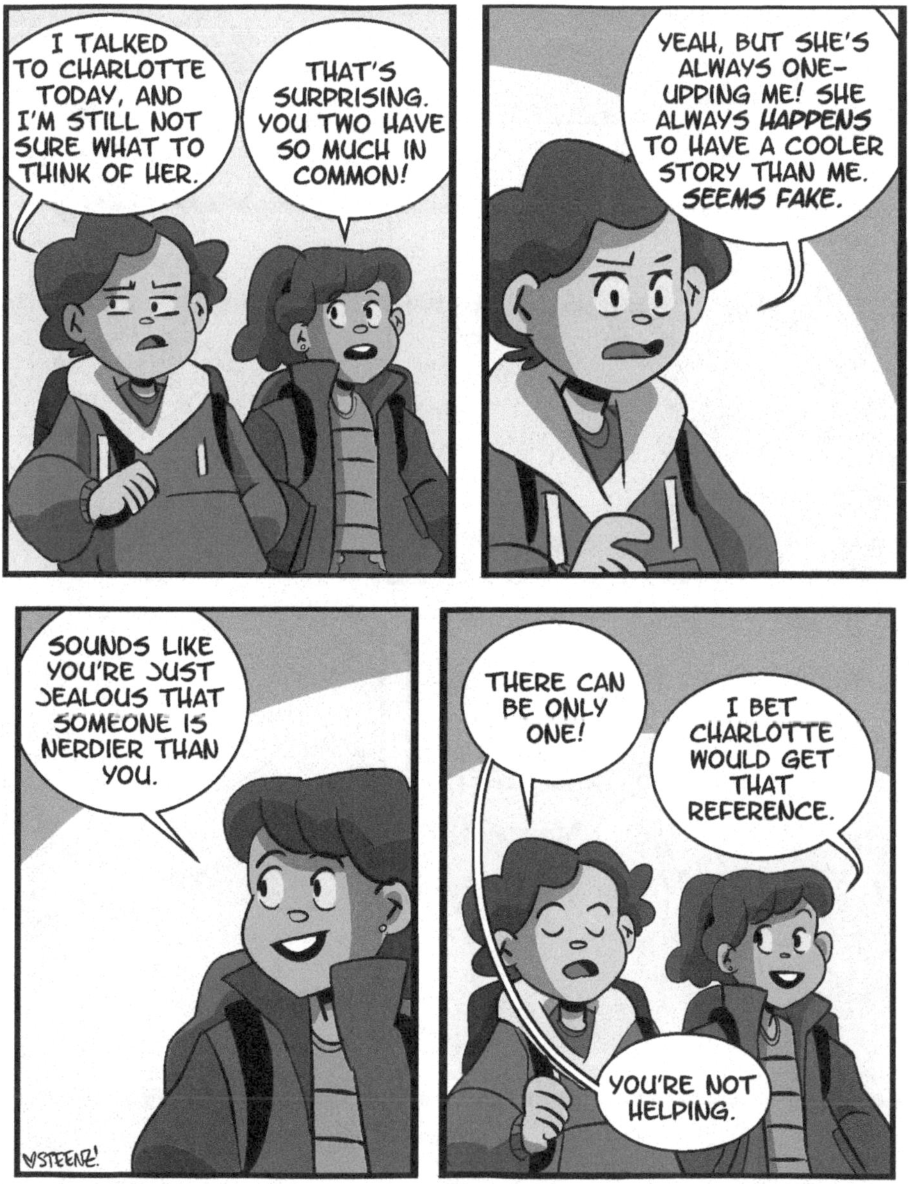
I TALKED TO CHARLOTTE TODAY, AND I'M STILL NOT SURE WHAT TO THINK OF HER.
THAT'S SURPRISING. YOU TWO HAVE SO MUCH IN COMMON!
YEAH, BUT SHE'S ALWAYS ONE-UPPING ME! SHE ALWAYS HAPPENS TO HAVE A COOLER STORY THAN ME. SEEMS FAKE.
SOUNDS LIKE YOU'RE JUST JEALOUS THAT SOMEONE IS NERDIER THAN YOU.
♡STEENZ!
THERE CAN BE ONLY ONE!
I BET CHARLOTTE WOULD GET THAT REFERENCE.
YOU'RE NOT HELPING.

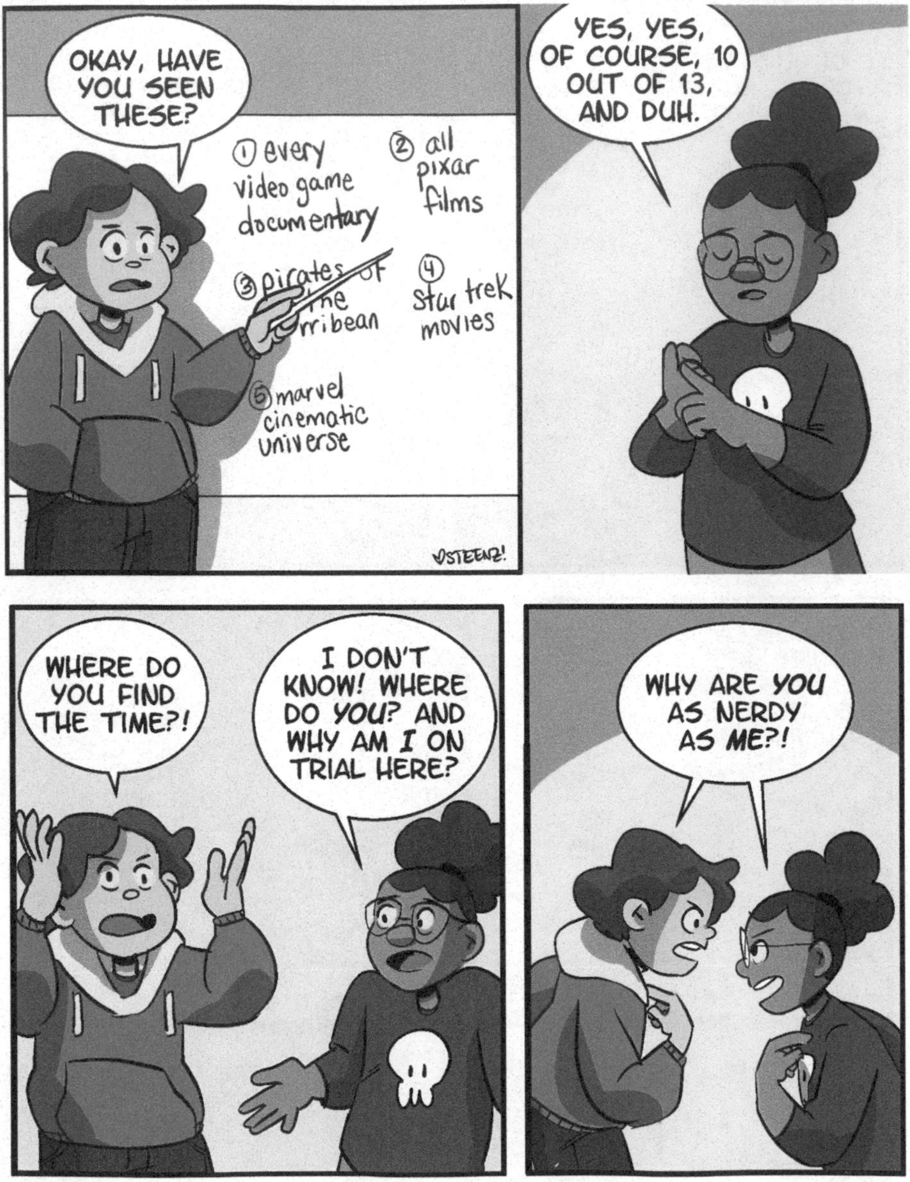
OKAY, HAVE YOU SEEN THESE?
① every video game documentary
② all pixar films
③ pirates of the ...rribean
④ star trek movies
⑤ marvel cinematic universe
STEENZ!
YES, YES, OF COURSE, 10 OUT OF 13, AND DUH.
WHERE DO YOU FIND THE TIME?!
I DON'T KNOW! WHERE DO YOU? AND WHY AM I ON TRIAL HERE?
WHY ARE YOU AS NERDY AS ME?!

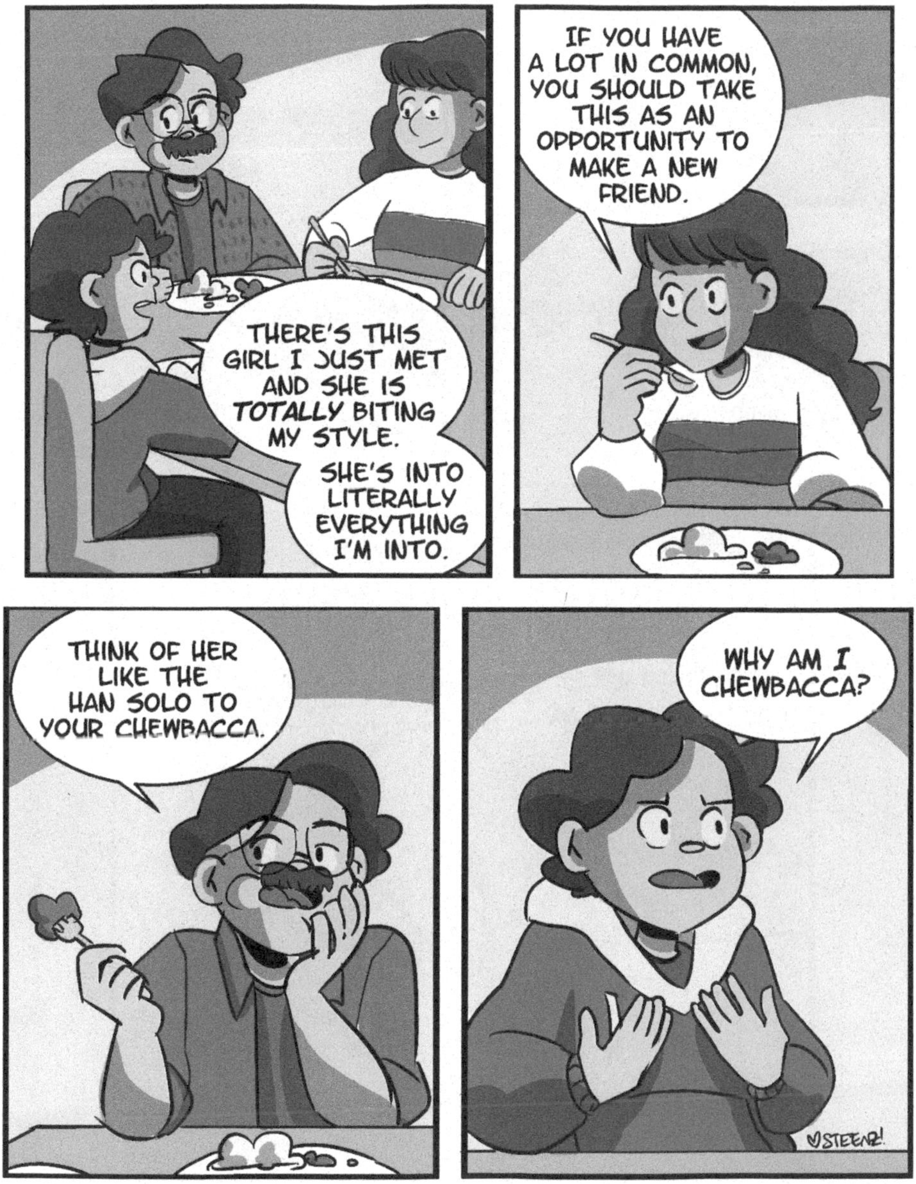
THERE'S THIS GIRL I JUST MET AND SHE IS *TOTALLY* BITING MY STYLE.
SHE'S INTO LITERALLY EVERYTHING I'M INTO.
IF YOU HAVE A LOT IN COMMON, YOU SHOULD TAKE THIS AS AN OPPORTUNITY TO MAKE A NEW FRIEND.
THINK OF HER LIKE THE HAN SOLO TO YOUR CHEWBACCA.
WHY AM *I* CHEWBACCA?
STEENZ!

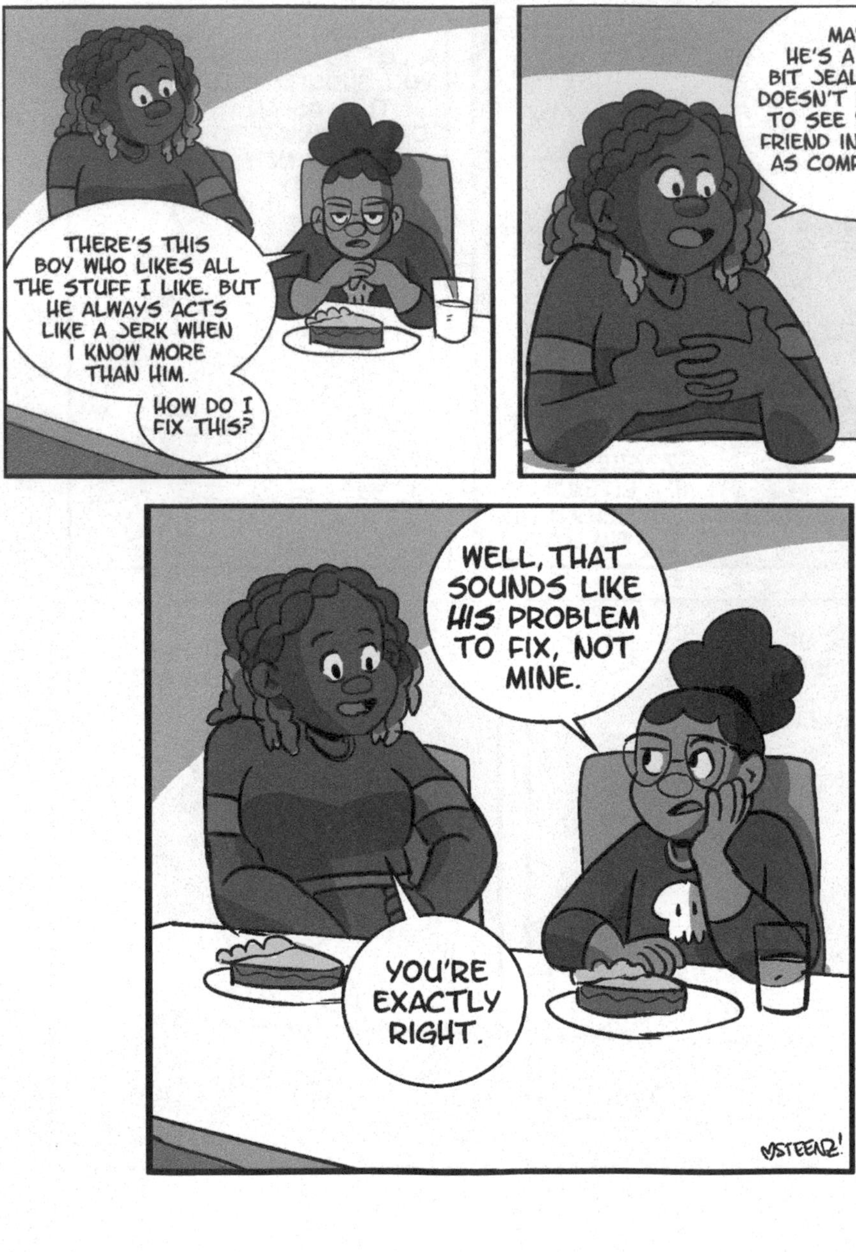
THERE'S THIS BOY WHO LIKES ALL THE STUFF I LIKE. BUT HE ALWAYS ACTS LIKE A JERK WHEN I KNOW MORE THAN HIM.
HOW DO I FIX THIS?
MAYBE HE'S A LITTLE BIT JEALOUS AND DOESN'T KNOW HOW TO SEE YOU AS A FRIEND INSTEAD OF AS COMPETITION.
WELL, THAT SOUNDS LIKE HIS PROBLEM TO FIX, NOT MINE.
YOU'RE EXACTLY RIGHT.
STEENZ!

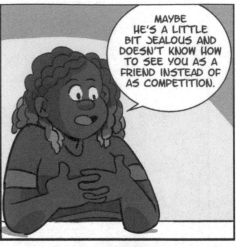

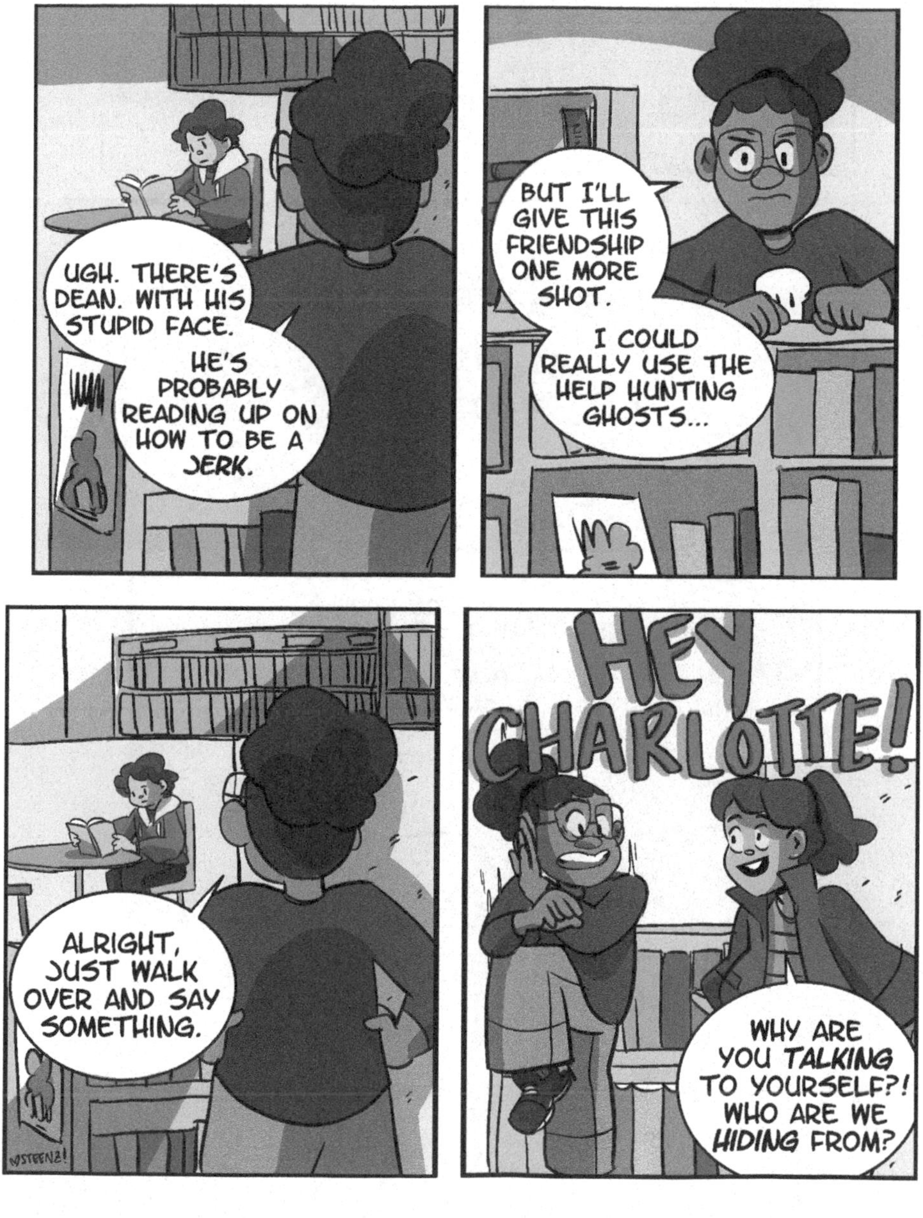
UGH. THERE'S DEAN. WITH HIS STUPID FACE.
HE'S PROBABLY READING UP ON HOW TO BE A JERK.
BUT I'LL GIVE THIS FRIENDSHIP ONE MORE SHOT.
I COULD REALLY USE THE HELP HUNTING GHOSTS...
ALRIGHT, JUST WALK OVER AND SAY SOMETHING.
HEY CHARLOTTE!
WHY ARE YOU TALKING TO YOURSELF?! WHO ARE WE HIDING FROM?

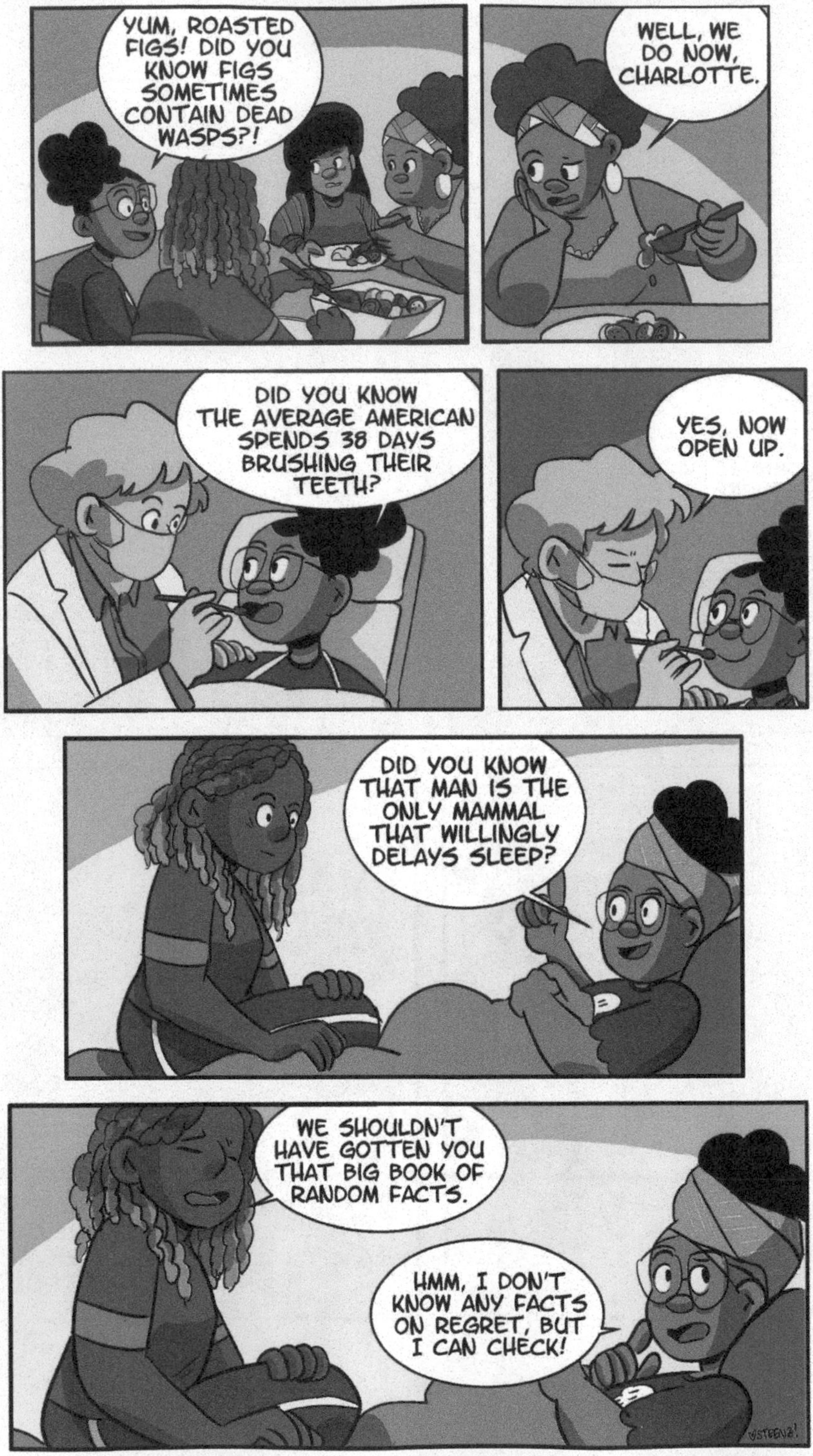
YUM, ROASTED FIGS! DID YOU KNOW FIGS SOMETIMES CONTAIN DEAD WASPS?!
WELL, WE DO NOW, CHARLOTTE.
DID YOU KNOW THE AVERAGE AMERICAN SPENDS 38 DAYS BRUSHING THEIR TEETH?
YES, NOW OPEN UP.
DID YOU KNOW THAT MAN IS THE ONLY MAMMAL THAT WILLINGLY DELAYS SLEEP?
WE SHOULDN'T HAVE GOTTEN YOU THAT BIG BOOK OF RANDOM FACTS.
HMM, I DON'T KNOW ANY FACTS ON REGRET, BUT I CAN CHECK!

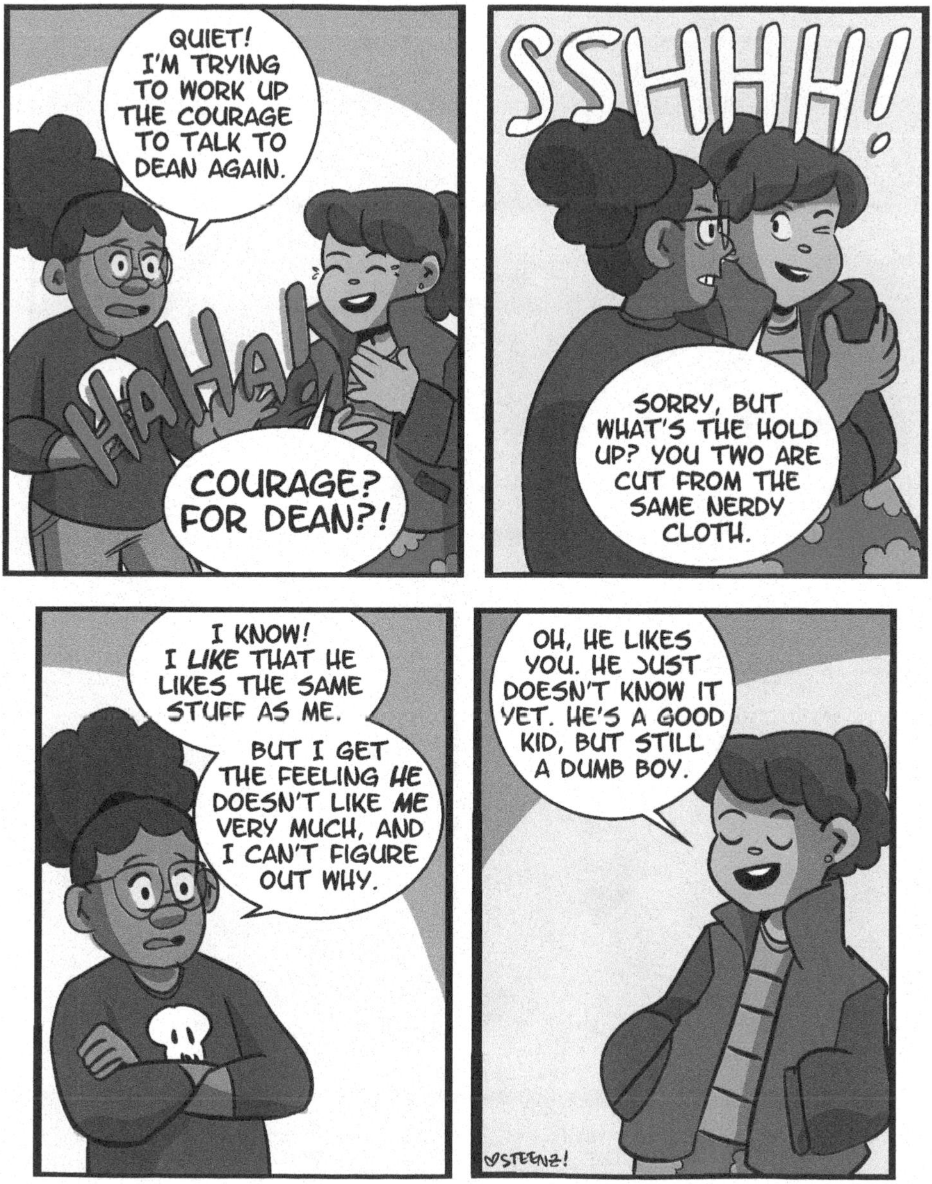
QUIET! I'M TRYING TO WORK UP THE COURAGE TO TALK TO DEAN AGAIN.
HAHA!
COURAGE? FOR DEAN?!
SSHHH!
SORRY, BUT WHAT'S THE HOLD UP? YOU TWO ARE CUT FROM THE SAME NERDY CLOTH.
I KNOW! I *LIKE* THAT HE LIKES THE SAME STUFF AS ME.
BUT I GET THE FEELING *HE* DOESN'T LIKE *ME* VERY MUCH, AND I CAN'T FIGURE OUT WHY.
OH, HE LIKES YOU. HE JUST DOESN'T KNOW IT YET. HE'S A GOOD KID, BUT STILL A DUMB BOY.
♡STEENZ!

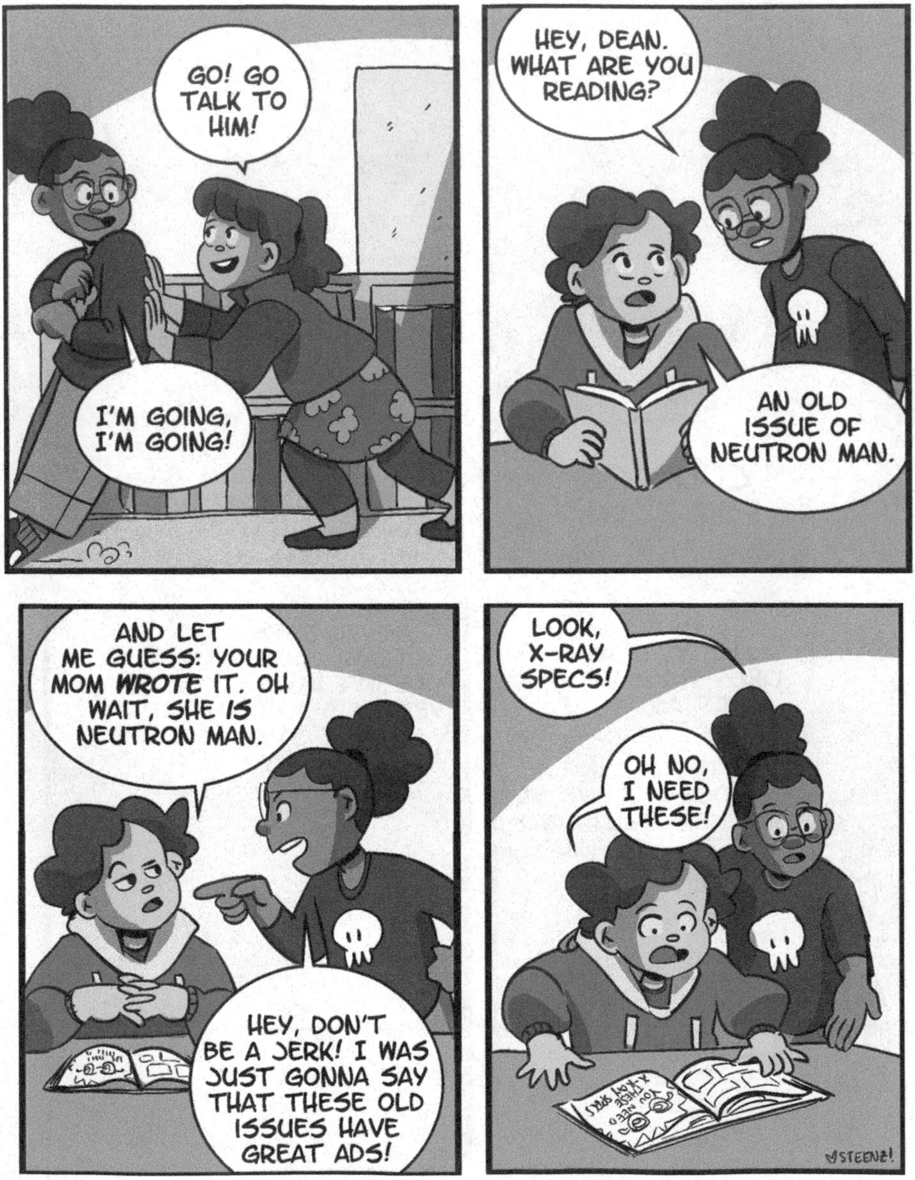
GO! GO TALK TO HIM!
I'M GOING, I'M GOING!
HEY, DEAN. WHAT ARE YOU READING?
AN OLD ISSUE OF NEUTRON MAN.
AND LET ME GUESS: YOUR MOM WROTE IT. OH WAIT, SHE IS NEUTRON MAN.
HEY, DON'T BE A JERK! I WAS JUST GONNA SAY THAT THESE OLD ISSUES HAVE GREAT ADS!
LOOK, X-RAY SPECS!
OH NO, I NEED THESE!
STEENZ!

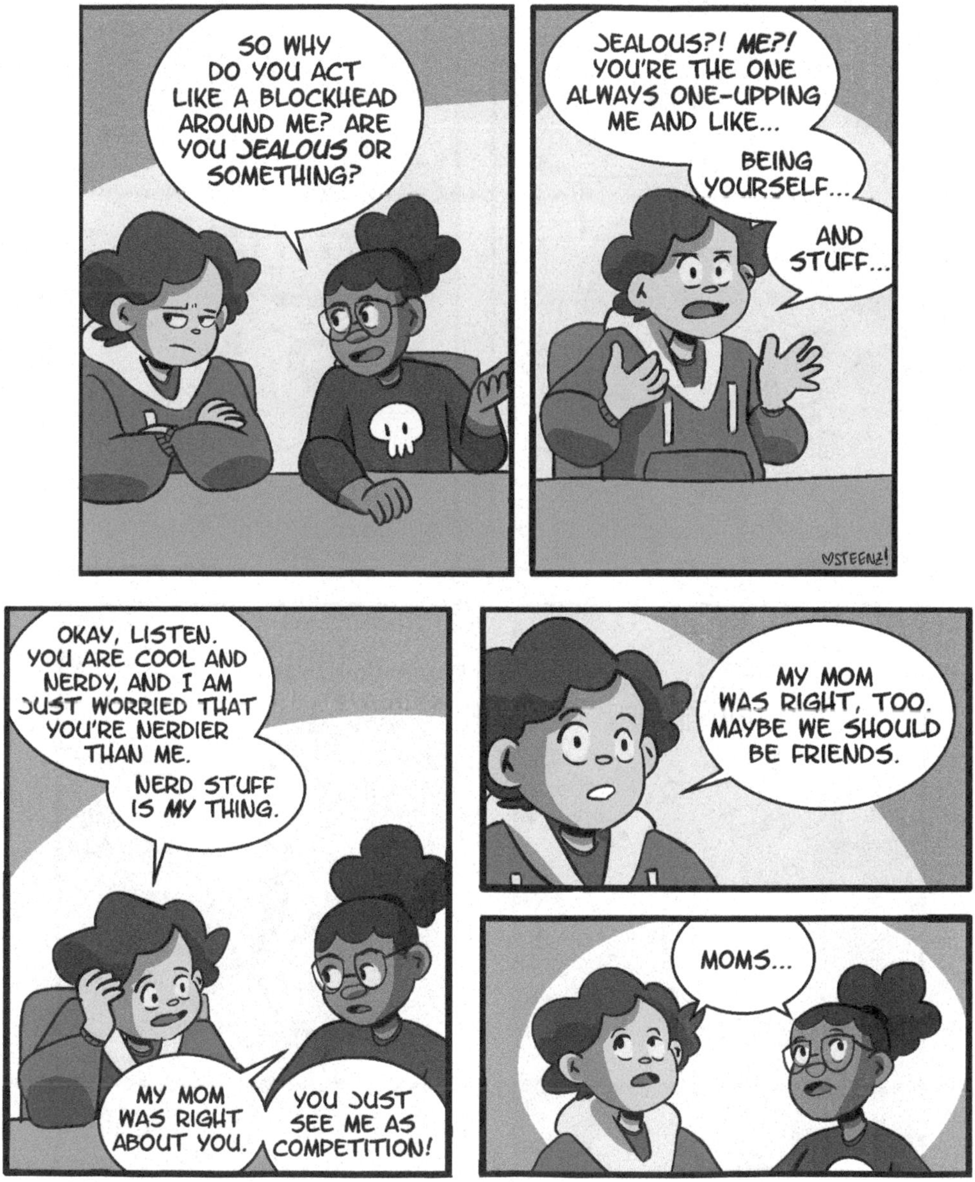
SO WHY DO YOU ACT LIKE A BLOCKHEAD AROUND ME? ARE YOU JEALOUS OR SOMETHING?
JEALOUS?! ME?! YOU'RE THE ONE ALWAYS ONE-UPPING ME AND LIKE...
BEING YOURSELF...
AND STUFF...
♡STEENZ!
OKAY, LISTEN. YOU ARE COOL AND NERDY, AND I AM JUST WORRIED THAT YOU'RE NERDIER THAN ME.
NERD STUFF IS MY THING.
MY MOM WAS RIGHT ABOUT YOU.
YOU JUST SEE ME AS COMPETITION!
MY MOM WAS RIGHT, TOO. MAYBE WE SHOULD BE FRIENDS.
MOMS...

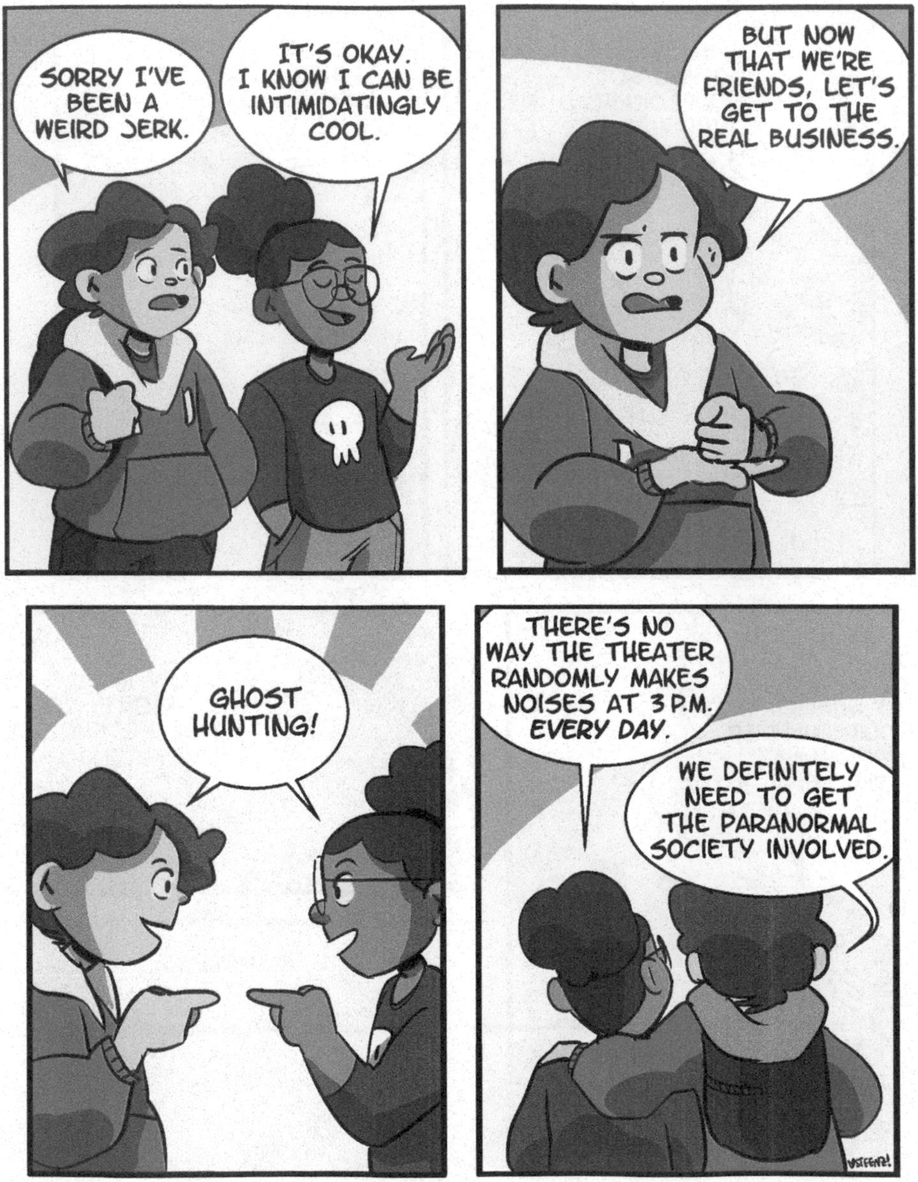
SORRY I'VE BEEN A WEIRD JERK.
IT'S OKAY. I KNOW I CAN BE INTIMIDATINGLY COOL.
BUT NOW THAT WE'RE FRIENDS, LET'S GET TO THE REAL BUSINESS.
GHOST HUNTING!
THERE'S NO WAY THE THEATER RANDOMLY MAKES NOISES AT 3 P.M. EVERY DAY.
WE DEFINITELY NEED TO GET THE PARANORMAL SOCIETY INVOLVED.

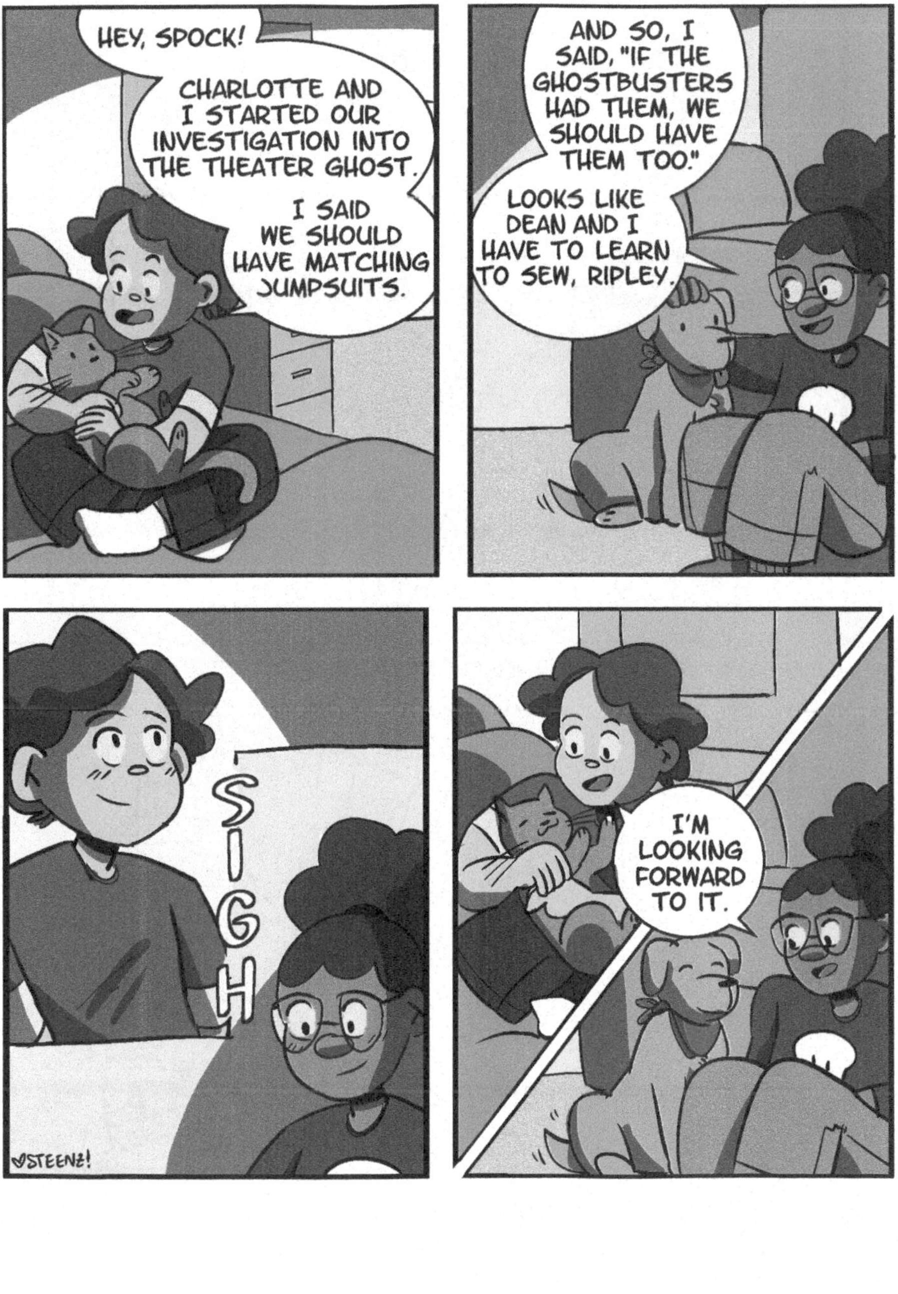
HEY, SPOCK!
CHARLOTTE AND I STARTED OUR INVESTIGATION INTO THE THEATER GHOST.
I SAID WE SHOULD HAVE MATCHING JUMPSUITS.
AND SO, I SAID, "IF THE GHOSTBUSTERS HAD THEM, WE SHOULD HAVE THEM TOO."
LOOKS LIKE DEAN AND I HAVE TO LEARN TO SEW, RIPLEY.
SIGH
♡STEENZ!
I'M LOOKING FORWARD TO IT.

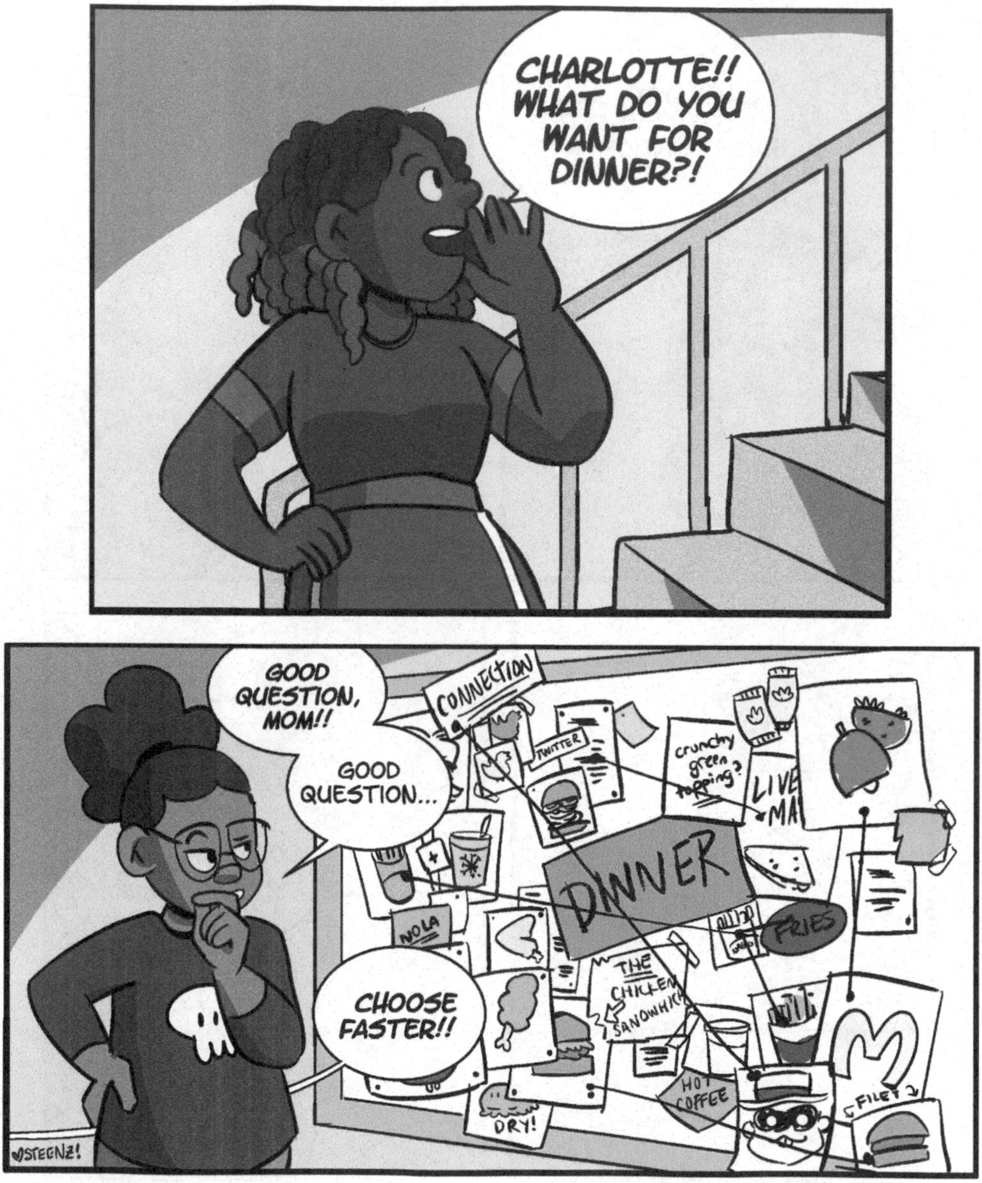
CHARLOTTE!! WHAT DO YOU WANT FOR DINNER?!
GOOD QUESTION, MOM!!
GOOD QUESTION...
CHOOSE FASTER!!
CONNECTION
TWITTER
crunchy green topping?
DINNER
FRIES
NOLA
HOT COFFEE
FILET
DRY!
STEENZ!

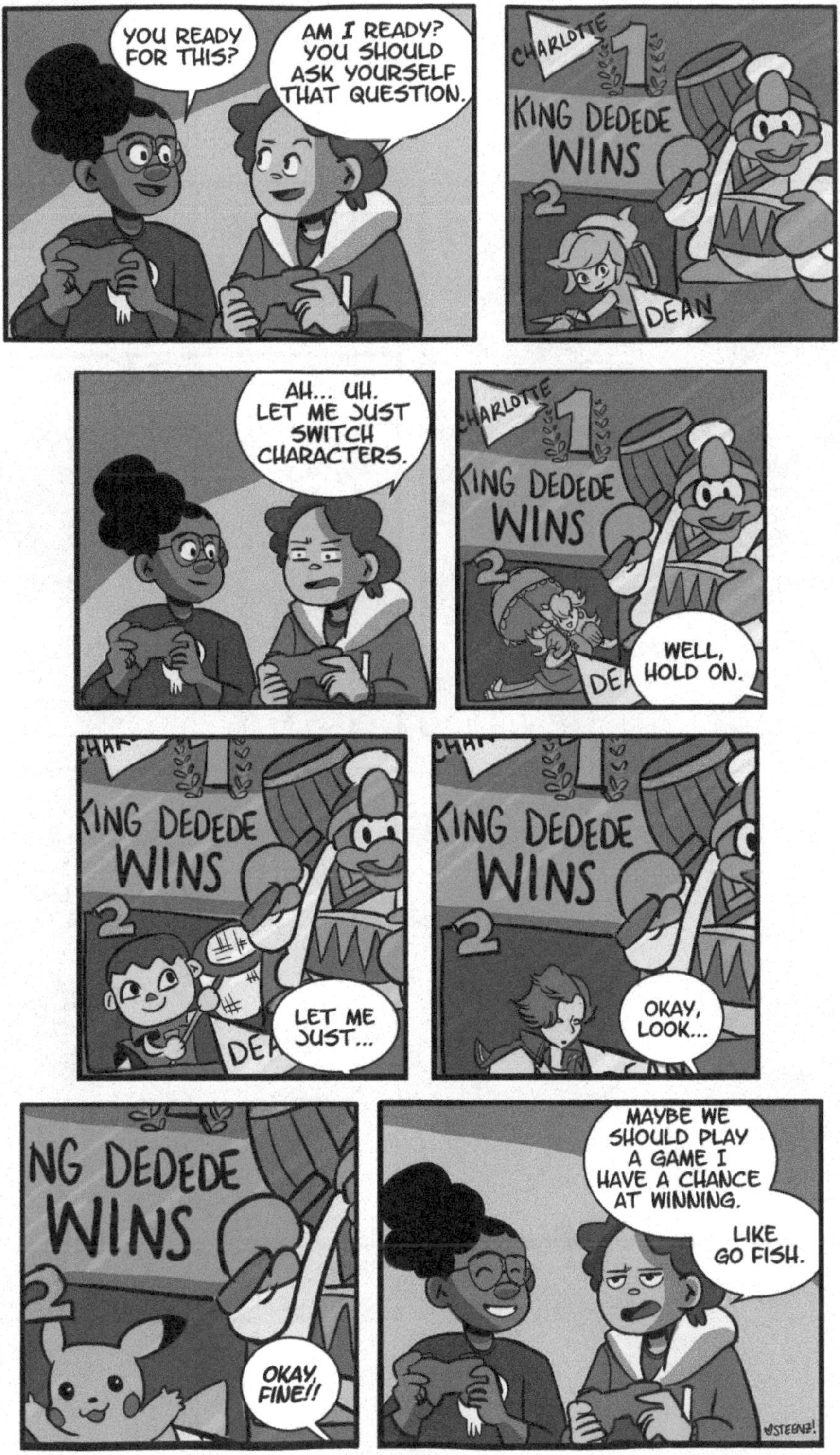

YOU READY FOR THIS?
AM I READY? YOU SHOULD ASK YOURSELF THAT QUESTION.
CHARLOTTE
KING DEDEDE WINS
DEAN
AH... UH. LET ME JUST SWITCH CHARACTERS.
CHARLOTTE
KING DEDEDE WINS
WELL, HOLD ON.
KING DEDEDE WINS
LET ME JUST...
KING DEDEDE WINS
OKAY, LOOK...
NG DEDEDE WINS
OKAY, FINE!!
MAYBE WE SHOULD PLAY A GAME I HAVE A CHANCE AT WINNING.
LIKE GO FISH.

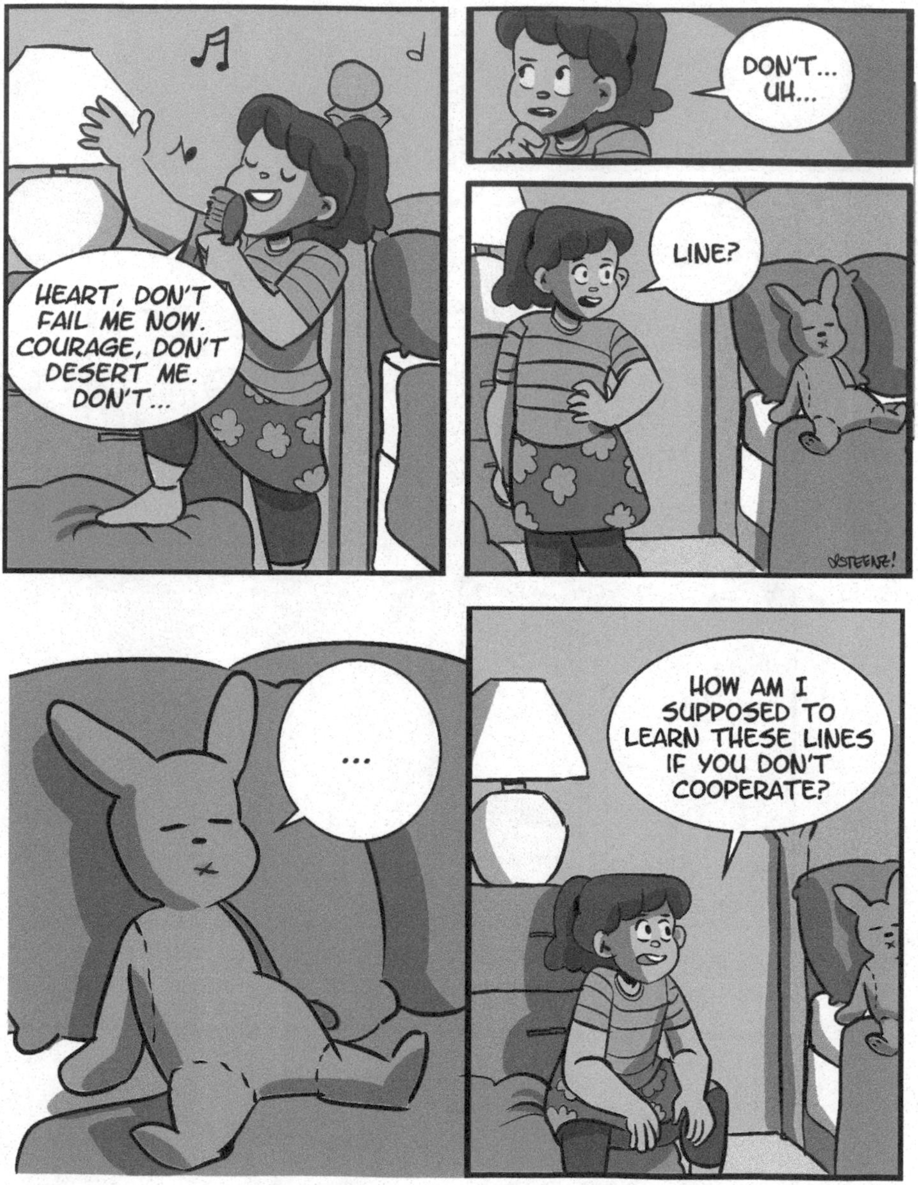
HEART, DON'T FAIL ME NOW. COURAGE, DON'T DESERT ME. DON'T...
DON'T... UH...
LINE?
STEENZ!
...
HOW AM I SUPPOSED TO LEARN THESE LINES IF YOU DON'T COOPERATE?

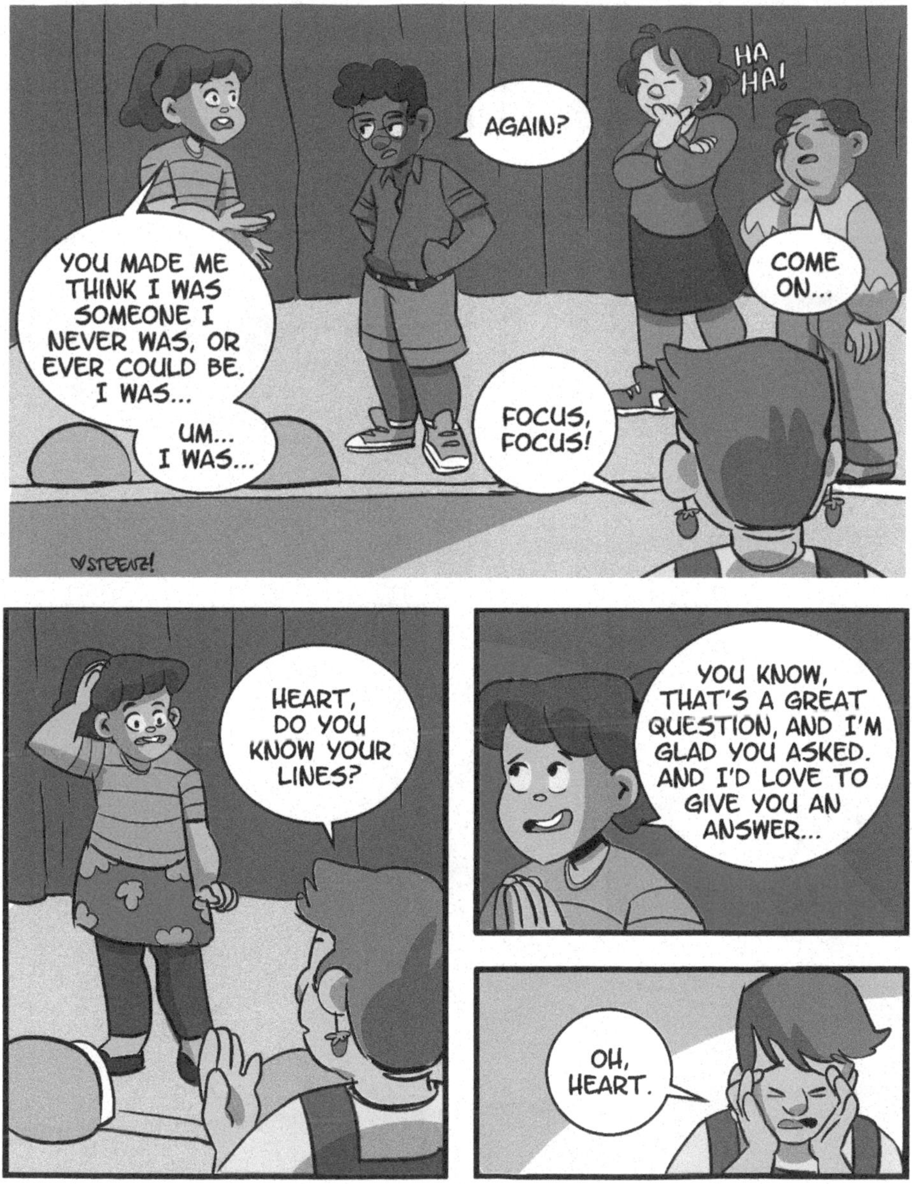
YOU MADE ME THINK I WAS SOMEONE I NEVER WAS, OR EVER COULD BE. I WAS...
UM... I WAS...
AGAIN?
HA HA!
COME ON...
FOCUS, FOCUS!
♡STEENZ!
HEART, DO YOU KNOW YOUR LINES?
YOU KNOW, THAT'S A GREAT QUESTION, AND I'M GLAD YOU ASKED. AND I'D LOVE TO GIVE YOU AN ANSWER...
OH, HEART.

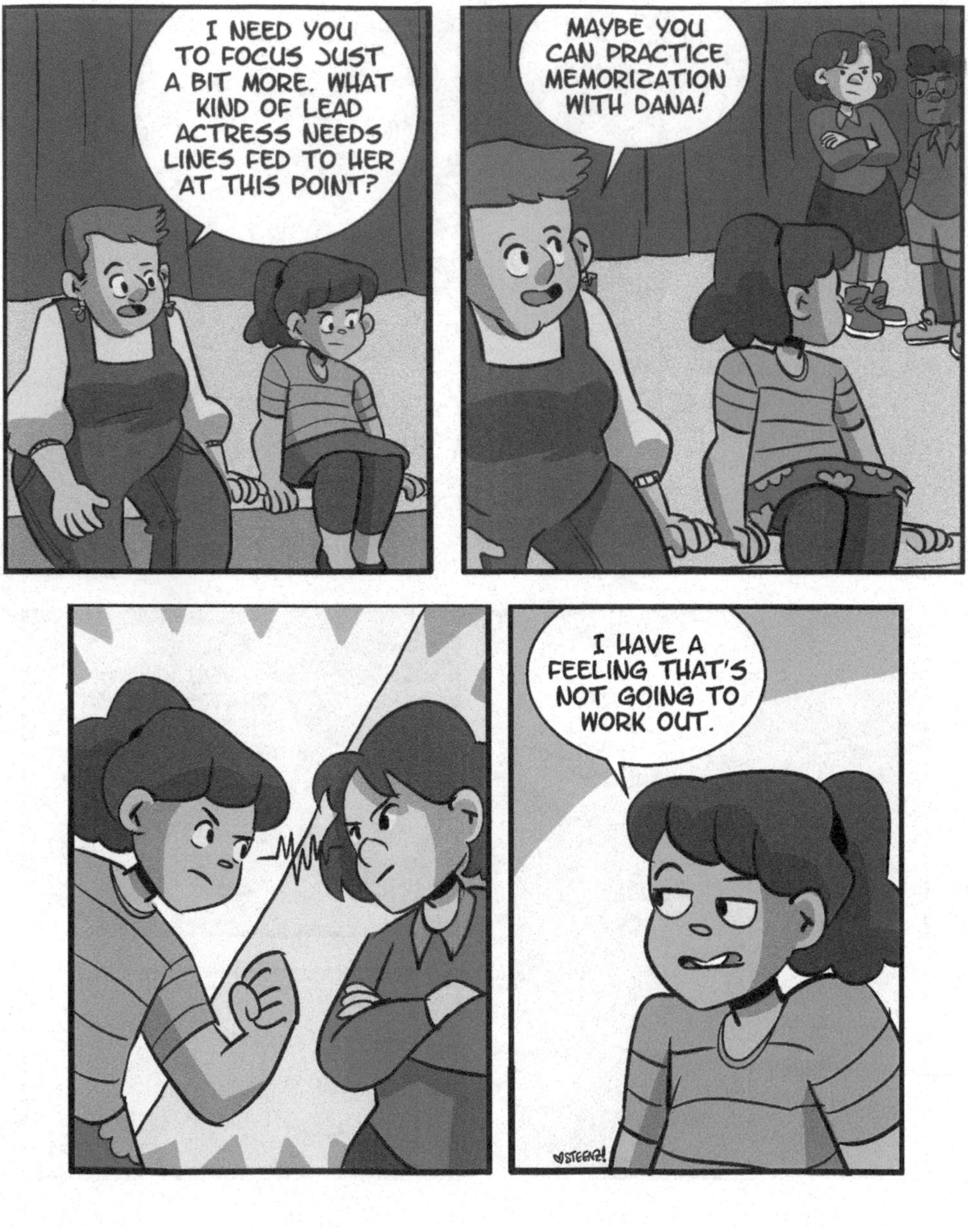
I NEED YOU TO FOCUS JUST A BIT MORE. WHAT KIND OF LEAD ACTRESS NEEDS LINES FED TO HER AT THIS POINT?
MAYBE YOU CAN PRACTICE MEMORIZATION WITH DANA!
I HAVE A FEELING THAT'S NOT GOING TO WORK OUT.
STEENZ!

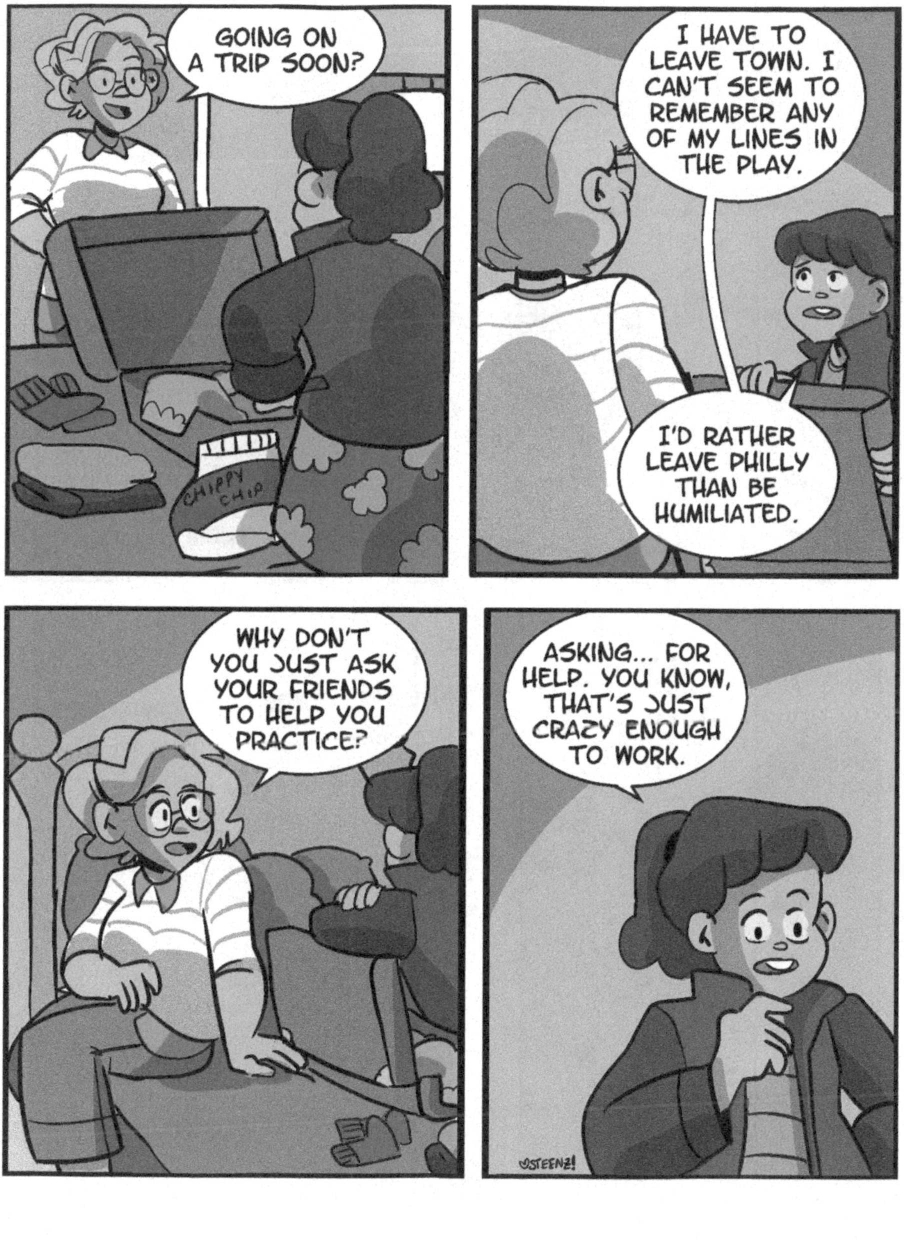
GOING ON A TRIP SOON?
CHIPPY CHIP
I HAVE TO LEAVE TOWN. I CAN'T SEEM TO REMEMBER ANY OF MY LINES IN THE PLAY.
I'D RATHER LEAVE PHILLY THAN BE HUMILIATED.
WHY DON'T YOU JUST ASK YOUR FRIENDS TO HELP YOU PRACTICE?
ASKING... FOR HELP. YOU KNOW, THAT'S JUST CRAZY ENOUGH TO WORK.
STEENZ!

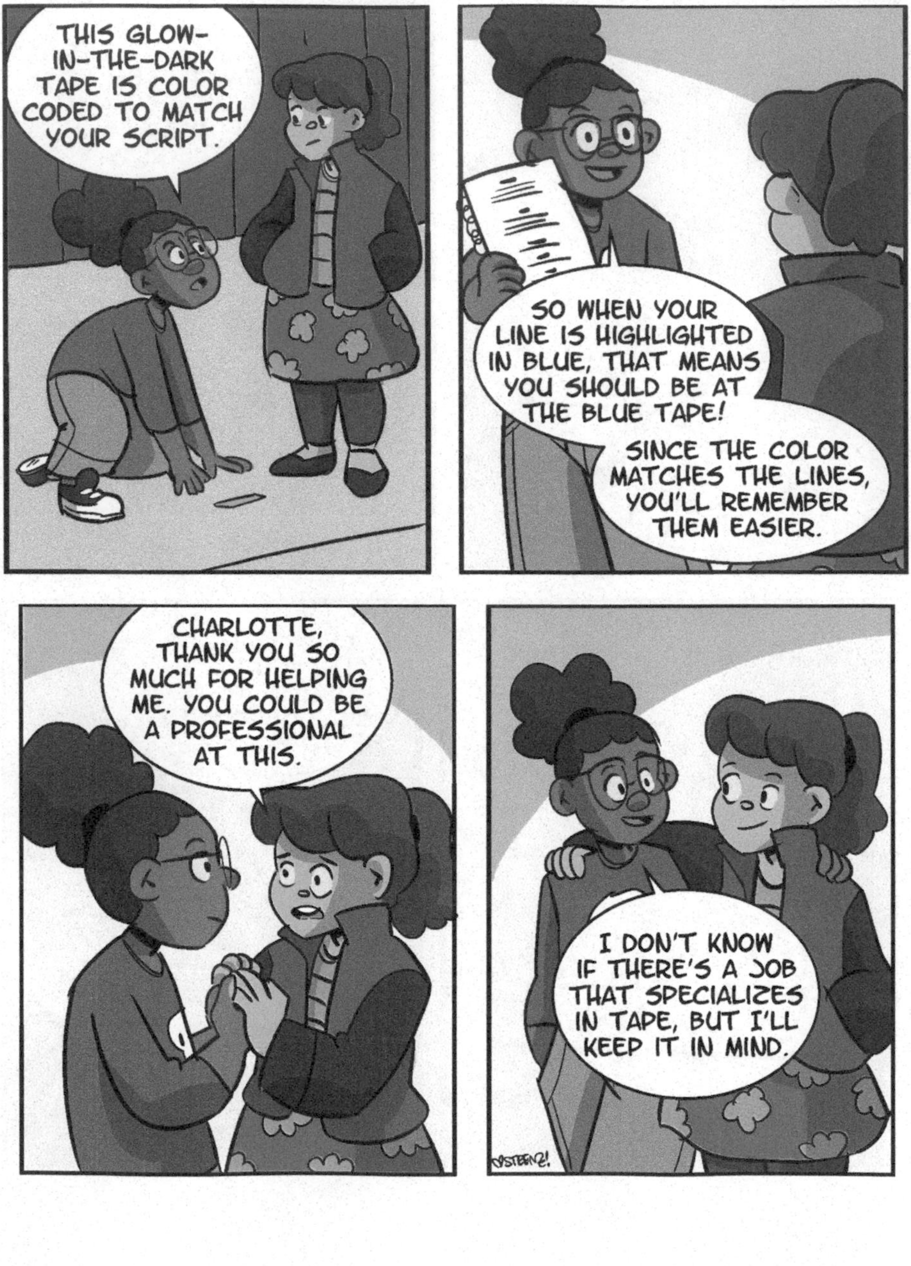
THIS GLOW-IN-THE-DARK TAPE IS COLOR CODED TO MATCH YOUR SCRIPT.
SO WHEN YOUR LINE IS HIGHLIGHTED IN BLUE, THAT MEANS YOU SHOULD BE AT THE BLUE TAPE!
SINCE THE COLOR MATCHES THE LINES, YOU'LL REMEMBER THEM EASIER.
CHARLOTTE, THANK YOU SO MUCH FOR HELPING ME. YOU COULD BE A PROFESSIONAL AT THIS.
I DON'T KNOW IF THERE'S A JOB THAT SPECIALIZES IN TAPE, BUT I'LL KEEP IT IN MIND.

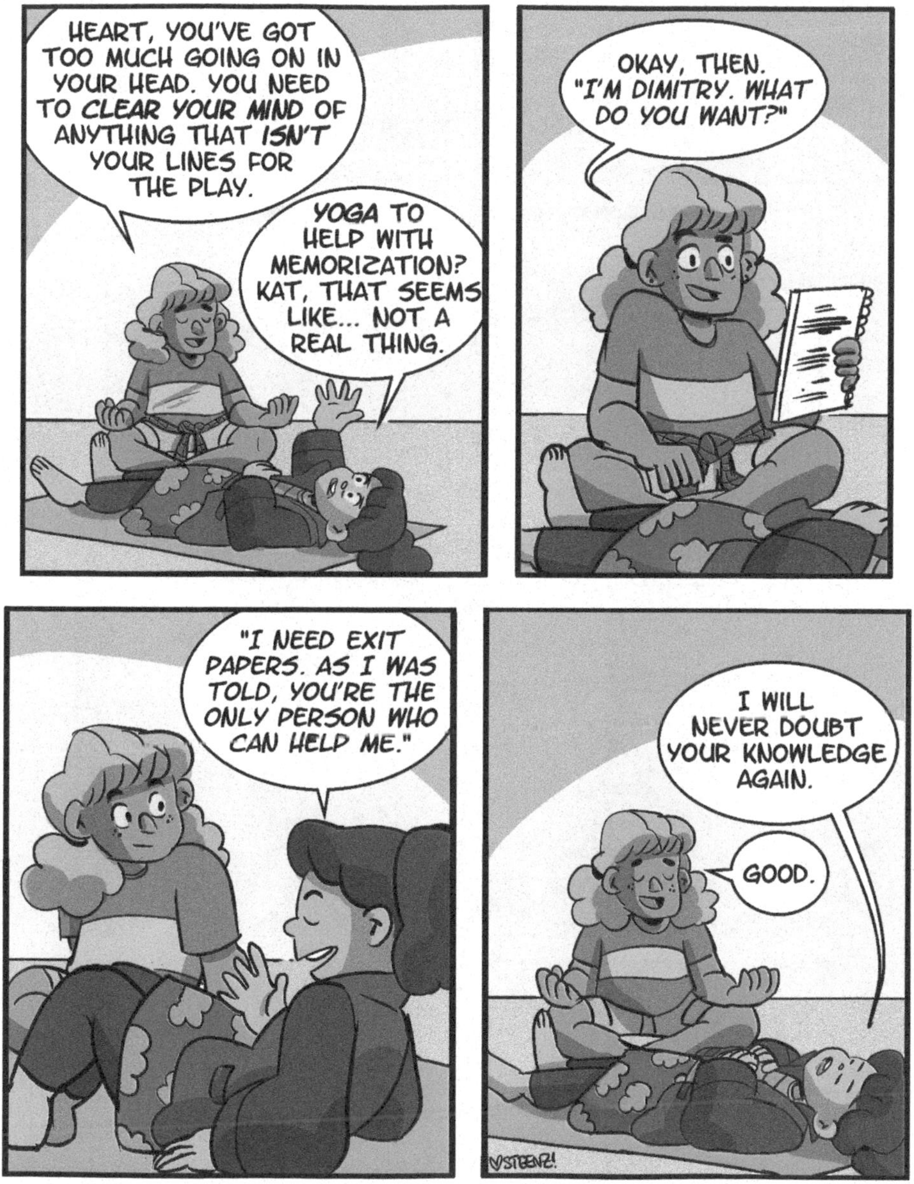
HEART, YOU'VE GOT TOO MUCH GOING ON IN YOUR HEAD. YOU NEED TO CLEAR YOUR MIND OF ANYTHING THAT ISN'T YOUR LINES FOR THE PLAY.
YOGA TO HELP WITH MEMORIZATION? KAT, THAT SEEMS LIKE... NOT A REAL THING.
OKAY, THEN. "I'M DIMITRY. WHAT DO YOU WANT?"
"I NEED EXIT PAPERS. AS I WAS TOLD, YOU'RE THE ONLY PERSON WHO CAN HELP ME."
I WILL NEVER DOUBT YOUR KNOWLEDGE AGAIN.
GOOD.

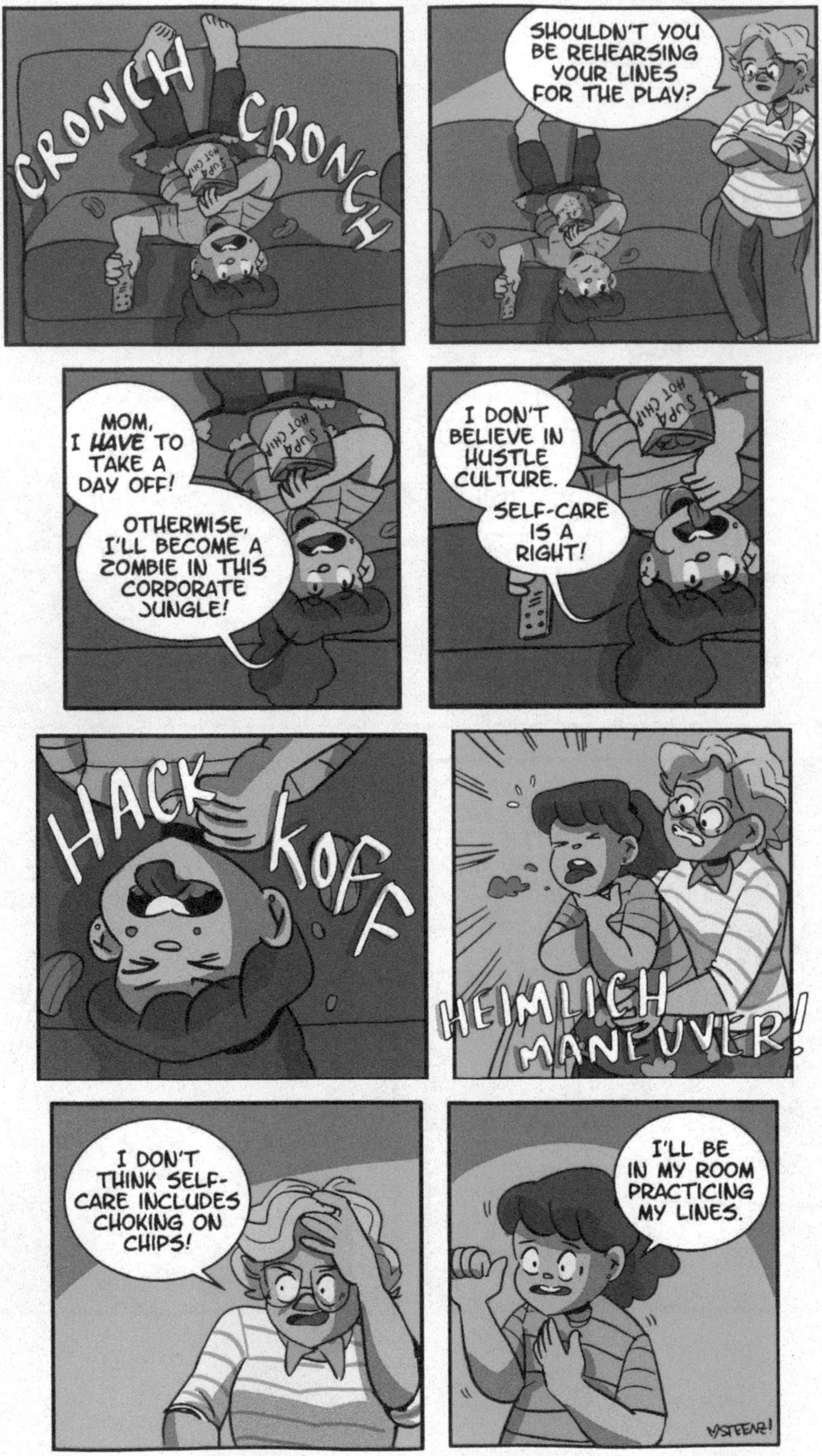
CRONCH CRONCH
SUPA HOT CHIP
SHOULDN'T YOU BE REHEARSING YOUR LINES FOR THE PLAY?
MOM, I *HAVE* TO TAKE A DAY OFF!
OTHERWISE, I'LL BECOME A ZOMBIE IN THIS CORPORATE JUNGLE!
I DON'T BELIEVE IN HUSTLE CULTURE.
SELF-CARE IS A RIGHT!
HACK KOFF
HEIMLICH MANEUVER!
I DON'T THINK SELF-CARE INCLUDES CHOKING ON CHIPS!
I'LL BE IN MY ROOM PRACTICING MY LINES.

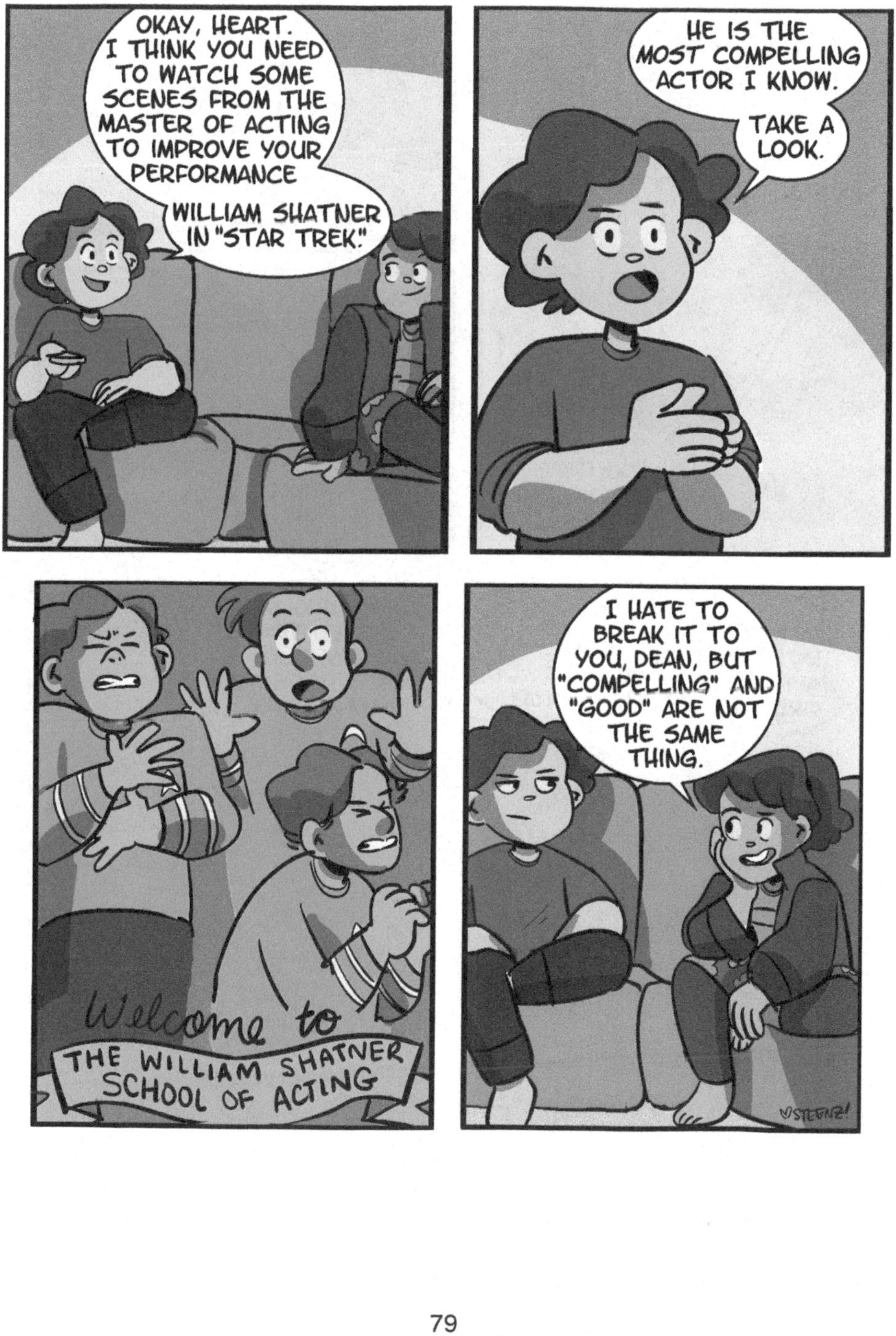
OKAY, HEART. I THINK YOU NEED TO WATCH SOME SCENES FROM THE MASTER OF ACTING TO IMPROVE YOUR PERFORMANCE
WILLIAM SHATNER IN "STAR TREK."
HE IS THE MOST COMPELLING ACTOR I KNOW.
TAKE A LOOK.
Welcome to
THE WILLIAM SHATNER SCHOOL OF ACTING
I HATE TO BREAK IT TO YOU, DEAN, BUT "COMPELLING" AND "GOOD" ARE NOT THE SAME THING.
STEENZ!

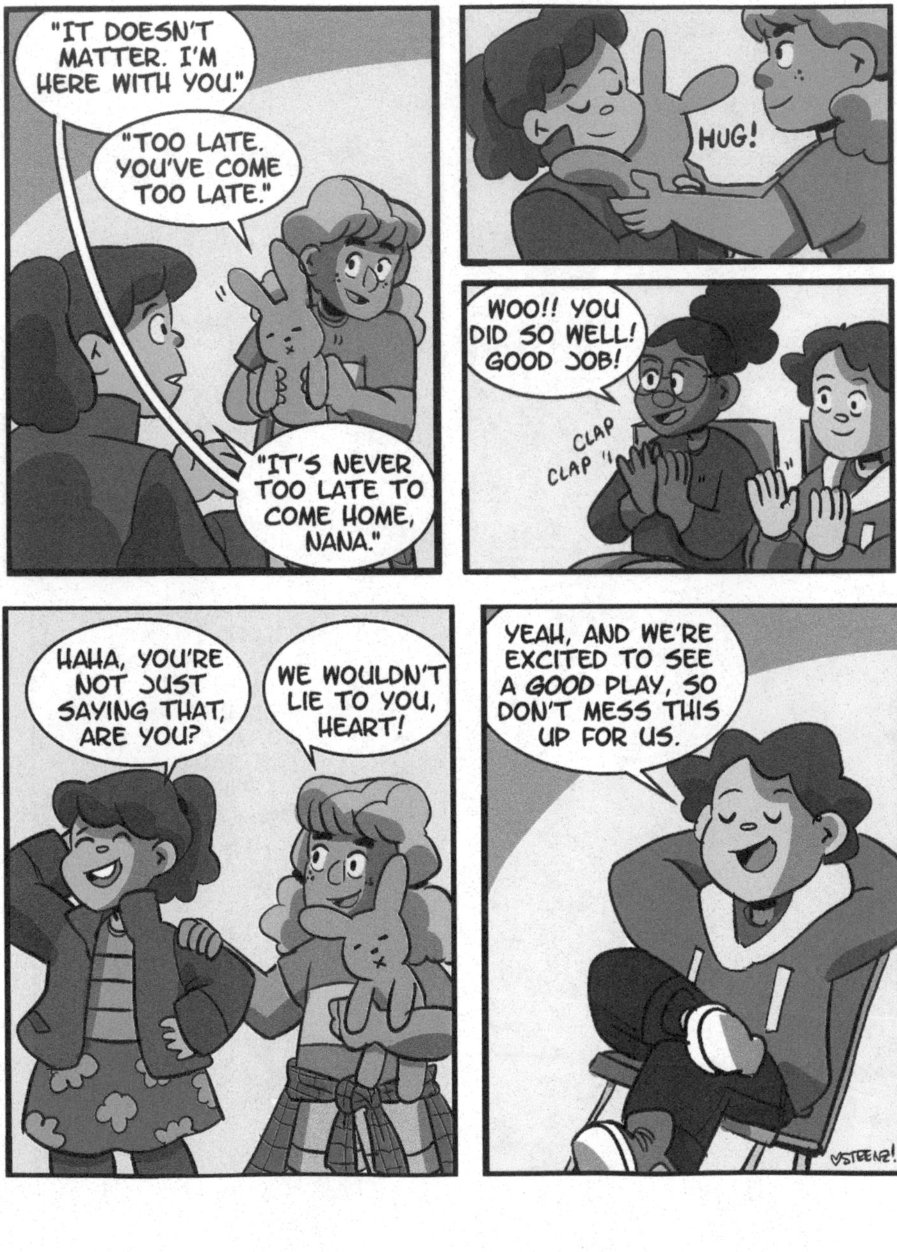

"IT DOESN'T MATTER. I'M HERE WITH YOU."
"TOO LATE. YOU'VE COME TOO LATE."
"IT'S NEVER TOO LATE TO COME HOME, NANA."
HUG!
WOO!! YOU DID SO WELL! GOOD JOB!
CLAP CLAP
HAHA, YOU'RE NOT JUST SAYING THAT, ARE YOU?
WE WOULDN'T LIE TO YOU, HEART!
YEAH, AND WE'RE EXCITED TO SEE A *GOOD* PLAY, SO DON'T MESS THIS UP FOR US.
STEENZ!

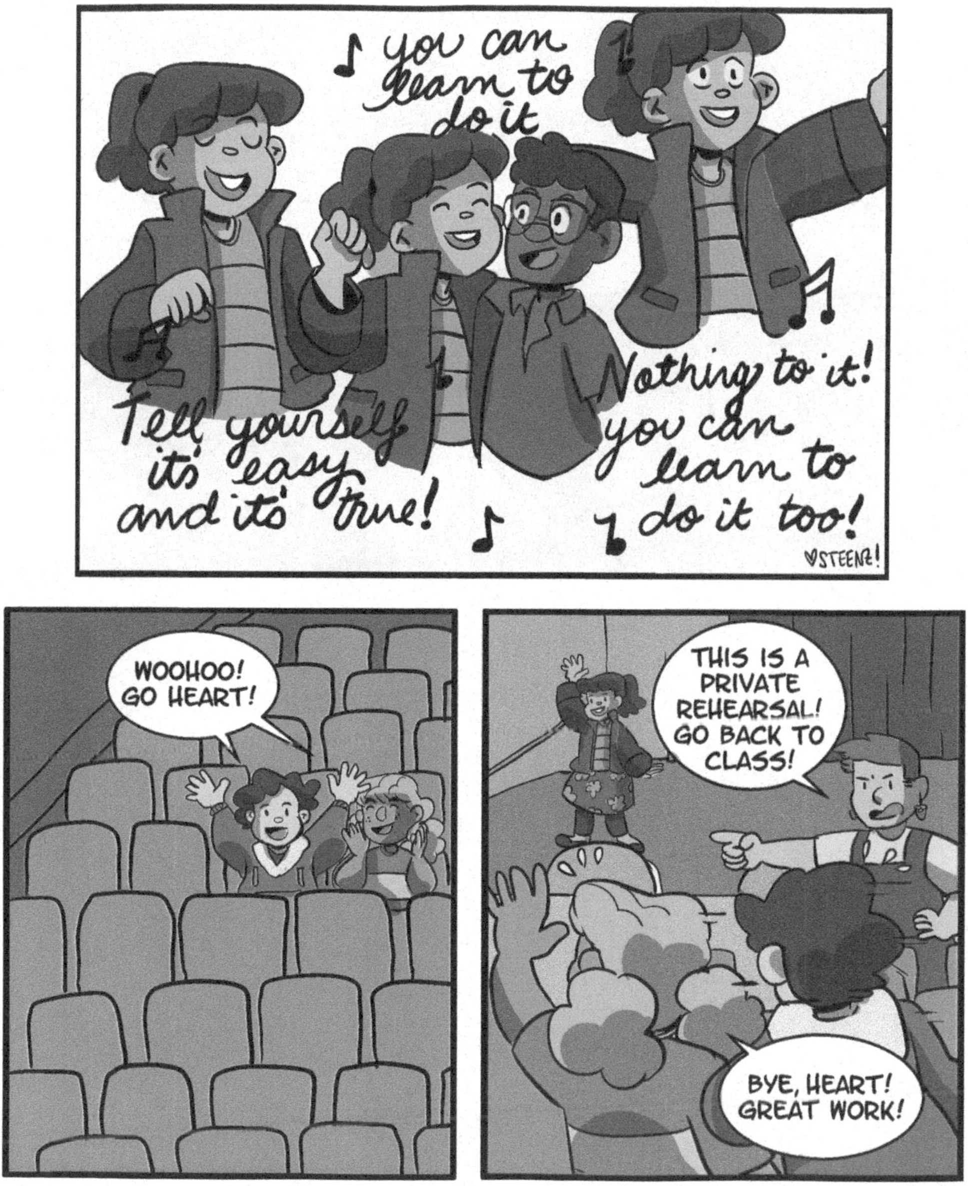
you can learn to do it
Tell yourself it's easy and it's true!
Nothing to it! you can learn to do it too!
STEENZ!
WOOHOO! GO HEART!
THIS IS A PRIVATE REHEARSAL! GO BACK TO CLASS!
BYE, HEART! GREAT WORK!

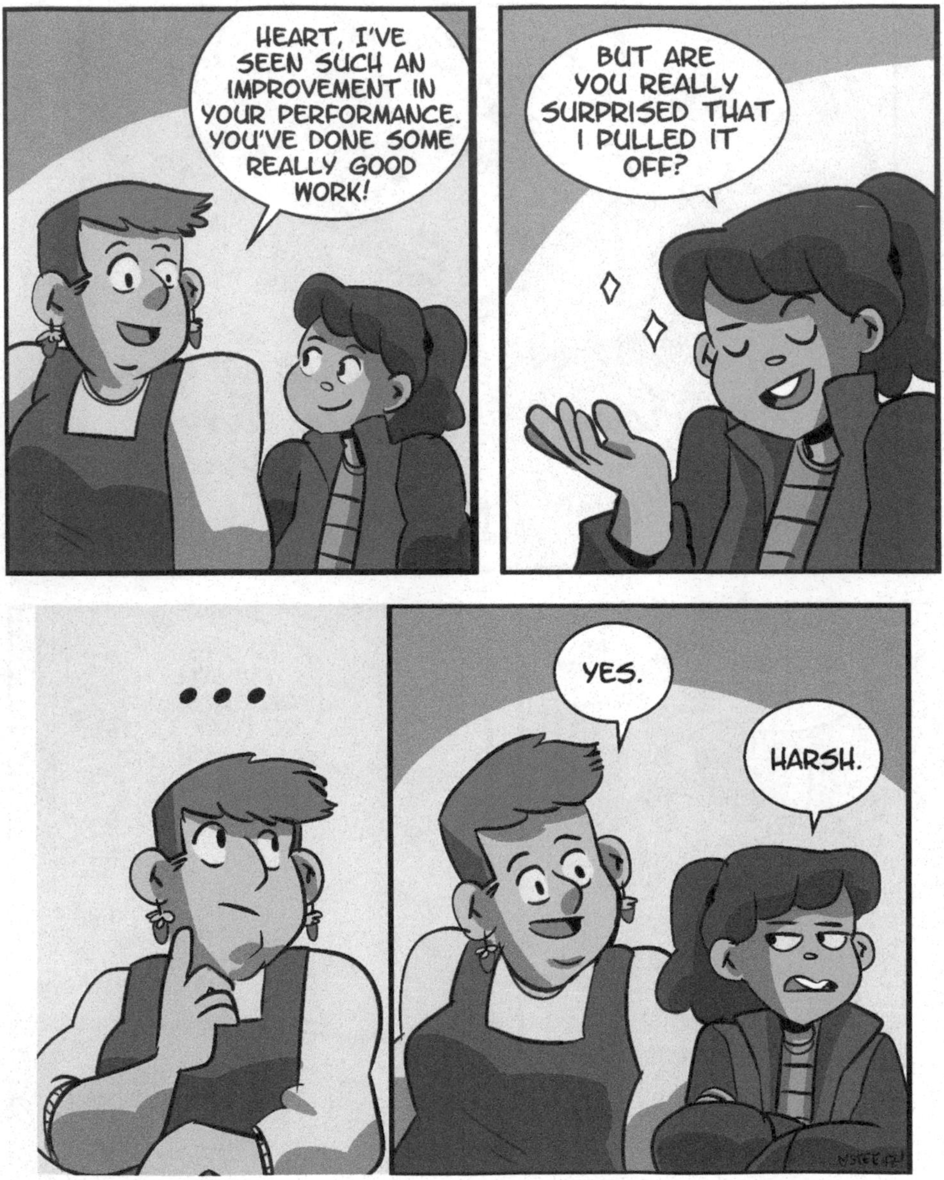
HEART, I'VE SEEN SUCH AN IMPROVEMENT IN YOUR PERFORMANCE. YOU'VE DONE SOME REALLY GOOD WORK!
BUT ARE YOU REALLY SURPRISED THAT I PULLED IT OFF?
...
YES.
HARSH.

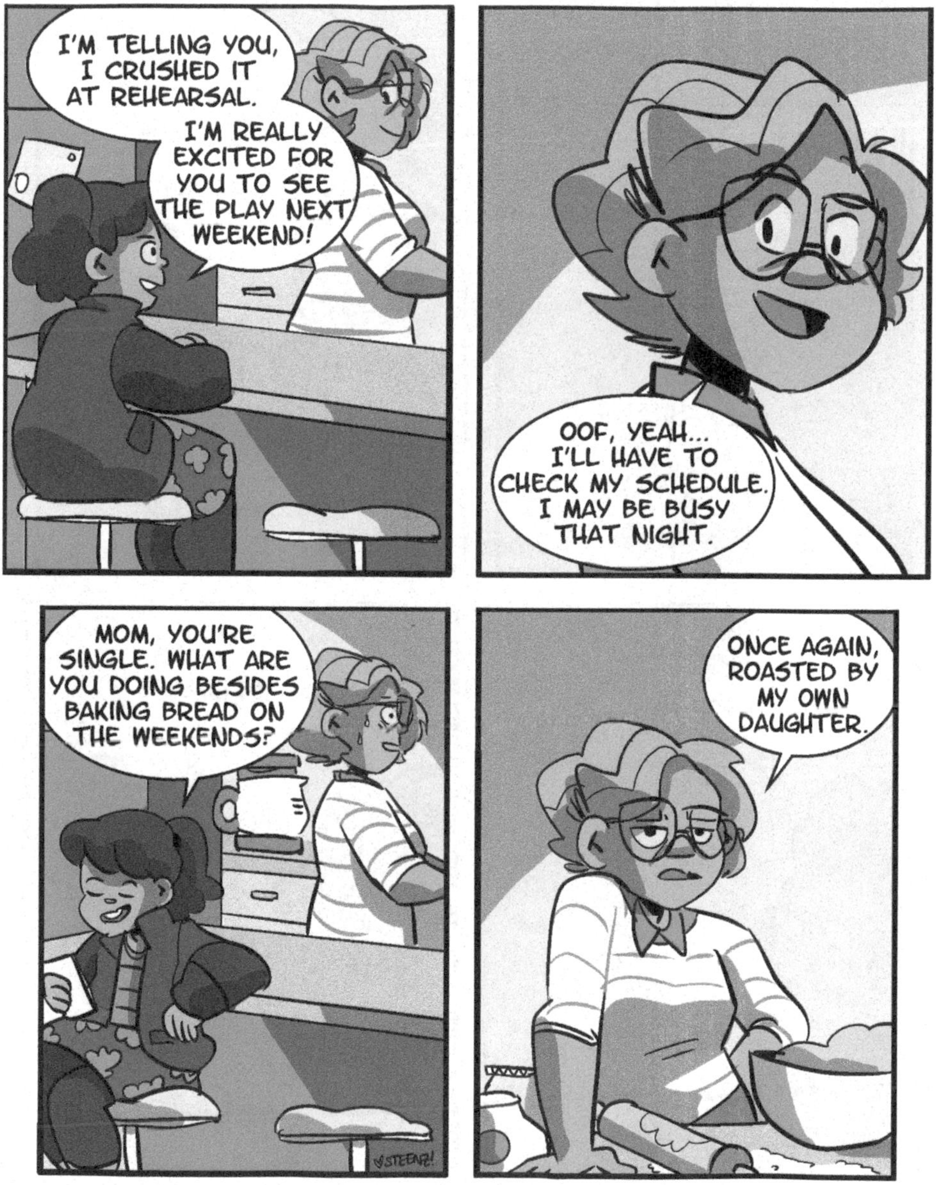
I'M TELLING YOU, I CRUSHED IT AT REHEARSAL.
I'M REALLY EXCITED FOR YOU TO SEE THE PLAY NEXT WEEKEND!
OOF, YEAH... I'LL HAVE TO CHECK MY SCHEDULE. I MAY BE BUSY THAT NIGHT.
MOM, YOU'RE SINGLE. WHAT ARE YOU DOING BESIDES BAKING BREAD ON THE WEEKENDS?
ONCE AGAIN, ROASTED BY MY OWN DAUGHTER.

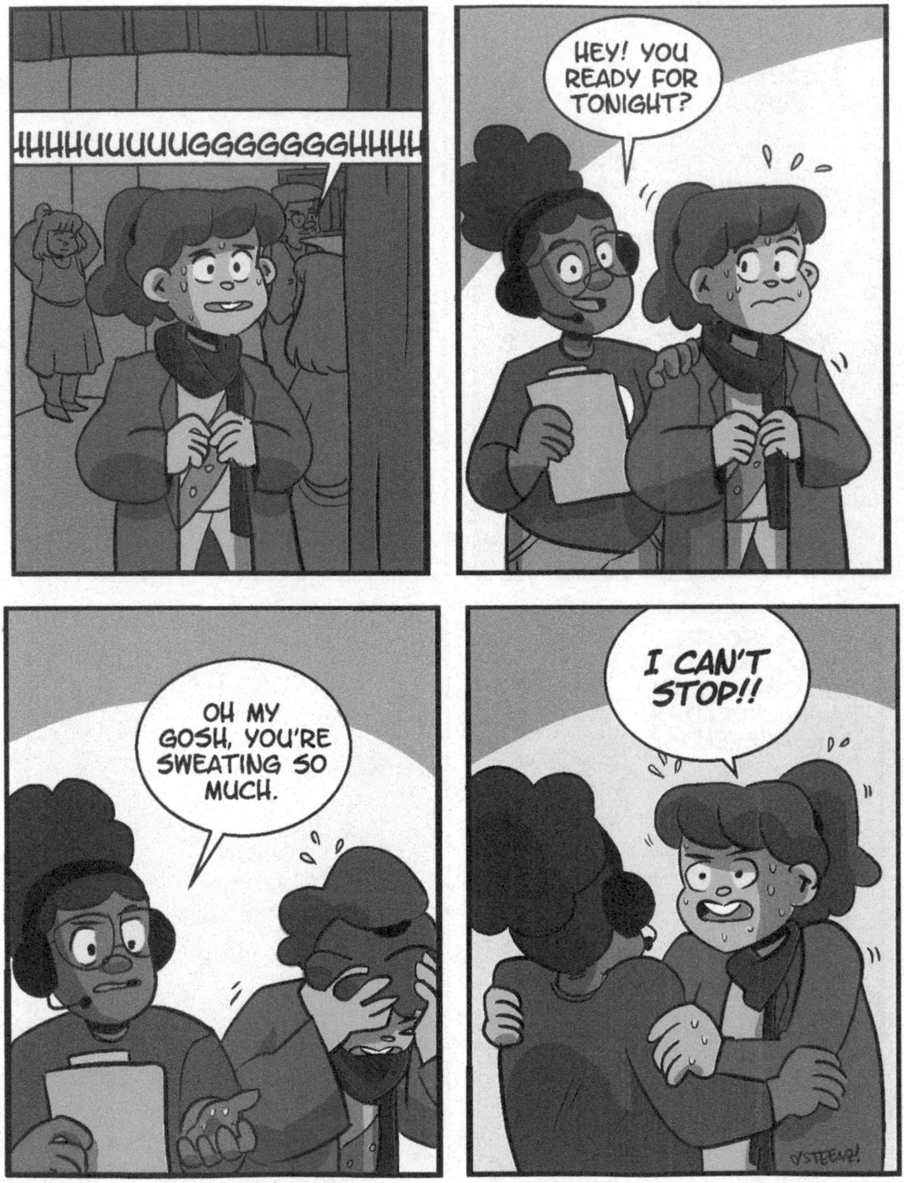
HHHHUUUUUGGGGGGGHHHH
HEY! YOU READY FOR TONIGHT?
OH MY GOSH, YOU'RE SWEATING SO MUCH.
I CAN'T STOP!!
♡STEENZ!

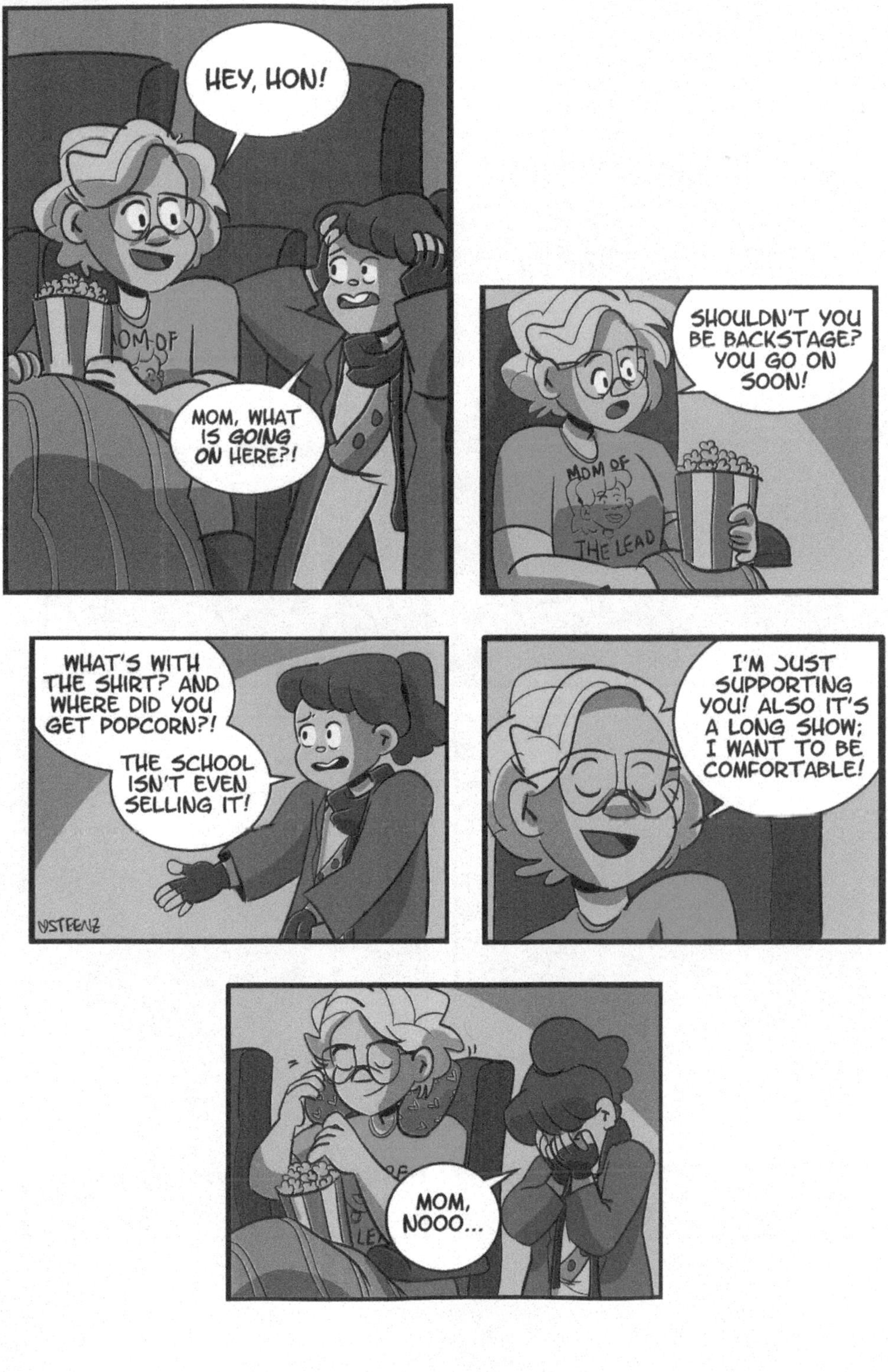
HEY, HON!
MOM, WHAT IS GOING ON HERE?!
SHOULDN'T YOU BE BACKSTAGE? YOU GO ON SOON!
MOM OF THE LEAD
WHAT'S WITH THE SHIRT? AND WHERE DID YOU GET POPCORN?!
THE SCHOOL ISN'T EVEN SELLING IT!
STEENZ
I'M JUST SUPPORTING YOU! ALSO IT'S A LONG SHOW; I WANT TO BE COMFORTABLE!
MOM, NOOO...

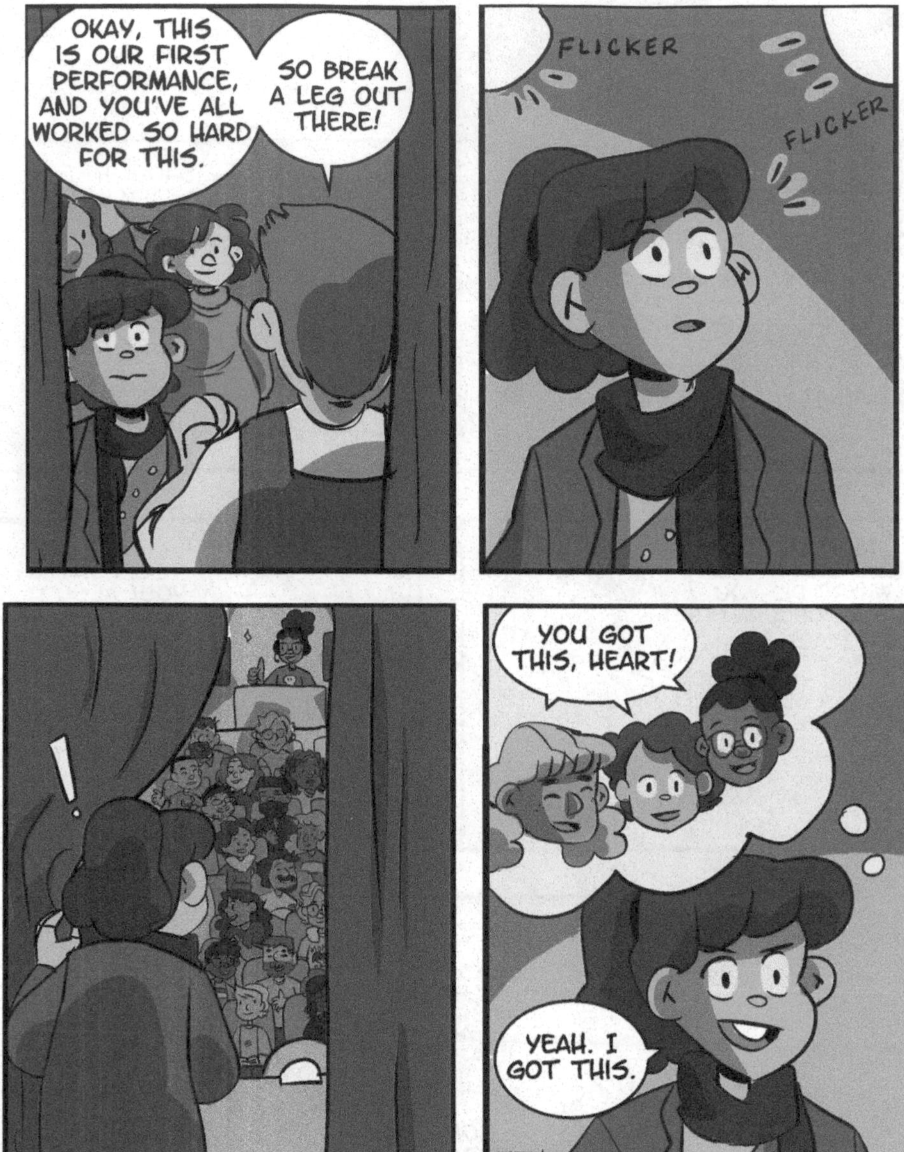
OKAY, THIS IS OUR FIRST PERFORMANCE, AND YOU'VE ALL WORKED SO HARD FOR THIS.
SO BREAK A LEG OUT THERE!
FLICKER
FLICKER
!
YOU GOT THIS, HEART!
YEAH. I GOT THIS.

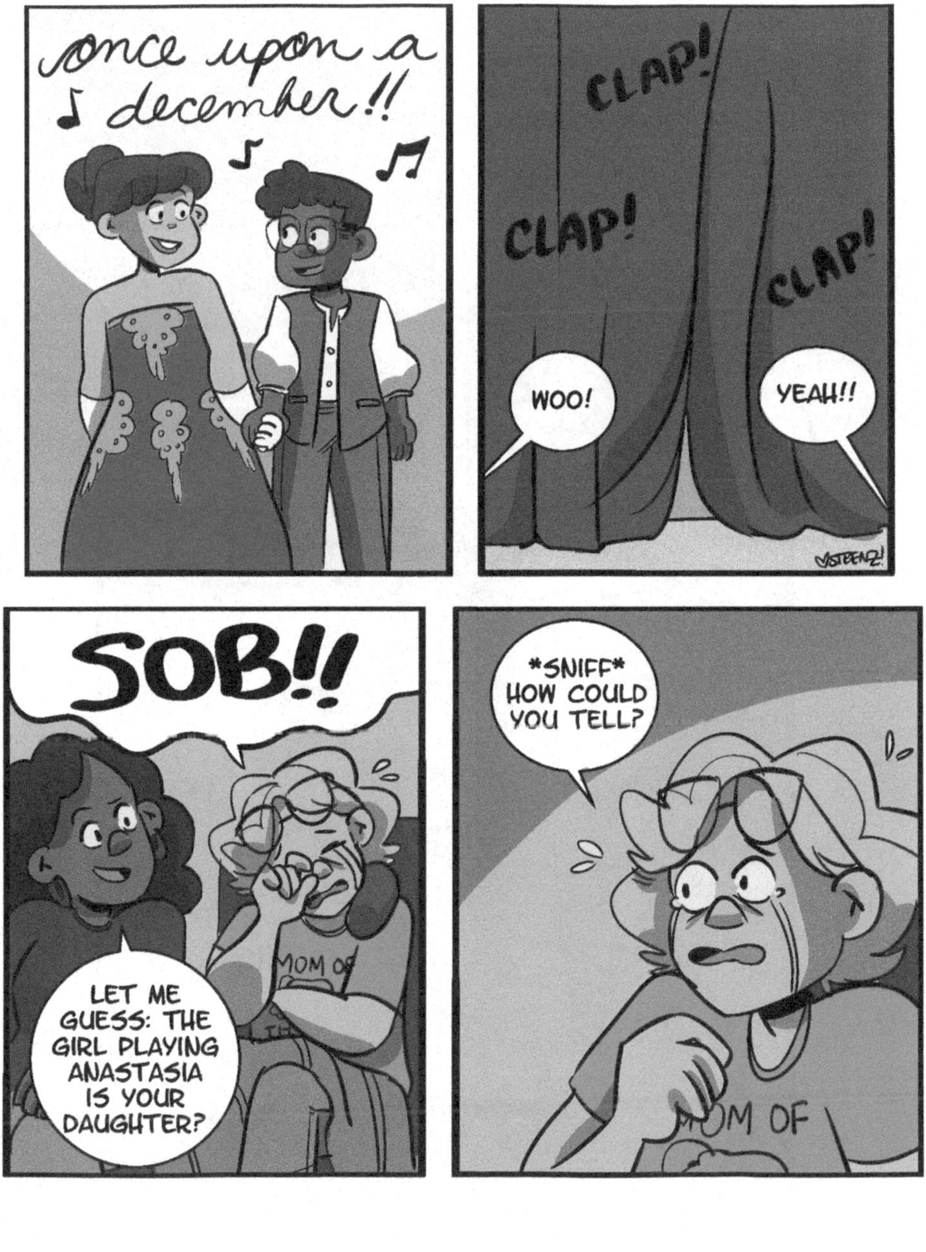
once upon a december!!
CLAP!
CLAP!
CLAP!
WOO!
YEAH!!
SOB!!
LET ME GUESS: THE GIRL PLAYING ANASTASIA IS YOUR DAUGHTER?
MOM OF
SNIFF HOW COULD YOU TELL?
MOM OF

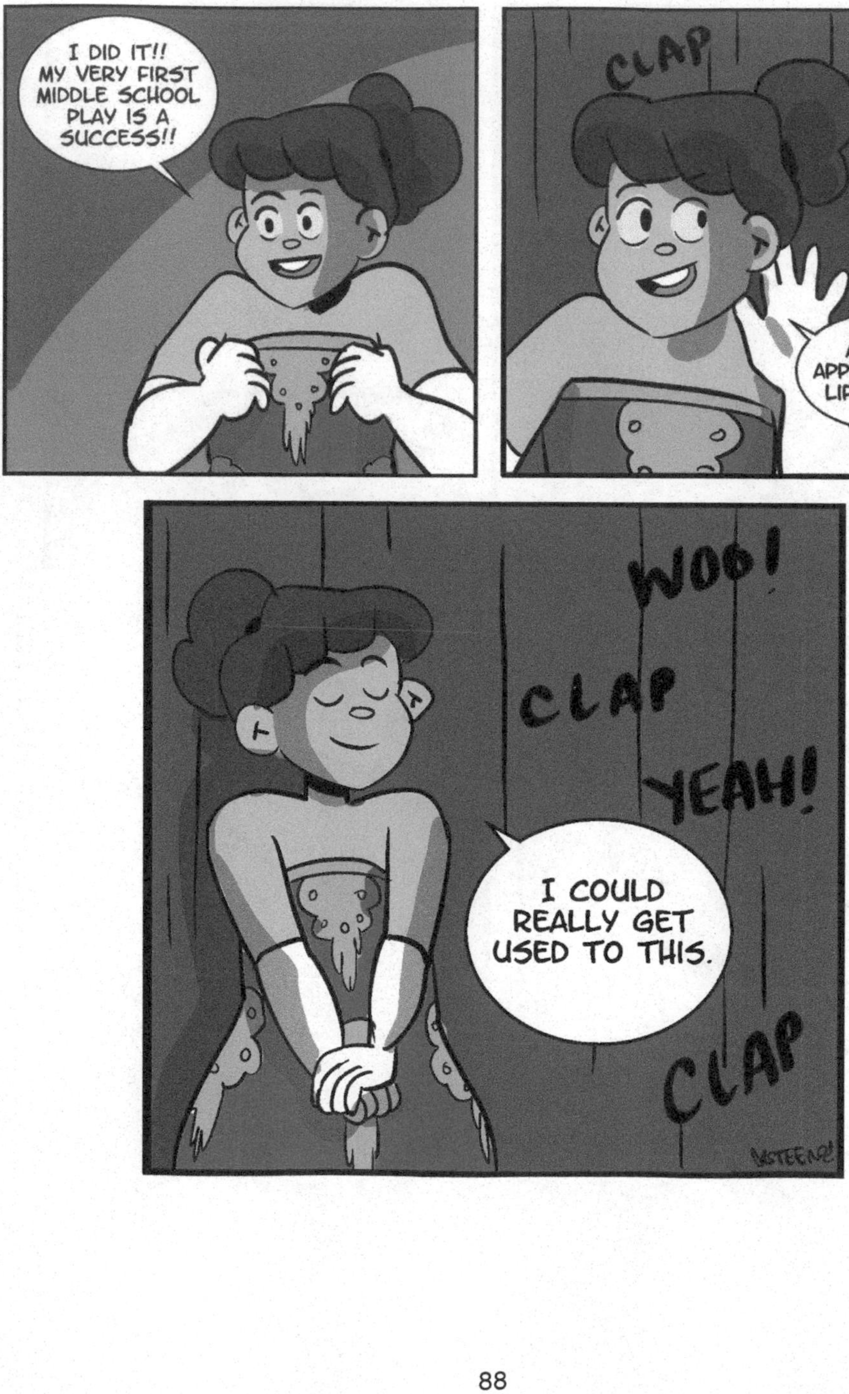
I DID IT!! MY VERY FIRST MIDDLE SCHOOL PLAY IS A SUCCESS!!
CLAP
CLAP
AH, THE APPLAUSE. MY LIFE BLOOD.
WOO!
CLAP
YEAH!
I COULD REALLY GET USED TO THIS.
CLAP

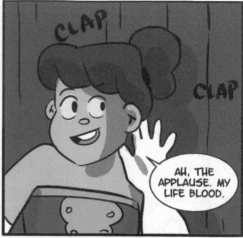

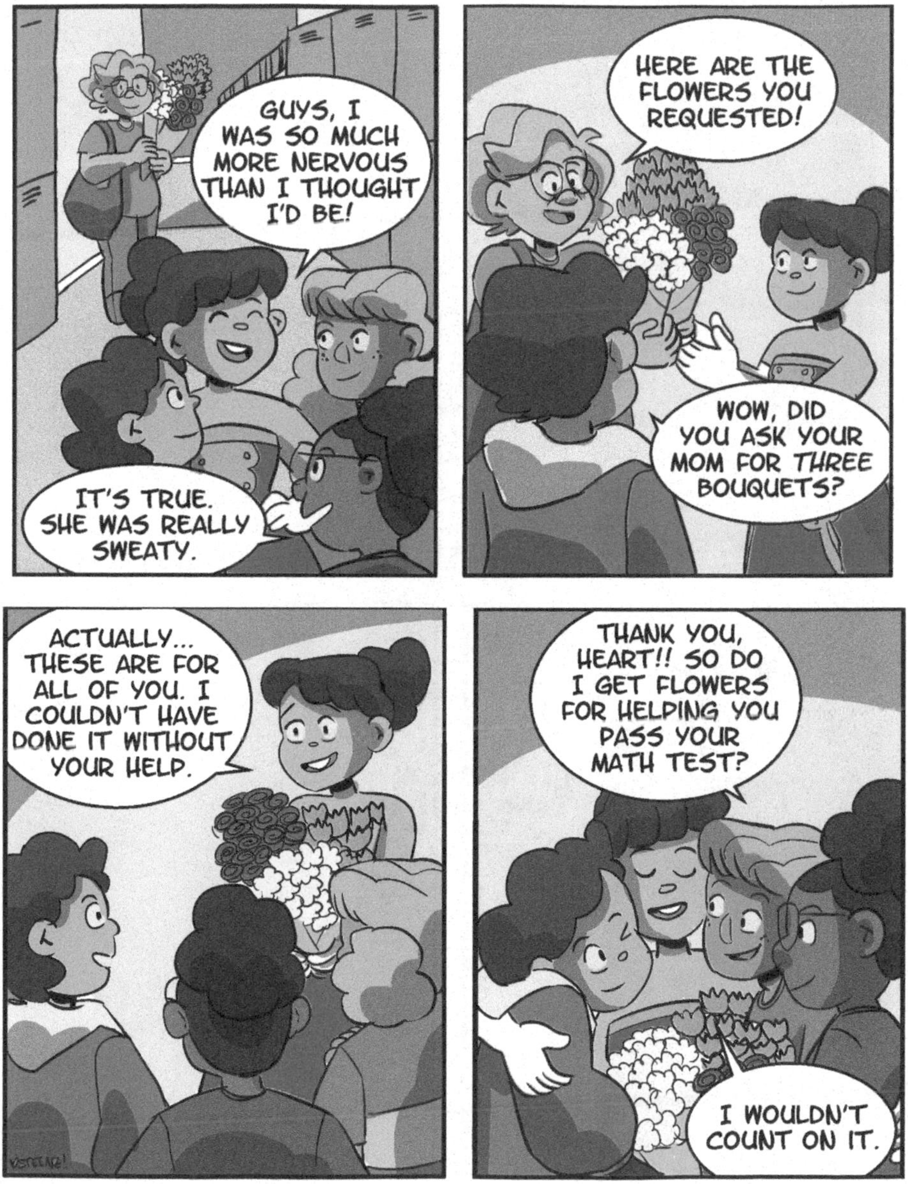
GUYS, I WAS SO MUCH MORE NERVOUS THAN I THOUGHT I'D BE!
IT'S TRUE. SHE WAS REALLY SWEATY.
HERE ARE THE FLOWERS YOU REQUESTED!
WOW, DID YOU ASK YOUR MOM FOR *THREE* BOUQUETS?
ACTUALLY... THESE ARE FOR ALL OF YOU. I COULDN'T HAVE DONE IT WITHOUT YOUR HELP.
THANK YOU, HEART!! SO DO I GET FLOWERS FOR HELPING YOU PASS YOUR MATH TEST?
I WOULDN'T COUNT ON IT.

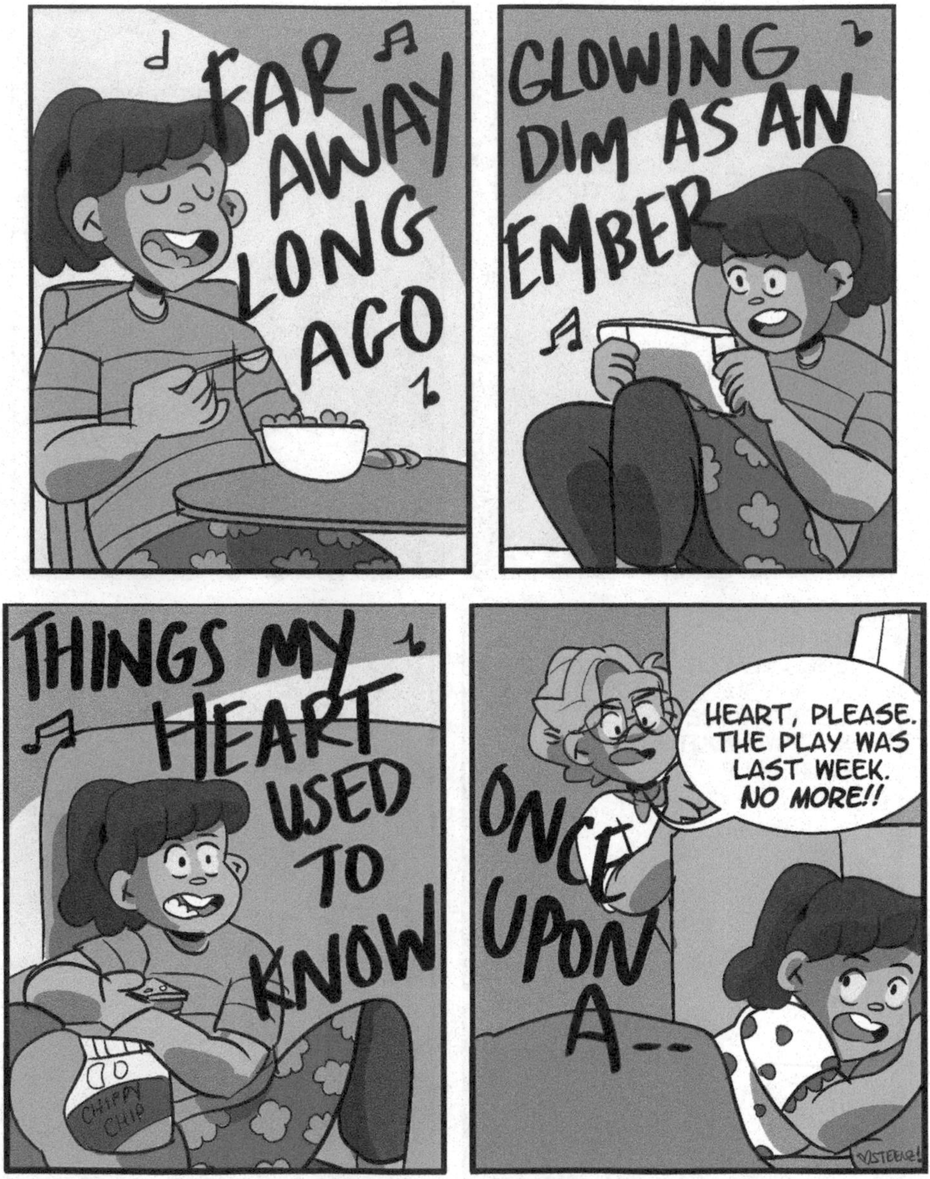
FAR AWAY LONG AGO
GLOWING DIM AS AN EMBER
THINGS MY HEART USED TO KNOW
CHIPPY CHIP
ONCE UPON A--
HEART, PLEASE. THE PLAY WAS LAST WEEK. NO MORE!!

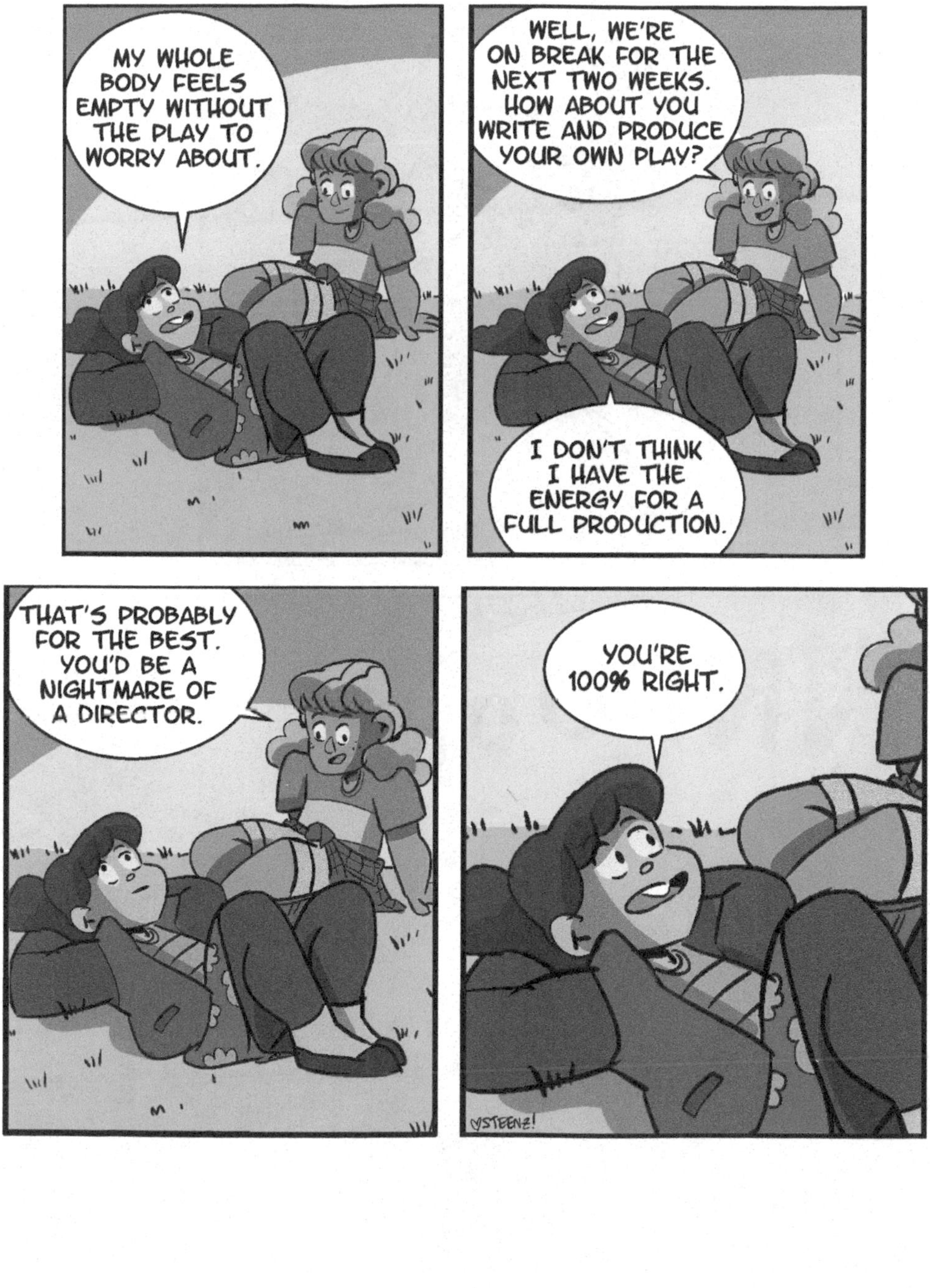
MY WHOLE BODY FEELS EMPTY WITHOUT THE PLAY TO WORRY ABOUT.
WELL, WE'RE ON BREAK FOR THE NEXT TWO WEEKS. HOW ABOUT YOU WRITE AND PRODUCE YOUR OWN PLAY?
I DON'T THINK I HAVE THE ENERGY FOR A FULL PRODUCTION.
THAT'S PROBABLY FOR THE BEST. YOU'D BE A NIGHTMARE OF A DIRECTOR.
YOU'RE 100% RIGHT.
♡STEENZ!

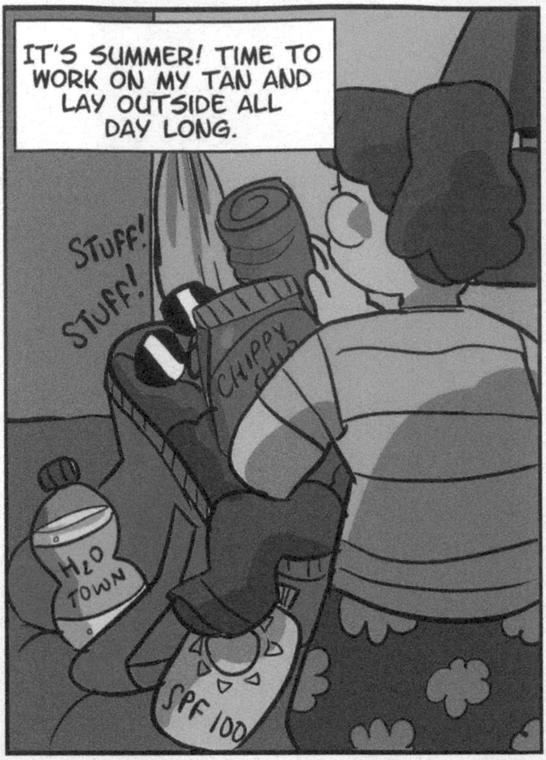
IT'S SUMMER! TIME TO WORK ON MY TAN AND LAY OUTSIDE ALL DAY LONG.
STUFF!
STUFF!
CHIPPY CHIP
H2O TOWN
SPF 100

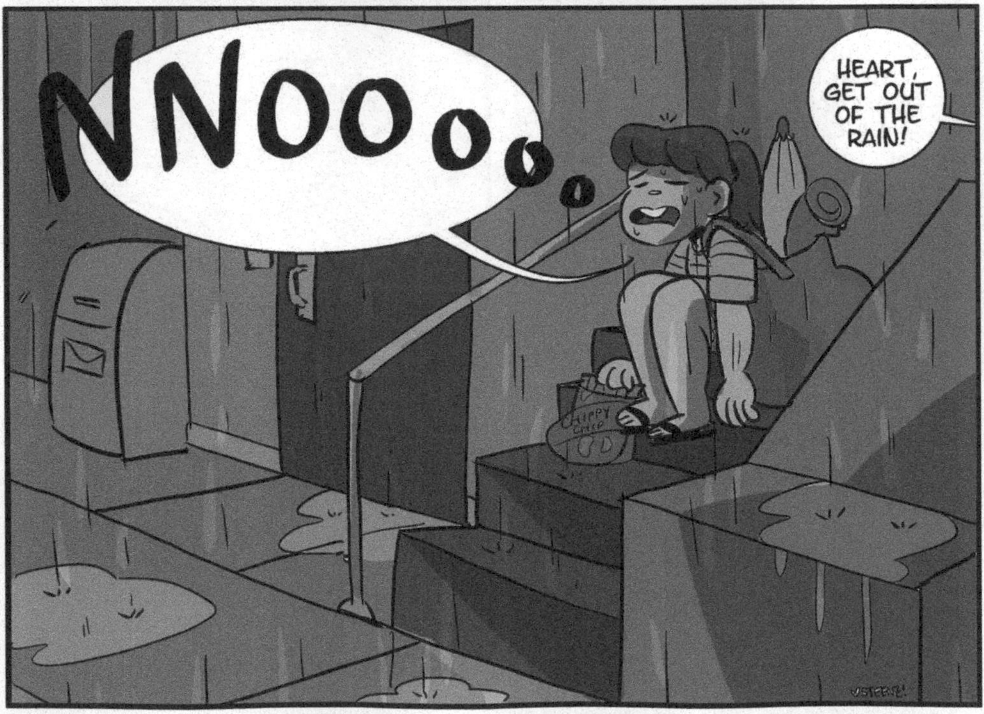
NNOOooo
HEART, GET OUT OF THE RAIN!
CHIPPY CHIP

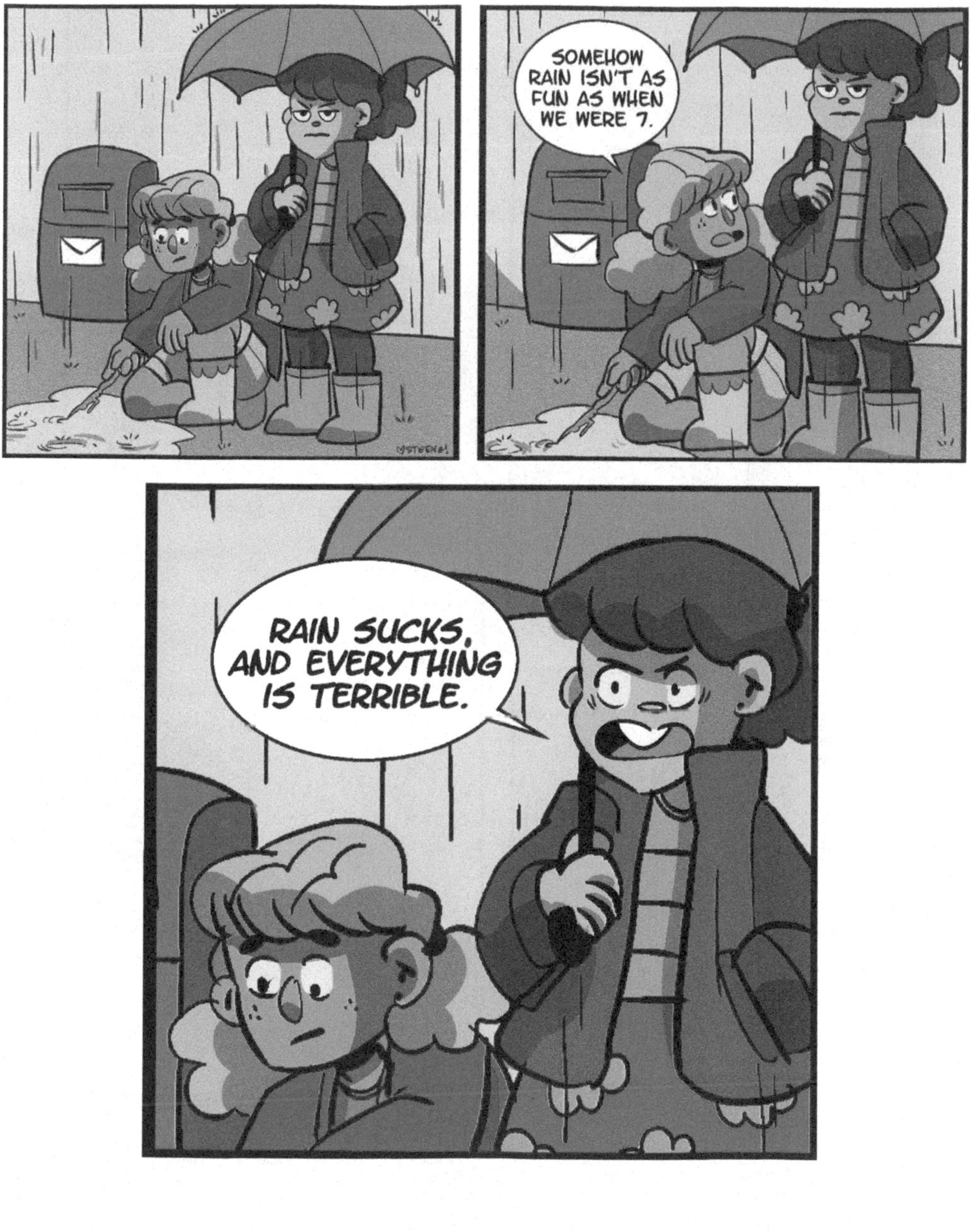
SOMEHOW RAIN ISN'T AS FUN AS WHEN WE WERE 7.
RAIN SUCKS, AND EVERYTHING IS TERRIBLE.

IF YOU KEEP THIS PACING UP, YOU'LL WEAR A HOLE IN THE FLOOR.

GREAT! THEN WE'LL GET SOME EXCITEMENT IN THIS HOUSE!

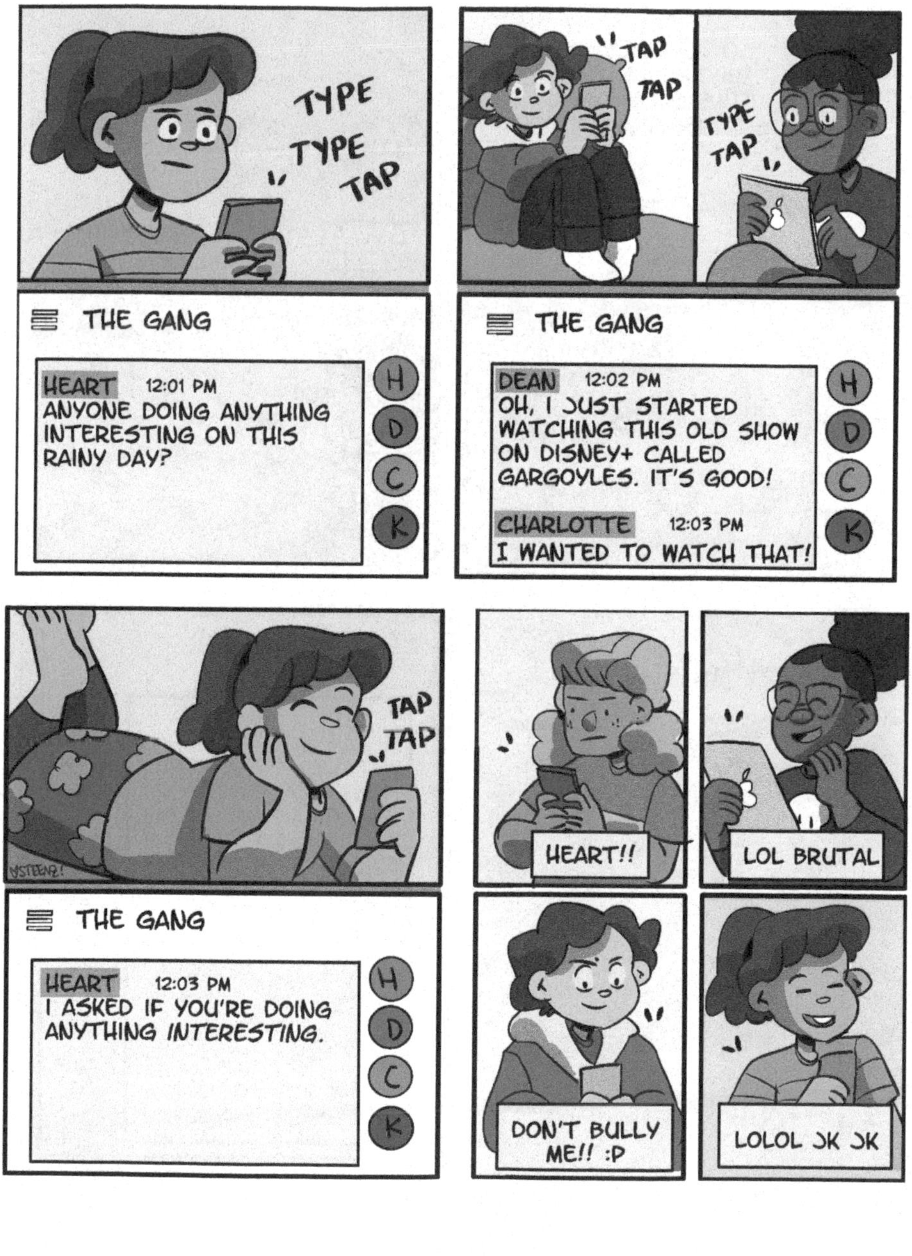
TYPE
TYPE
TAP
TAP
TAP
TYPE
TAP
THE GANG
HEART 12:01 PM
ANYONE DOING ANYTHING INTERESTING ON THIS RAINY DAY?
H
D
C
K
THE GANG
DEAN 12:02 PM
OH, I JUST STARTED WATCHING THIS OLD SHOW ON DISNEY+ CALLED GARGOYLES. IT'S GOOD!
CHARLOTTE 12:03 PM
I WANTED TO WATCH THAT!
H
D
C
K
TAP
TAP
THE GANG
HEART 12:03 PM
I ASKED IF YOU'RE DOING ANYTHING *INTERESTING*.
H
D
C
K
HEART!!
LOL BRUTAL
DON'T BULLY ME!! :P
LOLOL JK JK

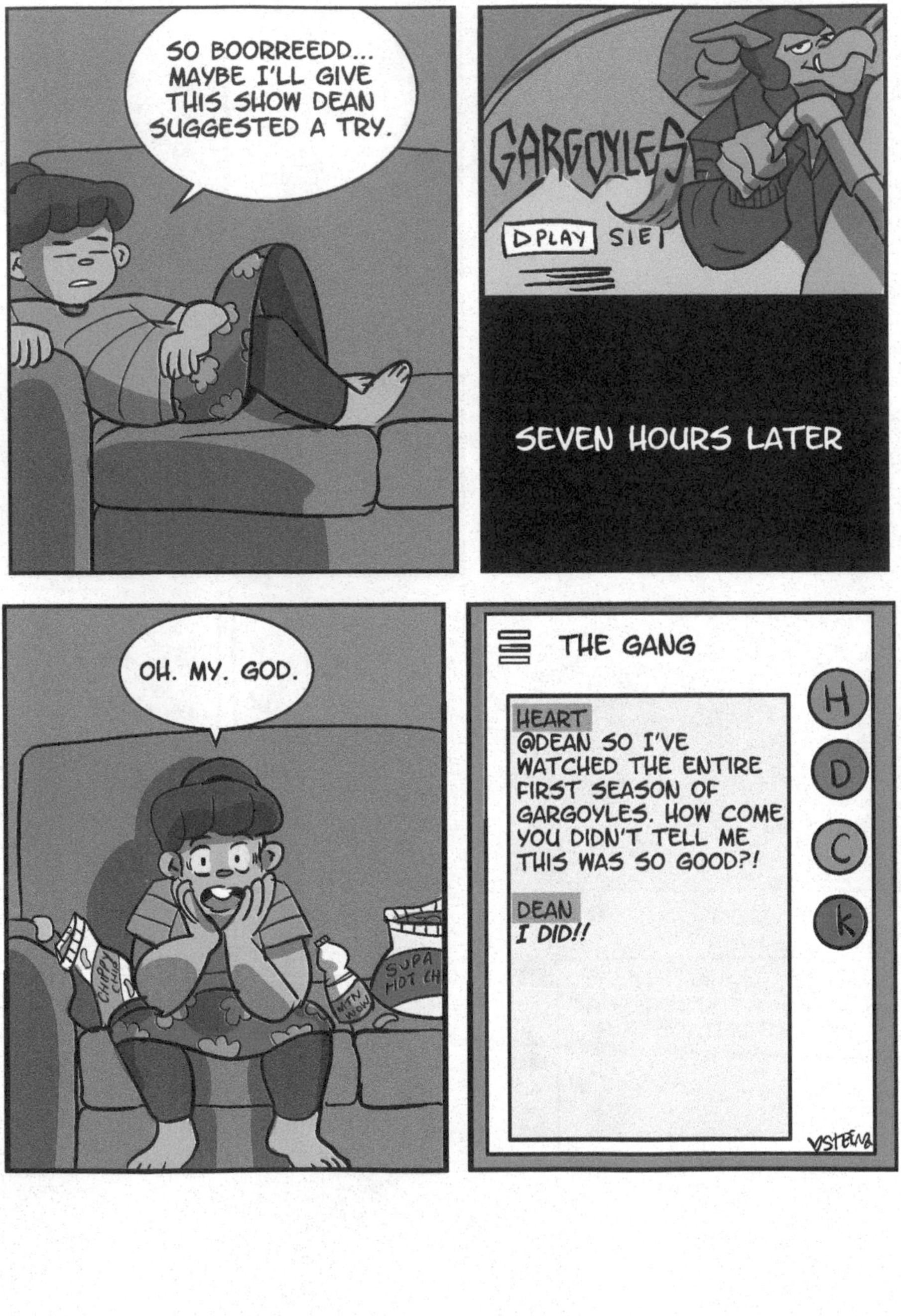
SO BOORREEDD... MAYBE I'LL GIVE THIS SHOW DEAN SUGGESTED A TRY.
GARGOYLES
PLAY
SEVEN HOURS LATER
OH. MY. GOD.
CHIPPY
MTN WOW
SUPA HOT CH
THE GANG
HEART
@DEAN SO I'VE WATCHED THE ENTIRE FIRST SEASON OF GARGOYLES. HOW COME YOU DIDN'T TELL ME THIS WAS SO GOOD?!
DEAN
I DID!!
H
D
C
k

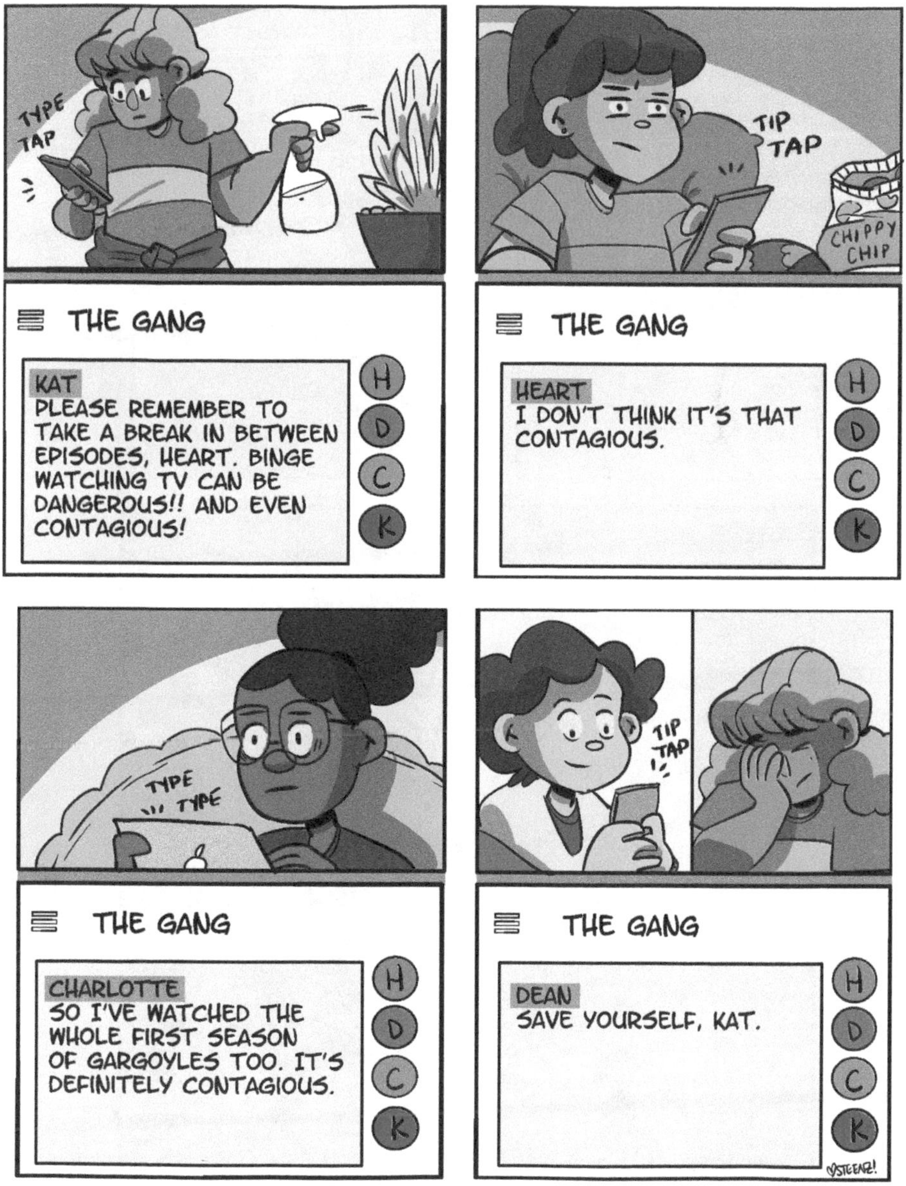
TYPE
TAP
THE GANG
KAT
PLEASE REMEMBER TO TAKE A BREAK IN BETWEEN EPISODES, HEART. BINGE WATCHING TV CAN BE DANGEROUS!! AND EVEN CONTAGIOUS!
H
D
C
K
TIP
TAP
CHIPPY CHIP
THE GANG
HEART
I DON'T THINK IT'S THAT CONTAGIOUS.
H
D
C
K
TYPE
TYPE
THE GANG
CHARLOTTE
SO I'VE WATCHED THE WHOLE FIRST SEASON OF GARGOYLES TOO. IT'S DEFINITELY CONTAGIOUS.
H
D
C
K
TIP
TAP
THE GANG
DEAN
SAVE YOURSELF, KAT.
H
D
C
K
STEEAR!

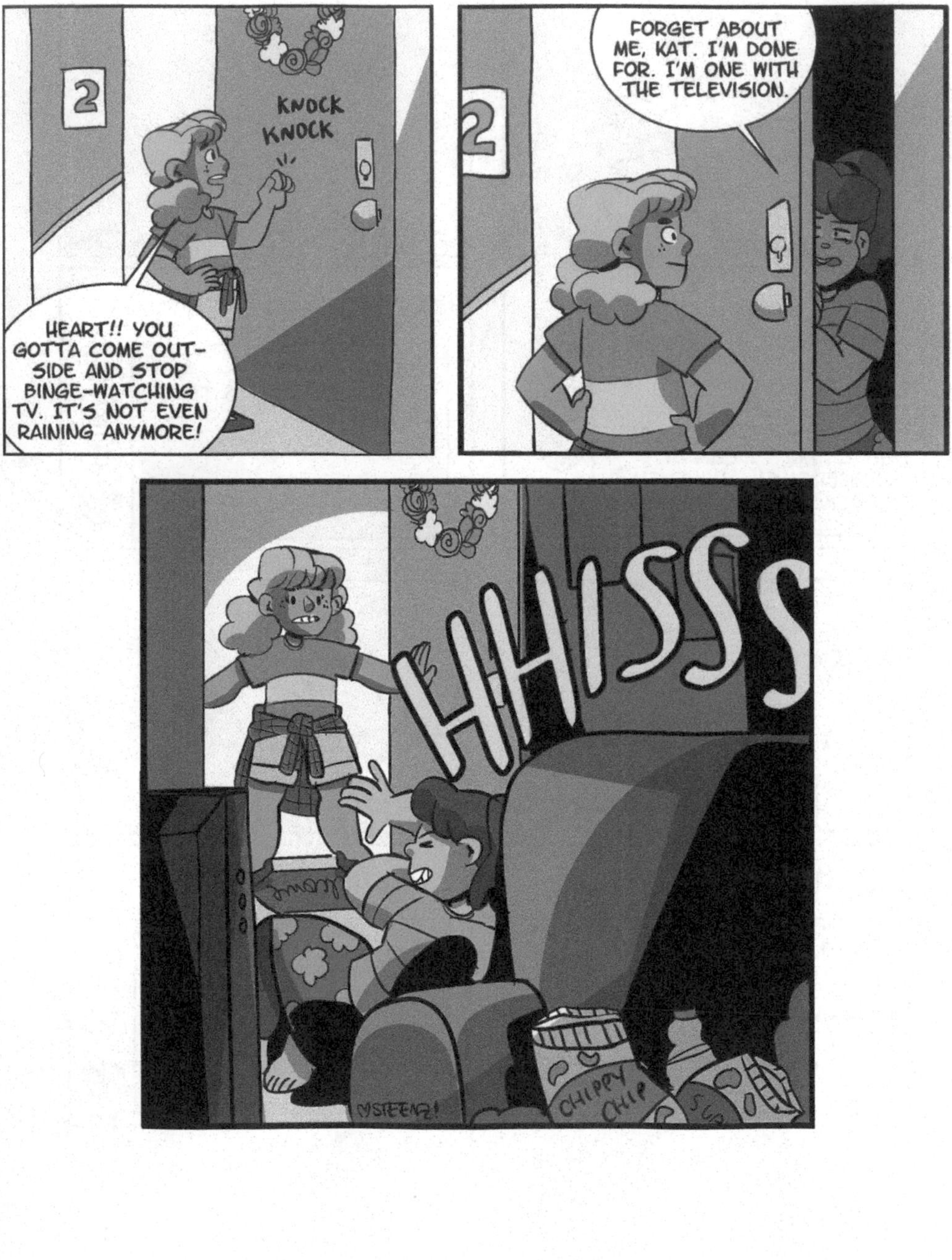
KNOCK KNOCK
HEART!! YOU GOTTA COME OUT-SIDE AND STOP BINGE-WATCHING TV. IT'S NOT EVEN RAINING ANYMORE!
FORGET ABOUT ME, KAT. I'M DONE FOR. I'M ONE WITH THE TELEVISION.
HHISSS
CHIPPY CHIP

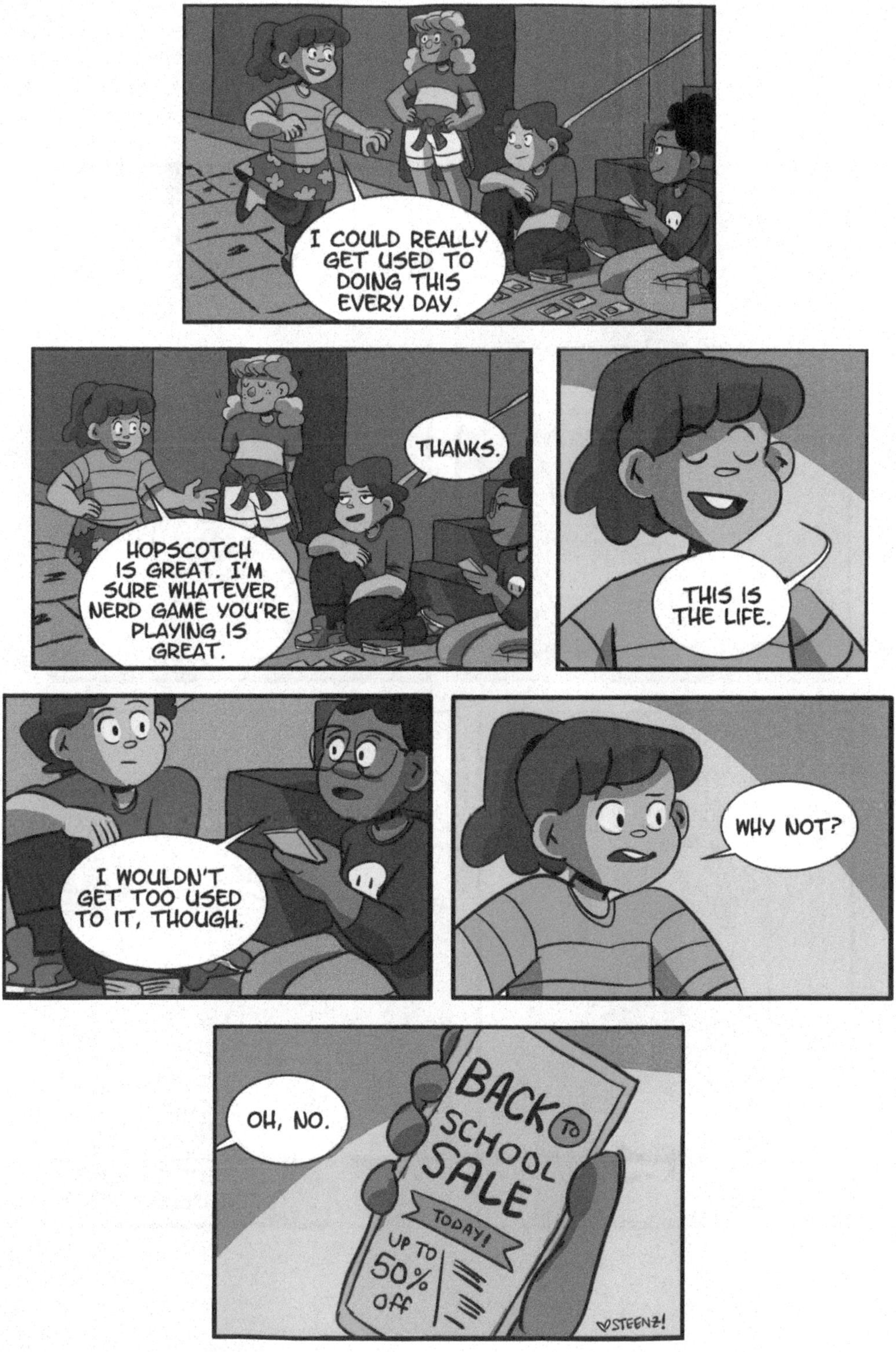
I COULD REALLY GET USED TO DOING THIS EVERY DAY.
THANKS.
HOPSCOTCH IS GREAT. I'M SURE WHATEVER NERD GAME YOU'RE PLAYING IS GREAT.
THIS IS THE LIFE.
I WOULDN'T GET TOO USED TO IT, THOUGH.
WHY NOT?
OH, NO.
BACK TO SCHOOL SALE
TODAY!
UP TO 50% OFF
♡STEENZ!

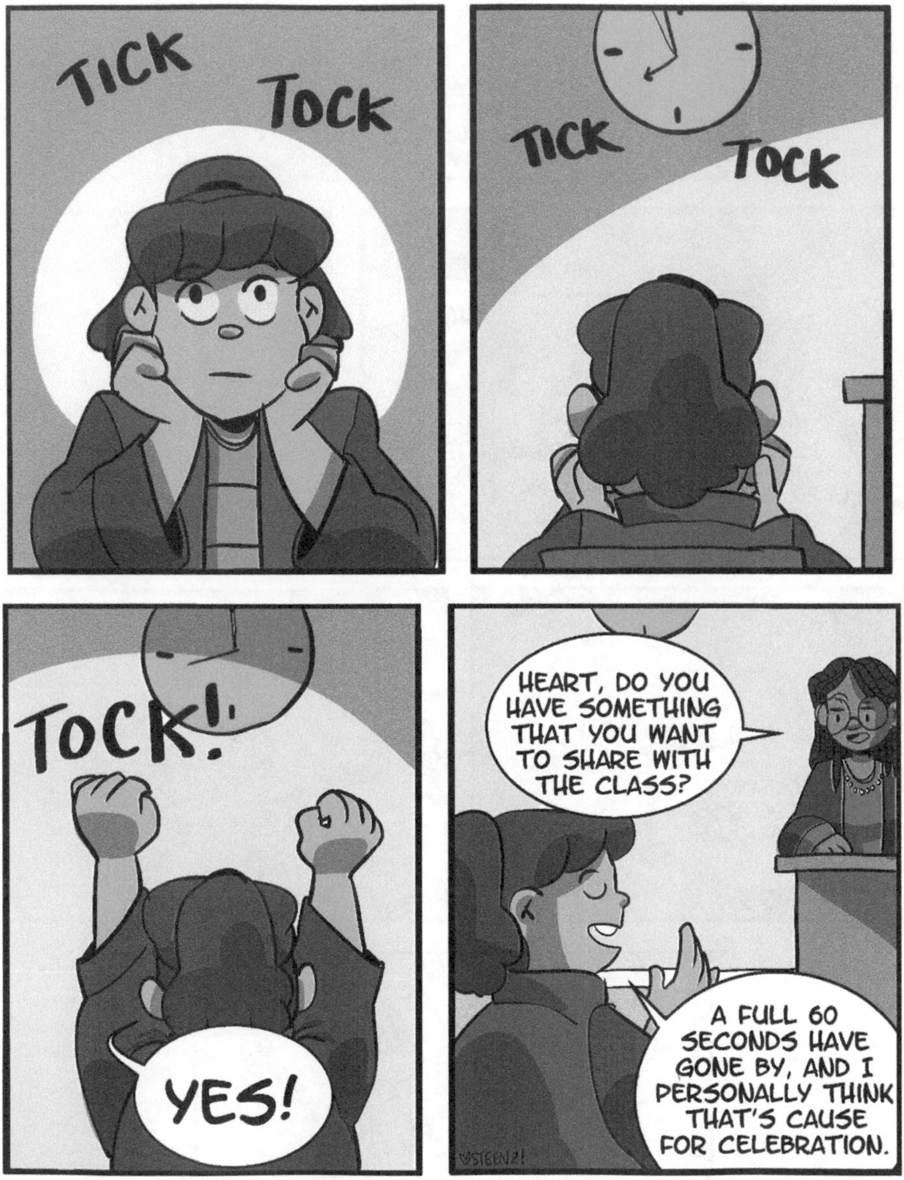
TICK
TOCK
TICK
TOCK
TOCK!
YES!
HEART, DO YOU HAVE SOMETHING THAT YOU WANT TO SHARE WITH THE CLASS?
A FULL 60 SECONDS HAVE GONE BY, AND I PERSONALLY THINK THAT'S CAUSE FOR CELEBRATION.
STEEN21

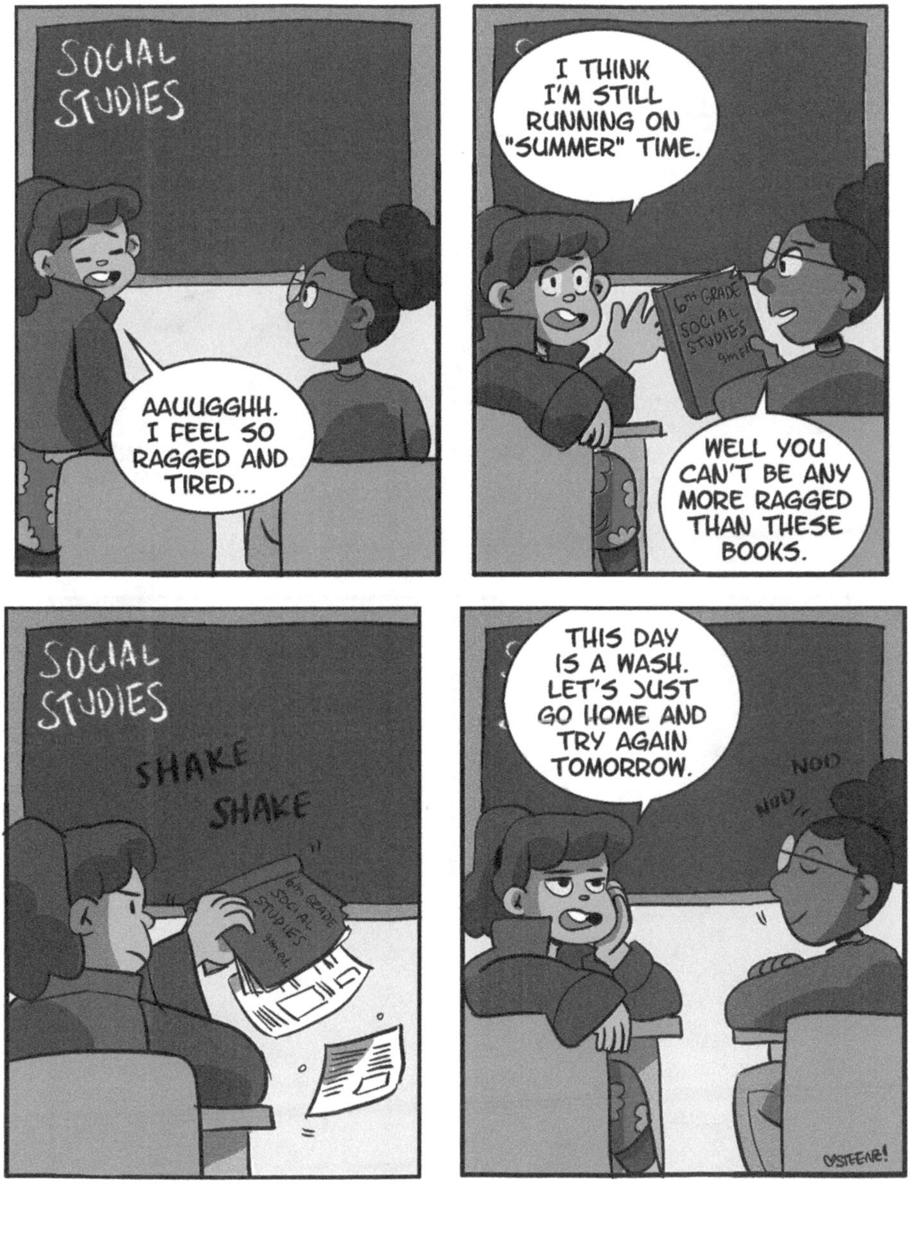
SOCIAL STUDIES
AAUUGGHH. I FEEL SO RAGGED AND TIRED...
I THINK I'M STILL RUNNING ON "SUMMER" TIME.
6TH GRADE SOCIAL STUDIES
WELL YOU CAN'T BE ANY MORE RAGGED THAN THESE BOOKS.
SOCIAL STUDIES
SHAKE
SHAKE
THIS DAY IS A WASH. LET'S JUST GO HOME AND TRY AGAIN TOMORROW.
NOD
NOD

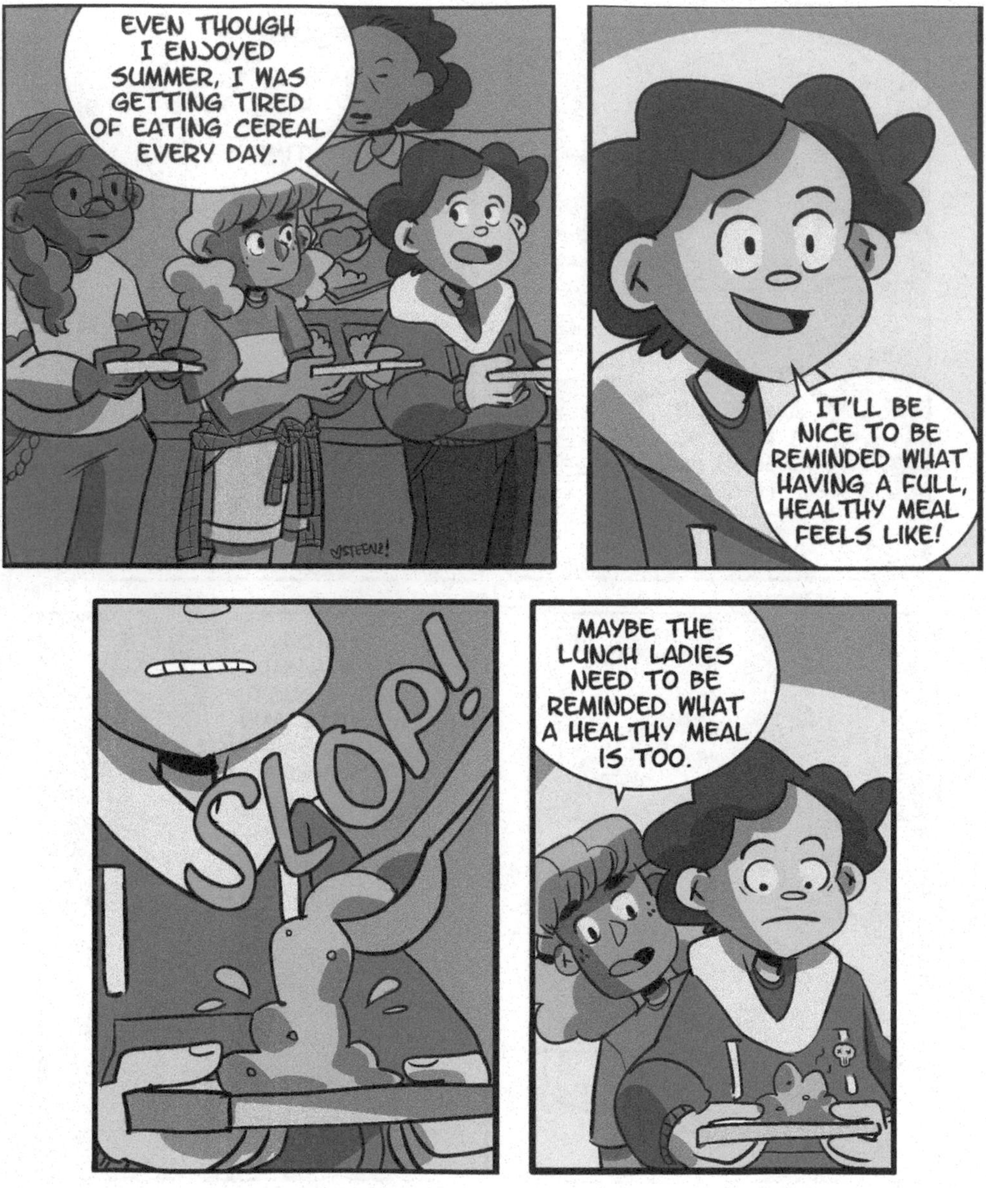
EVEN THOUGH I ENJOYED SUMMER, I WAS GETTING TIRED OF EATING CEREAL EVERY DAY.
IT'LL BE NICE TO BE REMINDED WHAT HAVING A FULL, HEALTHY MEAL FEELS LIKE!
SLOP!
MAYBE THE LUNCH LADIES NEED TO BE REMINDED WHAT A HEALTHY MEAL IS TOO.

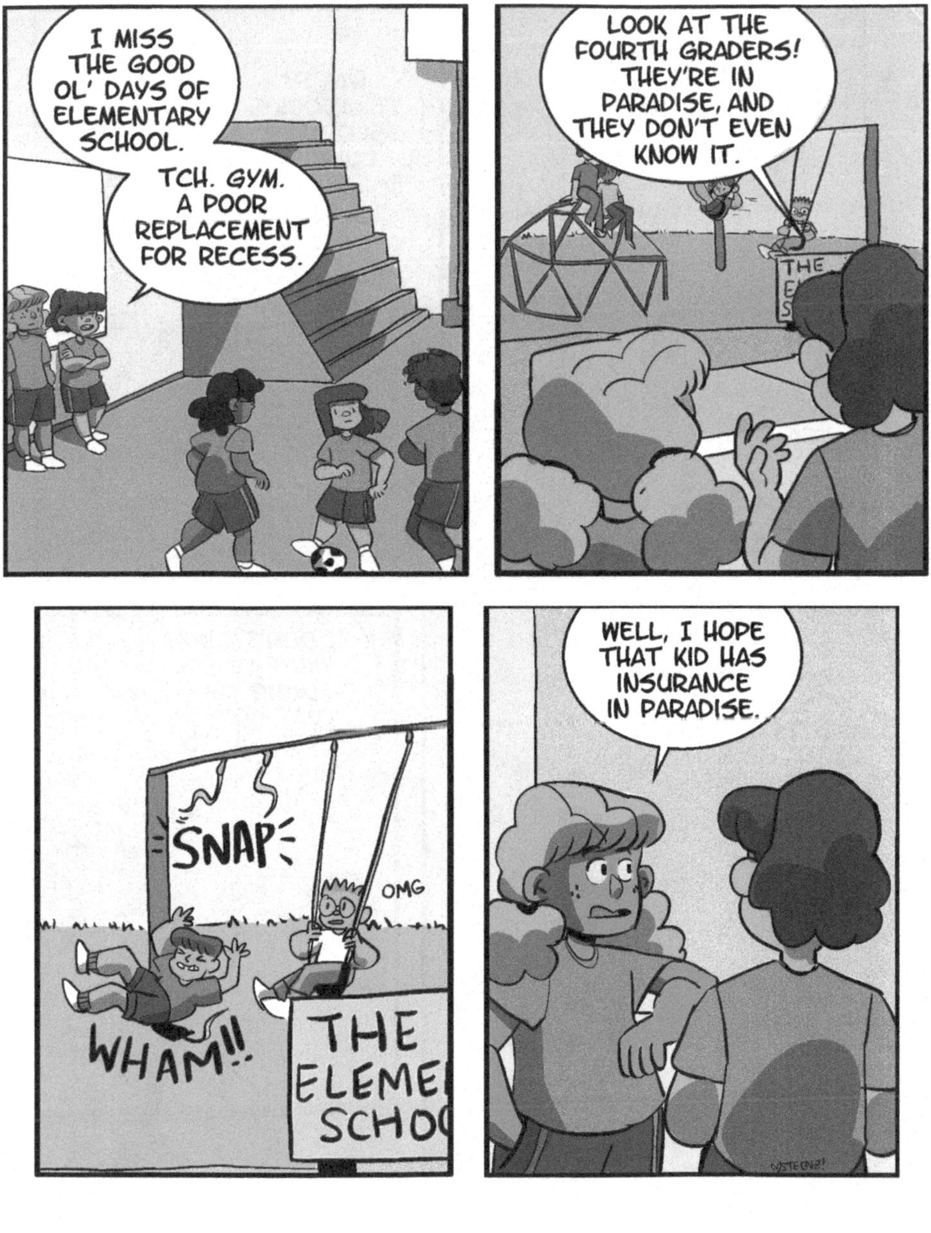

I MISS THE GOOD OL' DAYS OF ELEMENTARY SCHOOL.
TCH. GYM. A POOR REPLACEMENT FOR RECESS.
LOOK AT THE FOURTH GRADERS! THEY'RE IN PARADISE, AND THEY DON'T EVEN KNOW IT.
SNAP
OMG
WHAM!!
THE ELEME SCHO
WELL, I HOPE THAT KID HAS INSURANCE IN PARADISE.

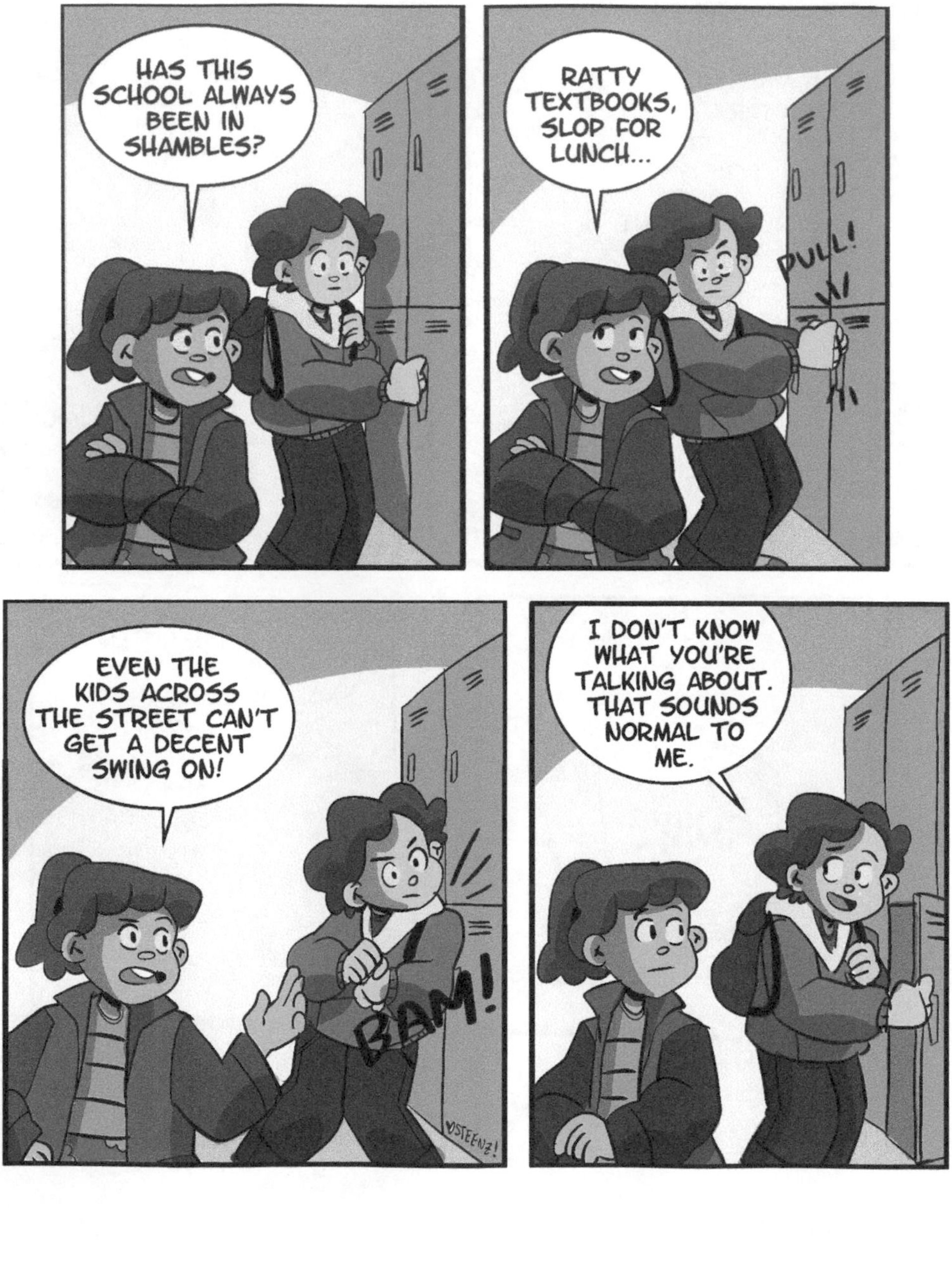
HAS THIS SCHOOL ALWAYS BEEN IN SHAMBLES?
RATTY TEXTBOOKS, SLOP FOR LUNCH...
PULL!
EVEN THE KIDS ACROSS THE STREET CAN'T GET A DECENT SWING ON!
BAM!
I DON'T KNOW WHAT YOU'RE TALKING ABOUT. THAT SOUNDS NORMAL TO ME.

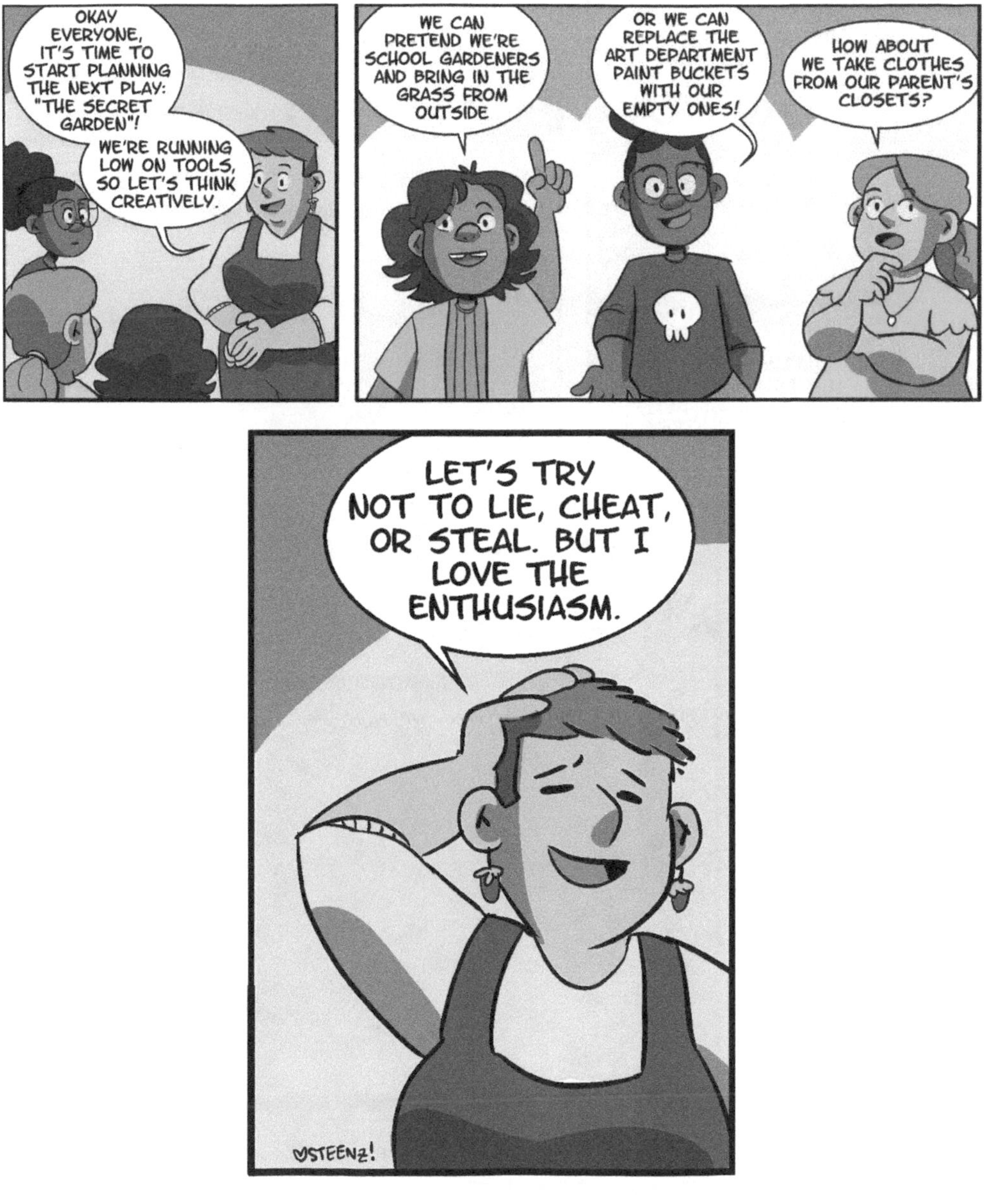
OKAY EVERYONE, IT'S TIME TO START PLANNING THE NEXT PLAY: "THE SECRET GARDEN"!
WE'RE RUNNING LOW ON TOOLS, SO LET'S THINK CREATIVELY.
WE CAN PRETEND WE'RE SCHOOL GARDENERS AND BRING IN THE GRASS FROM OUTSIDE
OR WE CAN REPLACE THE ART DEPARTMENT PAINT BUCKETS WITH OUR EMPTY ONES!
HOW ABOUT WE TAKE CLOTHES FROM OUR PARENT'S CLOSETS?
LET'S TRY NOT TO LIE, CHEAT, OR STEAL. BUT I LOVE THE ENTHUSIASM.
STEENZ!

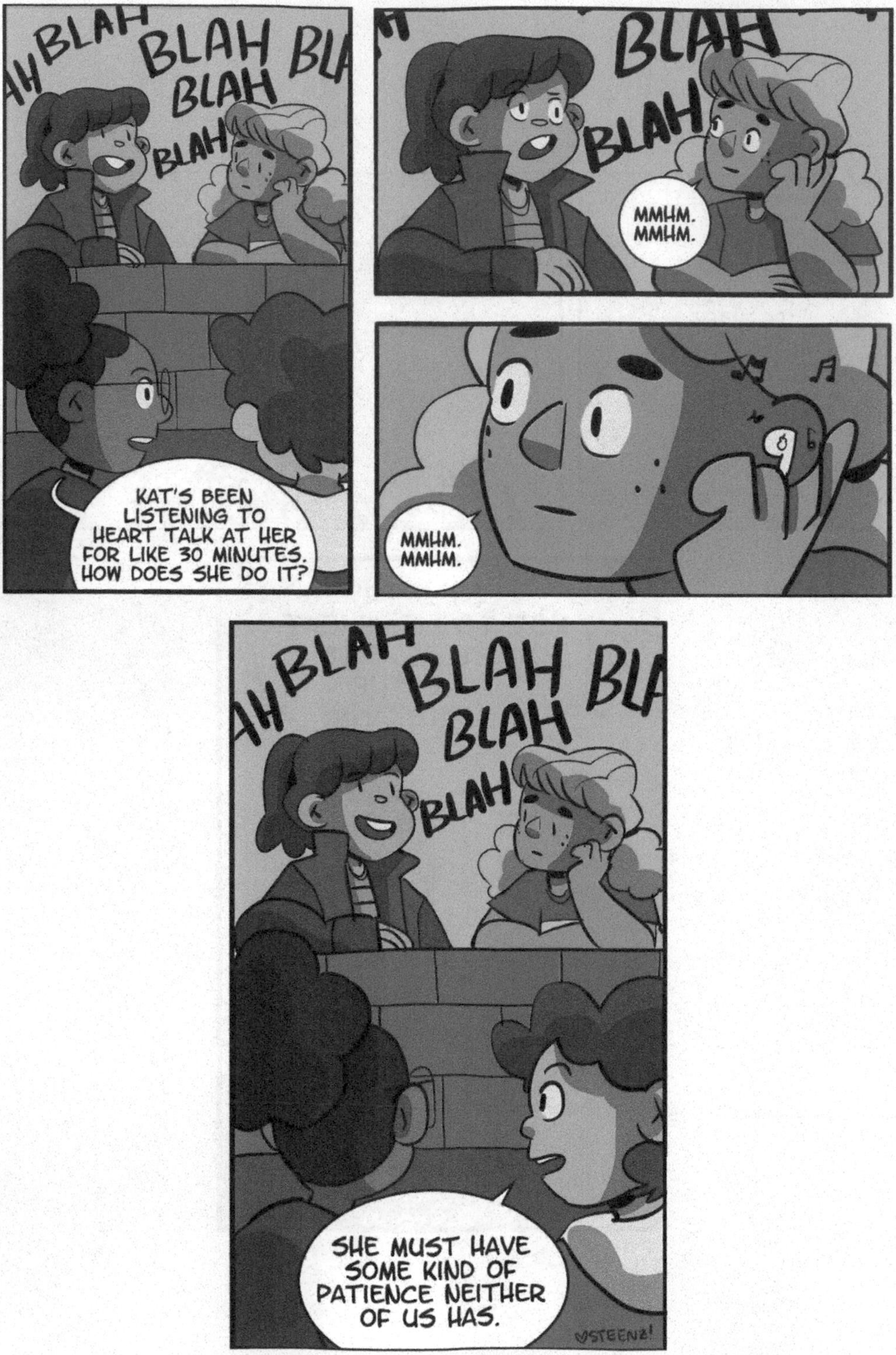
BLAH BLAH BLAH BLAH BLAH BLAH
KAT'S BEEN LISTENING TO HEART TALK AT HER FOR LIKE 30 MINUTES. HOW DOES SHE DO IT?
BLAH BLAH
MMHM. MMHM.
MMHM. MMHM.
BLAH BLAH BLAH BLAH BLAH BLAH
SHE MUST HAVE SOME KIND OF PATIENCE NEITHER OF US HAS.
STEENZ!

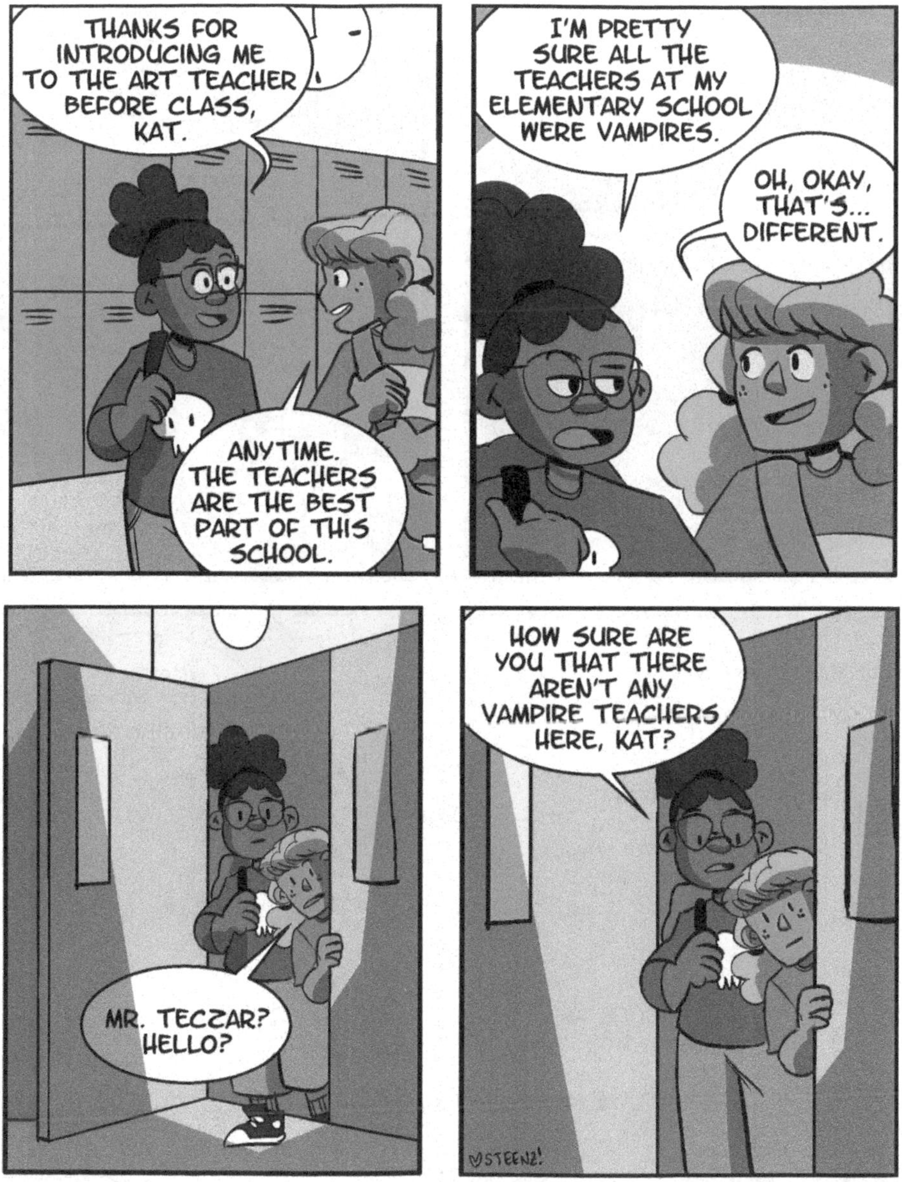
THANKS FOR INTRODUCING ME TO THE ART TEACHER BEFORE CLASS, KAT.
ANYTIME. THE TEACHERS ARE THE BEST PART OF THIS SCHOOL.
I'M PRETTY SURE ALL THE TEACHERS AT MY ELEMENTARY SCHOOL WERE VAMPIRES.
OH, OKAY, THAT'S... DIFFERENT.
MR. TECZAR? HELLO?
HOW SURE ARE YOU THAT THERE AREN'T ANY VAMPIRE TEACHERS HERE, KAT?
STEENZ!

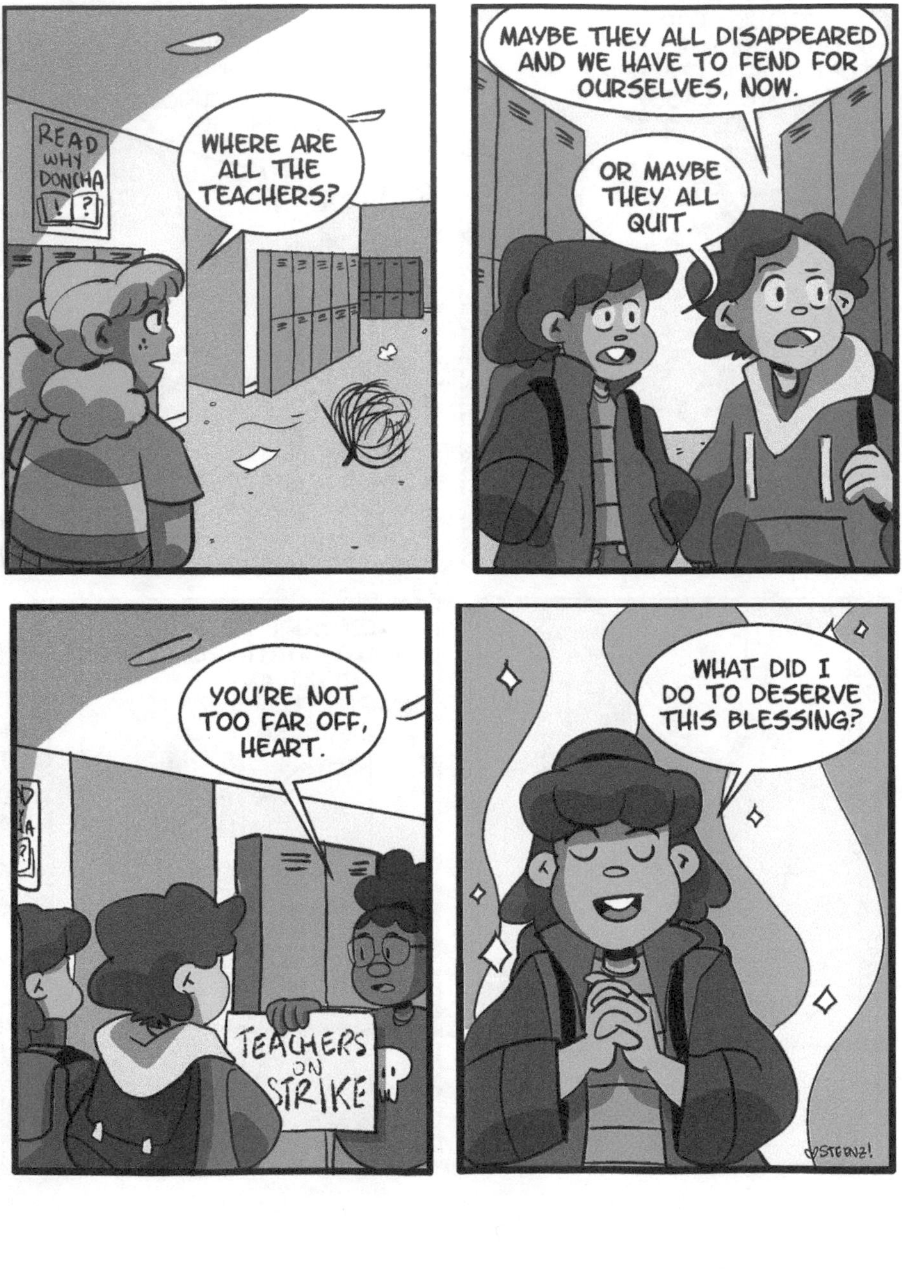
READ WHY DONCHA
WHERE ARE ALL THE TEACHERS?
MAYBE THEY ALL DISAPPEARED AND WE HAVE TO FEND FOR OURSELVES, NOW.
OR MAYBE THEY ALL QUIT.
YOU'RE NOT TOO FAR OFF, HEART.
TEACHERS ON STRIKE
WHAT DID I DO TO DESERVE THIS BLESSING?

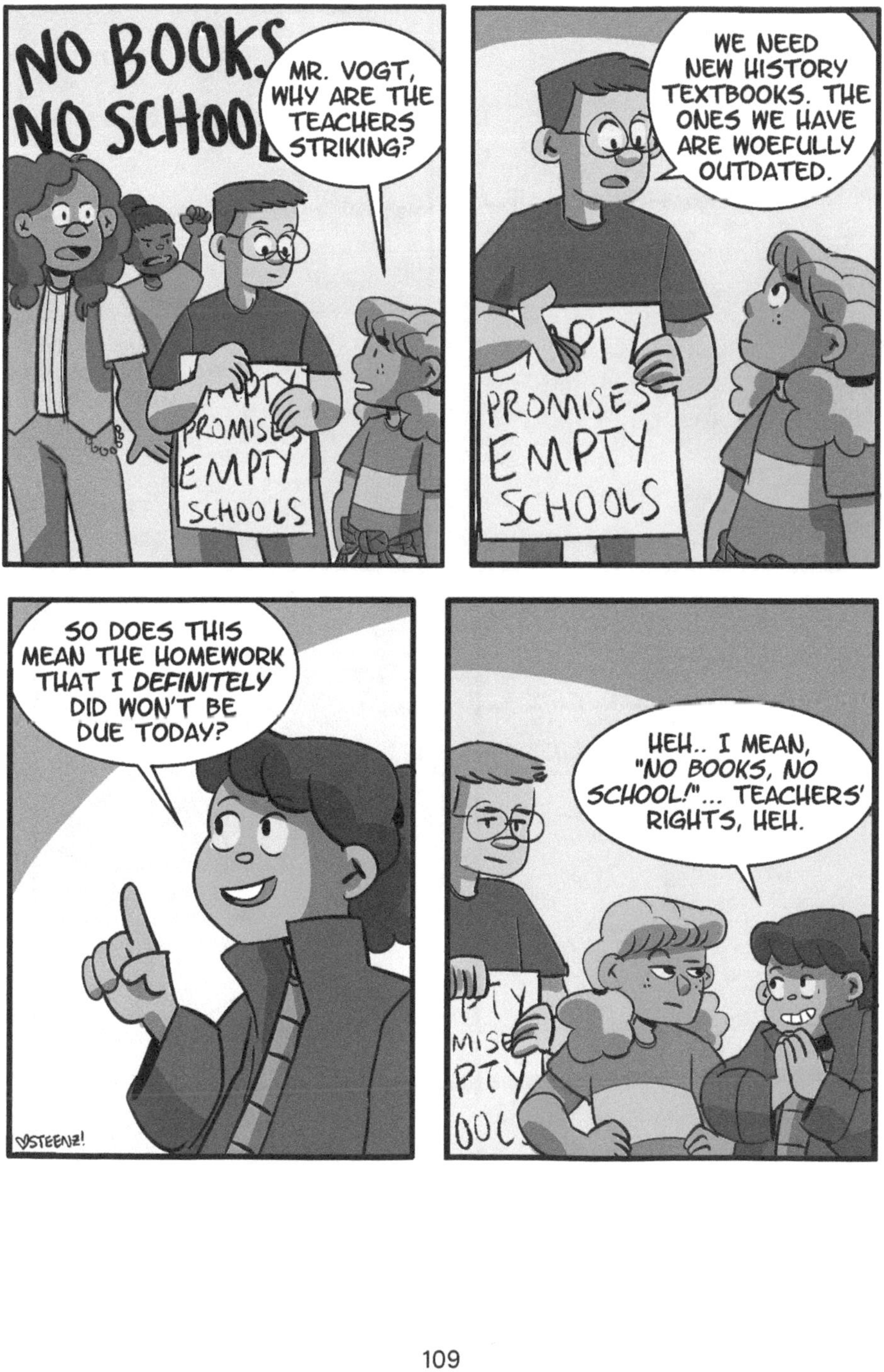
NO BOOKS NO SCHOOL
MR. VOGT, WHY ARE THE TEACHERS STRIKING?
EMPTY PROMISES EMPTY SCHOOLS
WE NEED NEW HISTORY TEXTBOOKS. THE ONES WE HAVE ARE WOEFULLY OUTDATED.
SO DOES THIS MEAN THE HOMEWORK THAT I *DEFINITELY* DID WON'T BE DUE TODAY?
STEENZ!
HEH.. I MEAN, *"NO BOOKS, NO SCHOOL!"*... TEACHERS' RIGHTS, HEH.

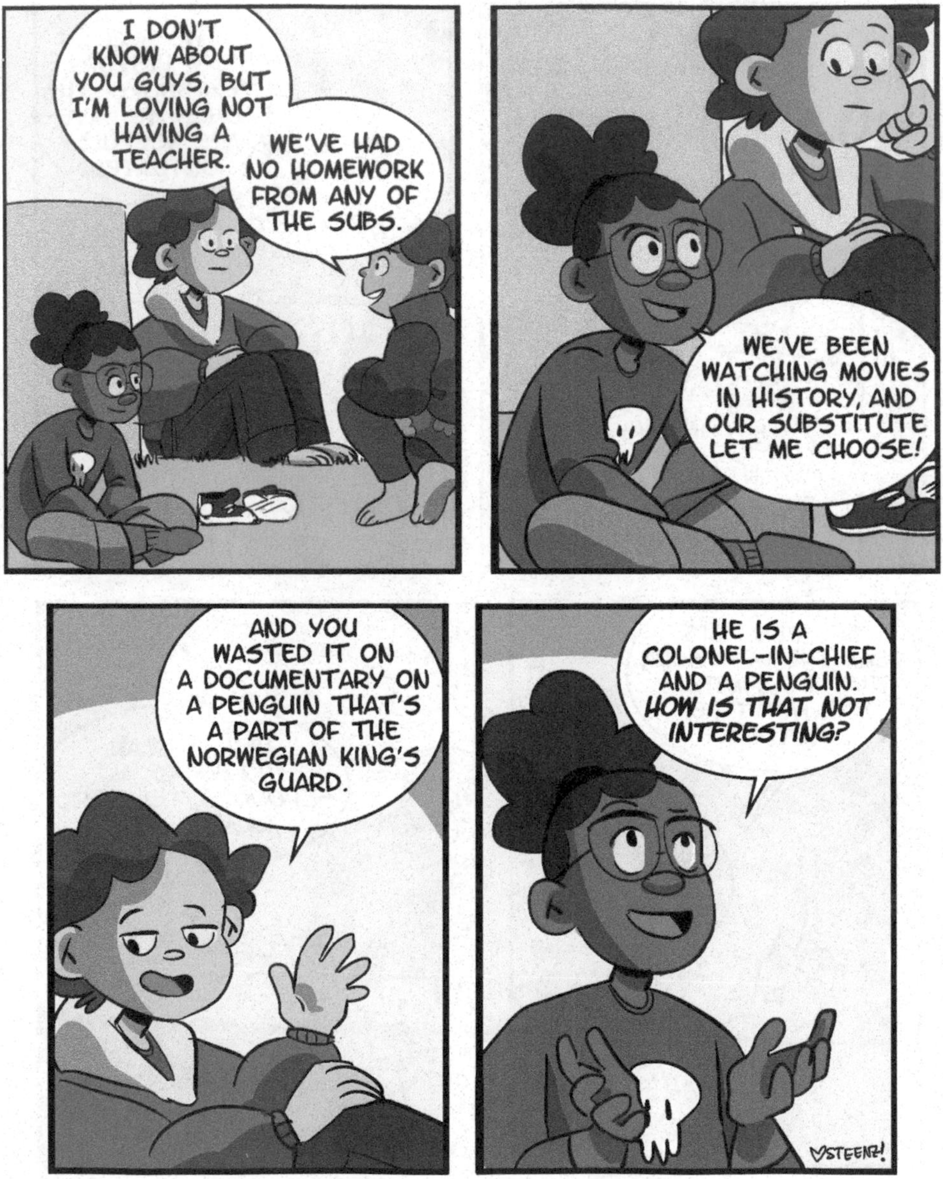
I DON'T KNOW ABOUT YOU GUYS, BUT I'M LOVING NOT HAVING A TEACHER.
WE'VE HAD NO HOMEWORK FROM ANY OF THE SUBS.
WE'VE BEEN WATCHING MOVIES IN HISTORY, AND OUR SUBSTITUTE LET ME CHOOSE!
AND YOU WASTED IT ON A DOCUMENTARY ON A PENGUIN THAT'S A PART OF THE NORWEGIAN KING'S GUARD.
HE IS A COLONEL-IN-CHIEF AND A PENGUIN. *HOW IS THAT NOT INTERESTING?*
♡STEENZ!

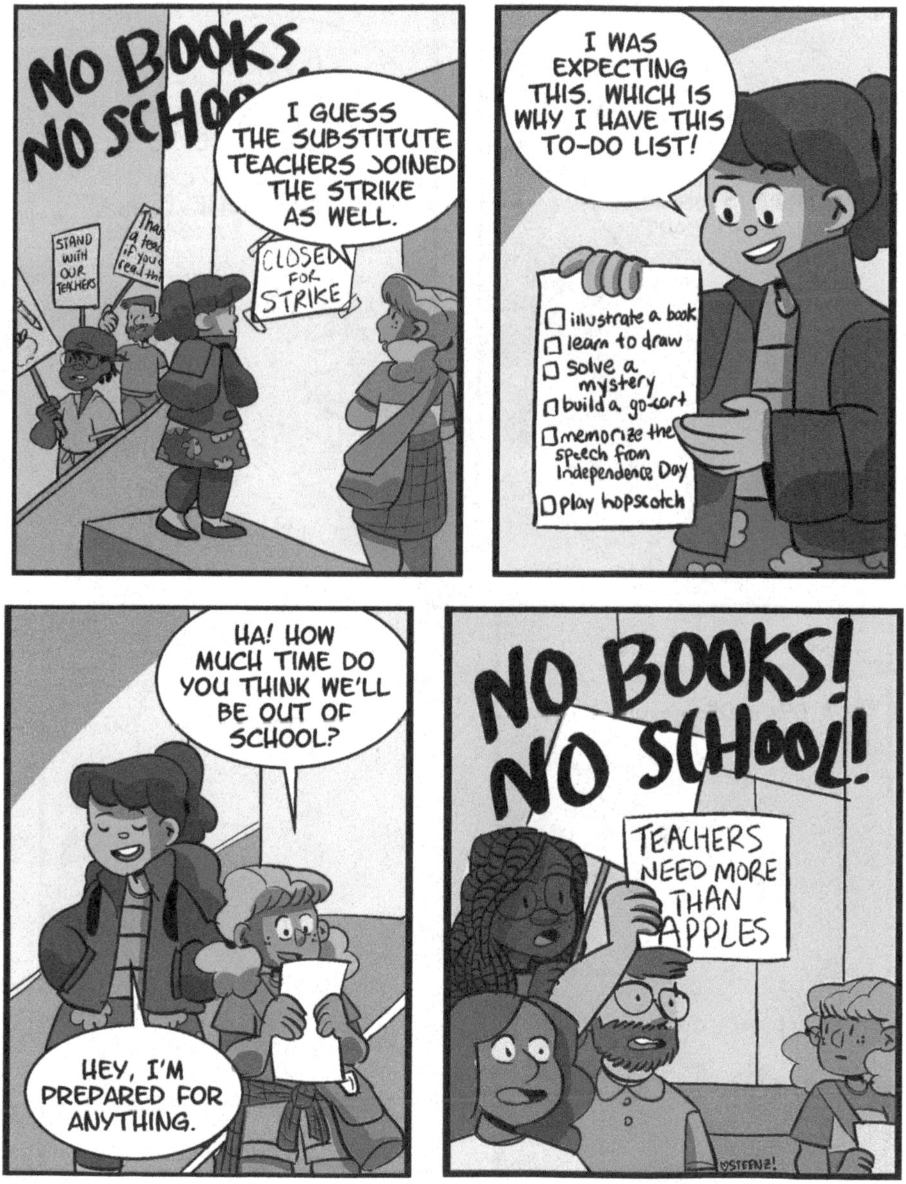
NO BOOKS NO SCHOOL
I GUESS THE SUBSTITUTE TEACHERS JOINED THE STRIKE AS WELL.
STAND WITH OUR TEACHERS
CLOSED FOR STRIKE
I WAS EXPECTING THIS. WHICH IS WHY I HAVE THIS TO-DO LIST!
illustrate a book
learn to draw
solve a mystery
build a go-cart
memorize the speech from Independence Day
play hopscotch
HA! HOW MUCH TIME DO YOU THINK WE'LL BE OUT OF SCHOOL?
HEY, I'M PREPARED FOR ANYTHING.
NO BOOKS! NO SCHOOL!
TEACHERS NEED MORE THAN APPLES

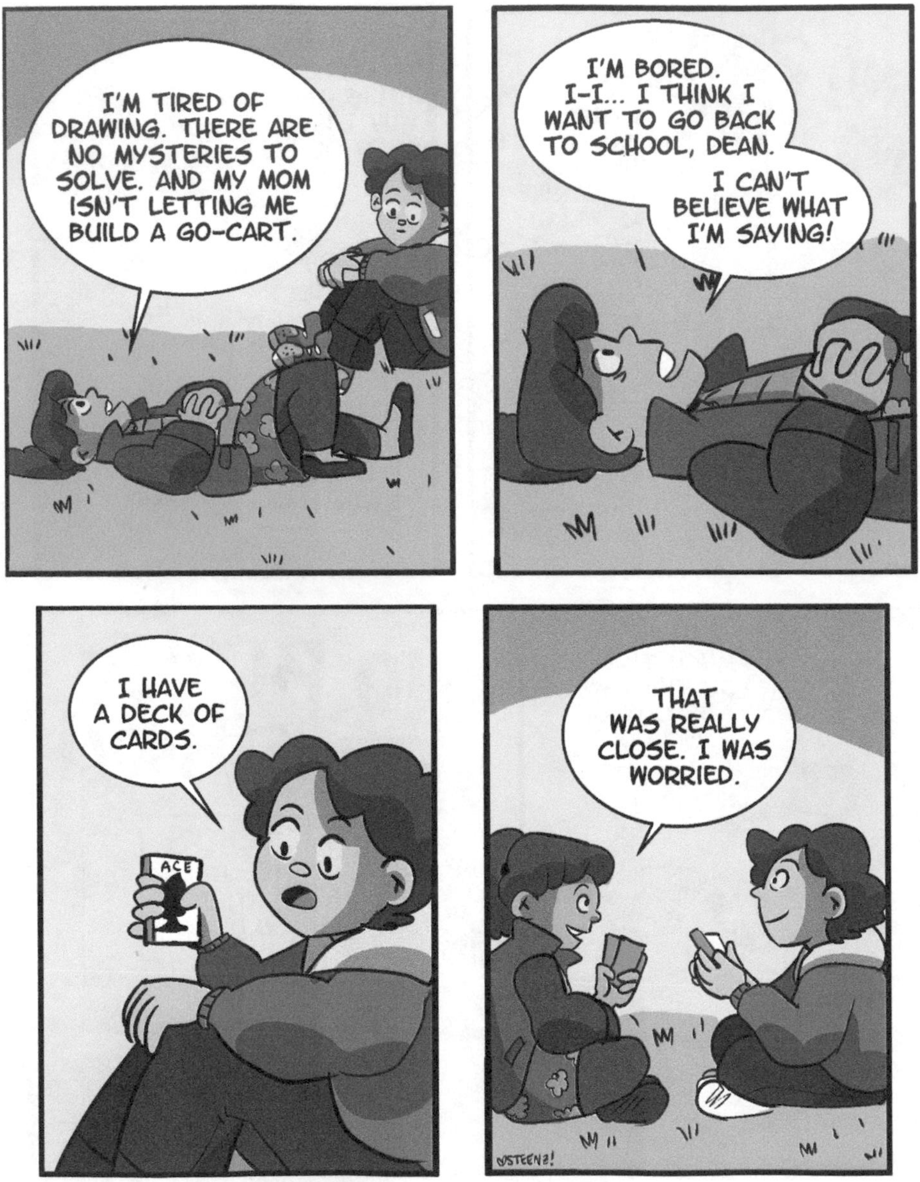
I'M TIRED OF DRAWING. THERE ARE NO MYSTERIES TO SOLVE. AND MY MOM ISN'T LETTING ME BUILD A GO-CART.
I'M BORED. I-I... I THINK I WANT TO GO BACK TO SCHOOL, DEAN.
I CAN'T BELIEVE WHAT I'M SAYING!
I HAVE A DECK OF CARDS.
ACE
THAT WAS REALLY CLOSE. I WAS WORRIED.
©STEENZ!

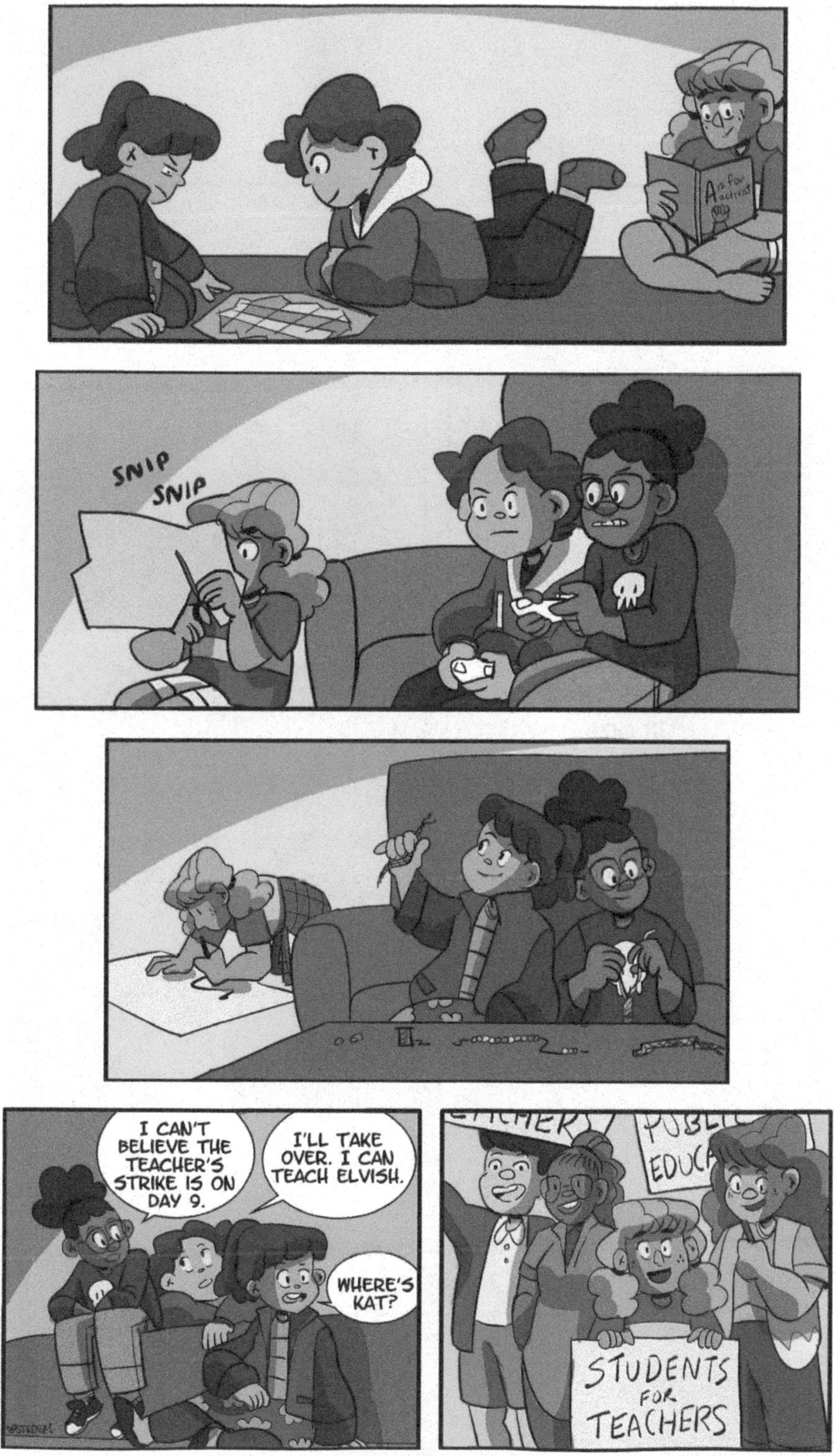
SNIP
SNIP
I CAN'T BELIEVE THE TEACHER'S STRIKE IS ON DAY 9.
I'LL TAKE OVER. I CAN TEACH ELVISH.
WHERE'S KAT?
STUDENTS FOR TEACHERS

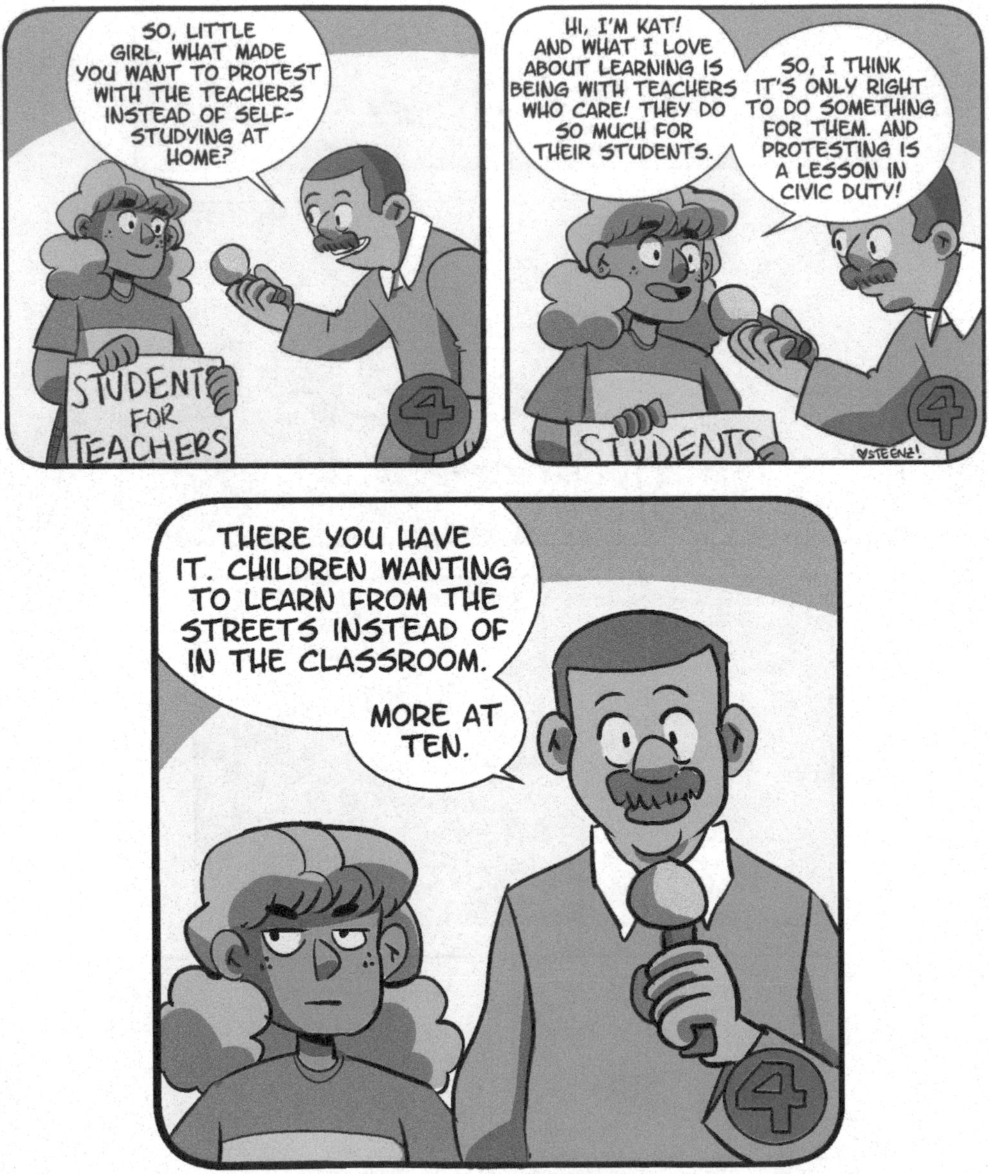
SO, LITTLE GIRL, WHAT MADE YOU WANT TO PROTEST WITH THE TEACHERS INSTEAD OF SELF-STUDYING AT HOME?
STUDENTS FOR TEACHERS
4
HI, I'M KAT! AND WHAT I LOVE ABOUT LEARNING IS BEING WITH TEACHERS WHO CARE! THEY DO SO MUCH FOR THEIR STUDENTS.
SO, I THINK IT'S ONLY RIGHT TO DO SOMETHING FOR THEM. AND PROTESTING IS A LESSON IN CIVIC DUTY!
STUDENTS
4
♥STEENZ!
THERE YOU HAVE IT. CHILDREN WANTING TO LEARN FROM THE STREETS INSTEAD OF IN THE CLASSROOM.
MORE AT TEN.
4

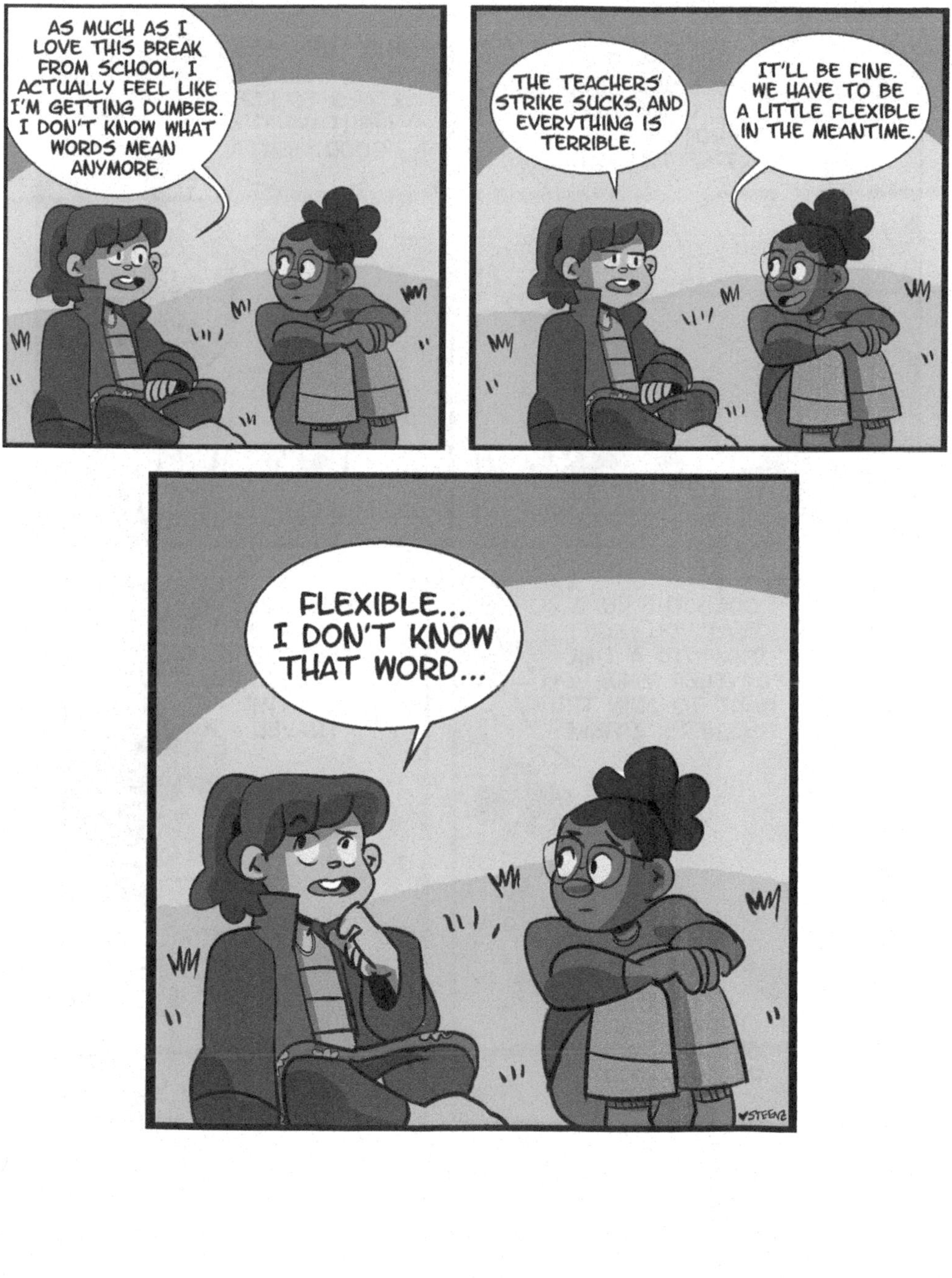
AS MUCH AS I LOVE THIS BREAK FROM SCHOOL, I ACTUALLY FEEL LIKE I'M GETTING DUMBER. I DON'T KNOW WHAT WORDS MEAN ANYMORE.
THE TEACHERS' STRIKE SUCKS, AND EVERYTHING IS TERRIBLE.
IT'LL BE FINE. WE HAVE TO BE A LITTLE FLEXIBLE IN THE MEANTIME.
FLEXIBLE... I DON'T KNOW THAT WORD...
♥STEENZ

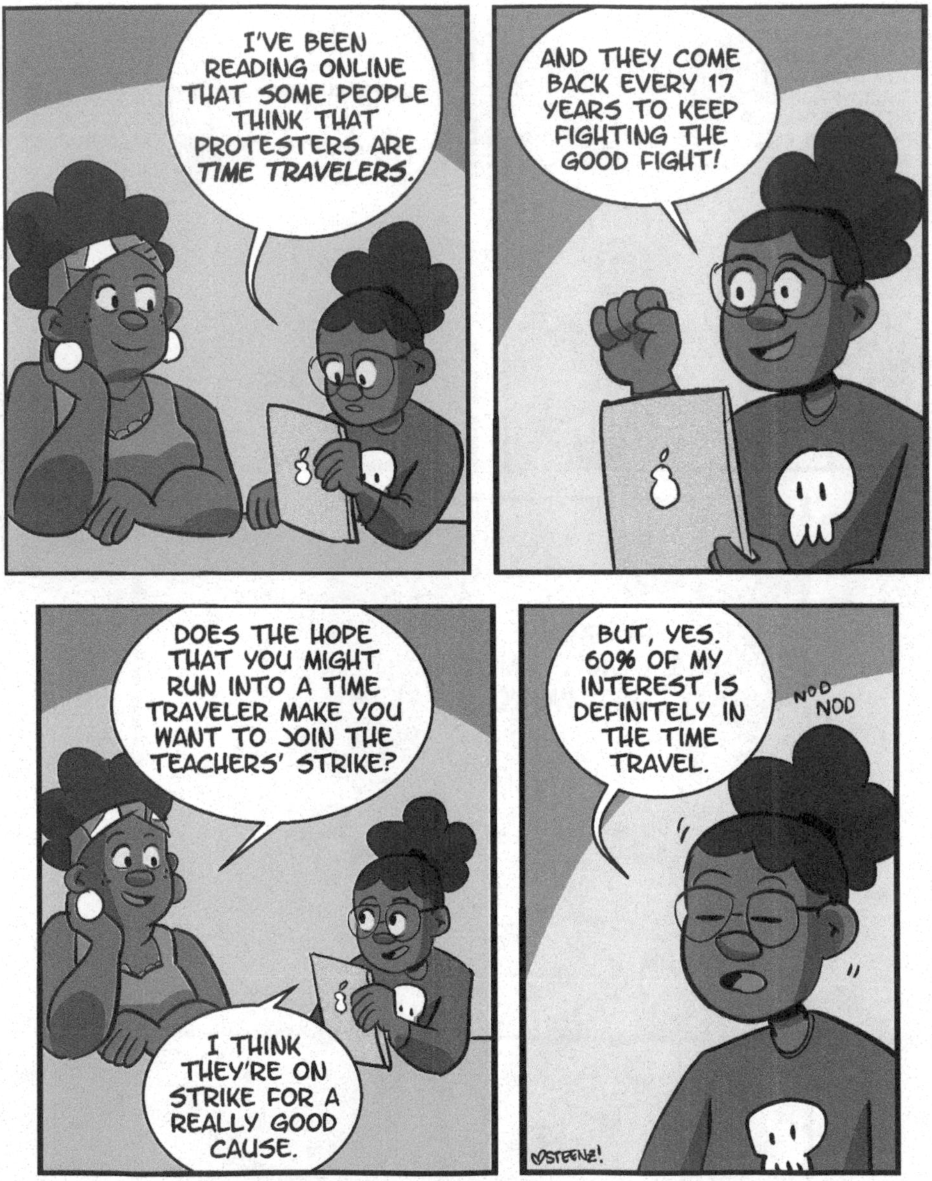
I'VE BEEN READING ONLINE THAT SOME PEOPLE THINK THAT PROTESTERS ARE *TIME TRAVELERS*.
AND THEY COME BACK EVERY 17 YEARS TO KEEP FIGHTING THE GOOD FIGHT!
DOES THE HOPE THAT YOU MIGHT RUN INTO A TIME TRAVELER MAKE YOU WANT TO JOIN THE TEACHERS' STRIKE?
I THINK THEY'RE ON STRIKE FOR A REALLY GOOD CAUSE.
BUT, YES. 60% OF MY INTEREST IS DEFINITELY IN THE TIME TRAVEL.
NOD NOD
♡STEENZ!

WHERE'S CHARLOTTE?
SHE SAID SHE WAS MAKING A SIGN TO CARRY AT THE TEACHERS' STRIKE.
OH, NOT HER, TOO! AND YOU FOLLOW HER AROUND LIKE A LOVESICK PUPPY, SO YOU'LL BE THERE NEXT.
I DO NOT!
BUT I DID TELL HER I'D MEET HER THERE TOMORROW.
STEENZ!

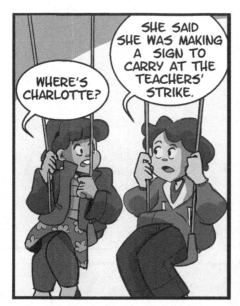

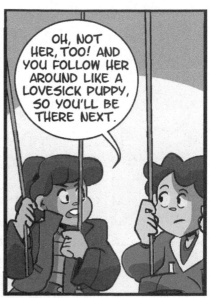

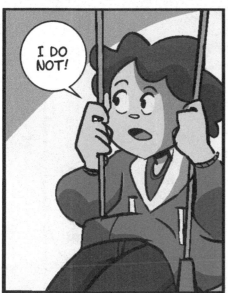

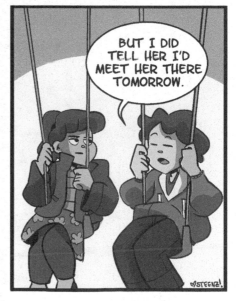

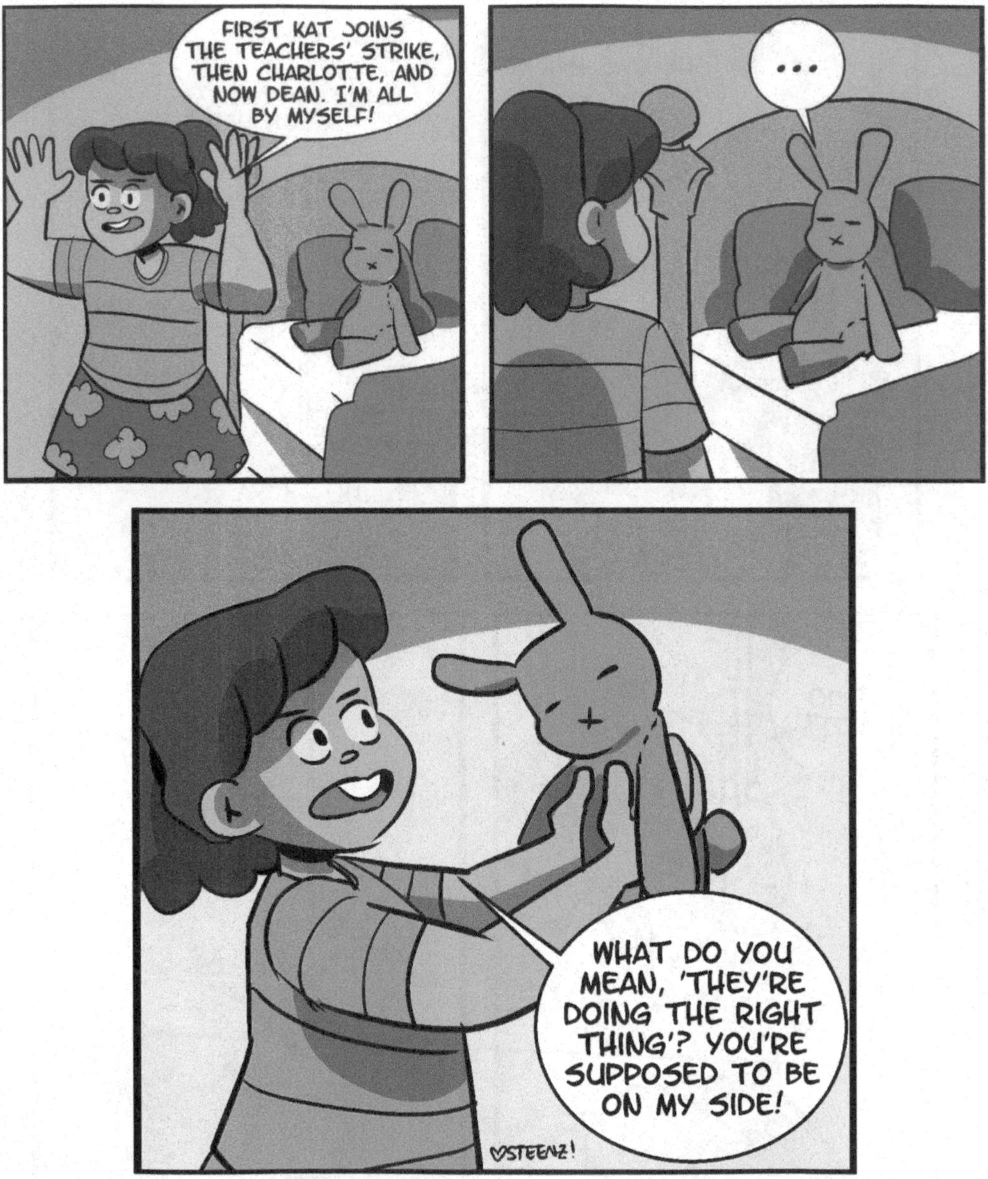
FIRST KAT JOINS THE TEACHERS' STRIKE, THEN CHARLOTTE, AND NOW DEAN. I'M ALL BY MYSELF!
...
WHAT DO YOU MEAN, 'THEY'RE DOING THE RIGHT THING'? YOU'RE SUPPOSED TO BE ON MY SIDE!
♡STEENZ!

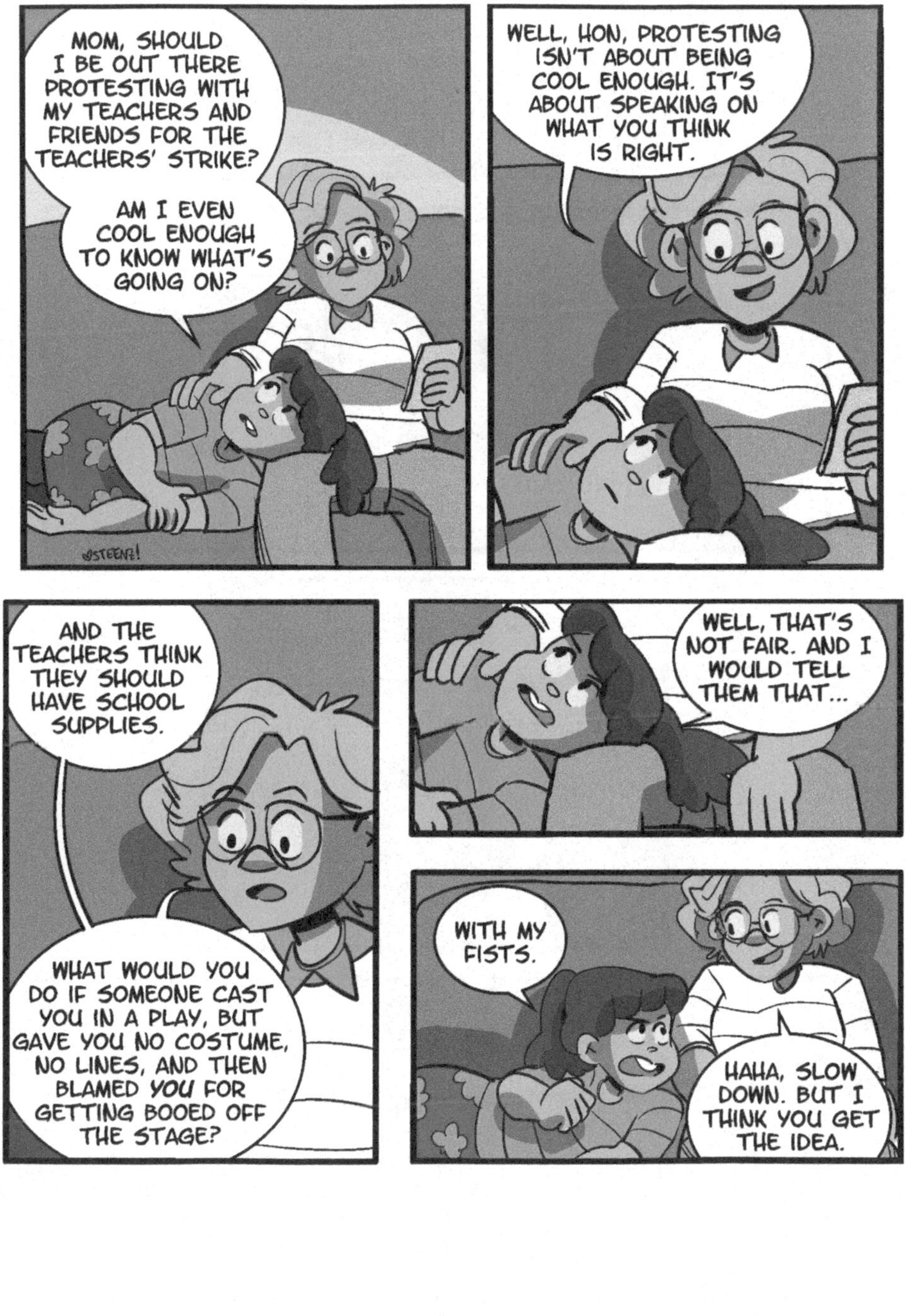
MOM, SHOULD I BE OUT THERE PROTESTING WITH MY TEACHERS AND FRIENDS FOR THE TEACHERS' STRIKE?
AM I EVEN COOL ENOUGH TO KNOW WHAT'S GOING ON?
©STEENZ!
WELL, HON, PROTESTING ISN'T ABOUT BEING COOL ENOUGH. IT'S ABOUT SPEAKING ON WHAT YOU THINK IS RIGHT.
AND THE TEACHERS THINK THEY SHOULD HAVE SCHOOL SUPPLIES.
WHAT WOULD YOU DO IF SOMEONE CAST YOU IN A PLAY, BUT GAVE YOU NO COSTUME, NO LINES, AND THEN BLAMED *YOU* FOR GETTING BOOED OFF THE STAGE?
WELL, THAT'S NOT FAIR. AND I WOULD TELL THEM THAT...
WITH MY FISTS.
HAHA, SLOW DOWN. BUT I THINK YOU GET THE IDEA.

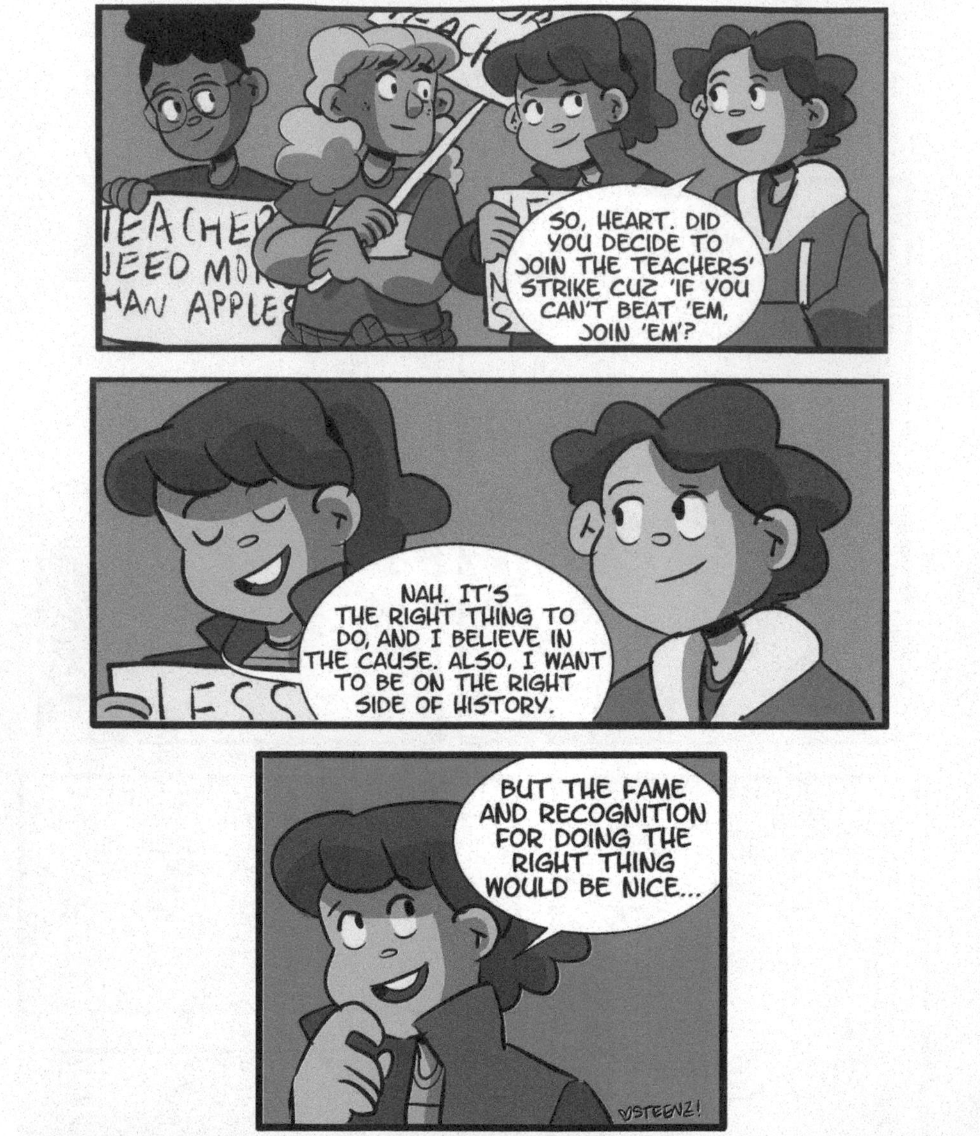
SO, HEART. DID YOU DECIDE TO JOIN THE TEACHERS' STRIKE CUZ 'IF YOU CAN'T BEAT 'EM, JOIN 'EM'?
NAH. IT'S THE RIGHT THING TO DO, AND I BELIEVE IN THE CAUSE. ALSO, I WANT TO BE ON THE RIGHT SIDE OF HISTORY.
BUT THE FAME AND RECOGNITION FOR DOING THE RIGHT THING WOULD BE NICE...
♡STEENZ!
THWAK!
STUDENTS
HEE HEE
HA HA
HEART, THAT'S NOT A GOOD REASON!!!
HAHA, I'M KIDDING! I'M KIDDING!

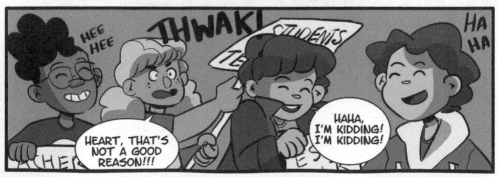

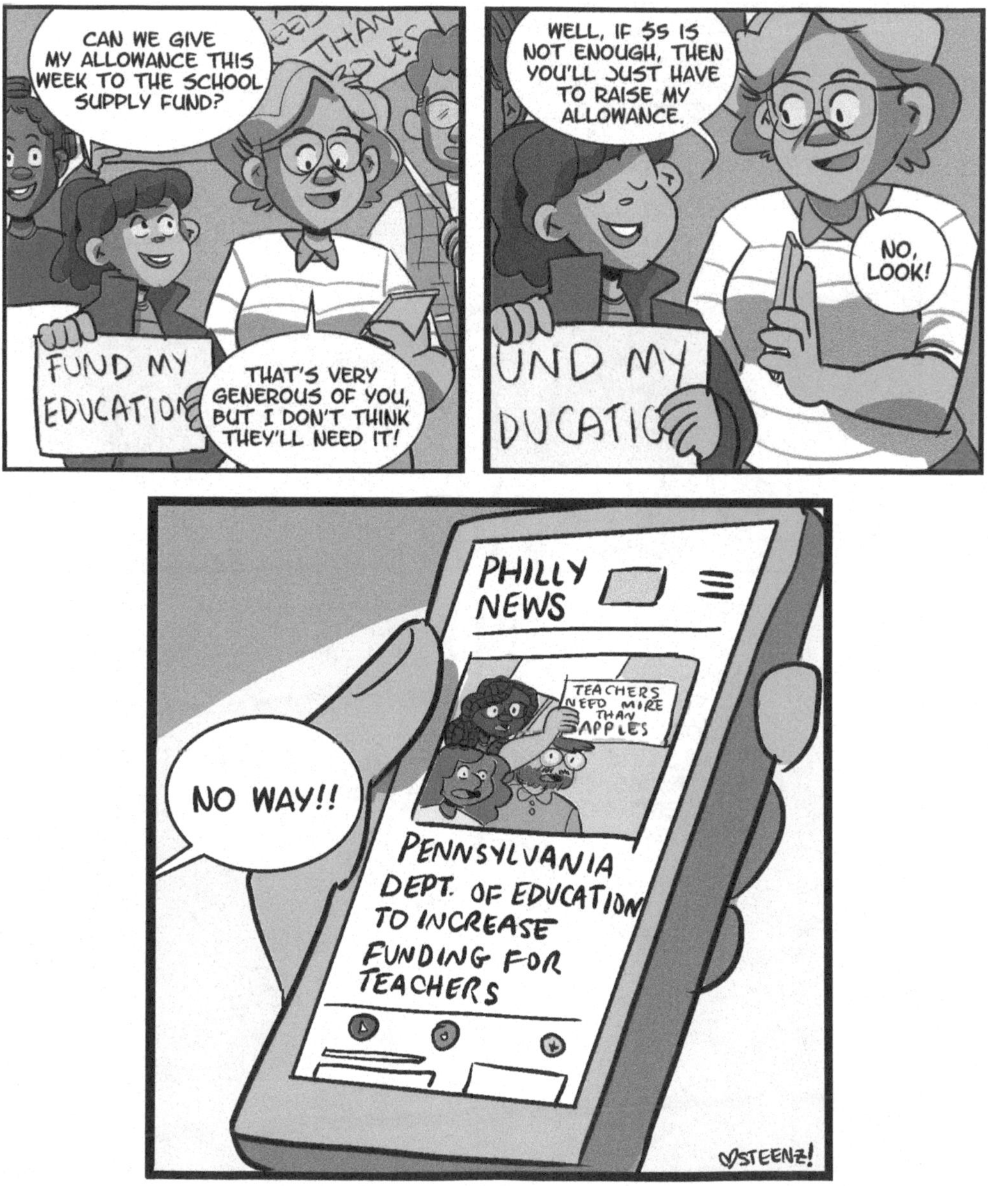
CAN WE GIVE MY ALLOWANCE THIS WEEK TO THE SCHOOL SUPPLY FUND?
FUND MY EDUCATIO
THAT'S VERY GENEROUS OF YOU, BUT I DON'T THINK THEY'LL NEED IT!
WELL, IF $5 IS NOT ENOUGH, THEN YOU'LL JUST HAVE TO RAISE MY ALLOWANCE.
UND MY DUCATIO
NO, LOOK!
PHILLY NEWS
TEACHERS NEED MORE THAN APPLES
PENNSYLVANIA DEPT. OF EDUCATION TO INCREASE FUNDING FOR TEACHERS
NO WAY!!
STEENZ!

NOW THAT THE TEACHERS STRIKE IS OVER, I GUESS WE'RE GOING BACK TO CLASS NEXT WEEK?
THAT'S RIGHT! WE FOUGHT FOR WHAT WE WANTED AND GOT IT!
SOOO... THIS PROTESTING THING COUNTS AS EXTRA CREDIT FOR HISTORY, RIGHT?
NO.
♡STEENZ!
UGH, HEART.
HEY, I'M FIGHTING FOR WHAT I WANT!

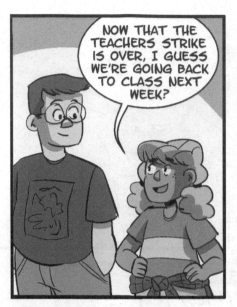

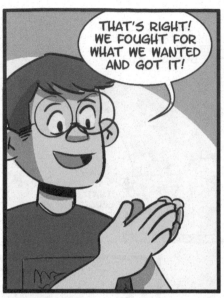

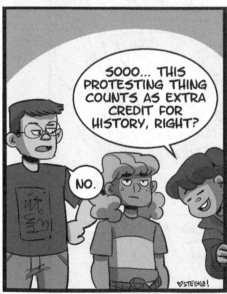

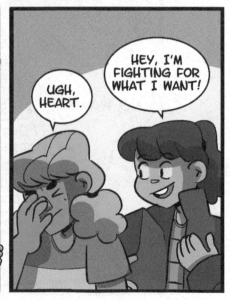

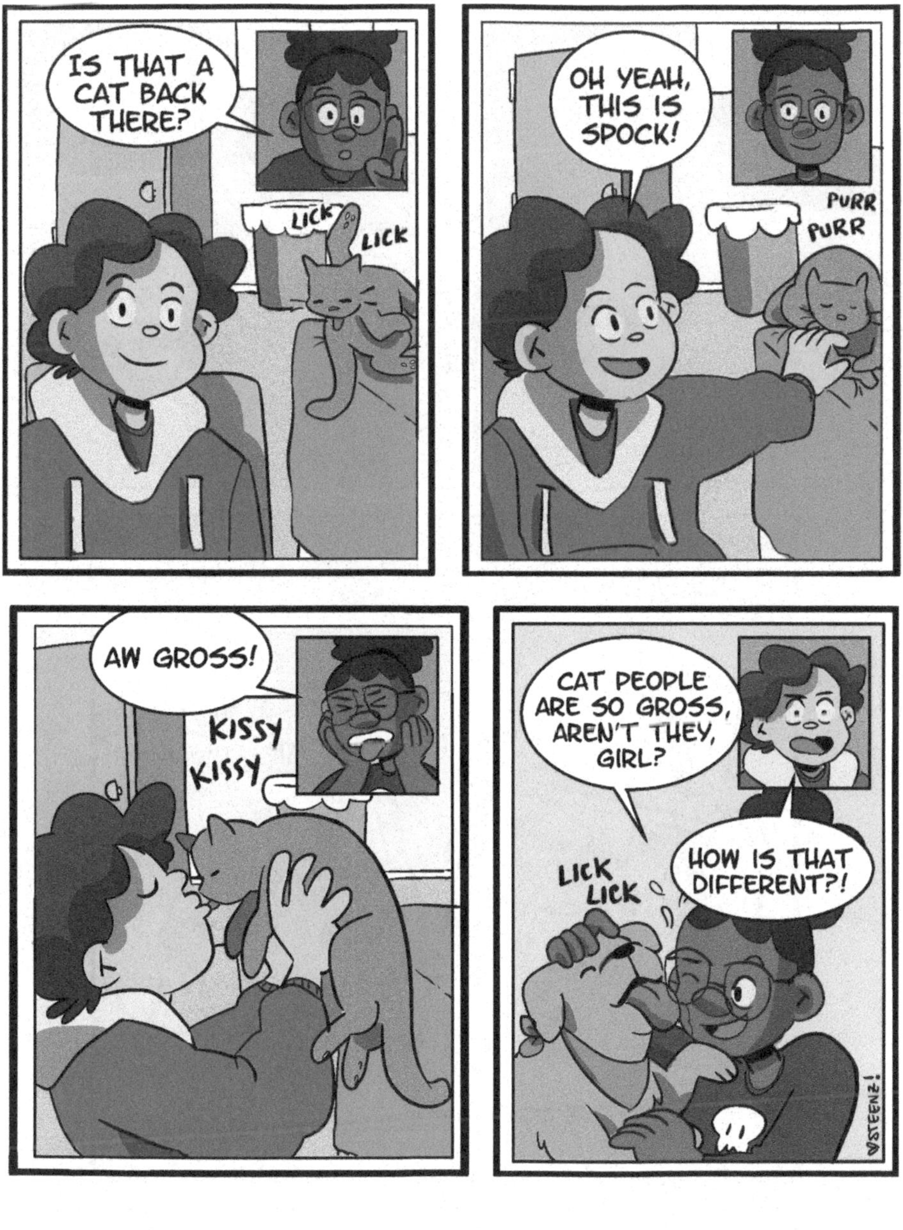
IS THAT A CAT BACK THERE?
LICK
LICK
OH YEAH, THIS IS SPOCK!
PURR
PURR
AW GROSS!
KISSY
KISSY
CAT PEOPLE ARE SO GROSS, AREN'T THEY, GIRL?
LICK
LICK
HOW IS THAT DIFFERENT?!
@STEENZ!

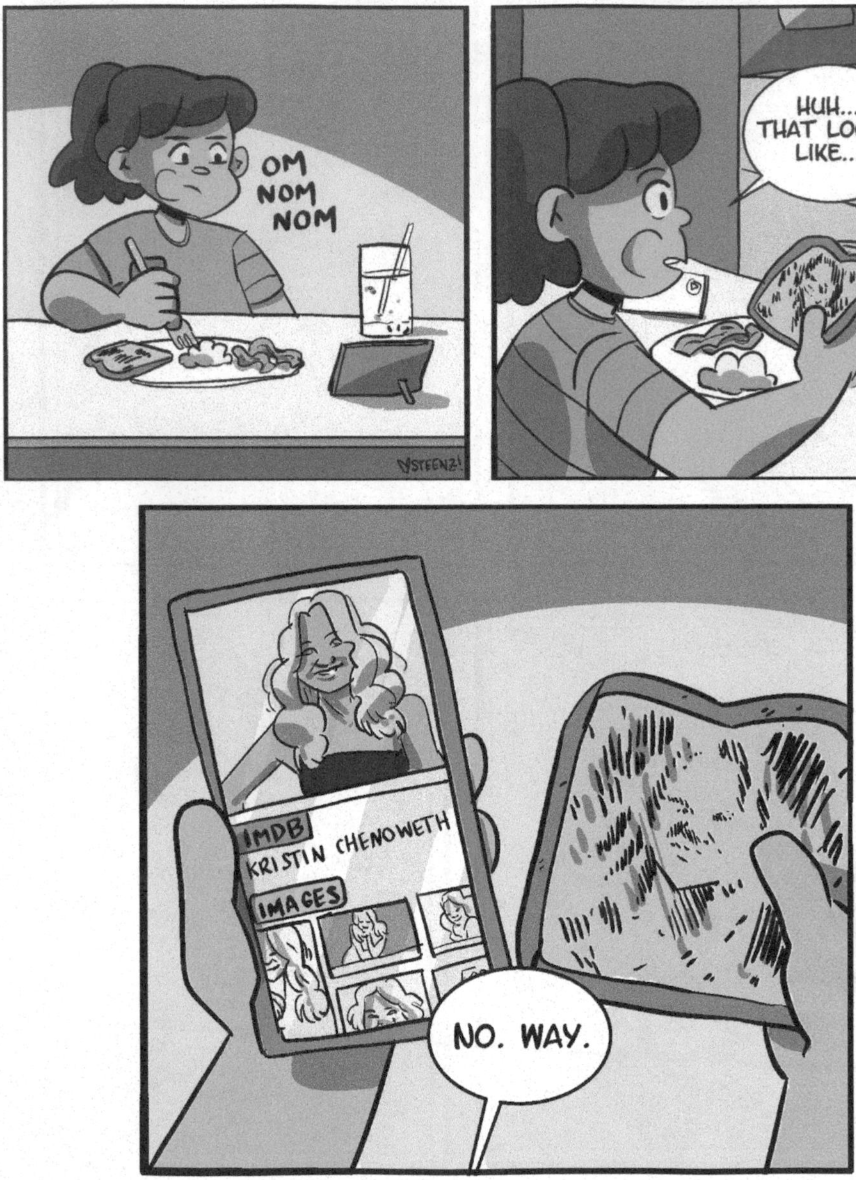
OM NOM NOM
STEENZ!
HUH... THAT LOOKS LIKE...
IMDB
KRISTIN CHENOWETH
IMAGES
NO. WAY.

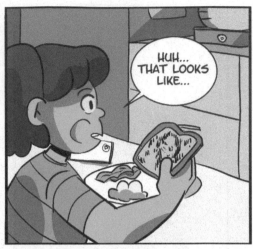

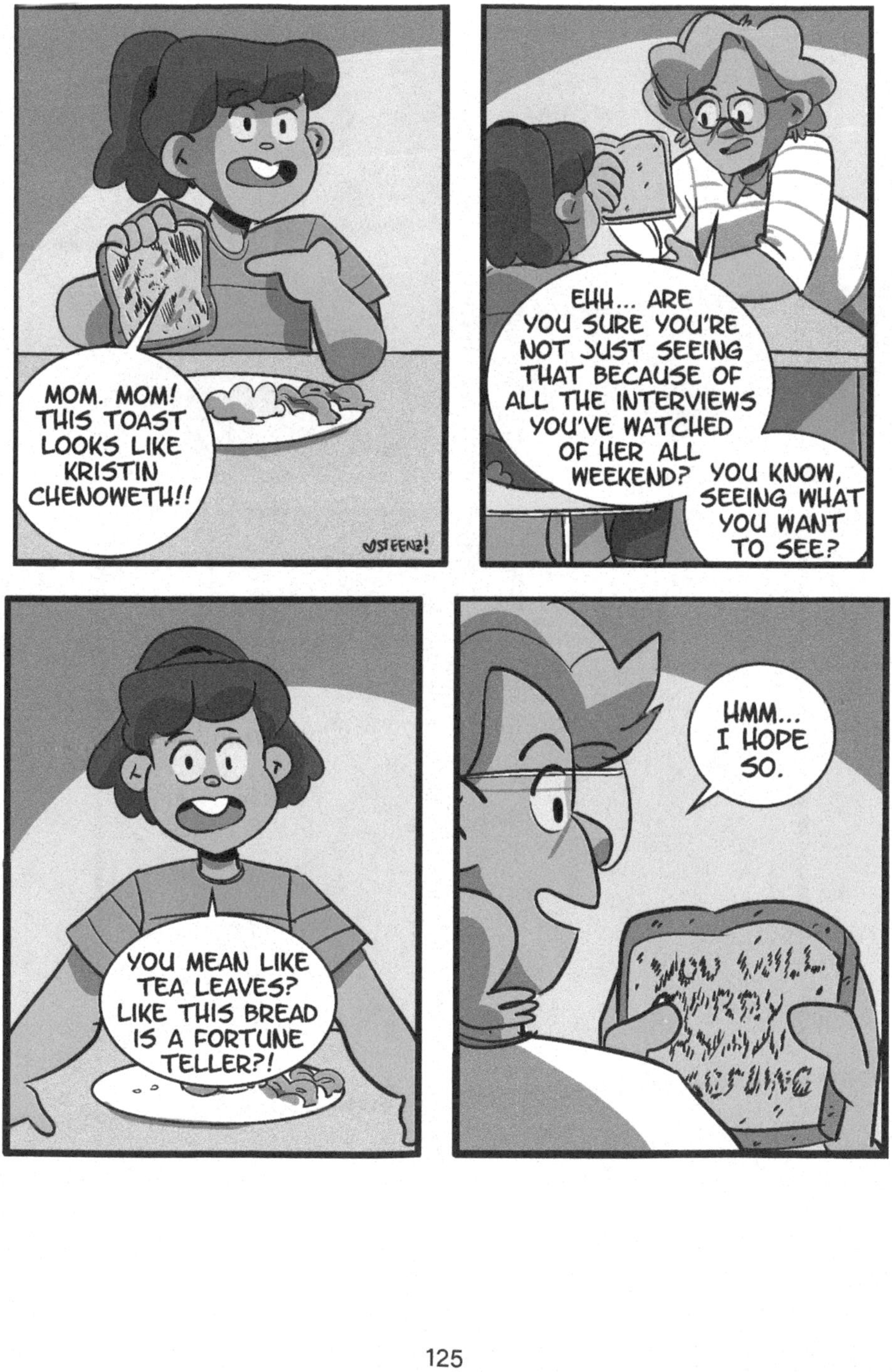
MOM. MOM! THIS TOAST LOOKS LIKE KRISTIN CHENOWETH!!
EHH... ARE YOU SURE YOU'RE NOT JUST SEEING THAT BECAUSE OF ALL THE INTERVIEWS YOU'VE WATCHED OF HER ALL WEEKEND?
YOU KNOW, SEEING WHAT YOU WANT TO SEE?
YOU MEAN LIKE TEA LEAVES? LIKE THIS BREAD IS A FORTUNE TELLER?!
HMM... I HOPE SO.

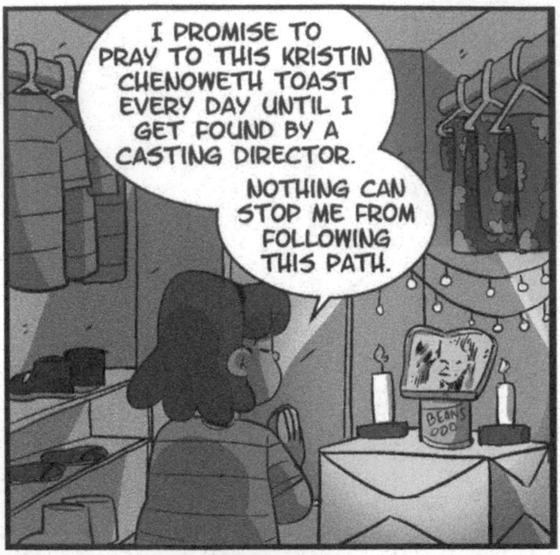
I PROMISE TO PRAY TO THIS KRISTIN CHENOWETH TOAST EVERY DAY UNTIL I GET FOUND BY A CASTING DIRECTOR.
NOTHING CAN STOP ME FROM FOLLOWING THIS PATH.
BEANS

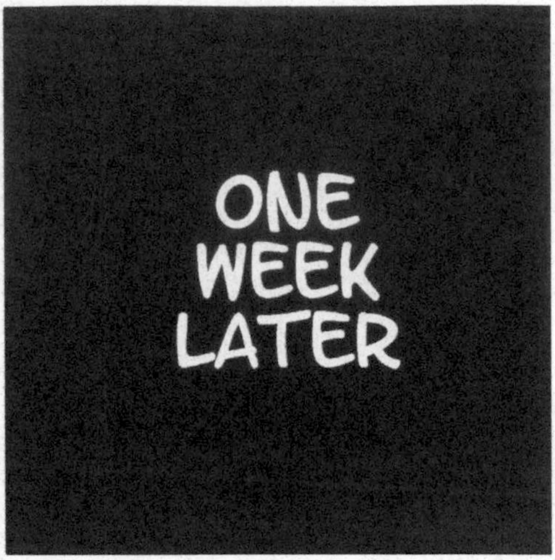
ONE WEEK LATER

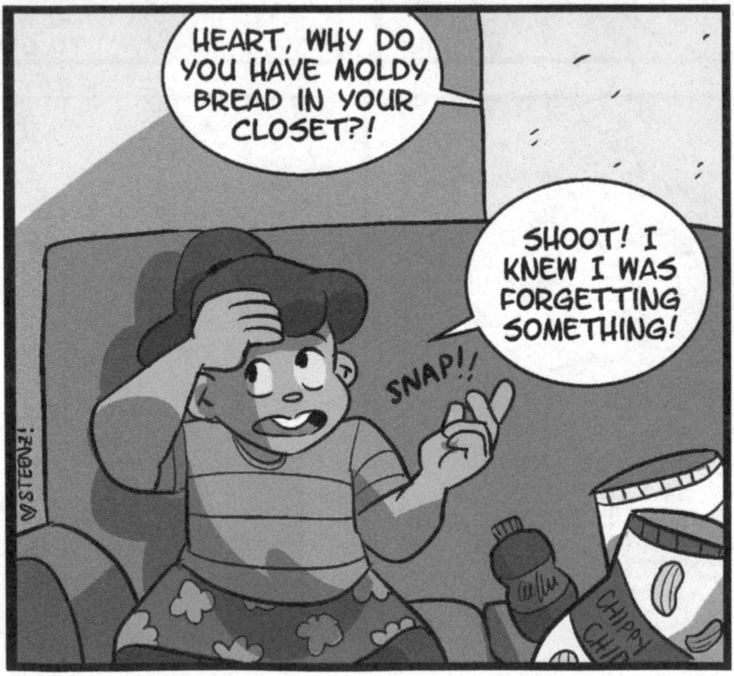
HEART, WHY DO YOU HAVE MOLDY BREAD IN YOUR CLOSET?!
SHOOT! I KNEW I WAS FORGETTING SOMETHING!
SNAP!!
CHIPPY

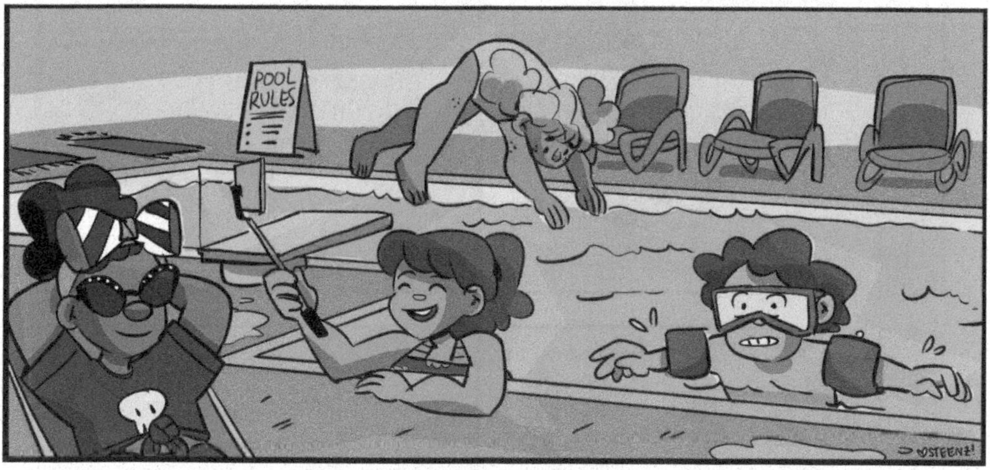
POOL RULES
©STEENZ!

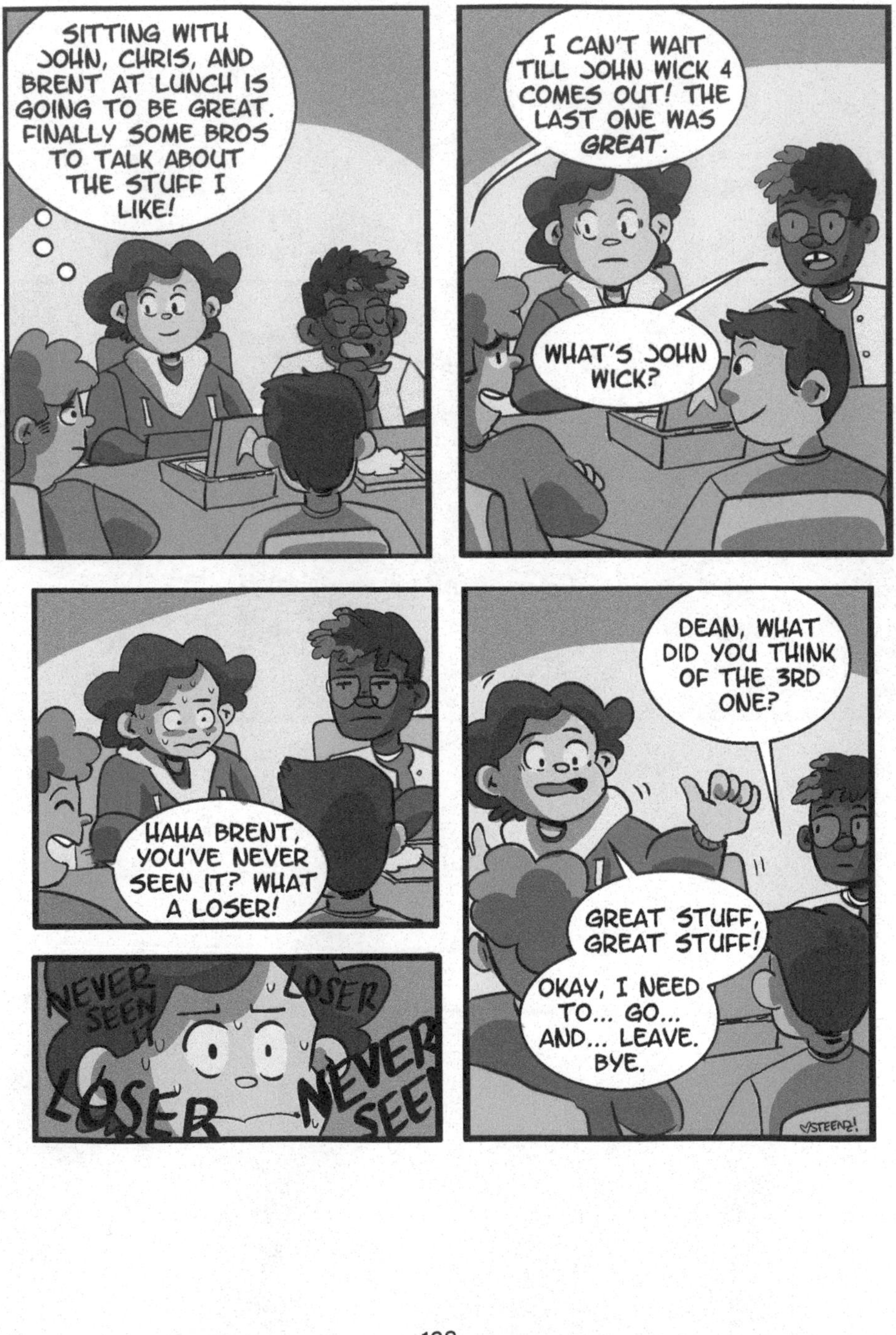
SITTING WITH JOHN, CHRIS, AND BRENT AT LUNCH IS GOING TO BE GREAT. FINALLY SOME BROS TO TALK ABOUT THE STUFF I LIKE!
I CAN'T WAIT TILL JOHN WICK 4 COMES OUT! THE LAST ONE WAS GREAT.
WHAT'S JOHN WICK?
HAHA BRENT, YOU'VE NEVER SEEN IT? WHAT A LOSER!
NEVER SEEN IT
LOSER
LOSER
NEVER SEE
DEAN, WHAT DID YOU THINK OF THE 3RD ONE?
GREAT STUFF, GREAT STUFF!
OKAY, I NEED TO... GO... AND... LEAVE. BYE.
STEENZ!

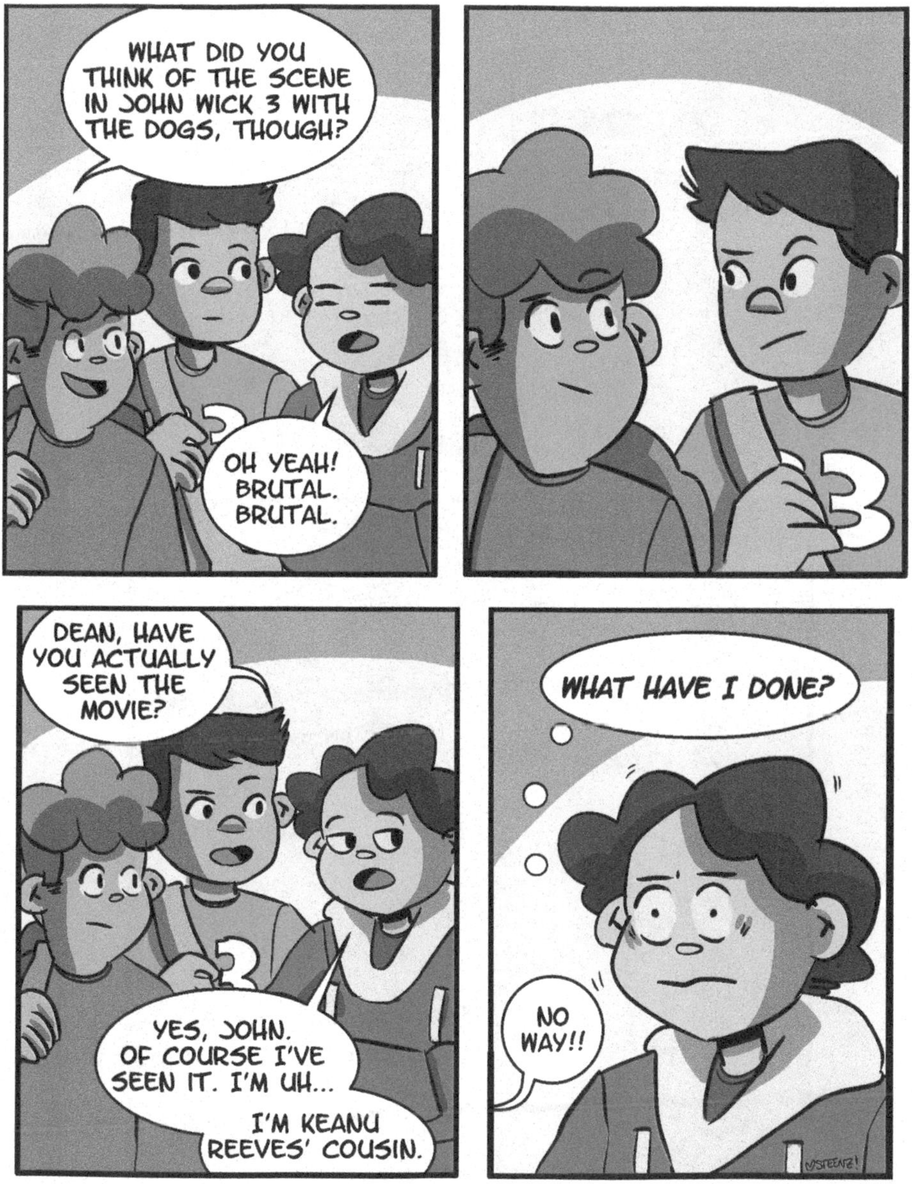
WHAT DID YOU THINK OF THE SCENE IN JOHN WICK 3 WITH THE DOGS, THOUGH?
OH YEAH! BRUTAL. BRUTAL.
DEAN, HAVE YOU ACTUALLY SEEN THE MOVIE?
YES, JOHN. OF COURSE I'VE SEEN IT. I'M UH...
I'M KEANU REEVES' COUSIN.
WHAT HAVE I DONE?
NO WAY!!

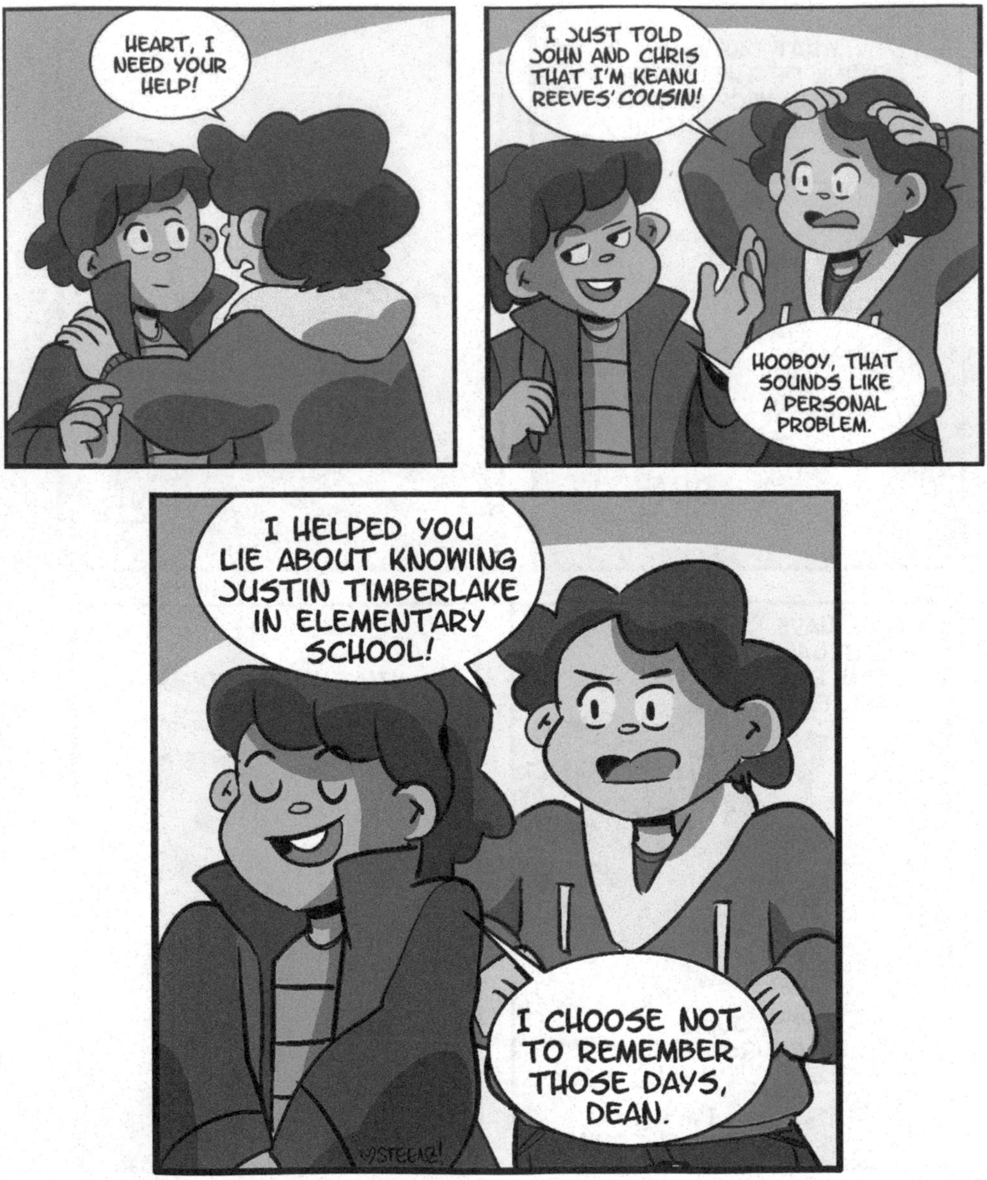
HEART, I NEED YOUR HELP!
I JUST TOLD JOHN AND CHRIS THAT I'M KEANU REEVES' COUSIN!
HOOBOY, THAT SOUNDS LIKE A PERSONAL PROBLEM.
I HELPED YOU LIE ABOUT KNOWING JUSTIN TIMBERLAKE IN ELEMENTARY SCHOOL!
I CHOOSE NOT TO REMEMBER THOSE DAYS, DEAN.

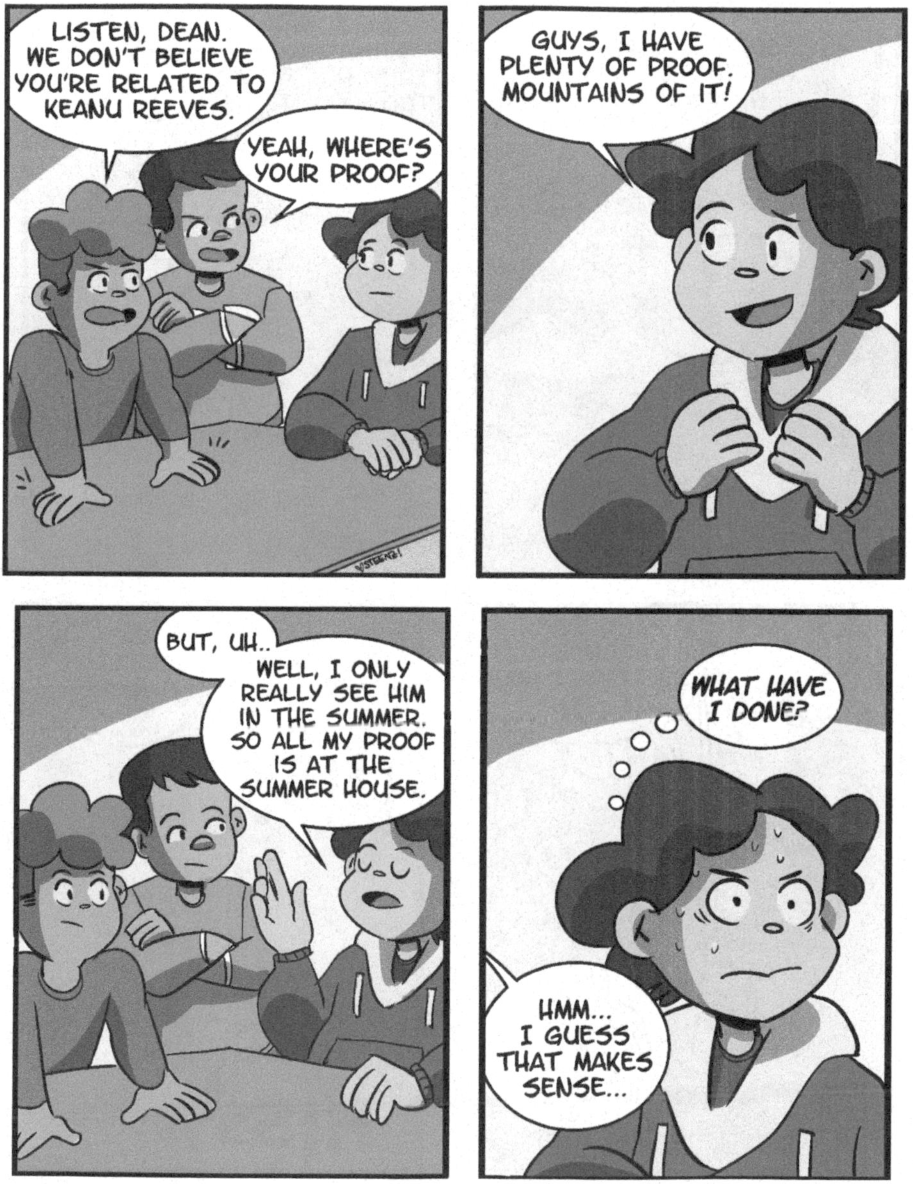
LISTEN, DEAN. WE DON'T BELIEVE YOU'RE RELATED TO KEANU REEVES.
YEAH, WHERE'S YOUR PROOF?
GUYS, I HAVE PLENTY OF PROOF. MOUNTAINS OF IT!
BUT, UH..
WELL, I ONLY REALLY SEE HIM IN THE SUMMER. SO ALL MY PROOF IS AT THE SUMMER HOUSE.
WHAT HAVE I DONE?
HMM... I GUESS THAT MAKES SENSE...

HEEYY MOOOMM. SO, UH... CAN I WATCH THE JOHN WICK MOVIES, PLEASE PLEASE PLEEEAASSE?
DEAN, WE'VE BEEN THROUGH THIS. NO. THEY'RE TOO VIOLENT! AND RATED R!
BUT I SEE VIOLENCE ALL THE TIME!! LOOK AT SPOCK!
ABSOLUTE CARNAGE, MOM.
HISS!
SCRATCH
SCRATCH
HISS!
STELENZ!

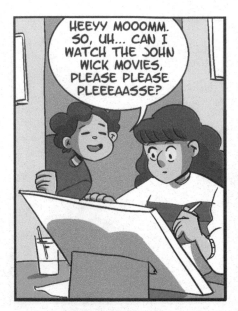

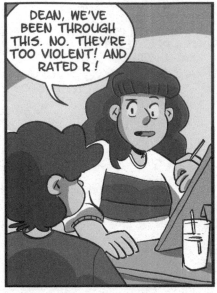

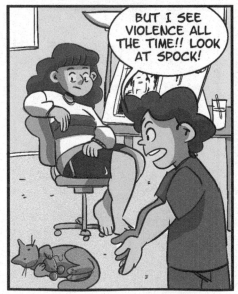

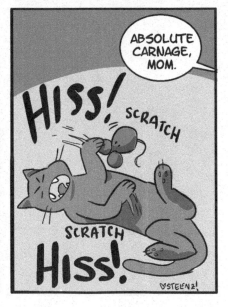

SO IF KEANU REEVES IS YOUR COUSIN, HOW COME HE DIDN'T TAKE YOU TO THE RELEASE OF JOHN WICK 3?
WELL, I DIDN'T... EXACTLY... SEE IT...
I KNEW IT!
HA! WOW.
I-I MEAN... I DIDN'T SEE IT BECAUSE I READ THE SCRIPT FOR IT AHEAD OF TIME!
WOW, THAT IS REALLY COOL.
HAHA, YUP!!
WHAT HAVE I DONE?!?
STEENZ!

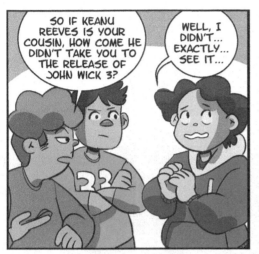

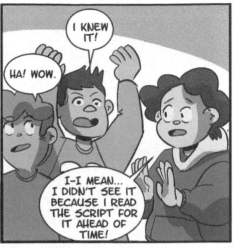

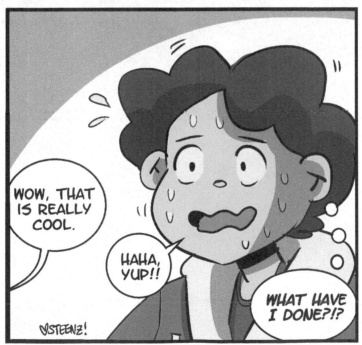

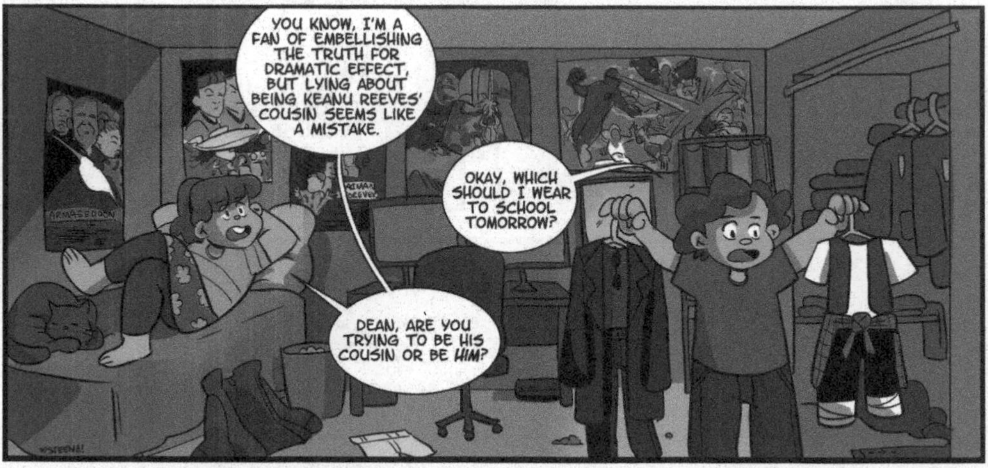
YOU KNOW, I'M A FAN OF EMBELLISHING THE TRUTH FOR DRAMATIC EFFECT, BUT LYING ABOUT BEING KEANU REEVES' COUSIN SEEMS LIKE A MISTAKE.
OKAY, WHICH SHOULD I WEAR TO SCHOOL TOMORROW?
DEAN, ARE YOU TRYING TO BE HIS COUSIN OR BE *HIM*?
ARMAGEDDON

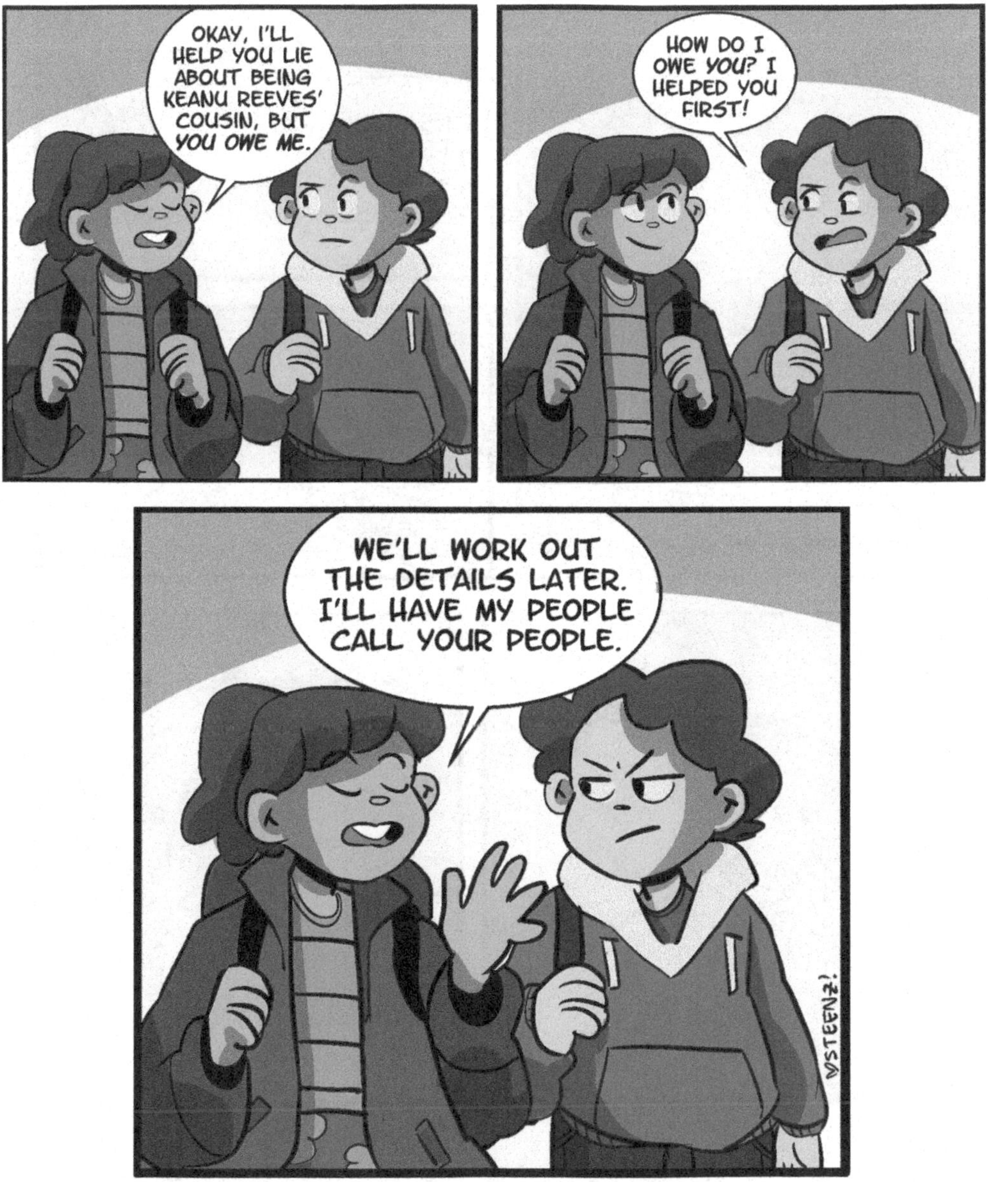
OKAY, I'LL HELP YOU LIE ABOUT BEING KEANU REEVES' COUSIN, BUT YOU OWE ME.
HOW DO I OWE YOU? I HELPED YOU FIRST!
WE'LL WORK OUT THE DETAILS LATER. I'LL HAVE MY PEOPLE CALL YOUR PEOPLE.
STEENZ!

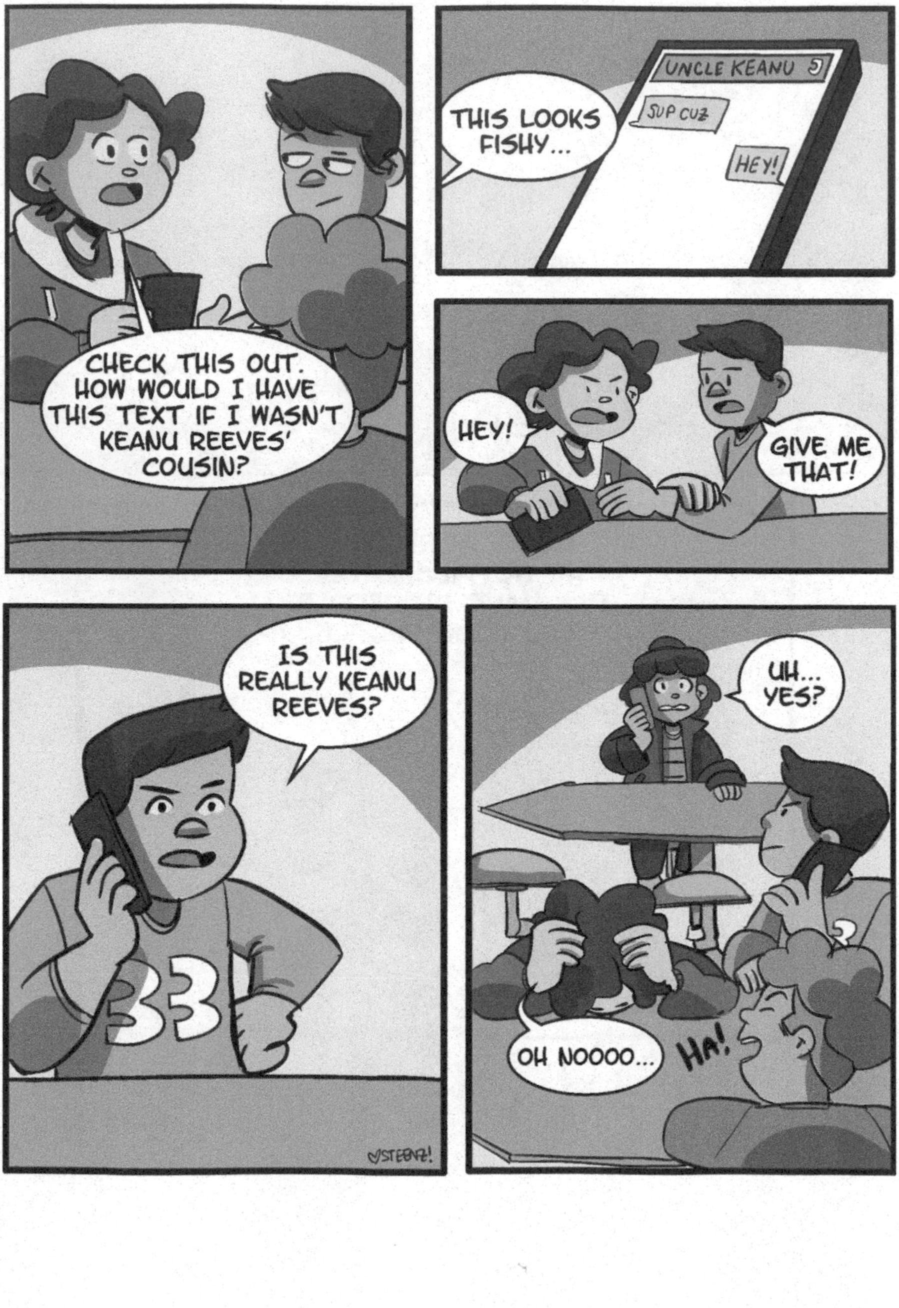
CHECK THIS OUT. HOW WOULD I HAVE THIS TEXT IF I WASN'T KEANU REEVES' COUSIN?
UNCLE KEANU
SUP CUZ
HEY!
THIS LOOKS FISHY...
HEY!
GIVE ME THAT!
IS THIS REALLY KEANU REEVES?
33
♡STEENZ!
UH... YES?
OH NOOOO...
HA!

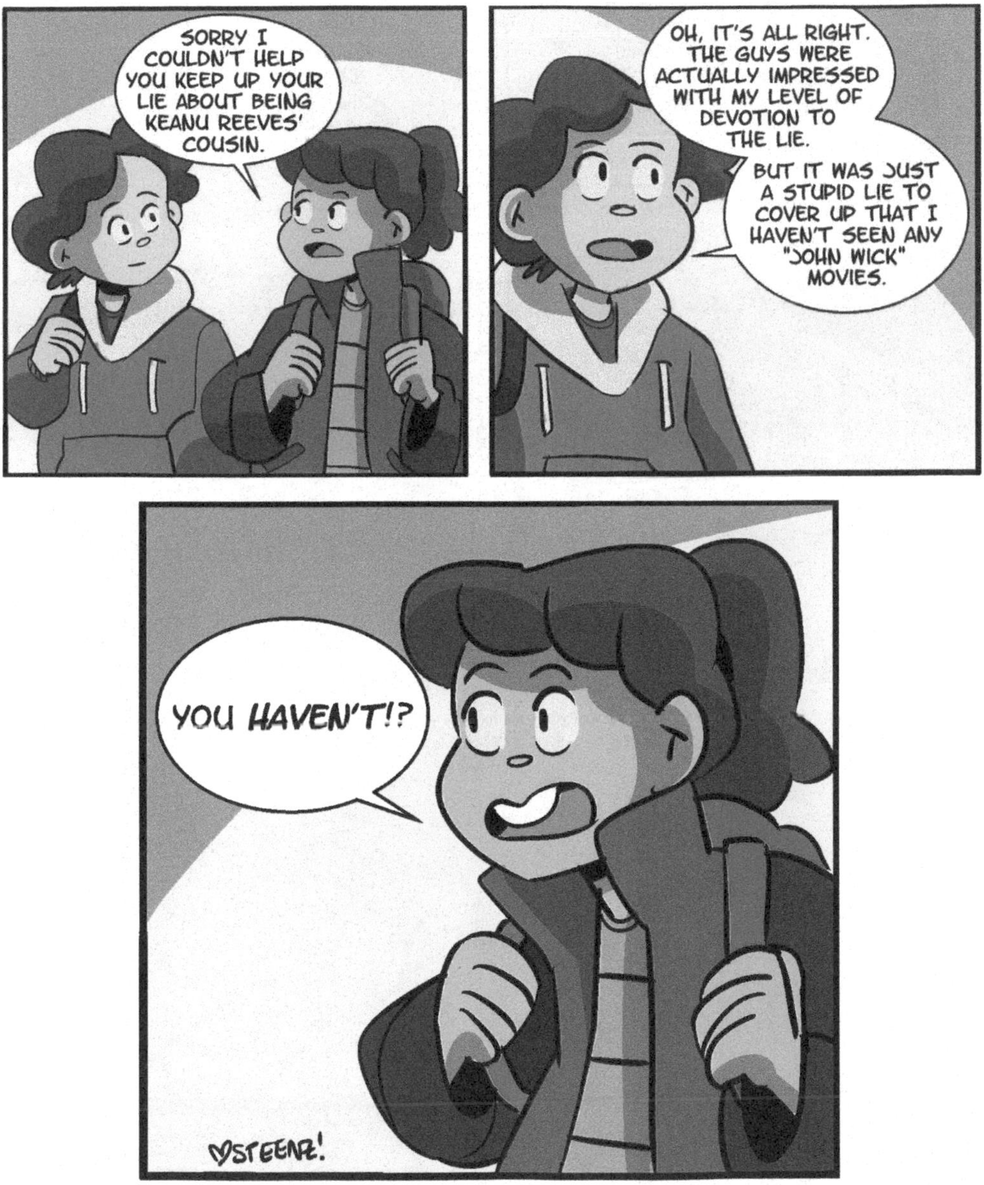
SORRY I COULDN'T HELP YOU KEEP UP YOUR LIE ABOUT BEING KEANU REEVES' COUSIN.
OH, IT'S ALL RIGHT. THE GUYS WERE ACTUALLY IMPRESSED WITH MY LEVEL OF DEVOTION TO THE LIE.
BUT IT WAS JUST A STUPID LIE TO COVER UP THAT I HAVEN'T SEEN ANY "JOHN WICK" MOVIES.
YOU HAVEN'T!?
STEENZ!

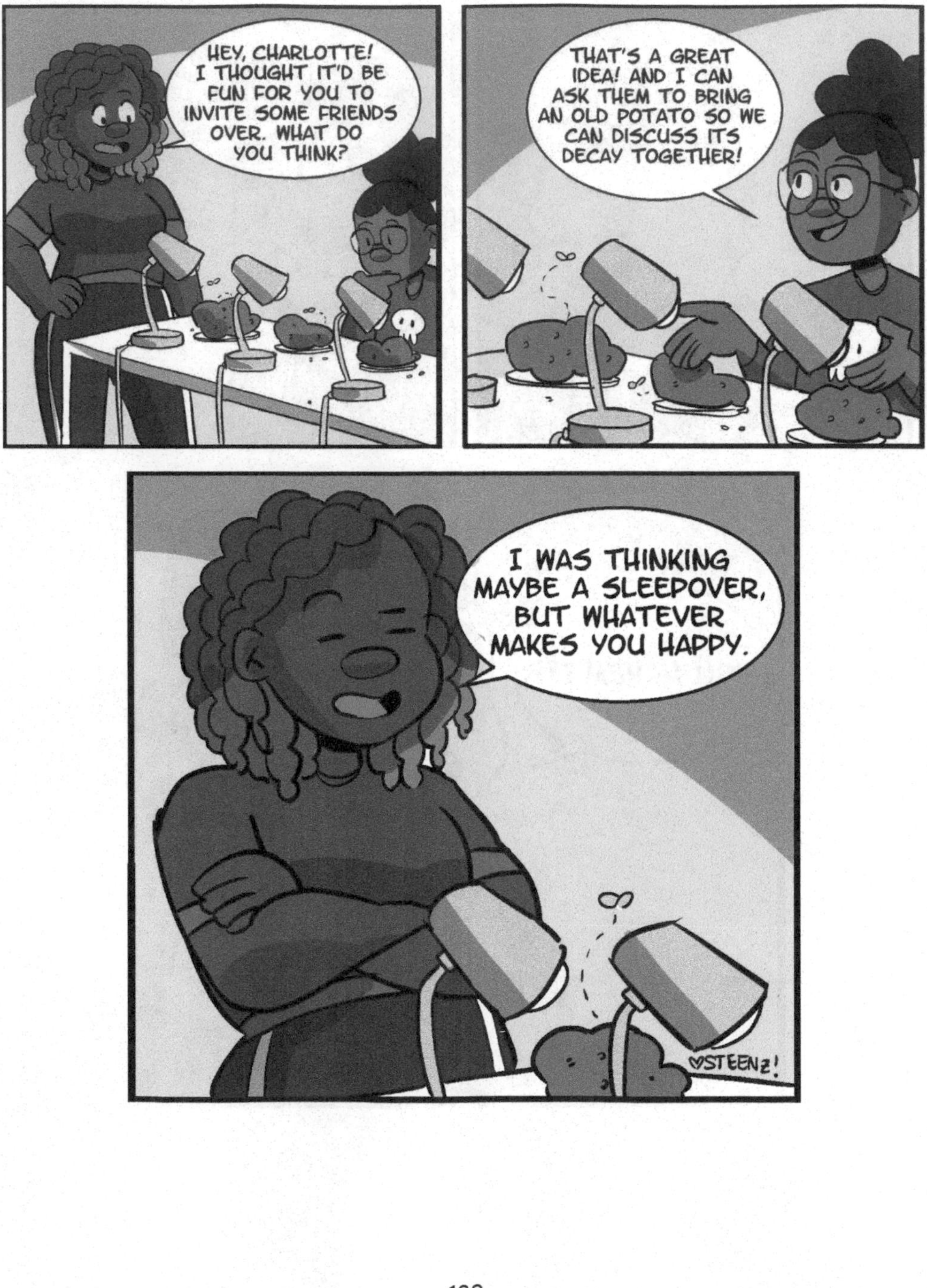
HEY, CHARLOTTE! I THOUGHT IT'D BE FUN FOR YOU TO INVITE SOME FRIENDS OVER. WHAT DO YOU THINK?
THAT'S A GREAT IDEA! AND I CAN ASK THEM TO BRING AN OLD POTATO SO WE CAN DISCUSS ITS DECAY TOGETHER!
I WAS THINKING MAYBE A SLEEPOVER, BUT WHATEVER MAKES YOU HAPPY.
STEENZ!

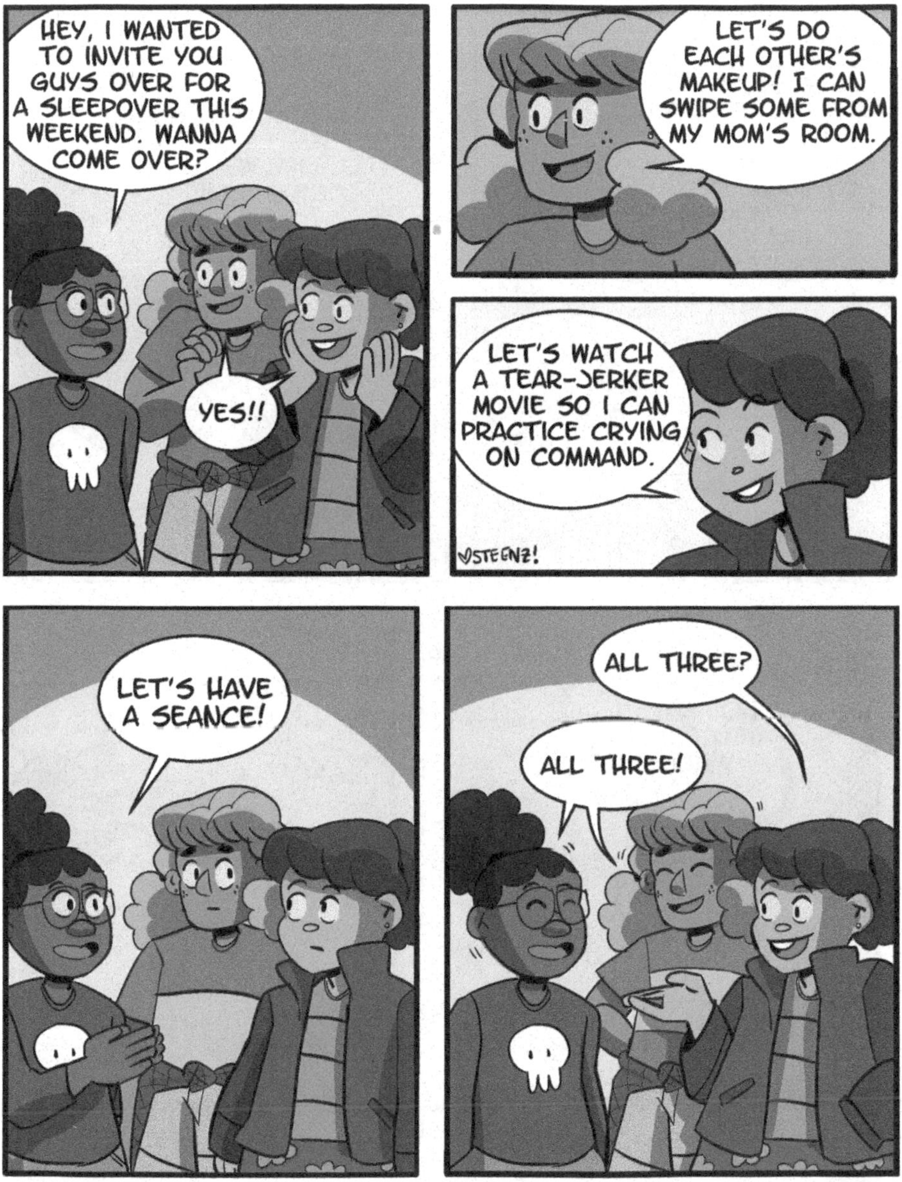
HEY, I WANTED TO INVITE YOU GUYS OVER FOR A SLEEPOVER THIS WEEKEND. WANNA COME OVER?
YES!!
LET'S DO EACH OTHER'S MAKEUP! I CAN SWIPE SOME FROM MY MOM'S ROOM.
LET'S WATCH A TEAR-JERKER MOVIE SO I CAN PRACTICE CRYING ON COMMAND.
♡STEENZ!
LET'S HAVE A SEANCE!
ALL THREE?
ALL THREE!

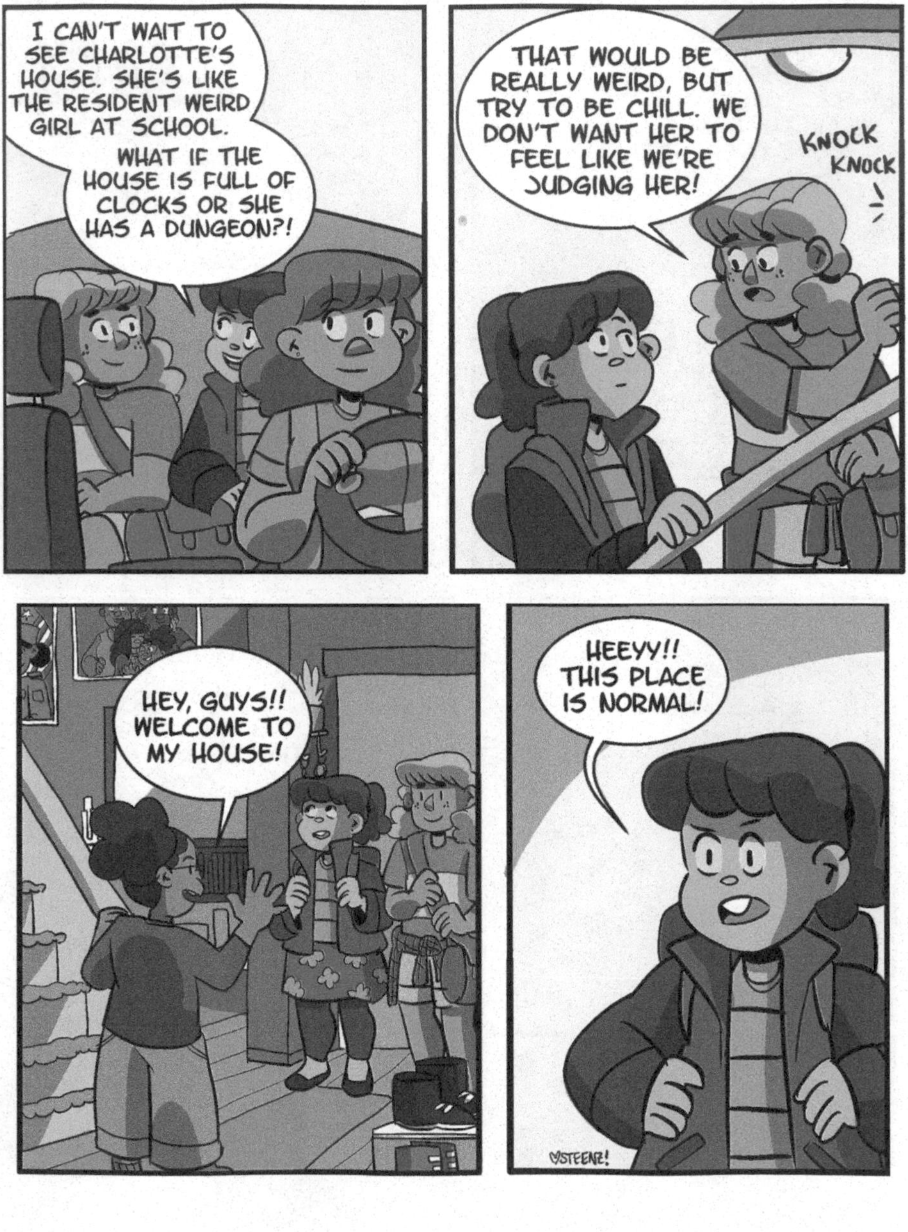
I CAN'T WAIT TO SEE CHARLOTTE'S HOUSE. SHE'S LIKE THE RESIDENT WEIRD GIRL AT SCHOOL.
WHAT IF THE HOUSE IS FULL OF CLOCKS OR SHE HAS A DUNGEON?!
THAT WOULD BE REALLY WEIRD, BUT TRY TO BE CHILL. WE DON'T WANT HER TO FEEL LIKE WE'RE JUDGING HER!
KNOCK KNOCK
HEY, GUYS!! WELCOME TO MY HOUSE!
HEEYY!! THIS PLACE IS NORMAL!
♡STEENZ!

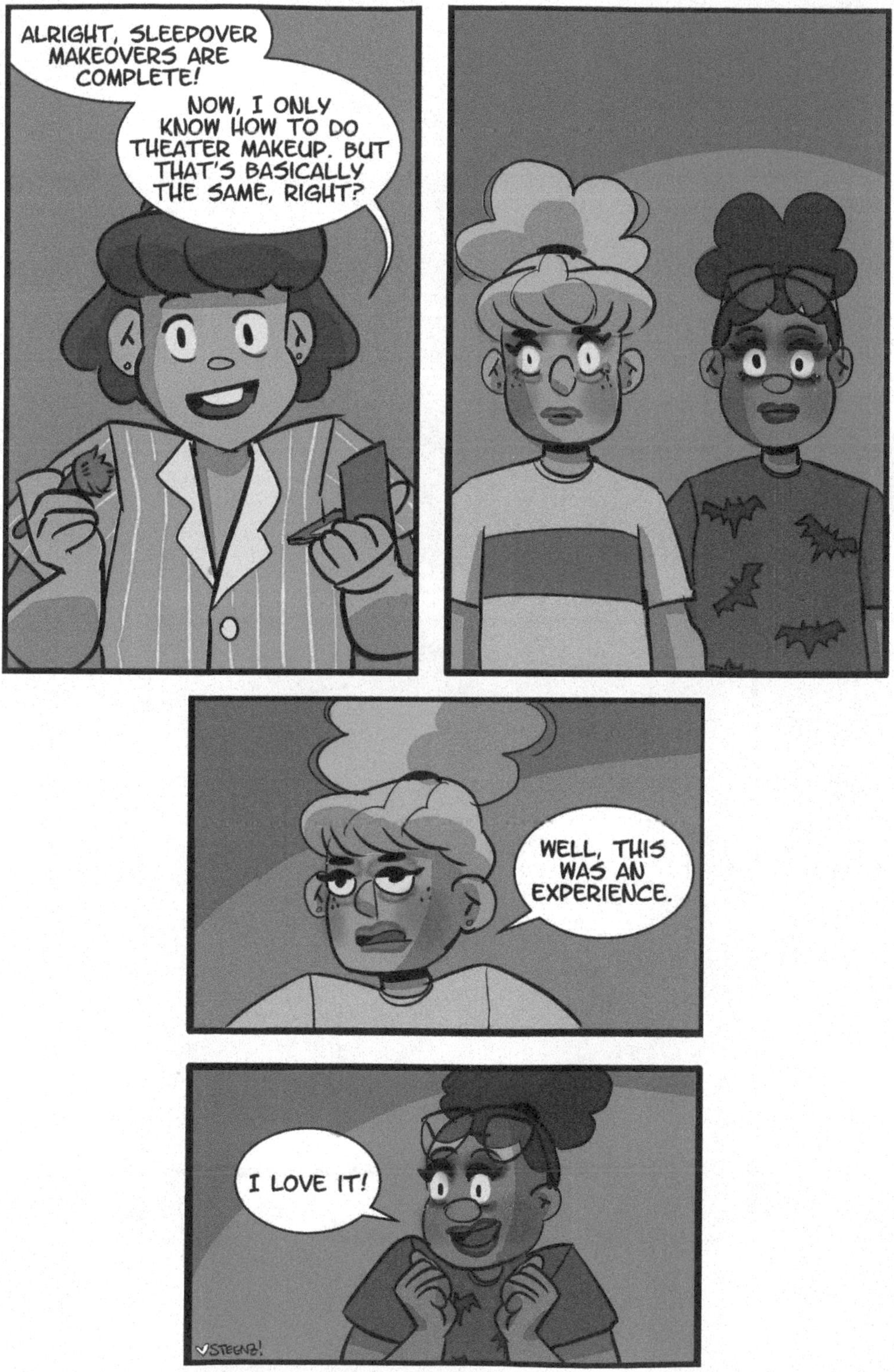
ALRIGHT, SLEEPOVER MAKEOVERS ARE COMPLETE!
NOW, I ONLY KNOW HOW TO DO THEATER MAKEUP. BUT THAT'S BASICALLY THE SAME, RIGHT?
WELL, THIS WAS AN EXPERIENCE.
I LOVE IT!
STEENZ!

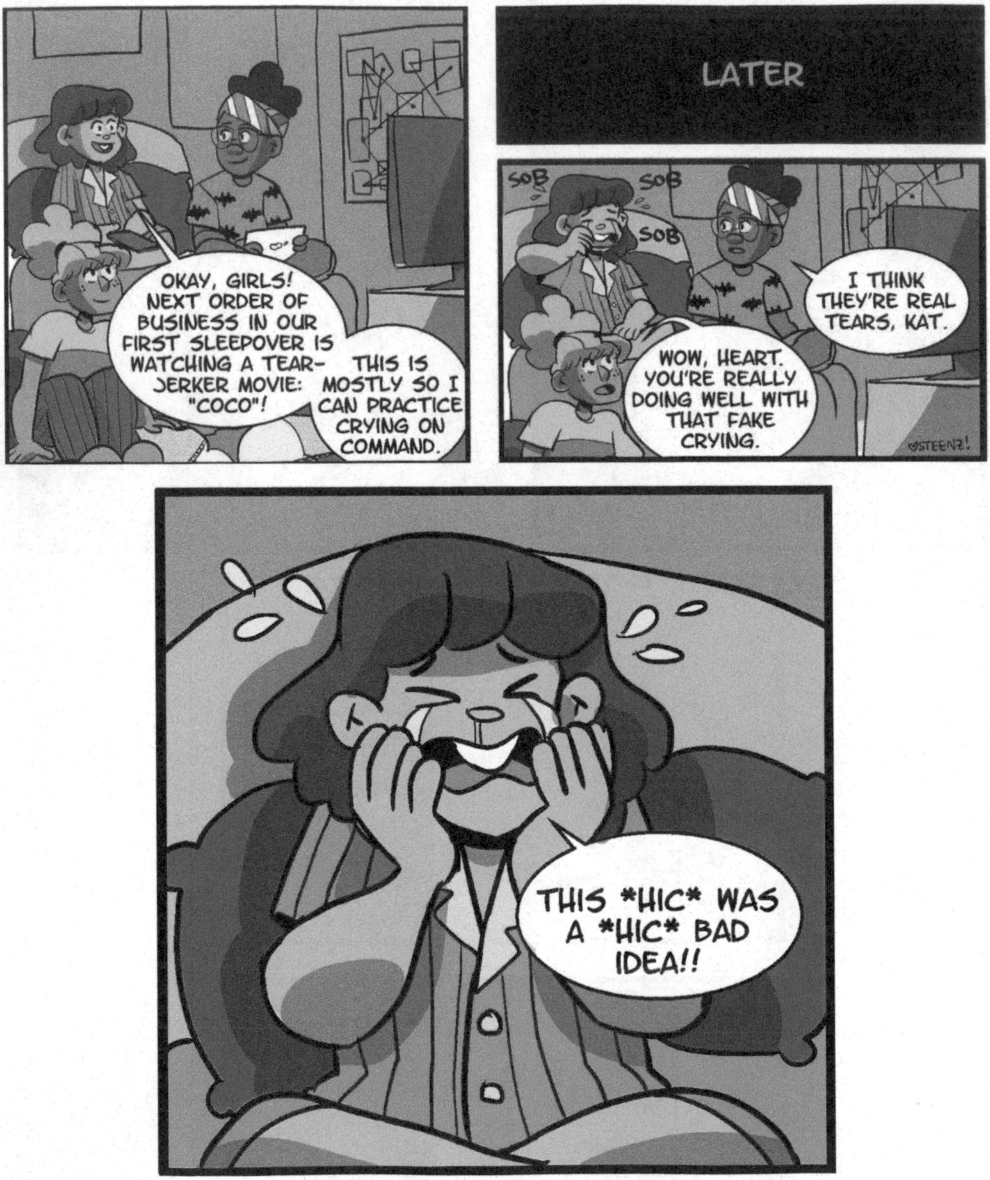
OKAY, GIRLS! NEXT ORDER OF BUSINESS IN OUR FIRST SLEEPOVER IS WATCHING A TEAR-JERKER MOVIE: "COCO"!
THIS IS MOSTLY SO I CAN PRACTICE CRYING ON COMMAND.
LATER
SOB
SOB
SOB
WOW, HEART. YOU'RE REALLY DOING WELL WITH THAT FAKE CRYING.
I THINK THEY'RE REAL TEARS, KAT.
♡STEENZ!
THIS *HIC* WAS A *HIC* BAD IDEA!!

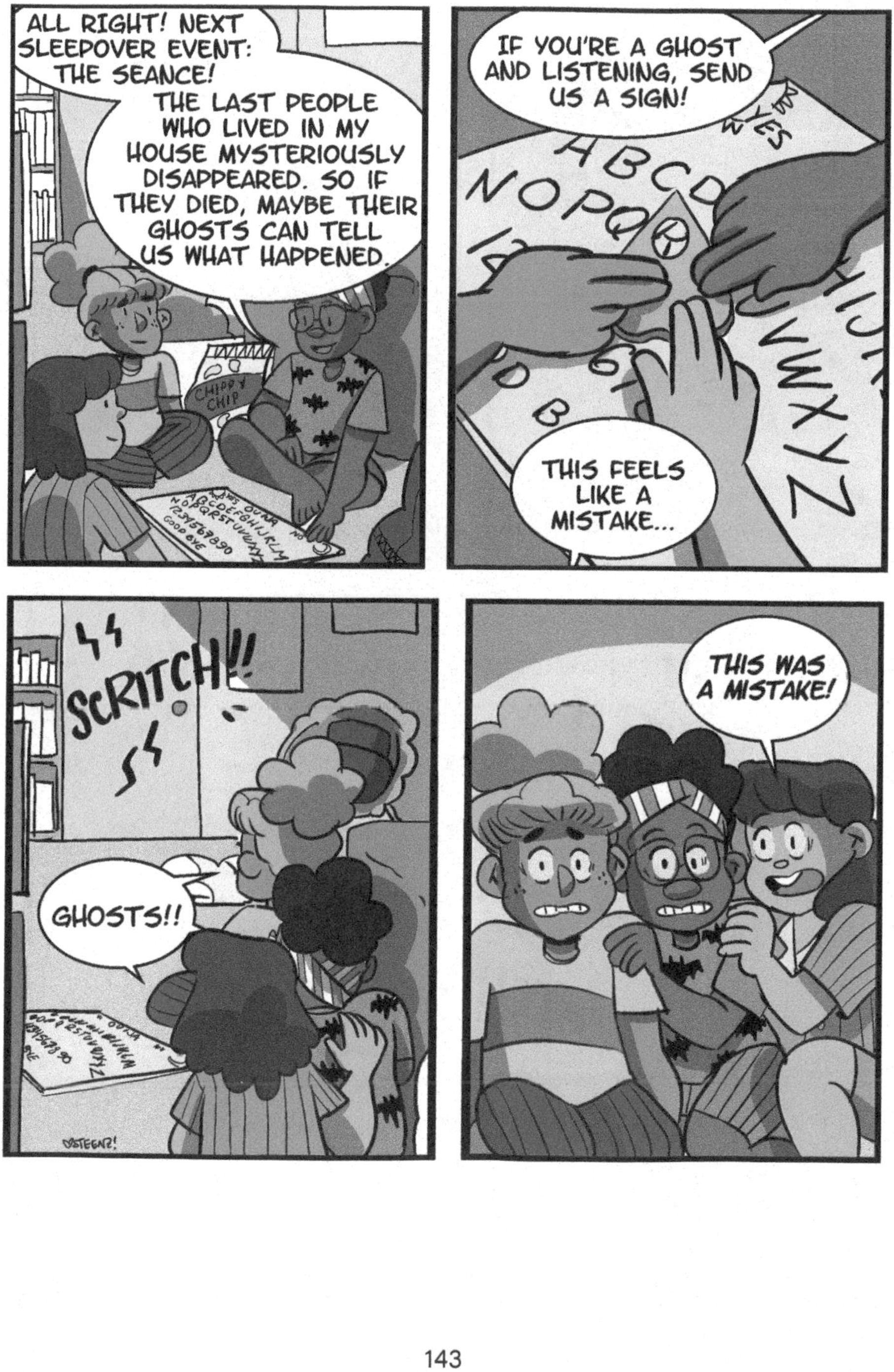
ALL RIGHT! NEXT SLEEPOVER EVENT: THE SEANCE!
THE LAST PEOPLE WHO LIVED IN MY HOUSE MYSTERIOUSLY DISAPPEARED. SO IF THEY DIED, MAYBE THEIR GHOSTS CAN TELL US WHAT HAPPENED.
CHIPPY CHIP
IF YOU'RE A GHOST AND LISTENING, SEND US A SIGN!
THIS FEELS LIKE A MISTAKE...
SCRITCH!!
GHOSTS!!
THIS WAS A MISTAKE!

SCRITCH!!
WHAT IS THAT? A GHOST?
FAMOUS PEOPLE ARE SUPPOSED TO DIE AT 27, NOT AT 11!
SCRITCH
SCRATCH
BAM!
HA HA
AW, RIPLEY!
THIS IS WHY I DON'T HAVE PETS.
STEENZ!

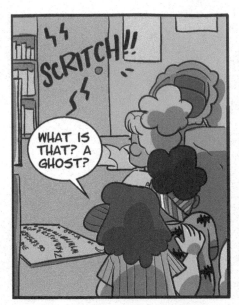

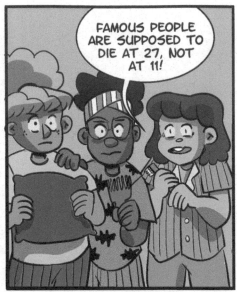

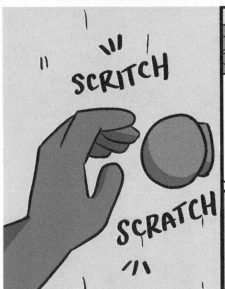

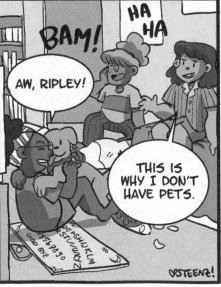

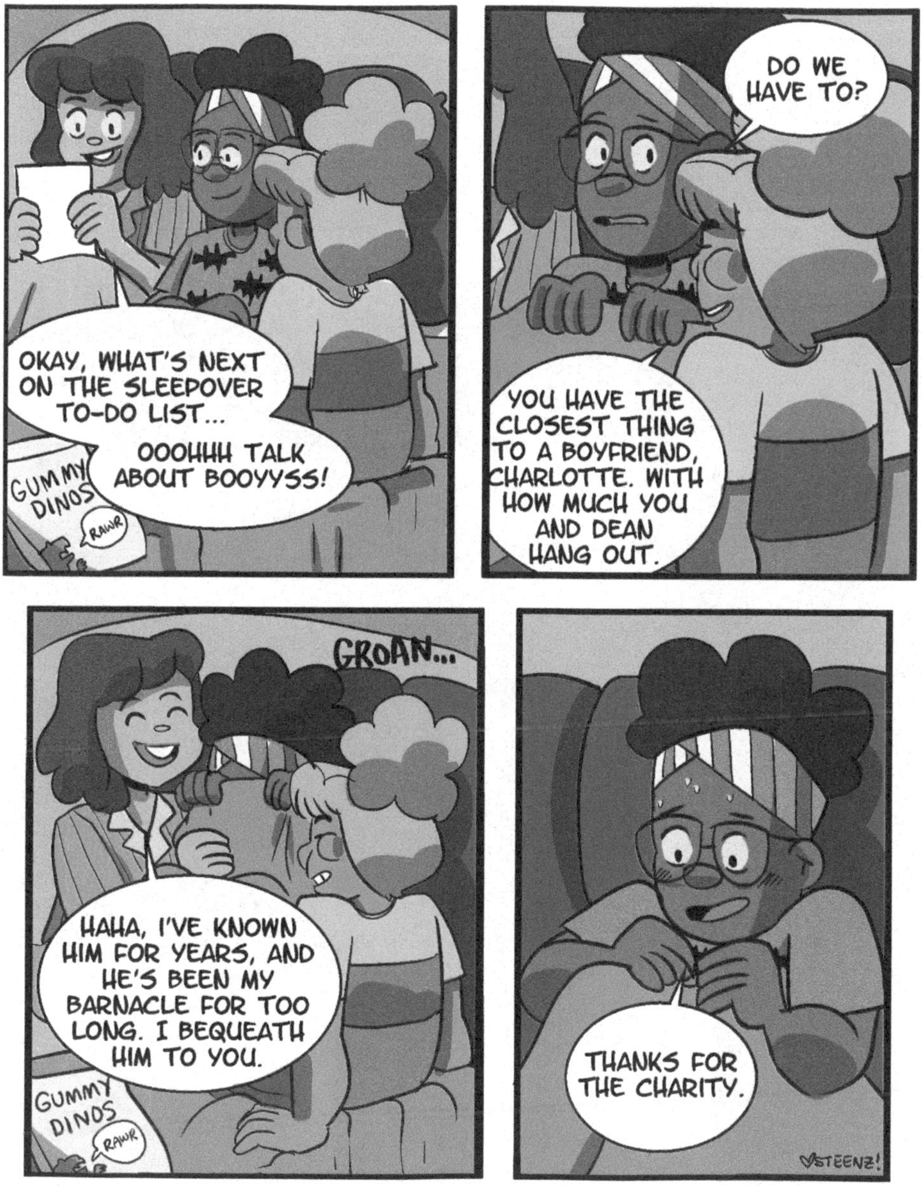
OKAY, WHAT'S NEXT ON THE SLEEPOVER TO-DO LIST...
OOOHHH TALK ABOUT BOOYYSS!
GUMMY DINOS
RAWR
DO WE HAVE TO?
YOU HAVE THE CLOSEST THING TO A BOYFRIEND, CHARLOTTE. WITH HOW MUCH YOU AND DEAN HANG OUT.
GROAN...
HAHA, I'VE KNOWN HIM FOR YEARS, AND HE'S BEEN MY BARNACLE FOR TOO LONG. I BEQUEATH HIM TO YOU.
GUMMY DINOS
RAWR
THANKS FOR THE CHARITY.
STEENZ!

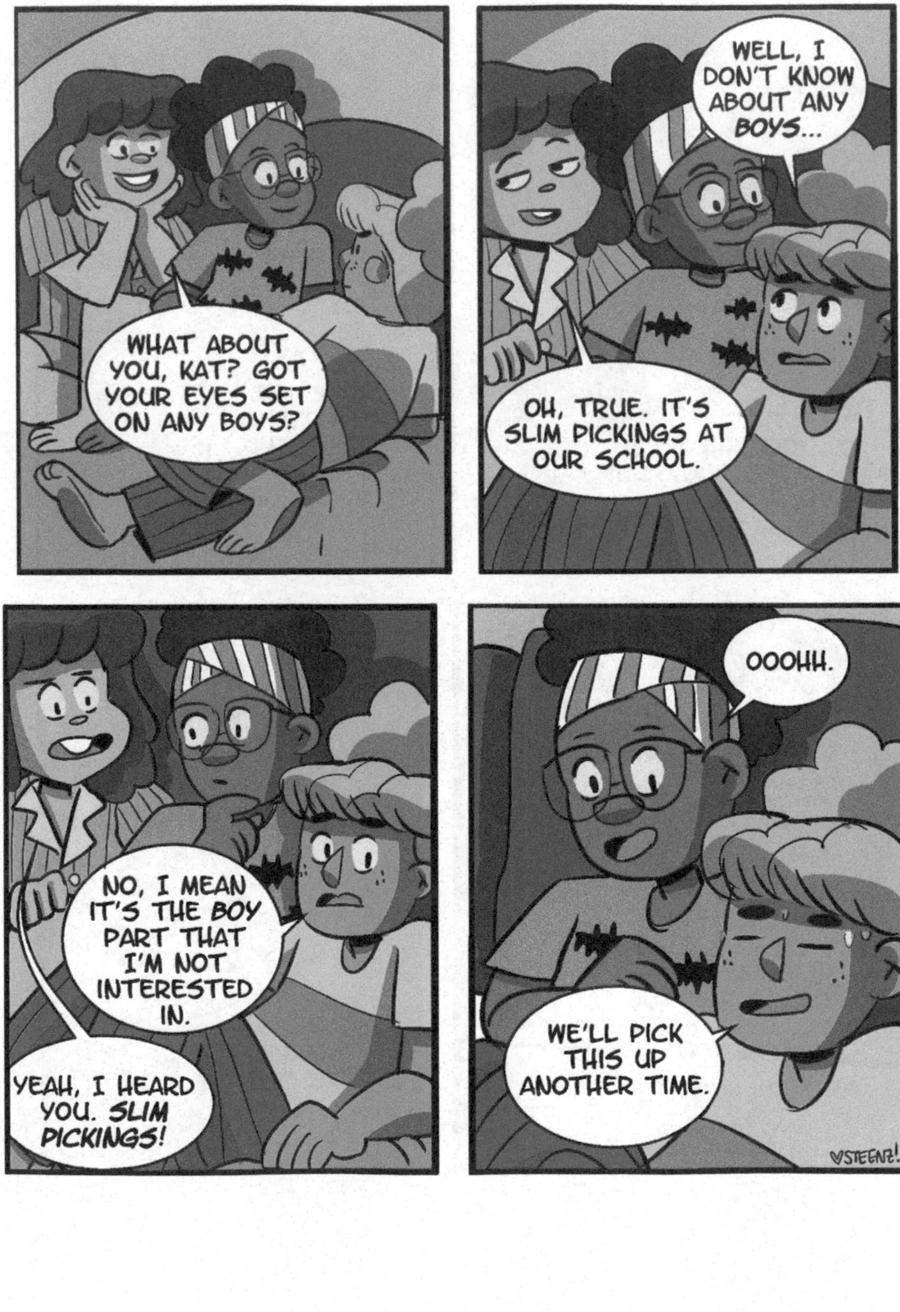
WHAT ABOUT YOU, KAT? GOT YOUR EYES SET ON ANY BOYS?
WELL, I DON'T KNOW ABOUT ANY BOYS...
OH, TRUE. IT'S SLIM PICKINGS AT OUR SCHOOL.
NO, I MEAN IT'S THE BOY PART THAT I'M NOT INTERESTED IN.
YEAH, I HEARD YOU. SLIM PICKINGS!
OOOHH.
WE'LL PICK THIS UP ANOTHER TIME.
♡STEENZ!

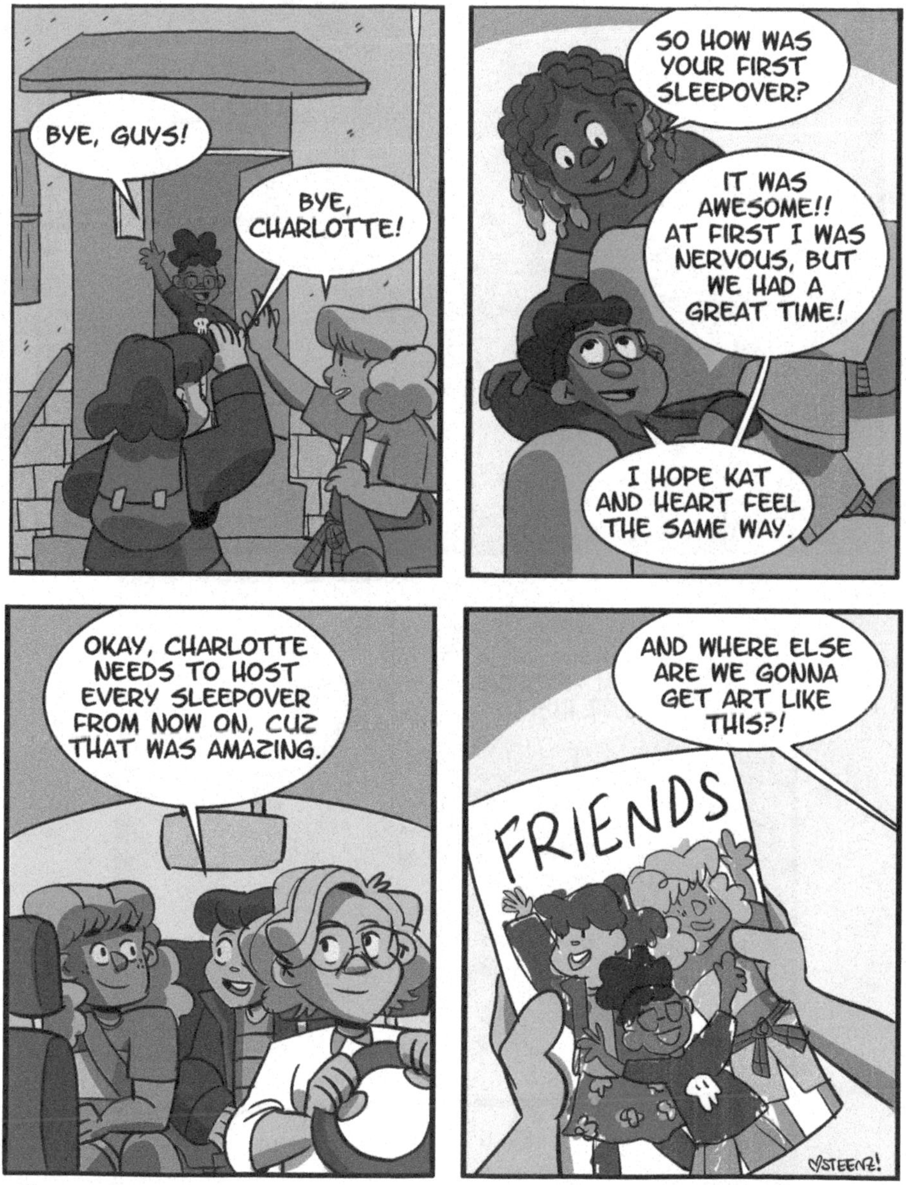
BYE, GUYS!
BYE, CHARLOTTE!
SO HOW WAS YOUR FIRST SLEEPOVER?
IT WAS AWESOME!! AT FIRST I WAS NERVOUS, BUT WE HAD A GREAT TIME!
I HOPE KAT AND HEART FEEL THE SAME WAY.
OKAY, CHARLOTTE NEEDS TO HOST EVERY SLEEPOVER FROM NOW ON, CUZ THAT WAS AMAZING.
AND WHERE ELSE ARE WE GONNA GET ART LIKE THIS?!
FRIENDS
STEENZ!

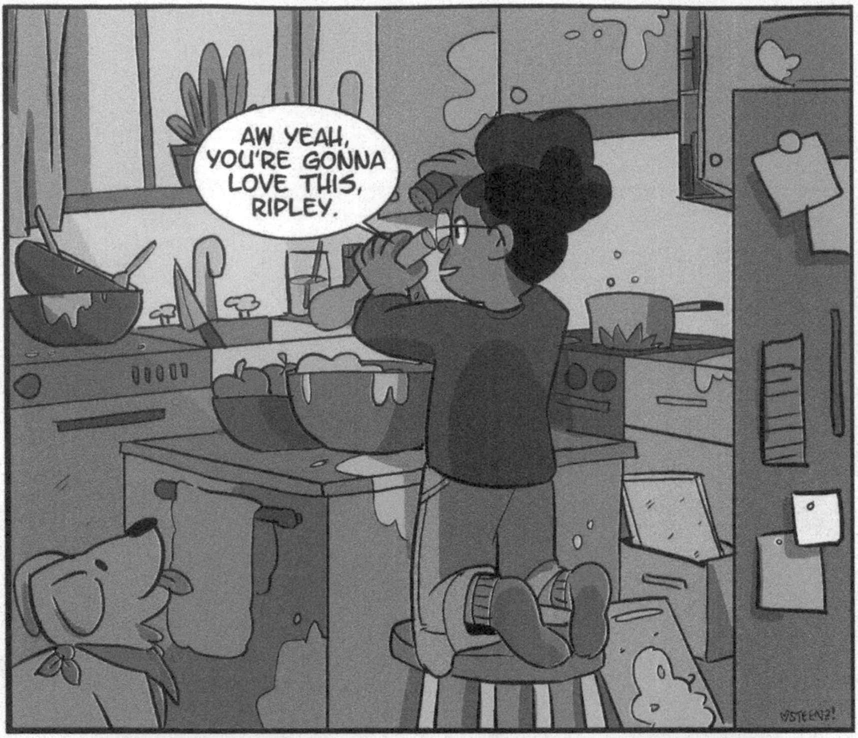
AW YEAH, YOU'RE GONNA LOVE THIS, RIPLEY.

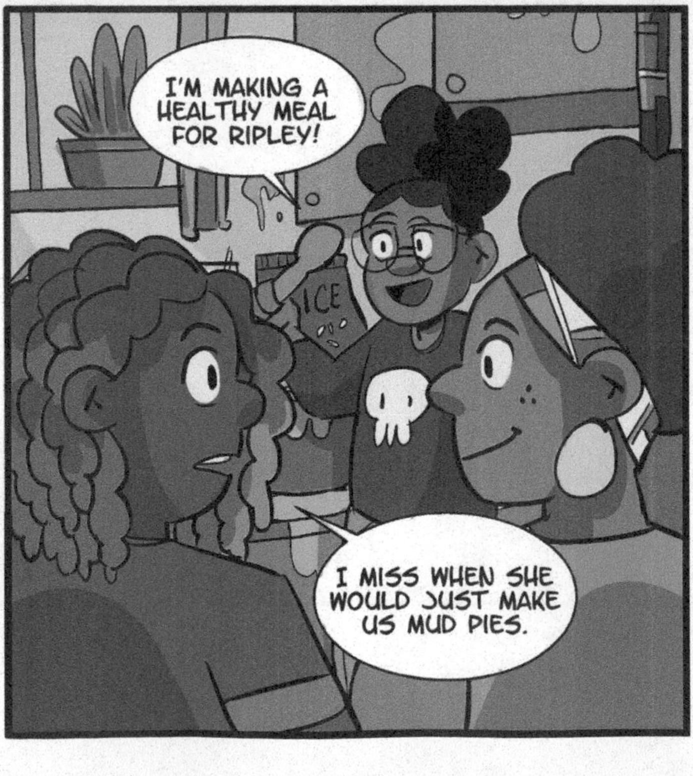
I'M MAKING A HEALTHY MEAL FOR RIPLEY!
ICE
I MISS WHEN SHE WOULD JUST MAKE US MUD PIES.

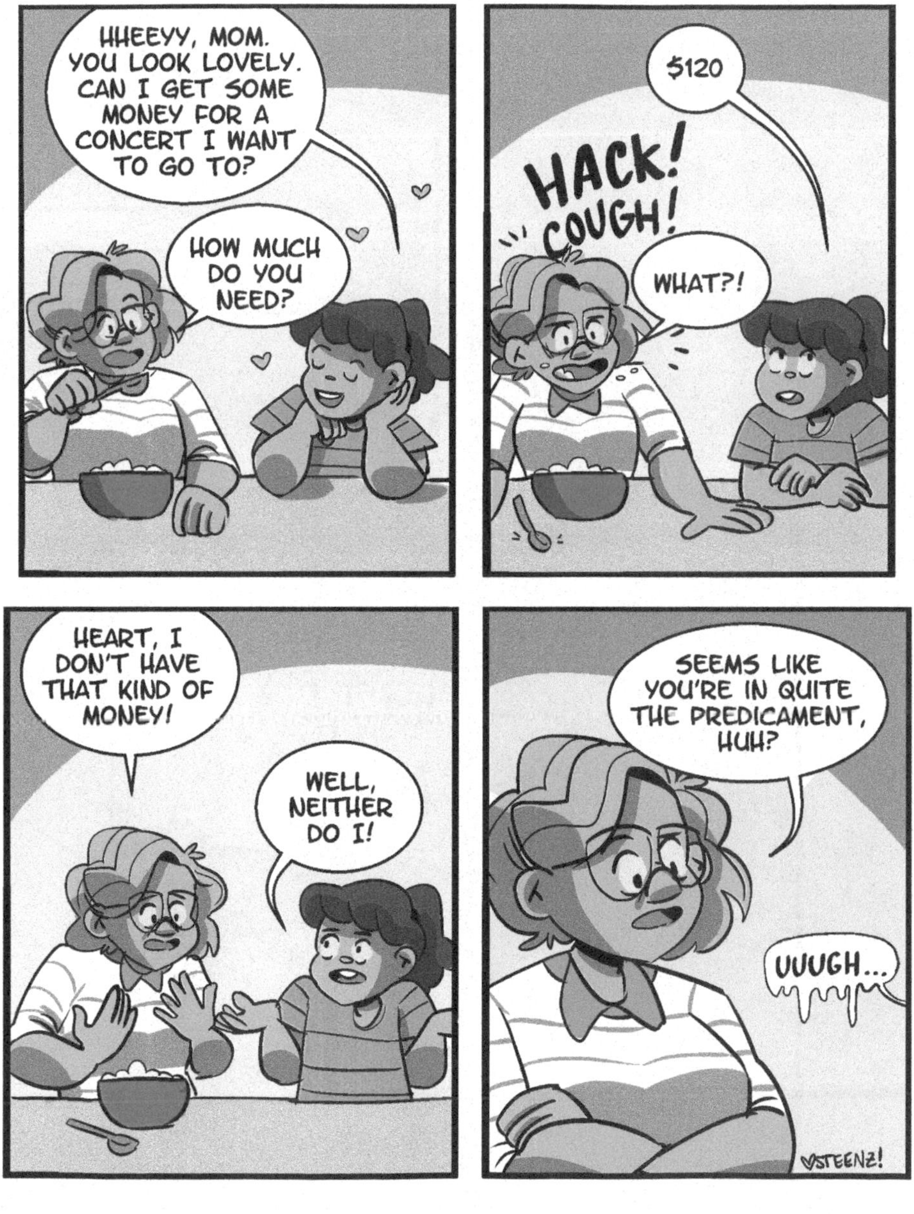
HHEEYY, MOM. YOU LOOK LOVELY. CAN I GET SOME MONEY FOR A CONCERT I WANT TO GO TO?
HOW MUCH DO YOU NEED?
$120
HACK!
COUGH!
WHAT?!
HEART, I DON'T HAVE THAT KIND OF MONEY!
WELL, NEITHER DO I!
SEEMS LIKE YOU'RE IN QUITE THE PREDICAMENT, HUH?
UUUGH...
STEENZ!

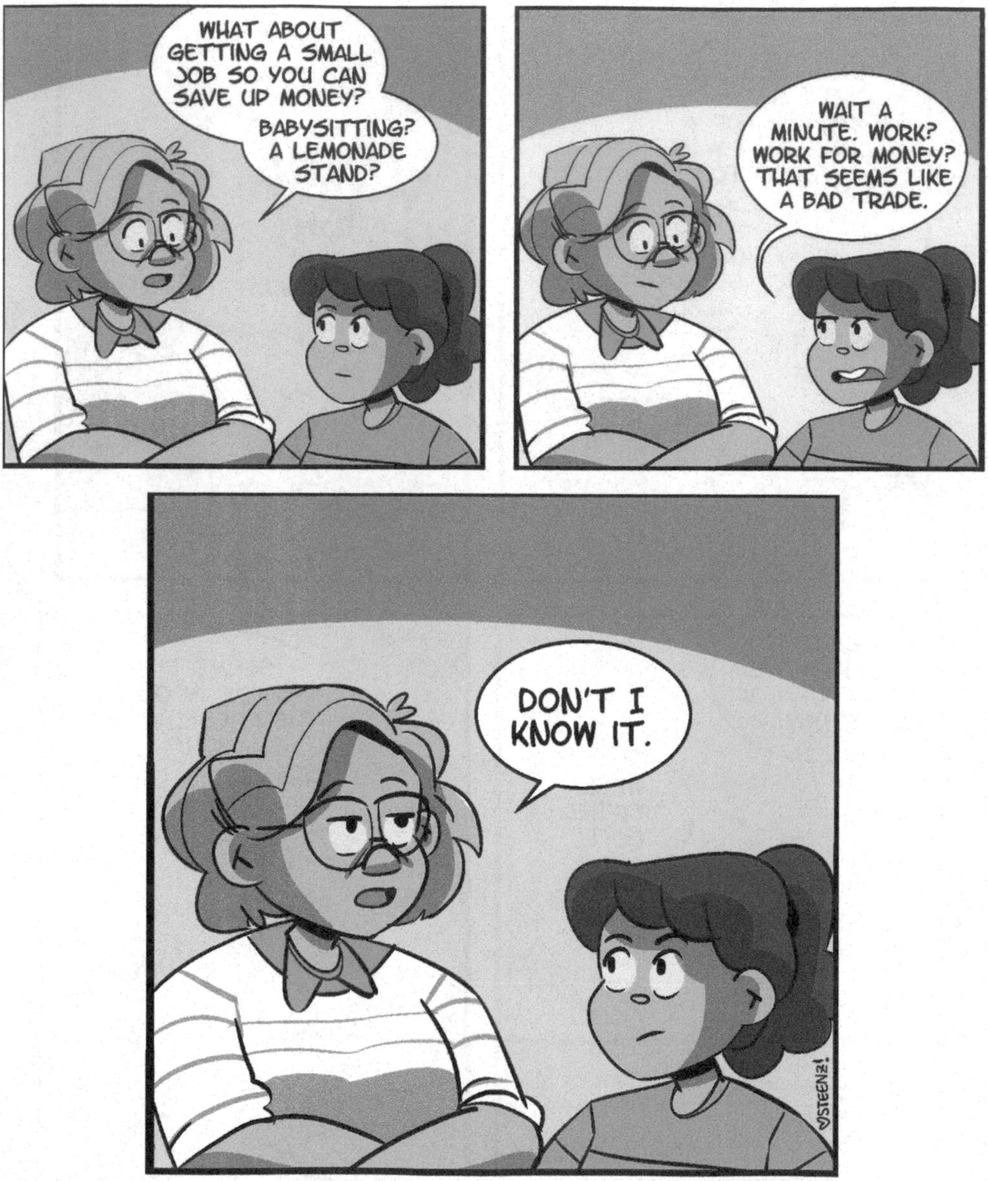
WHAT ABOUT GETTING A SMALL JOB SO YOU CAN SAVE UP MONEY?
BABYSITTING? A LEMONADE STAND?
WAIT A MINUTE. WORK? WORK FOR MONEY? THAT SEEMS LIKE A BAD TRADE.
DON'T I KNOW IT.

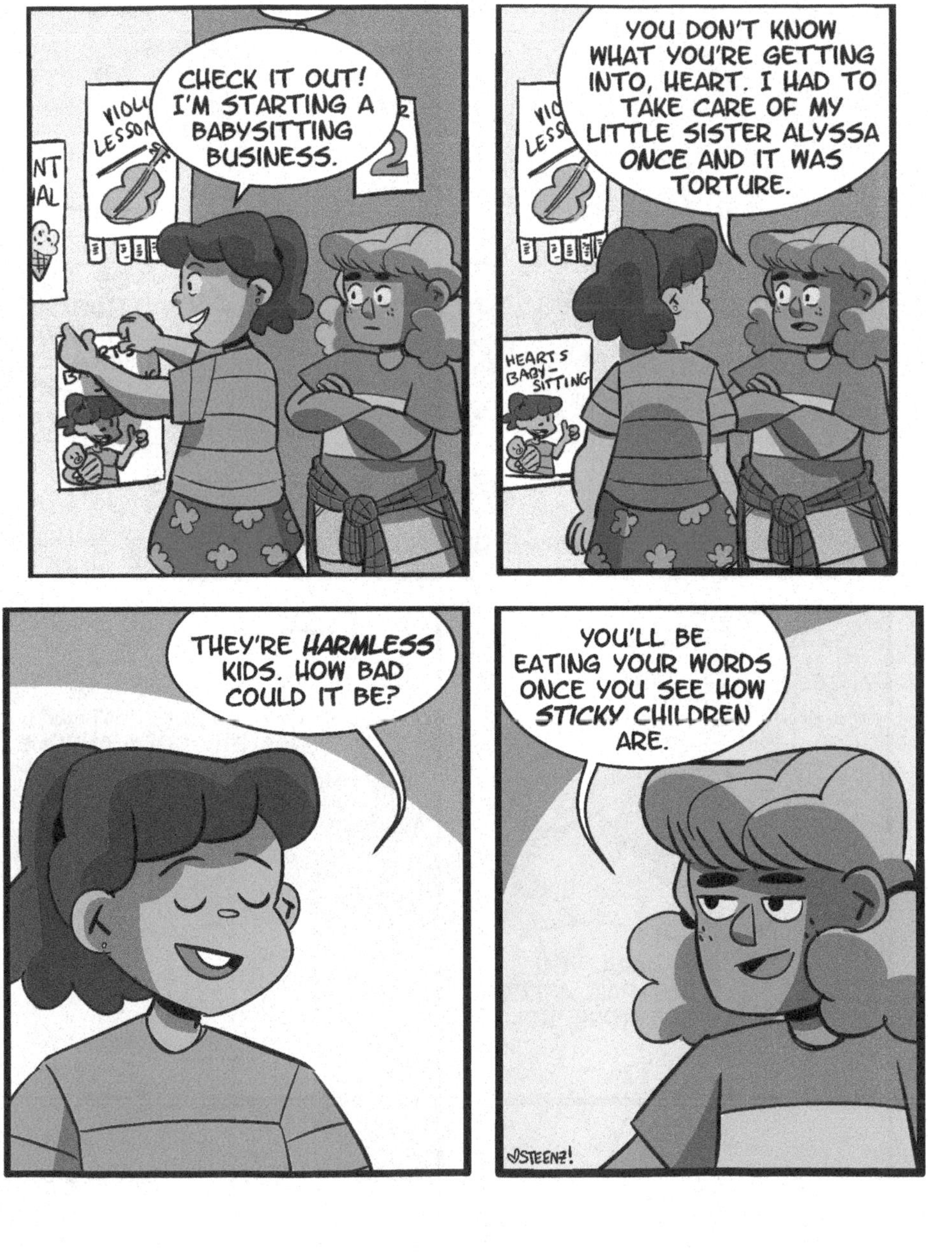
CHECK IT OUT! I'M STARTING A BABYSITTING BUSINESS.
YOU DON'T KNOW WHAT YOU'RE GETTING INTO, HEART. I HAD TO TAKE CARE OF MY LITTLE SISTER ALYSSA *ONCE* AND IT WAS TORTURE.
HEARTS BABY-SITTING
THEY'RE ***HARMLESS*** KIDS. HOW BAD COULD IT BE?
YOU'LL BE EATING YOUR WORDS ONCE YOU SEE HOW ***STICKY*** CHILDREN ARE.
STEENZ!

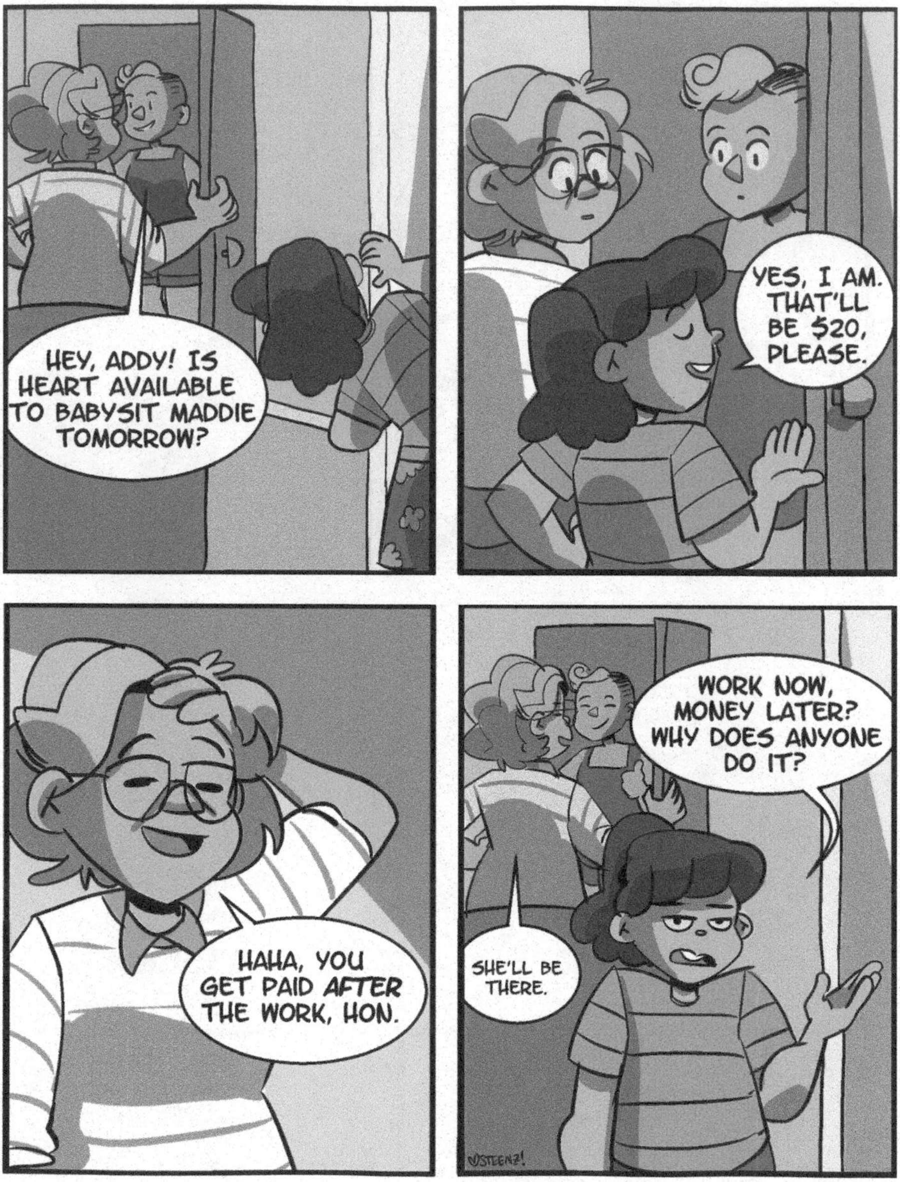
HEY, ADDY! IS HEART AVAILABLE TO BABYSIT MADDIE TOMORROW?
YES, I AM. THAT'LL BE $20, PLEASE.
HAHA, YOU GET PAID AFTER THE WORK, HON.
WORK NOW, MONEY LATER? WHY DOES ANYONE DO IT?
SHE'LL BE THERE.
STEENZ!

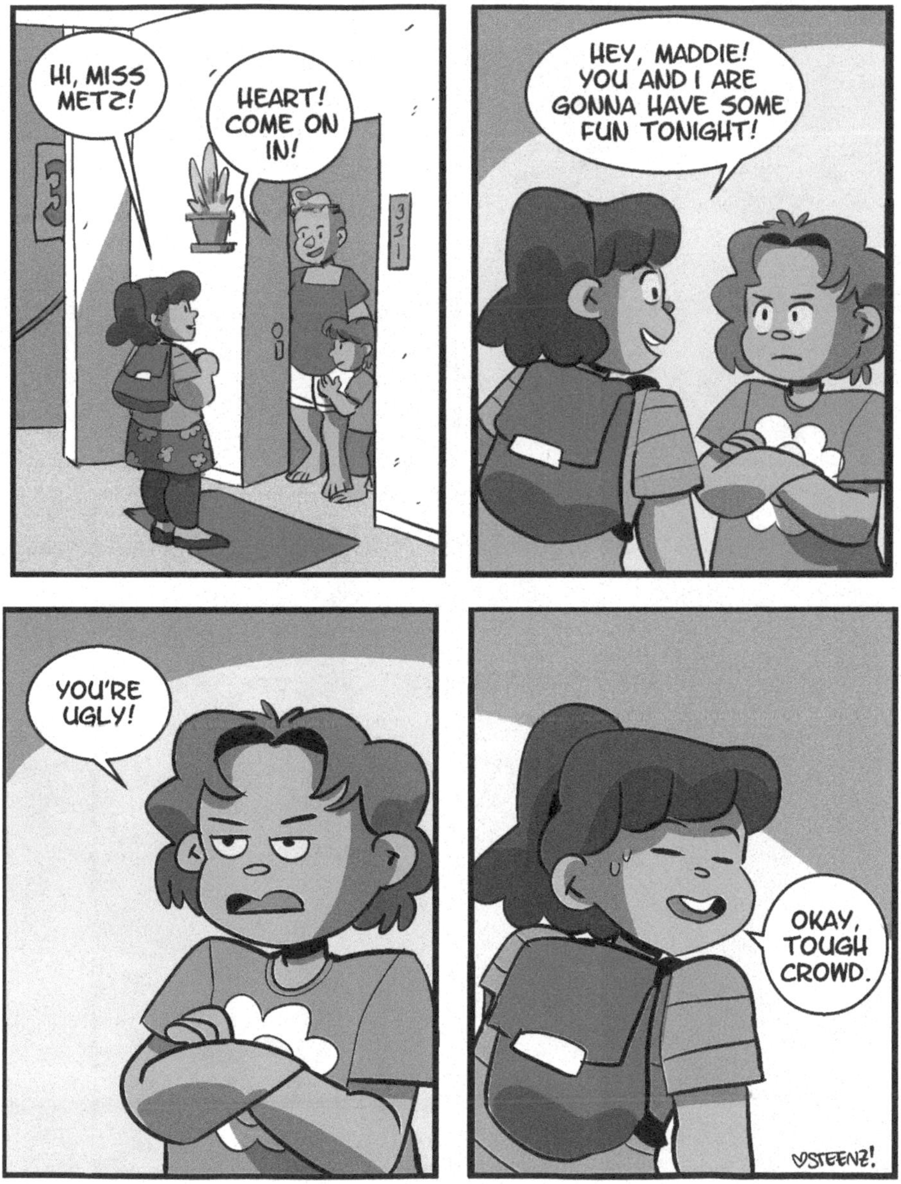
HI, MISS METZ!
HEART! COME ON IN!
331
HEY, MADDIE! YOU AND I ARE GONNA HAVE SOME FUN TONIGHT!
YOU'RE UGLY!
OKAY, TOUGH CROWD.
STEENZ!

OKAY, HEART, I'LL BE ON THE FIFTH FLOOR AT A FRIEND'S PLACE IF YOU NEED ANYTHING.

MADDIE GOES TO BED AT 9 P.M. AND I'LL BE BACK NO LATER THAN 10 P.M. ANY QUESTIONS?

9 P.M. IS MY BEDTIME! I GET TO STAY UP LATE!!

I'M ALL SET TO BE UP AND AWAKE AND DEFINITELY NOT ASLEEP!

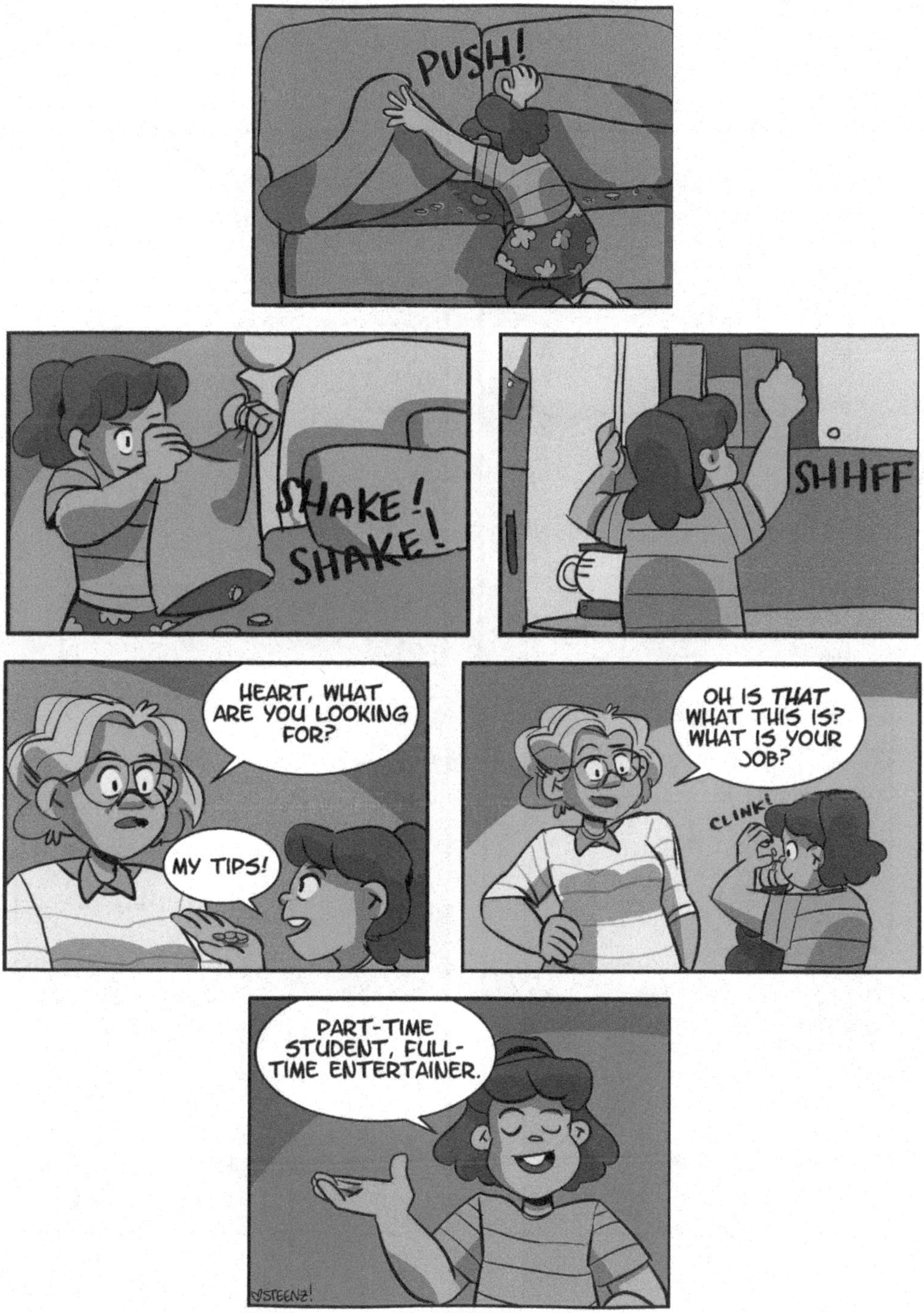
PUSH!
SHAKE!
SHAKE!
SHHFF
HEART, WHAT ARE YOU LOOKING FOR?
MY TIPS!
OH IS *THAT* WHAT THIS IS? WHAT IS YOUR JOB?
CLINK!
PART-TIME STUDENT, FULL-TIME ENTERTAINER.
STEENZ!

THIS SUCKS. BABYSITTERS SUCK. YOU SUCK!!
WOULD A SUCKY BABYSITTER HAVE... CANDY?
GUMMY DINOS RAWR
!!
GUMMY DINOS?!
HMM... THIS IS A GOOD START FOR YOU.
SHE'S SO BOSSY! REMINDS ME OF MYSELF AT THAT AGE.
OM NOM NOM
STEENZ!

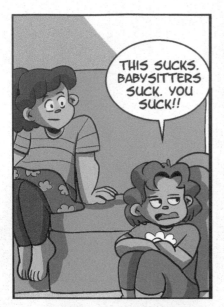

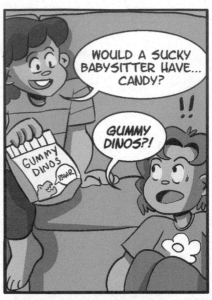

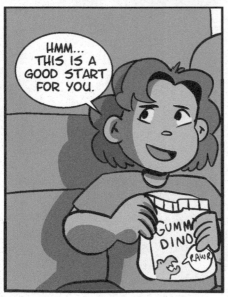

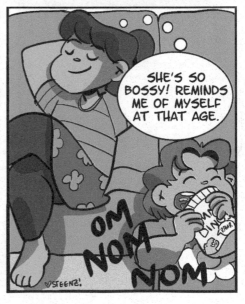

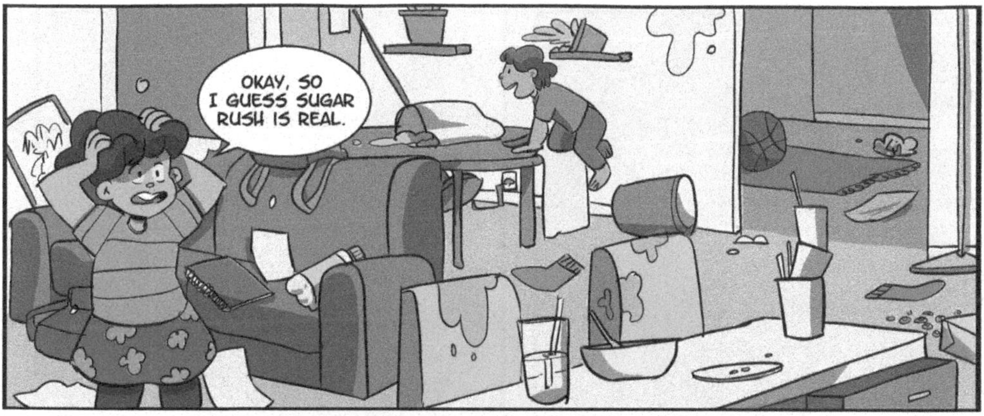
OKAY, SO
I GUESS SUGAR
RUSH IS REAL.

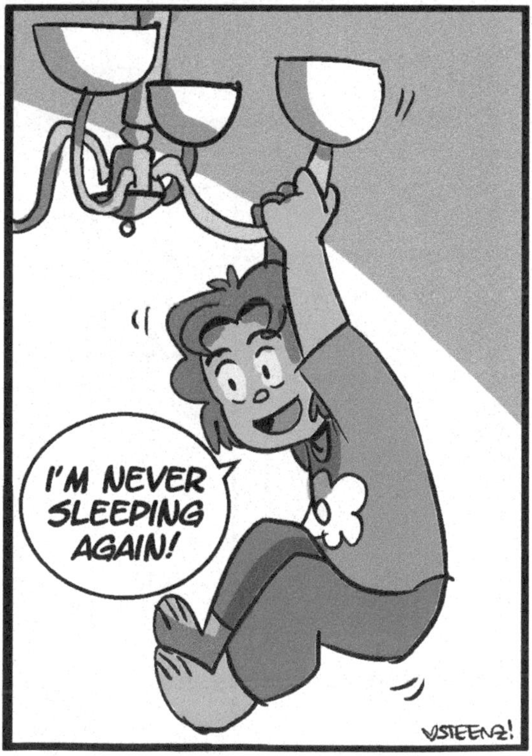
I'M NEVER
SLEEPING
AGAIN!
VJSTEENZ!

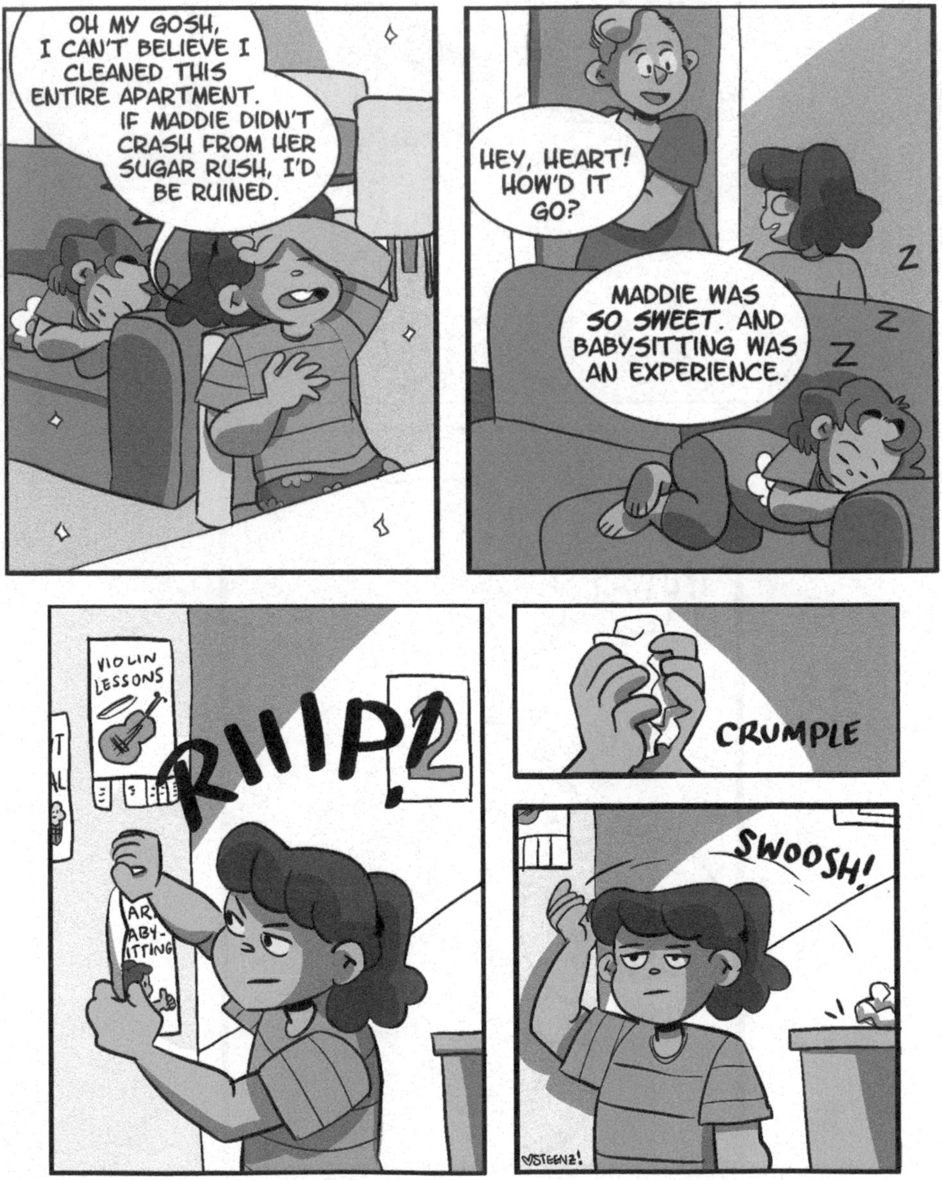
OH MY GOSH, I CAN'T BELIEVE I CLEANED THIS ENTIRE APARTMENT.
IF MADDIE DIDN'T CRASH FROM HER SUGAR RUSH, I'D BE RUINED.
HEY, HEART! HOW'D IT GO?
MADDIE WAS SO SWEET. AND BABYSITTING WAS AN EXPERIENCE.
Z
Z
Z
VIOLIN LESSONS
RIIIP!
CRUMPLE
SWOOSH!
STEENZ!

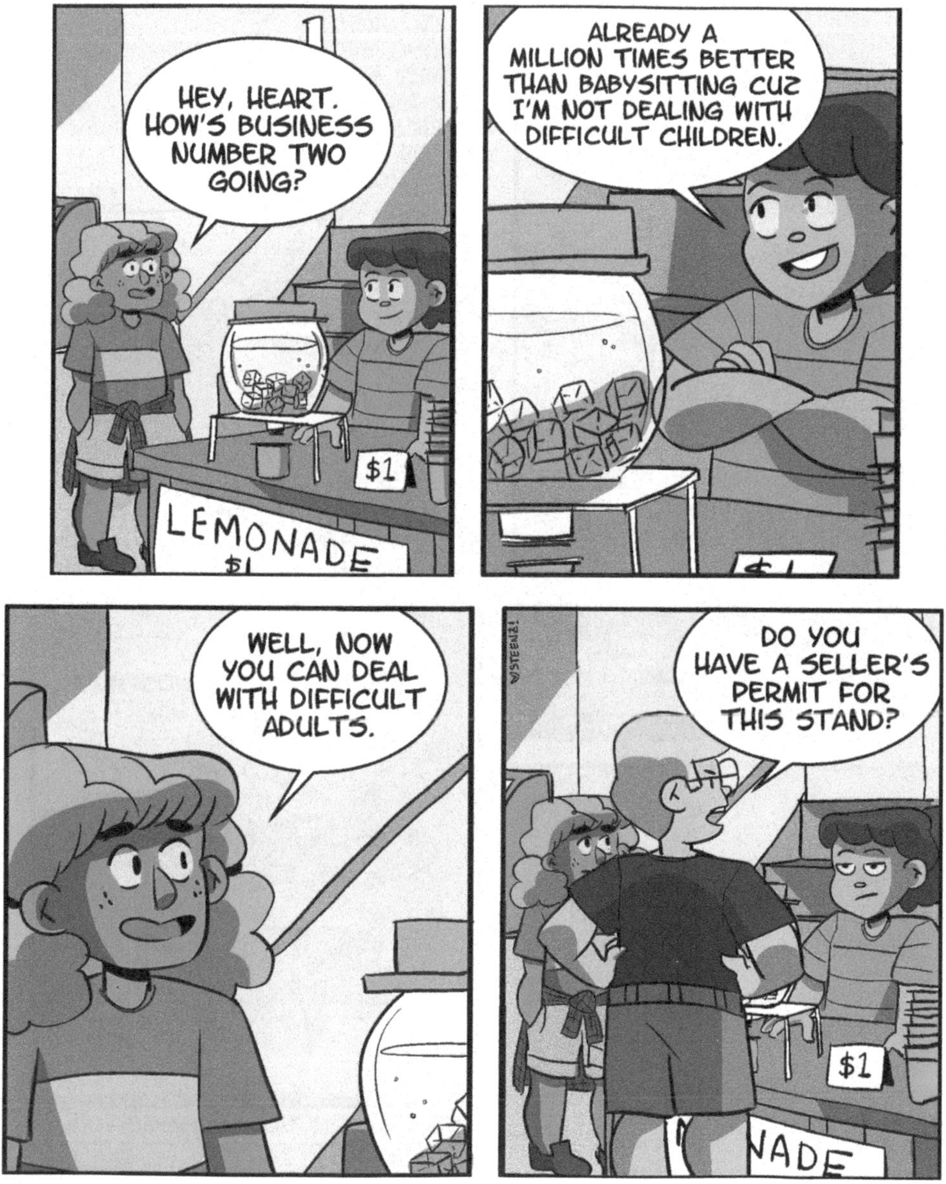
HEY, HEART. HOW'S BUSINESS NUMBER TWO GOING?
$1
LEMONADE $1
ALREADY A MILLION TIMES BETTER THAN BABYSITTING CUZ I'M NOT DEALING WITH DIFFICULT CHILDREN.
WELL, NOW YOU CAN DEAL WITH DIFFICULT ADULTS.
DO YOU HAVE A SELLER'S PERMIT FOR THIS STAND?
$1
NADE

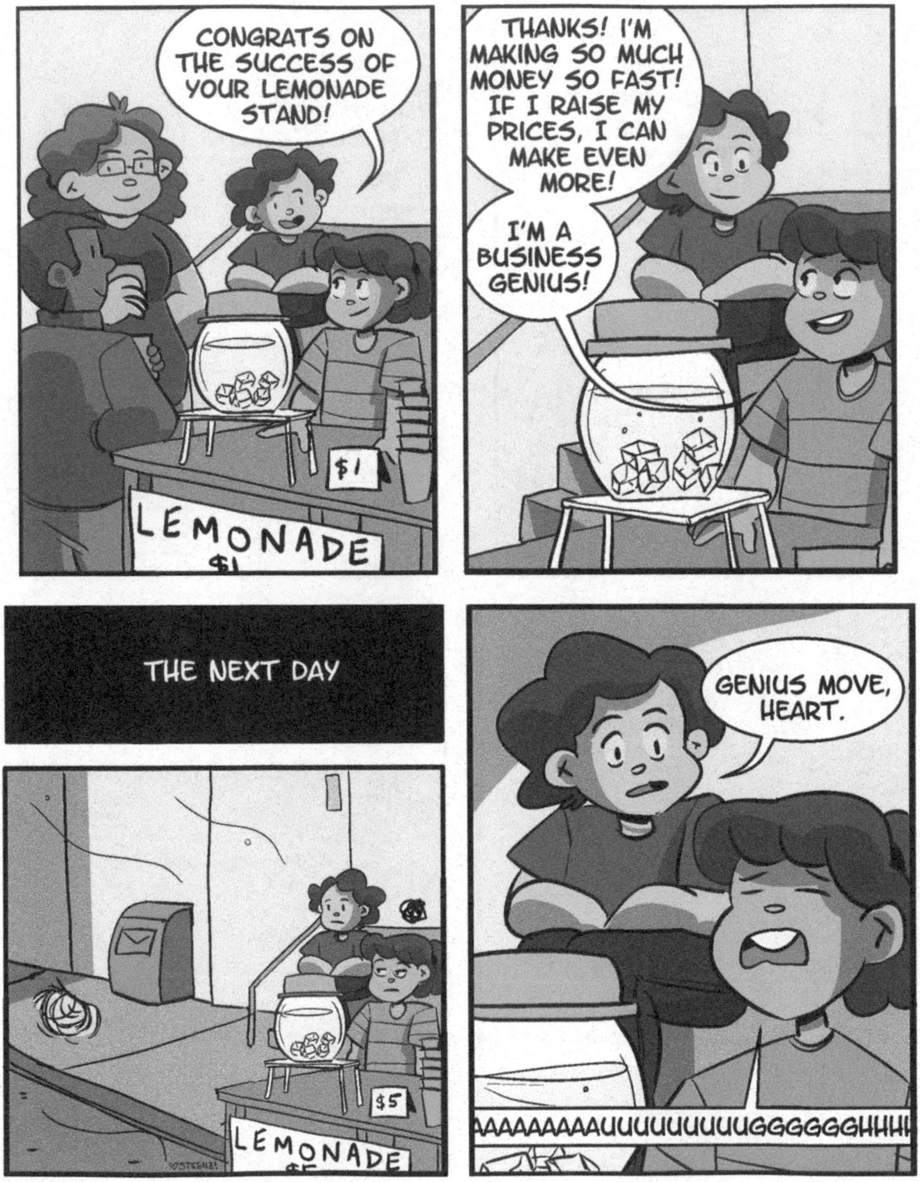
CONGRATS ON THE SUCCESS OF YOUR LEMONADE STAND!
$1
LEMONADE
THANKS! I'M MAKING SO MUCH MONEY SO FAST! IF I RAISE MY PRICES, I CAN MAKE EVEN MORE!
I'M A BUSINESS GENIUS!
THE NEXT DAY
$5
LEMONADE
GENIUS MOVE, HEART.
AAAAAAAAAUUUUUUUUUGGGGGGHHHH

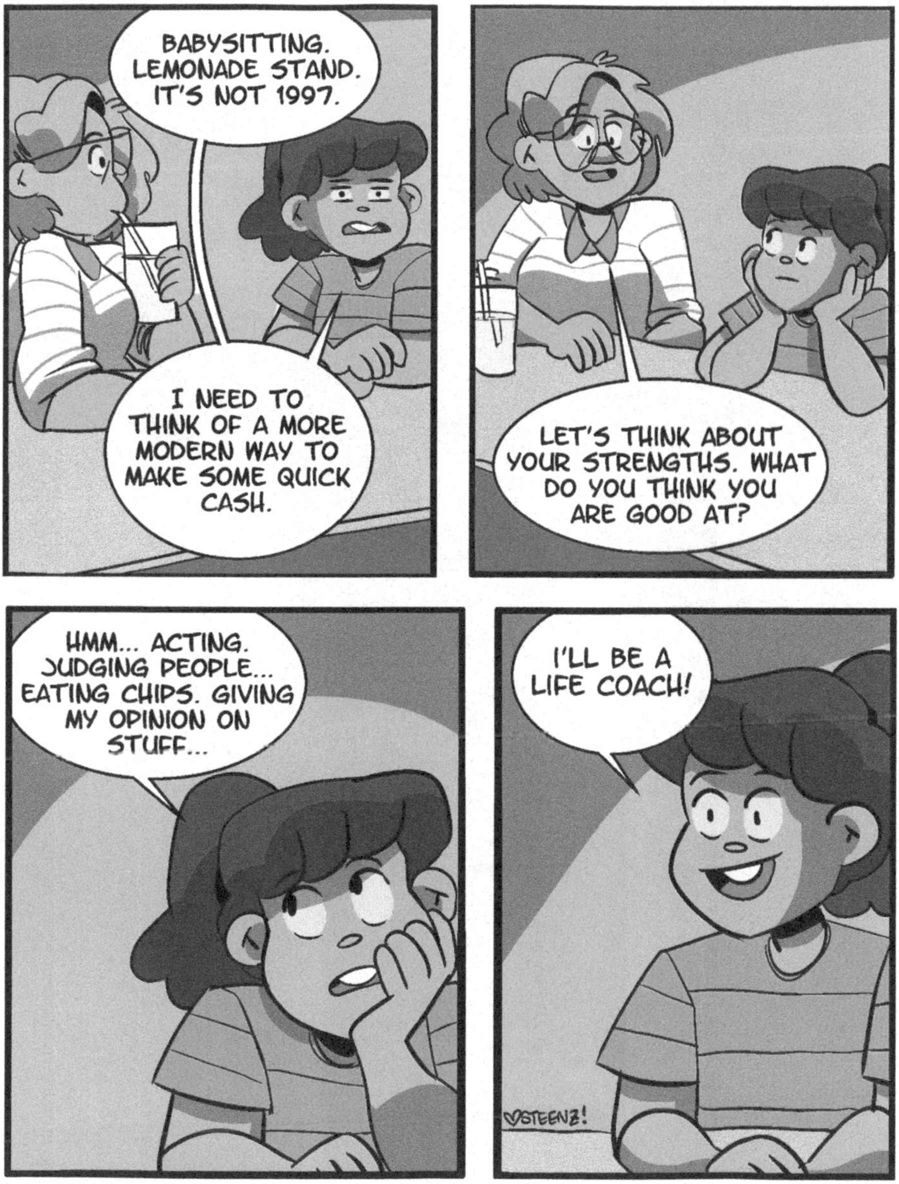
BABYSITTING. LEMONADE STAND. IT'S NOT 1997.
I NEED TO THINK OF A MORE MODERN WAY TO MAKE SOME QUICK CASH.
LET'S THINK ABOUT YOUR STRENGTHS. WHAT DO YOU THINK YOU ARE GOOD AT?
HMM... ACTING. JUDGING PEOPLE... EATING CHIPS. GIVING MY OPINION ON STUFF...
I'LL BE A LIFE COACH!
STEENZ!

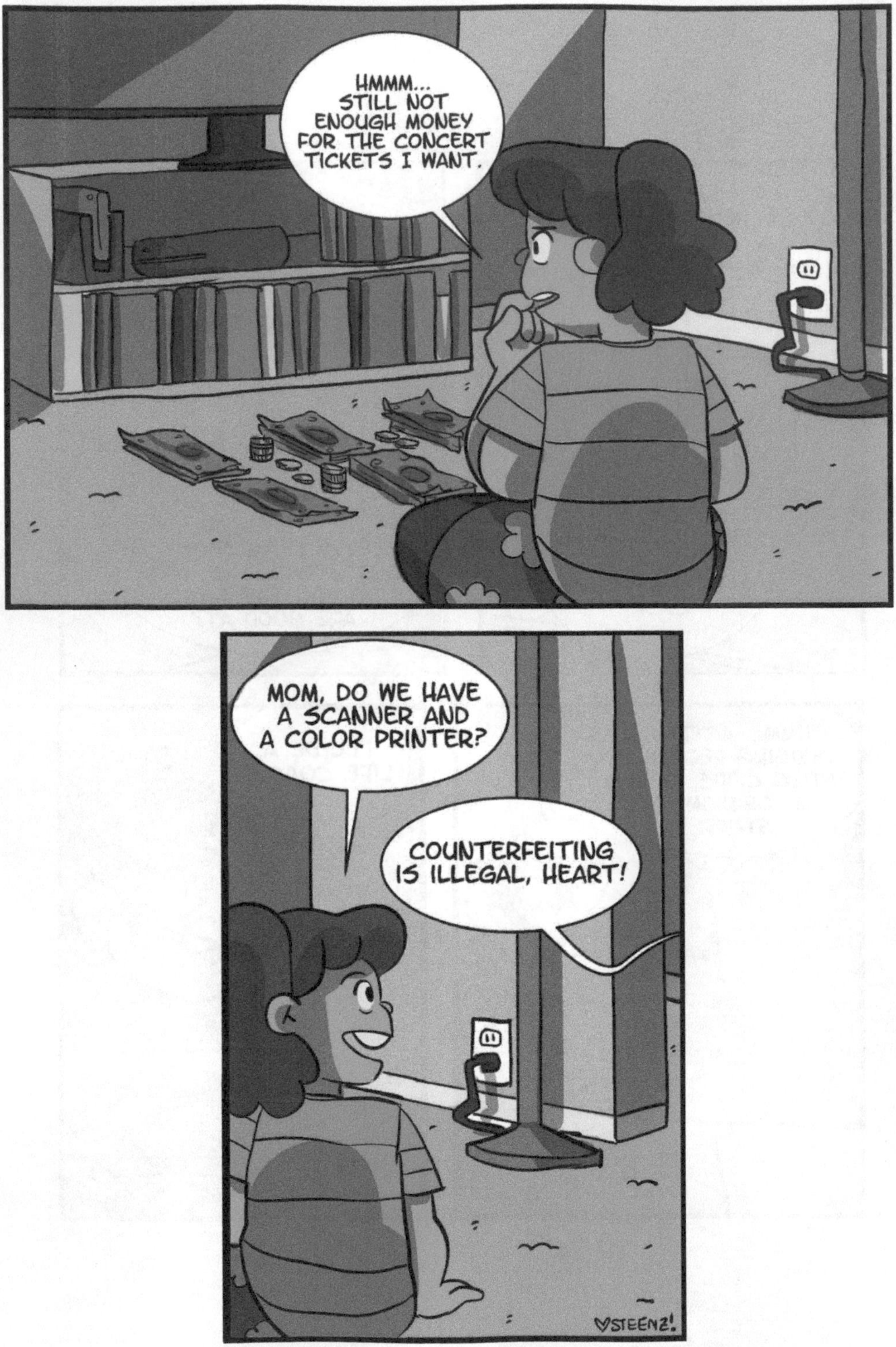
HMMM... STILL NOT ENOUGH MONEY FOR THE CONCERT TICKETS I WANT.
MOM, DO WE HAVE A SCANNER AND A COLOR PRINTER?
COUNTERFEITING IS ILLEGAL, HEART!
♥STEENZ!

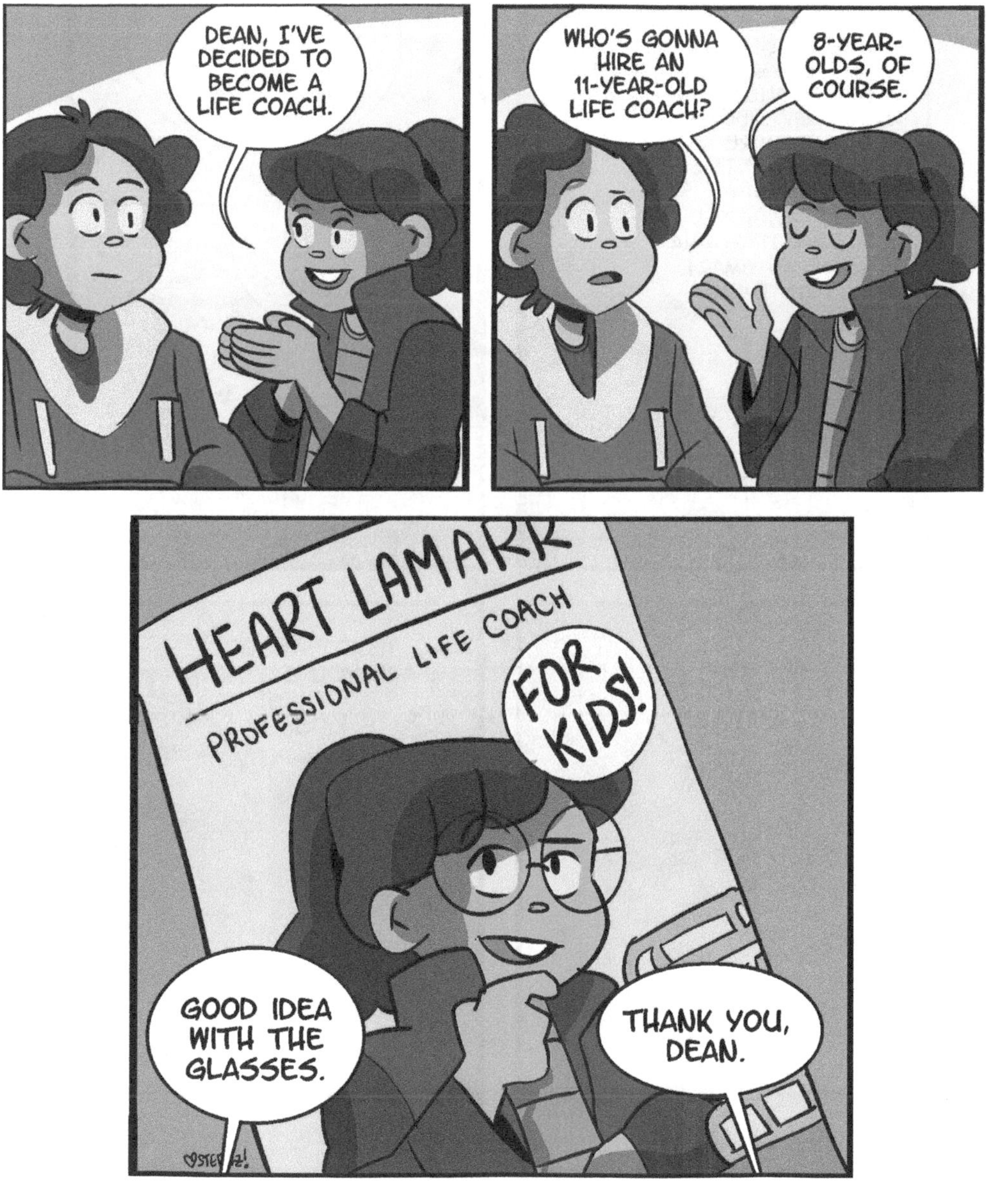
DEAN, I'VE DECIDED TO BECOME A LIFE COACH.
WHO'S GONNA HIRE AN 11-YEAR-OLD LIFE COACH?
8-YEAR-OLDS, OF COURSE.
HEART LAMARR
PROFESSIONAL LIFE COACH
FOR KIDS!
GOOD IDEA WITH THE GLASSES.
THANK YOU, DEAN.

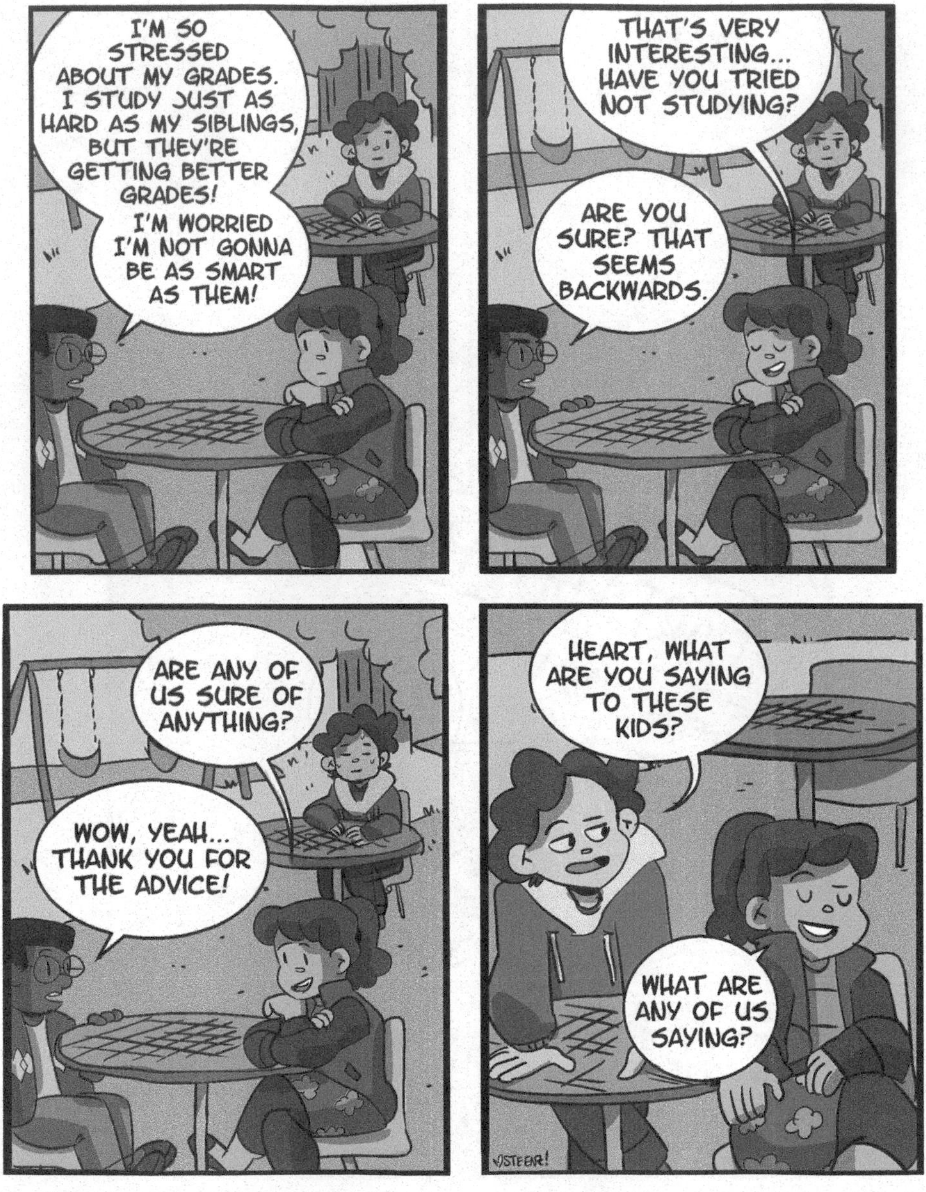
I'M SO STRESSED ABOUT MY GRADES. I STUDY JUST AS HARD AS MY SIBLINGS, BUT THEY'RE GETTING BETTER GRADES!
I'M WORRIED I'M NOT GONNA BE AS SMART AS THEM!
THAT'S VERY INTERESTING... HAVE YOU TRIED NOT STUDYING?
ARE YOU SURE? THAT SEEMS BACKWARDS.
ARE ANY OF US SURE OF ANYTHING?
WOW, YEAH... THANK YOU FOR THE ADVICE!
HEART, WHAT ARE YOU SAYING TO THESE KIDS?
WHAT ARE ANY OF US SAYING?
STEENZ!

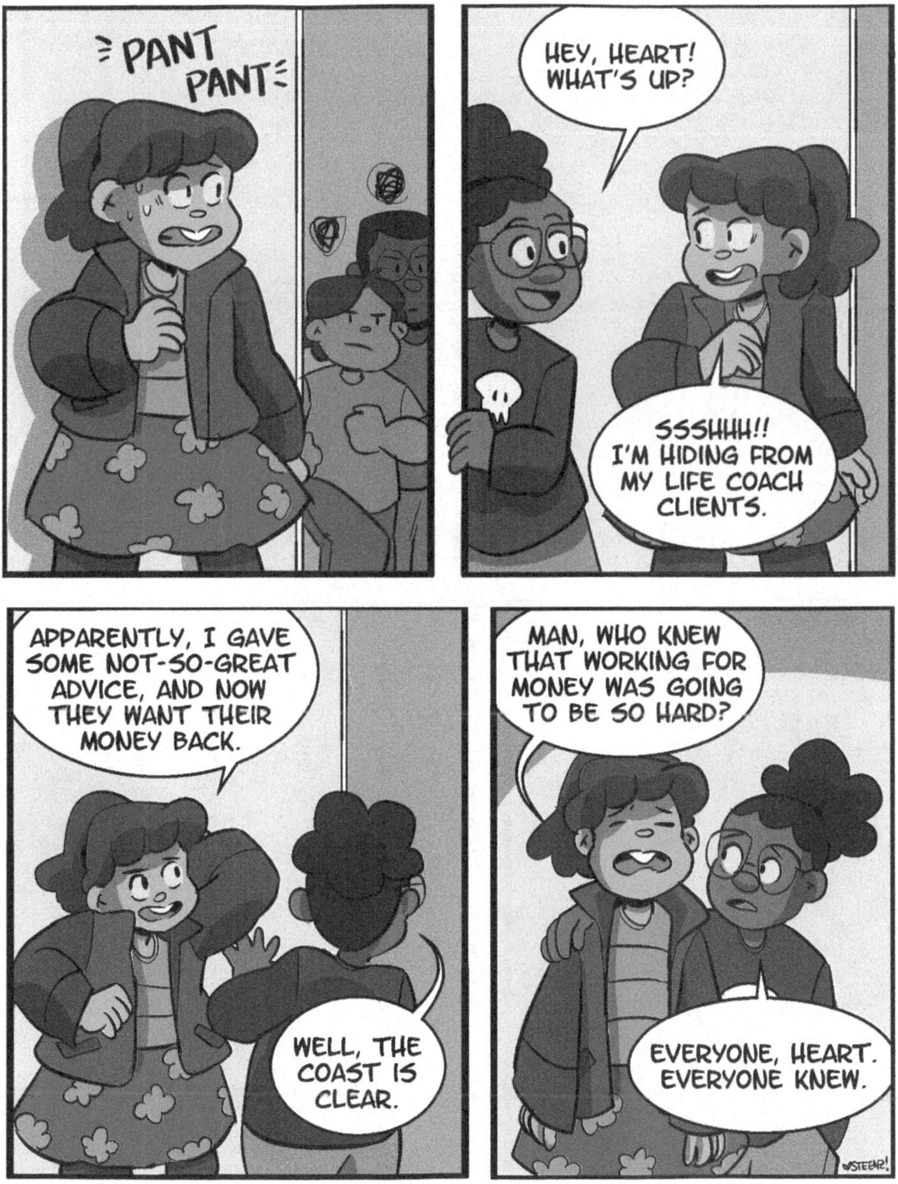
PANT PANT
HEY, HEART! WHAT'S UP?
SSSHHH!! I'M HIDING FROM MY LIFE COACH CLIENTS.
APPARENTLY, I GAVE SOME NOT-SO-GREAT ADVICE, AND NOW THEY WANT THEIR MONEY BACK.
WELL, THE COAST IS CLEAR.
MAN, WHO KNEW THAT WORKING FOR MONEY WAS GOING TO BE SO HARD?
EVERYONE, HEART. EVERYONE KNEW.

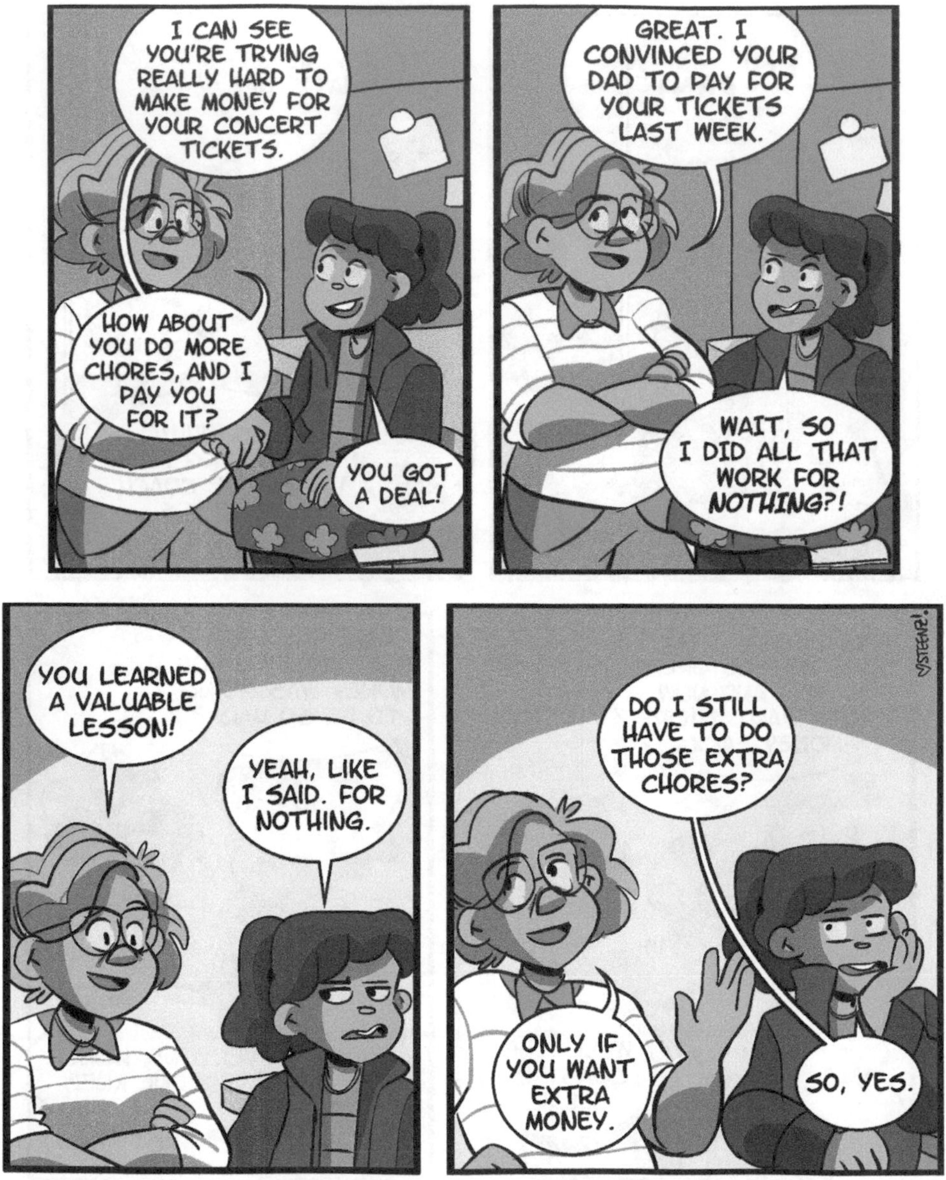
I CAN SEE YOU'RE TRYING REALLY HARD TO MAKE MONEY FOR YOUR CONCERT TICKETS.
HOW ABOUT YOU DO MORE CHORES, AND I PAY YOU FOR IT?
YOU GOT A DEAL!
GREAT. I CONVINCED YOUR DAD TO PAY FOR YOUR TICKETS LAST WEEK.
WAIT, SO I DID ALL THAT WORK FOR *NOTHING*?!
YOU LEARNED A VALUABLE LESSON!
YEAH, LIKE I SAID. FOR NOTHING.
DO I STILL HAVE TO DO THOSE EXTRA CHORES?
ONLY IF YOU WANT EXTRA MONEY.
SO, YES.

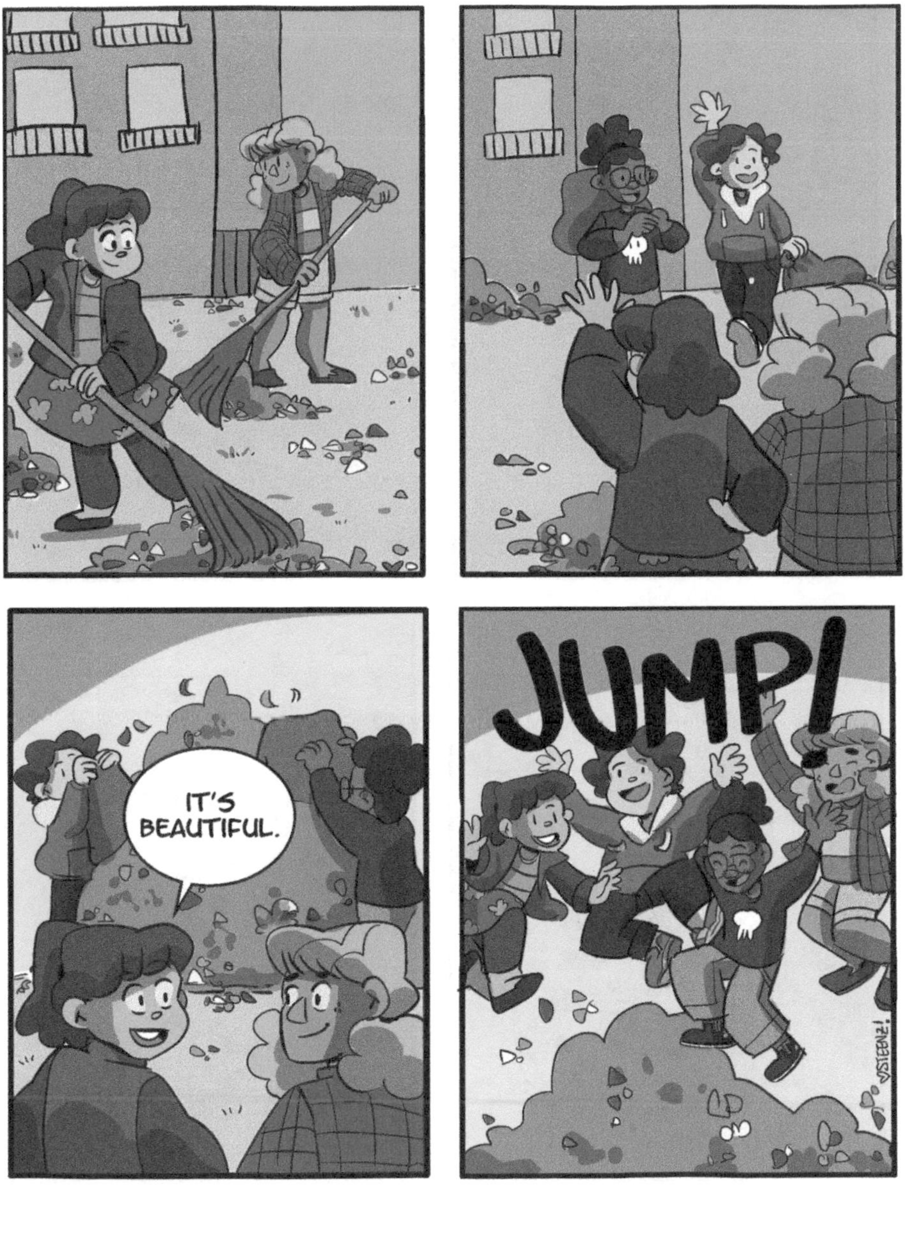
IT'S BEAUTIFUL.
JUMP!

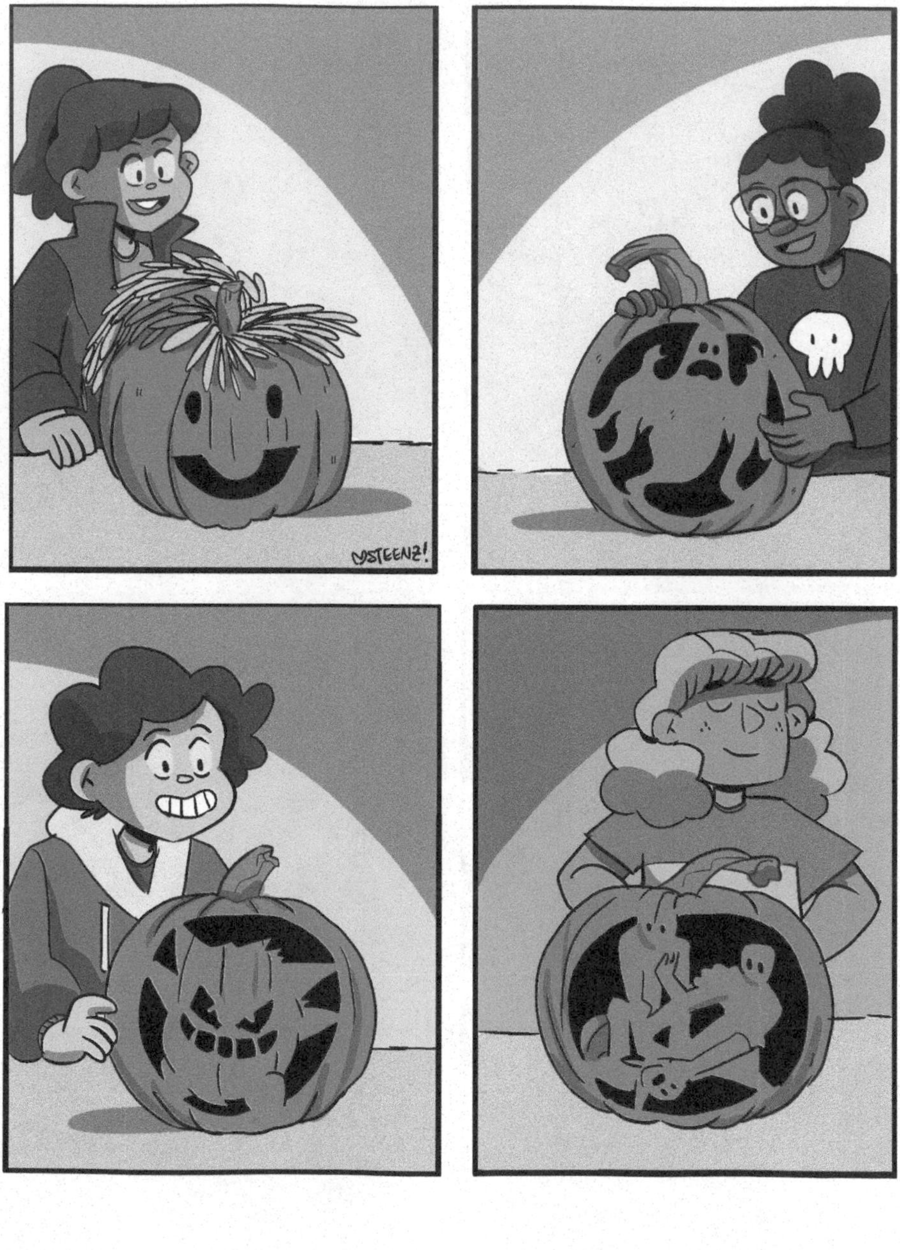
STEENZ!

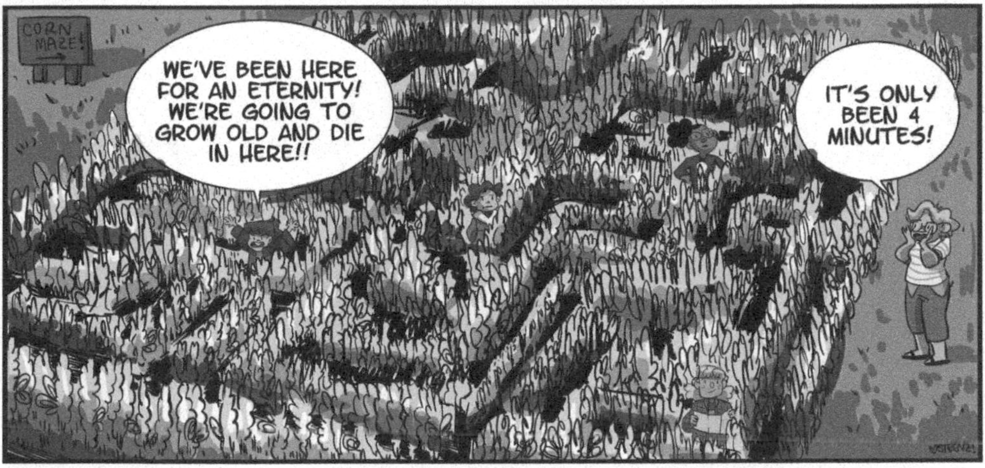
CORN MAZE!
WE'VE BEEN HERE FOR AN ETERNITY! WE'RE GOING TO GROW OLD AND DIE IN HERE!!
IT'S ONLY BEEN 4 MINUTES!

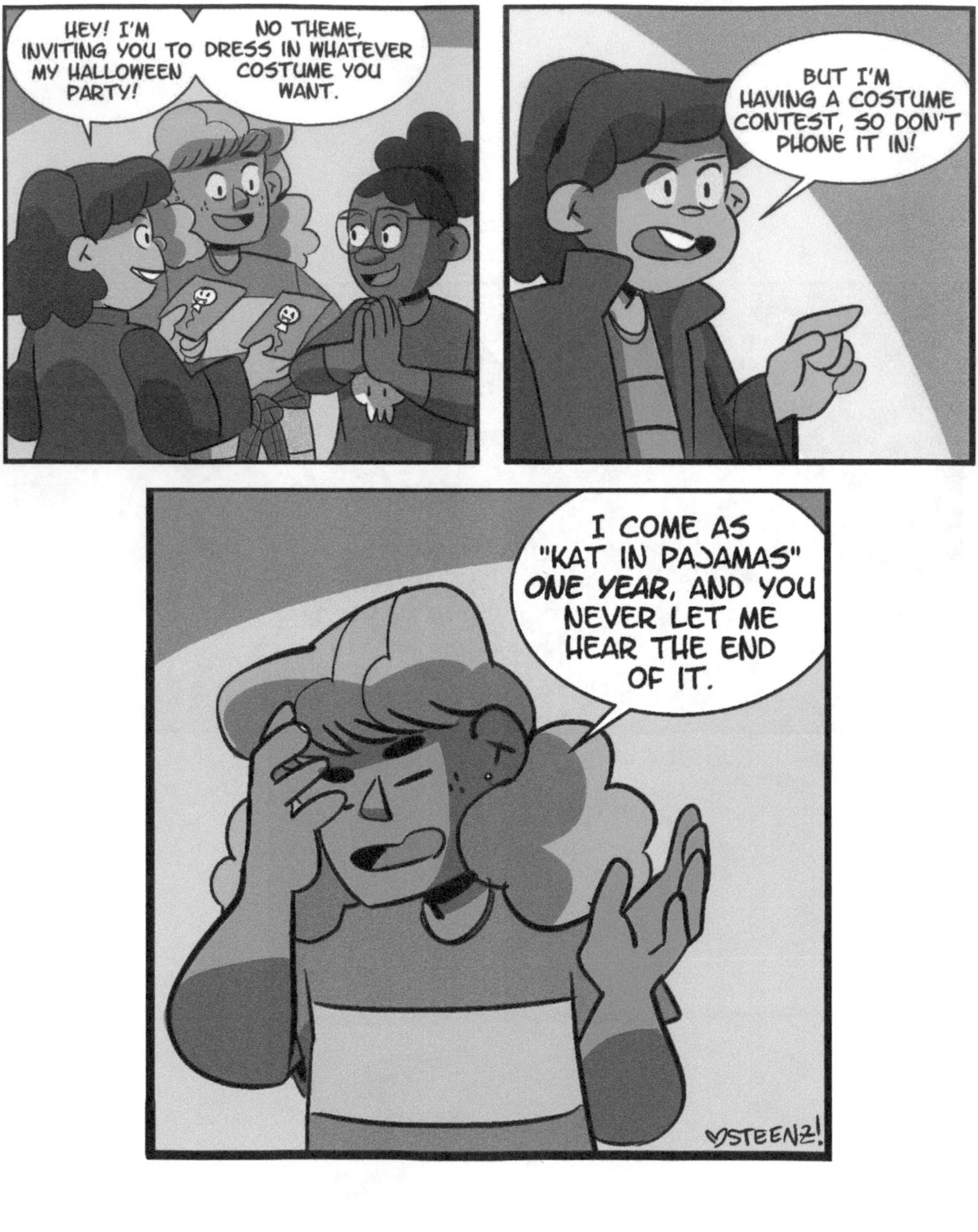
HEY! I'M INVITING YOU TO MY HALLOWEEN PARTY!
NO THEME, DRESS IN WHATEVER COSTUME YOU WANT.
BUT I'M HAVING A COSTUME CONTEST, SO DON'T PHONE IT IN!
I COME AS "KAT IN PAJAMAS" ONE YEAR, AND YOU NEVER LET ME HEAR THE END OF IT.
STEENZ!

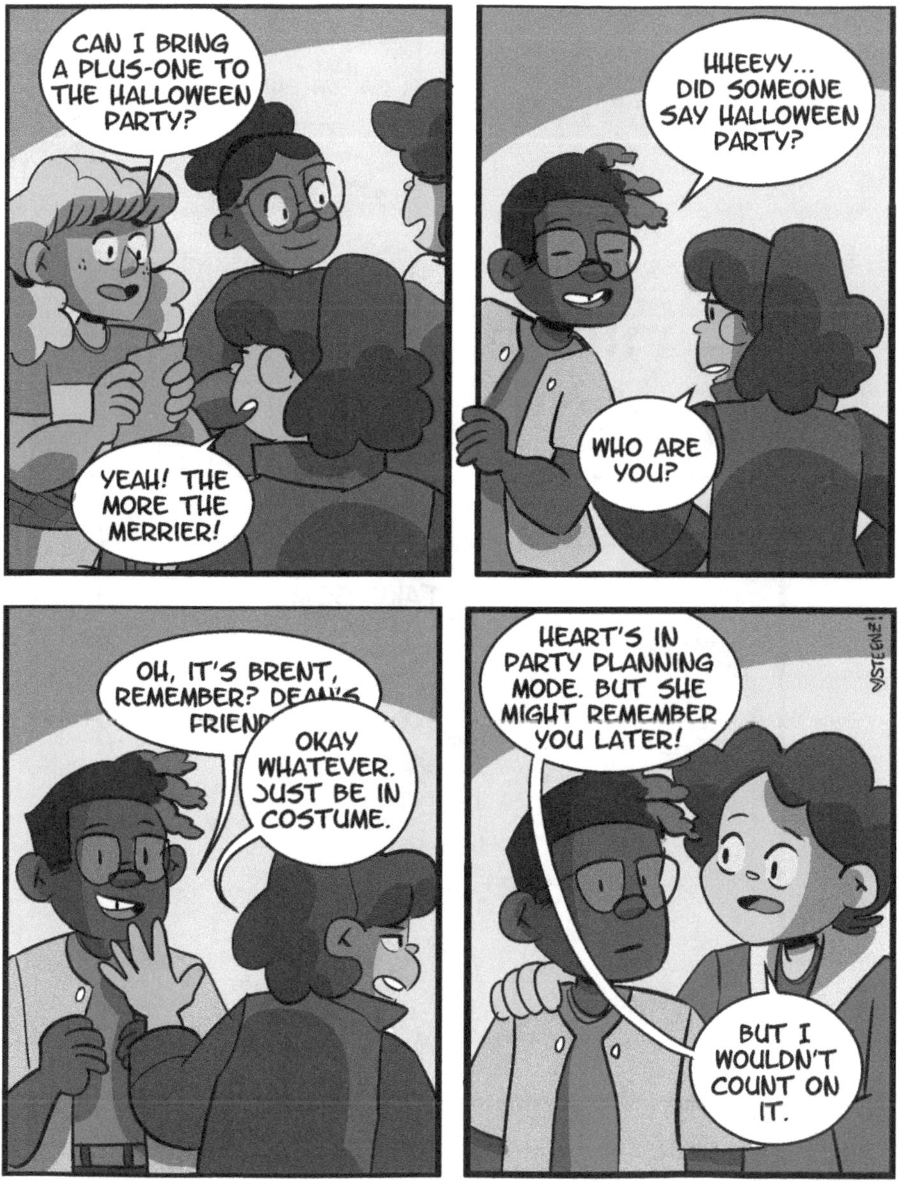
CAN I BRING A PLUS-ONE TO THE HALLOWEEN PARTY?
YEAH! THE MORE THE MERRIER!
HHEEYY... DID SOMEONE SAY HALLOWEEN PARTY?
WHO ARE YOU?
OH, IT'S BRENT, REMEMBER? DEAN'S
OKAY WHATEVER. JUST BE IN COSTUME.
HEART'S IN PARTY PLANNING MODE. BUT SHE MIGHT REMEMBER YOU LATER!
BUT I WOULDN'T COUNT ON IT.

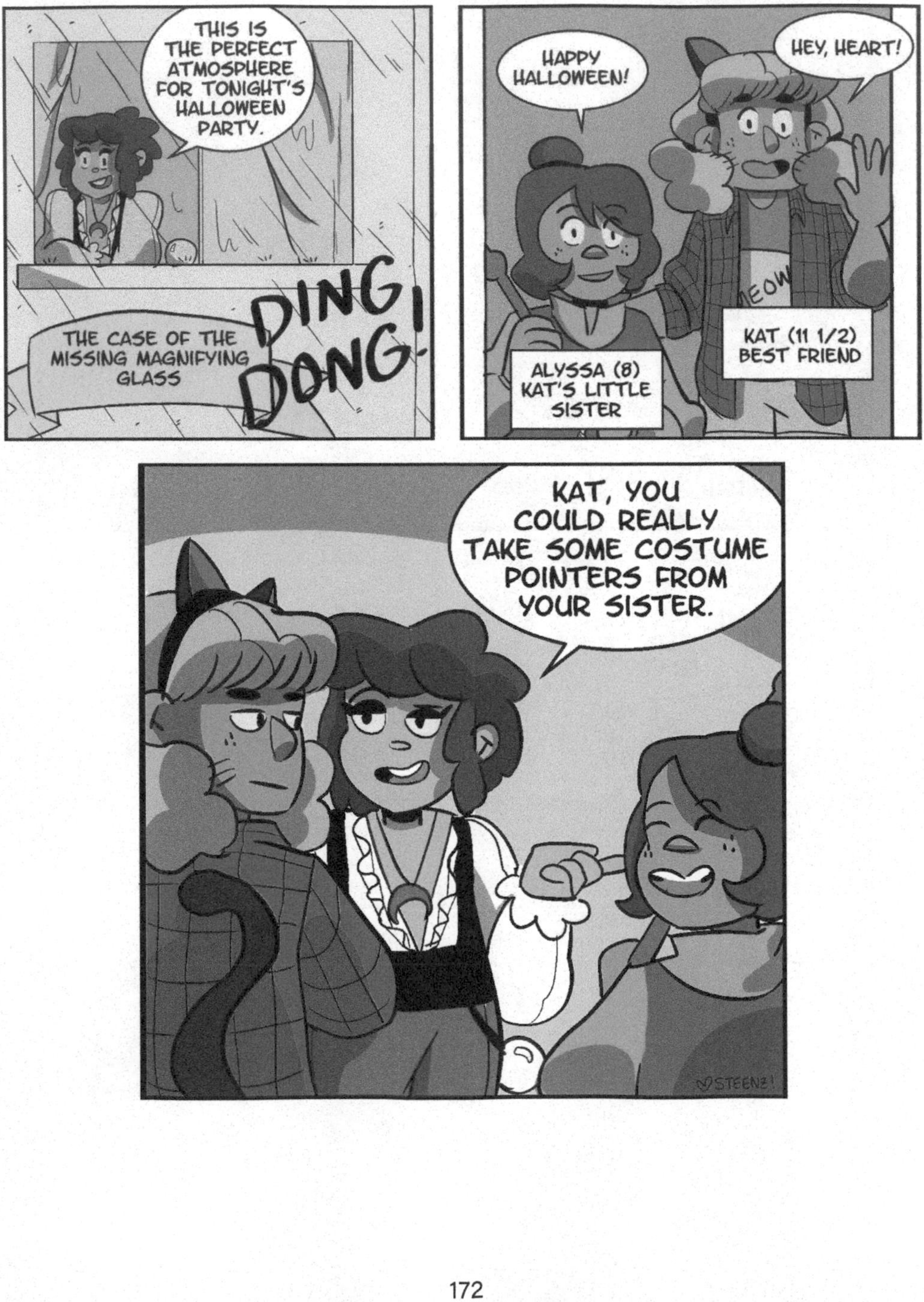
THIS IS THE PERFECT ATMOSPHERE FOR TONIGHT'S HALLOWEEN PARTY.
THE CASE OF THE MISSING MAGNIFYING GLASS
DING DONG!
HAPPY HALLOWEEN!
HEY, HEART!
ALYSSA (8) KAT'S LITTLE SISTER
KAT (11 1/2) BEST FRIEND
MEOW
KAT, YOU COULD REALLY TAKE SOME COSTUME POINTERS FROM YOUR SISTER.
STEENZ!

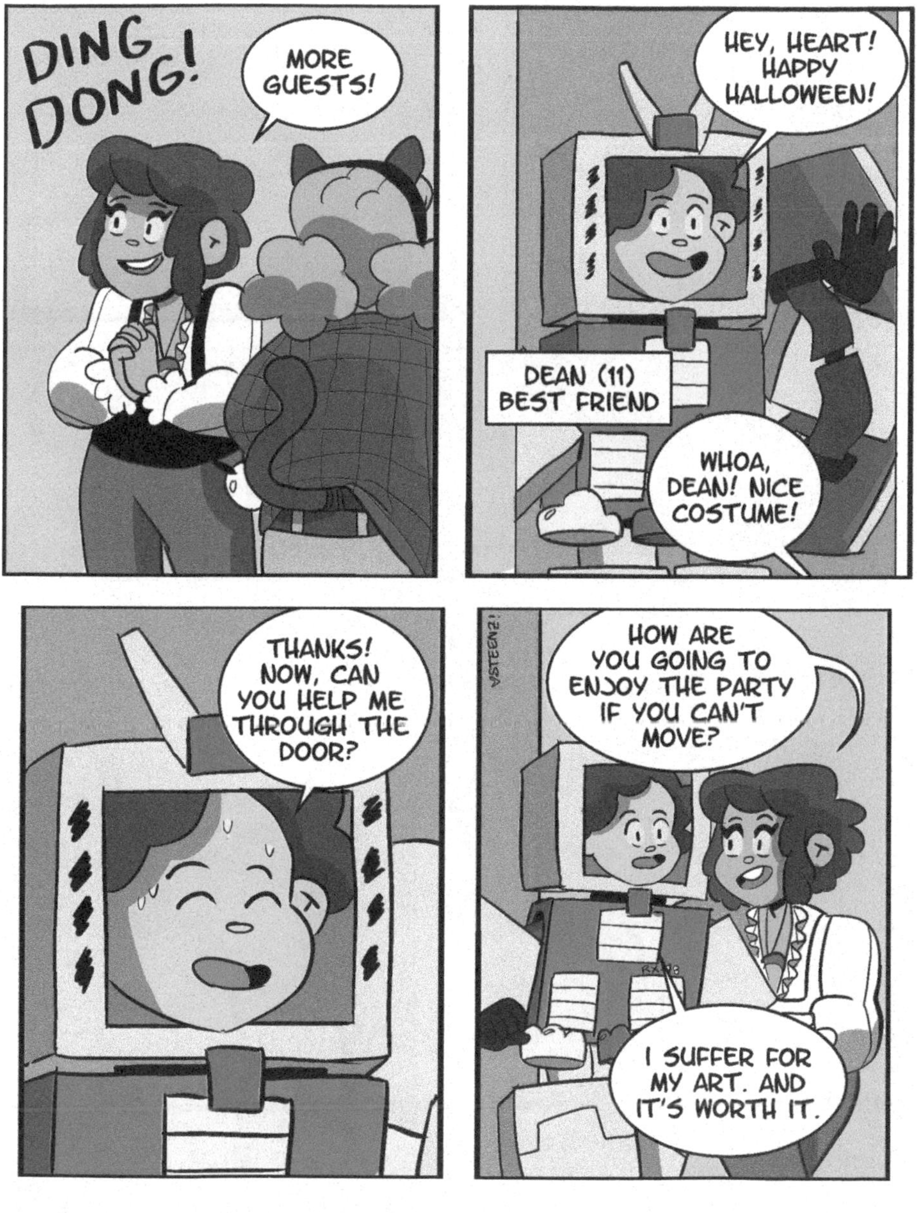
DING DONG!
MORE GUESTS!
HEY, HEART! HAPPY HALLOWEEN!
DEAN (11) BEST FRIEND
WHOA, DEAN! NICE COSTUME!
THANKS! NOW, CAN YOU HELP ME THROUGH THE DOOR?
HOW ARE YOU GOING TO ENJOY THE PARTY IF YOU CAN'T MOVE?
I SUFFER FOR MY ART. AND IT'S WORTH IT.

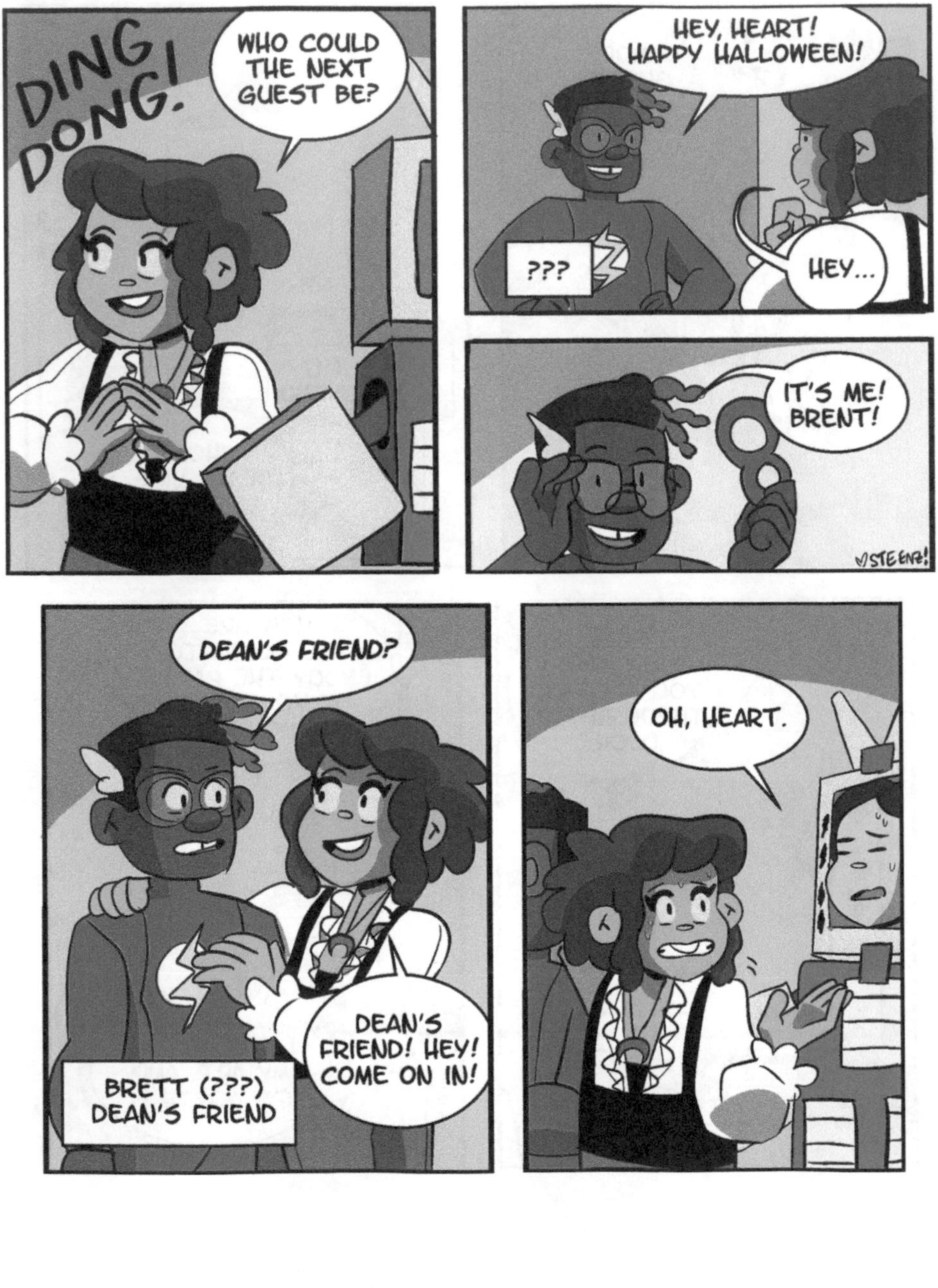
DING DONG!
WHO COULD THE NEXT GUEST BE?
HEY, HEART! HAPPY HALLOWEEN!
???
HEY...
IT'S ME! BRENT!
STEENZ!
DEAN'S FRIEND?
BRETT (???) DEAN'S FRIEND
DEAN'S FRIEND! HEY! COME ON IN!
OH, HEART.

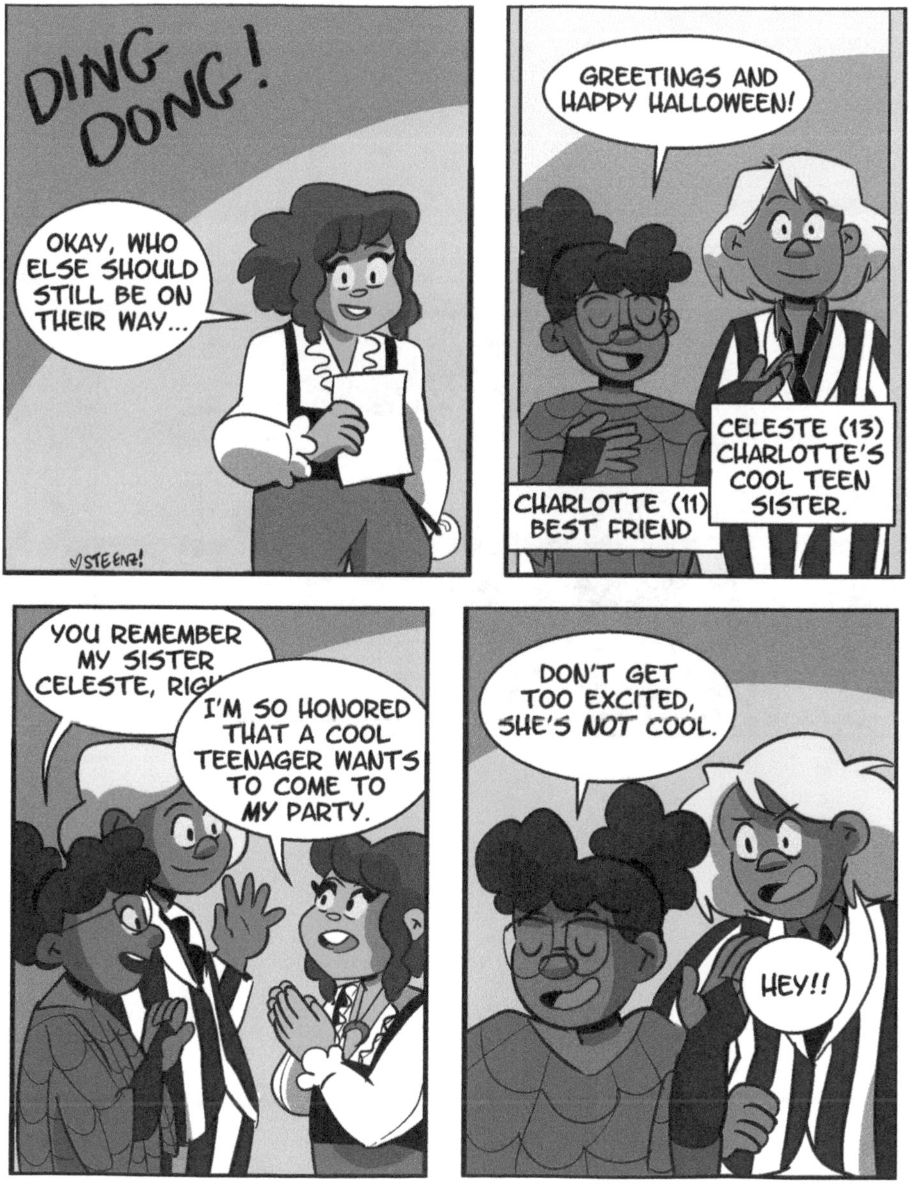
DING DONG!
OKAY, WHO ELSE SHOULD STILL BE ON THEIR WAY...
♡STEENZ!
GREETINGS AND HAPPY HALLOWEEN!
CHARLOTTE (11) BEST FRIEND
CELESTE (13) CHARLOTTE'S COOL TEEN SISTER.
YOU REMEMBER MY SISTER CELESTE, RIG
I'M SO HONORED THAT A COOL TEENAGER WANTS TO COME TO MY PARTY.
DON'T GET TOO EXCITED, SHE'S NOT COOL.
HEY!!

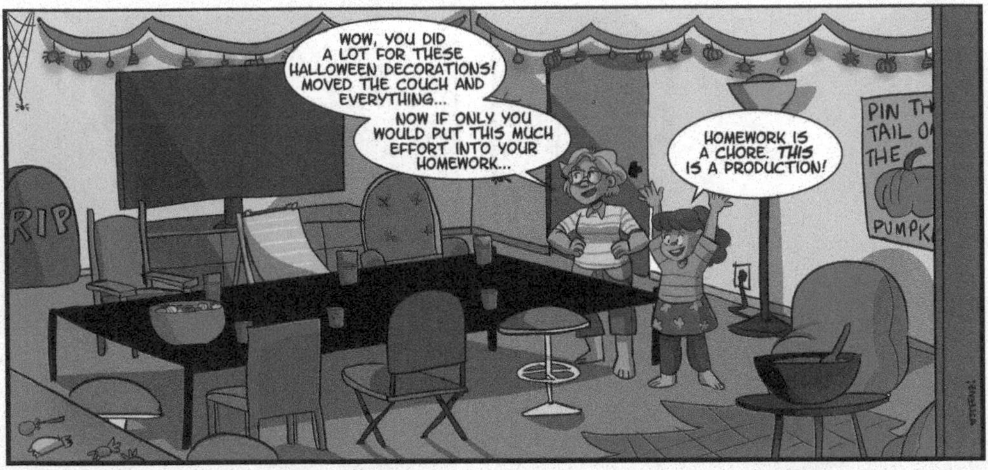
WOW, YOU DID A LOT FOR THESE HALLOWEEN DECORATIONS! MOVED THE COUCH AND EVERYTHING...
NOW IF ONLY YOU WOULD PUT THIS MUCH EFFORT INTO YOUR HOMEWORK...
HOMEWORK IS A CHORE. THIS IS A PRODUCTION!
RIP
PIN TH
TAIL O
THE
PUMPK

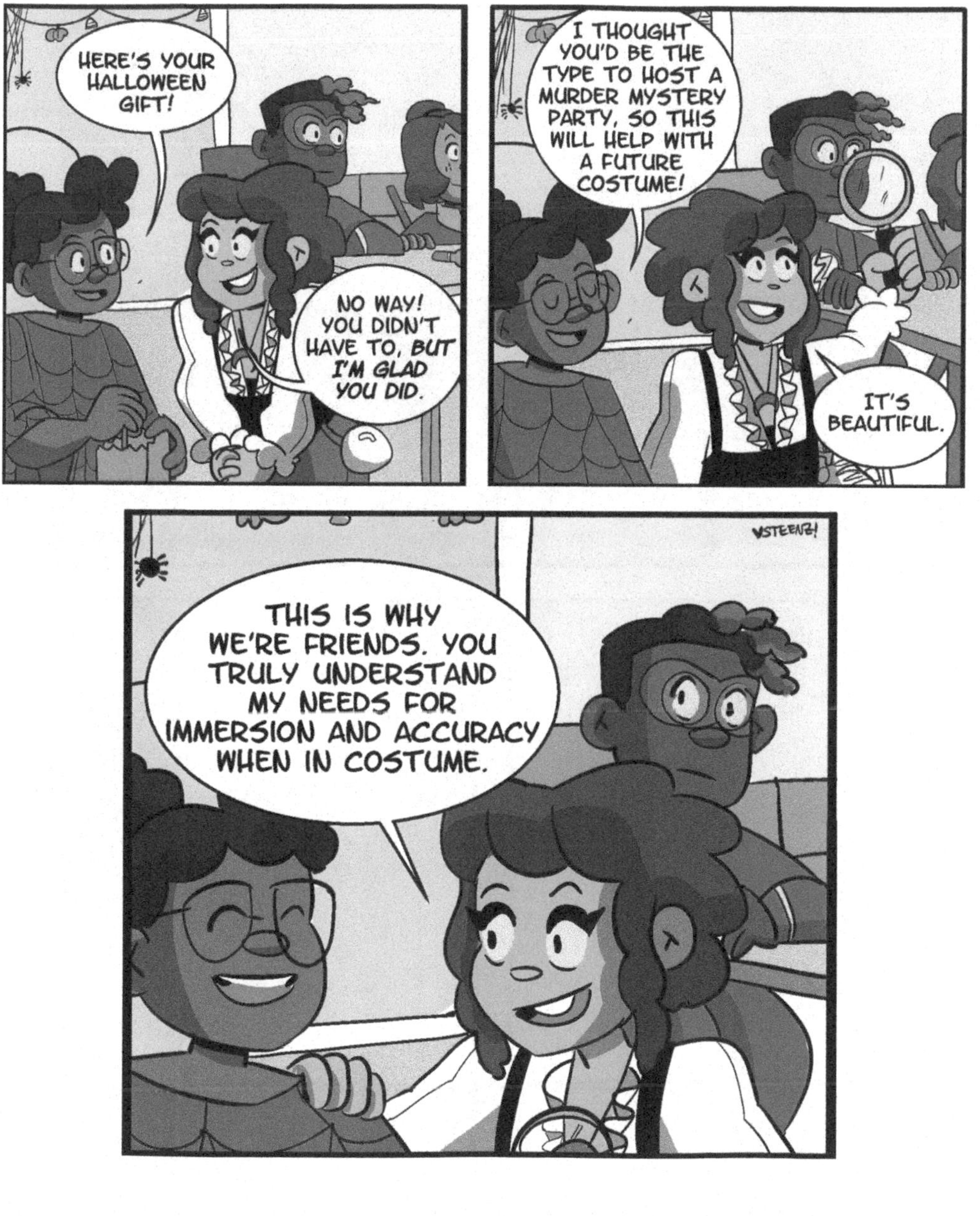
HERE'S YOUR HALLOWEEN GIFT!
NO WAY! YOU DIDN'T HAVE TO, BUT I'M GLAD YOU DID.
I THOUGHT YOU'D BE THE TYPE TO HOST A MURDER MYSTERY PARTY, SO THIS WILL HELP WITH A FUTURE COSTUME!
IT'S BEAUTIFUL.
THIS IS WHY WE'RE FRIENDS. YOU TRULY UNDERSTAND MY NEEDS FOR IMMERSION AND ACCURACY WHEN IN COSTUME.

ALYSSA, I'M IMPRESSED WITH YOUR BO STAFF.
DID YOU MAKE IT?
HA! OF COURSE. THIS STAFF ISN'T SOMETHING YOU CAN JUST BUY.
THE DETAILING, THE WEIGHT... IT'S PERFECTION.
I REGRET ASKING.

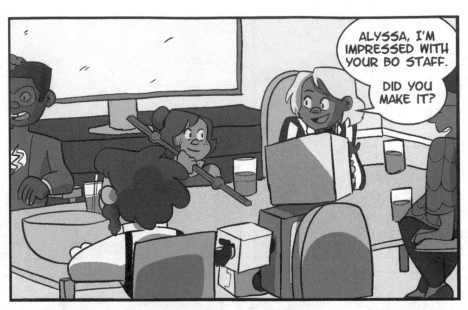

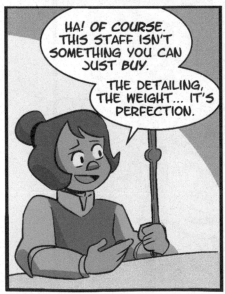

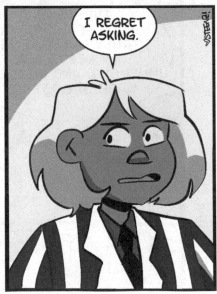

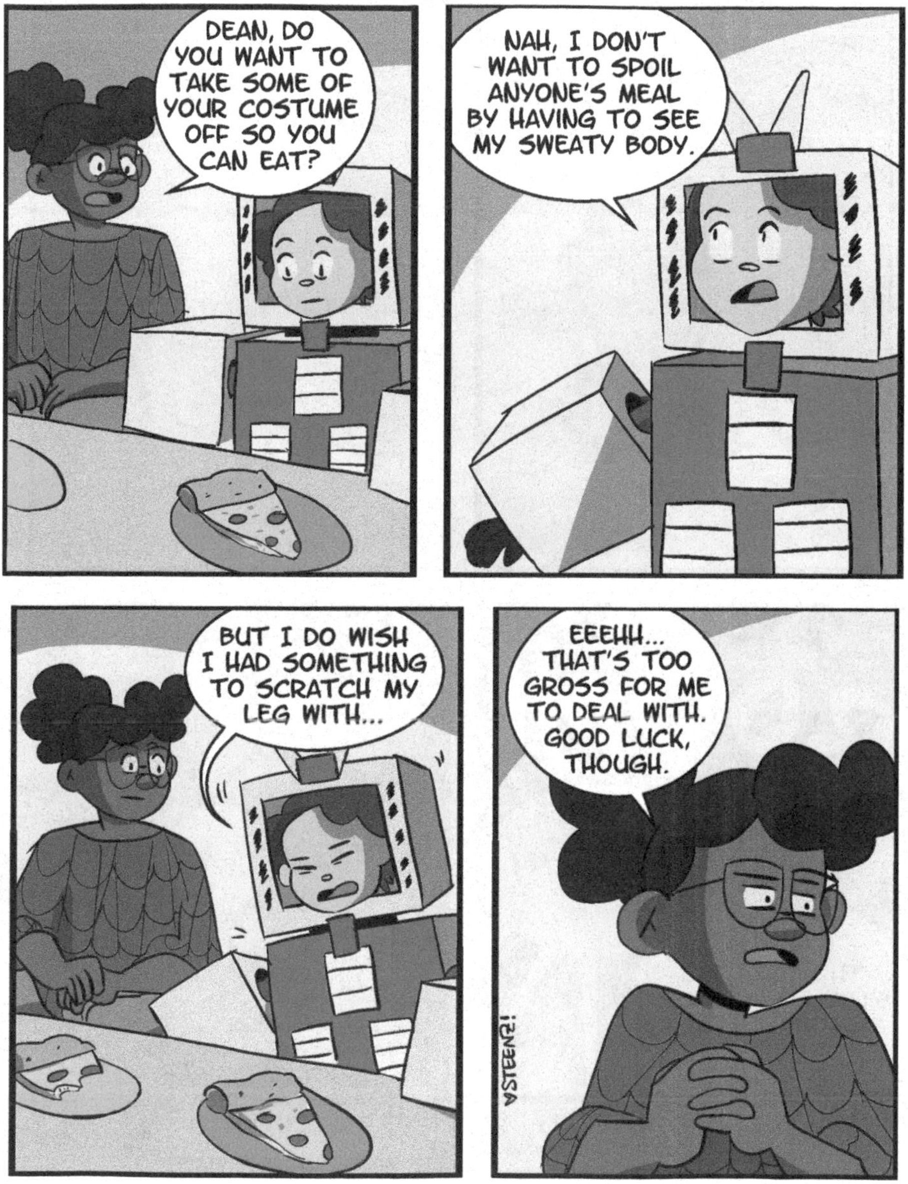
DEAN, DO YOU WANT TO TAKE SOME OF YOUR COSTUME OFF SO YOU CAN EAT?
NAH, I DON'T WANT TO SPOIL ANYONE'S MEAL BY HAVING TO SEE MY SWEATY BODY.
BUT I DO WISH I HAD SOMETHING TO SCRATCH MY LEG WITH...
EEEHH... THAT'S TOO GROSS FOR ME TO DEAL WITH. GOOD LUCK, THOUGH.

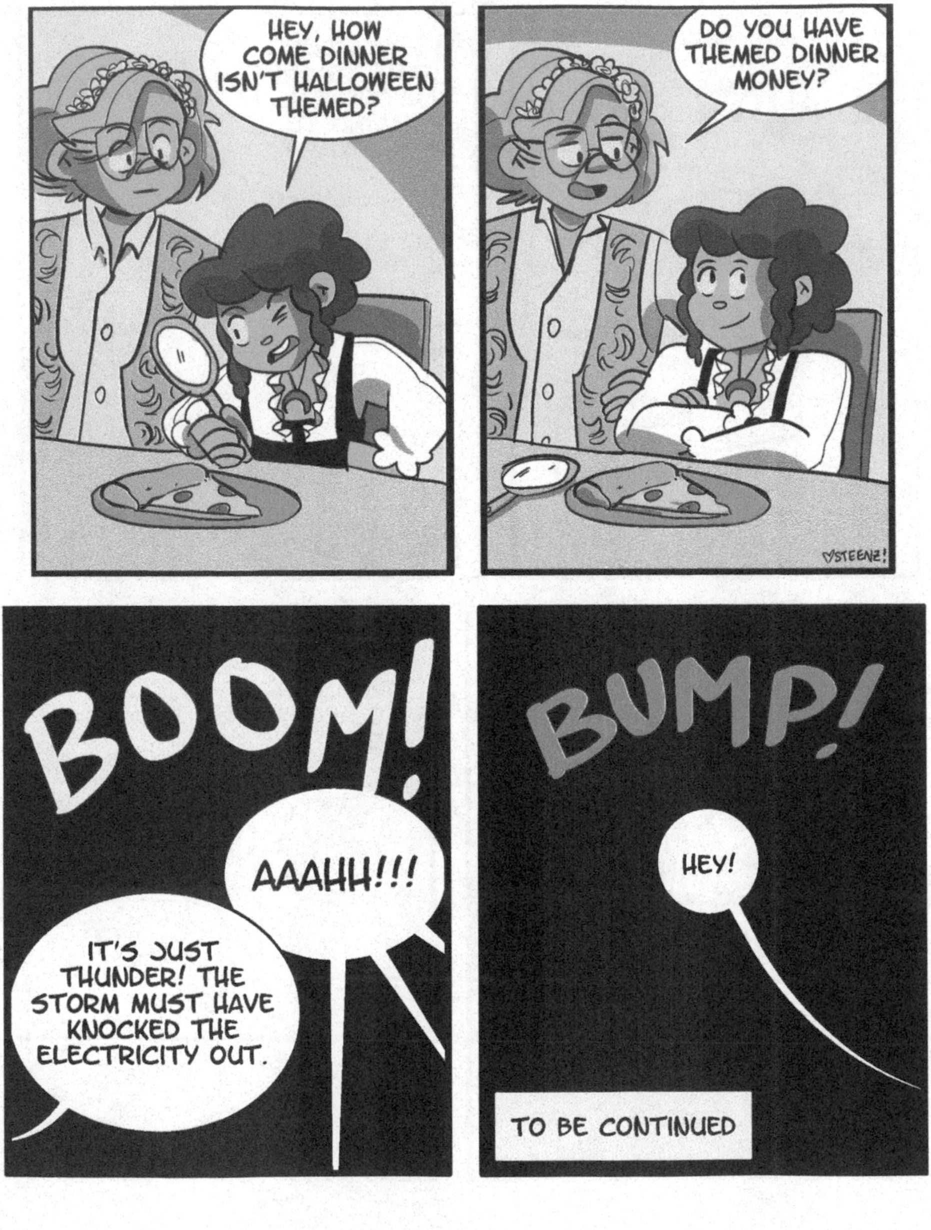
HEY, HOW COME DINNER ISN'T HALLOWEEN THEMED?
DO YOU HAVE THEMED DINNER MONEY?
♡STEENZ!
BOOM!
AAAHH!!!
IT'S JUST THUNDER! THE STORM MUST HAVE KNOCKED THE ELECTRICITY OUT.
BUMP!
HEY!
TO BE CONTINUED

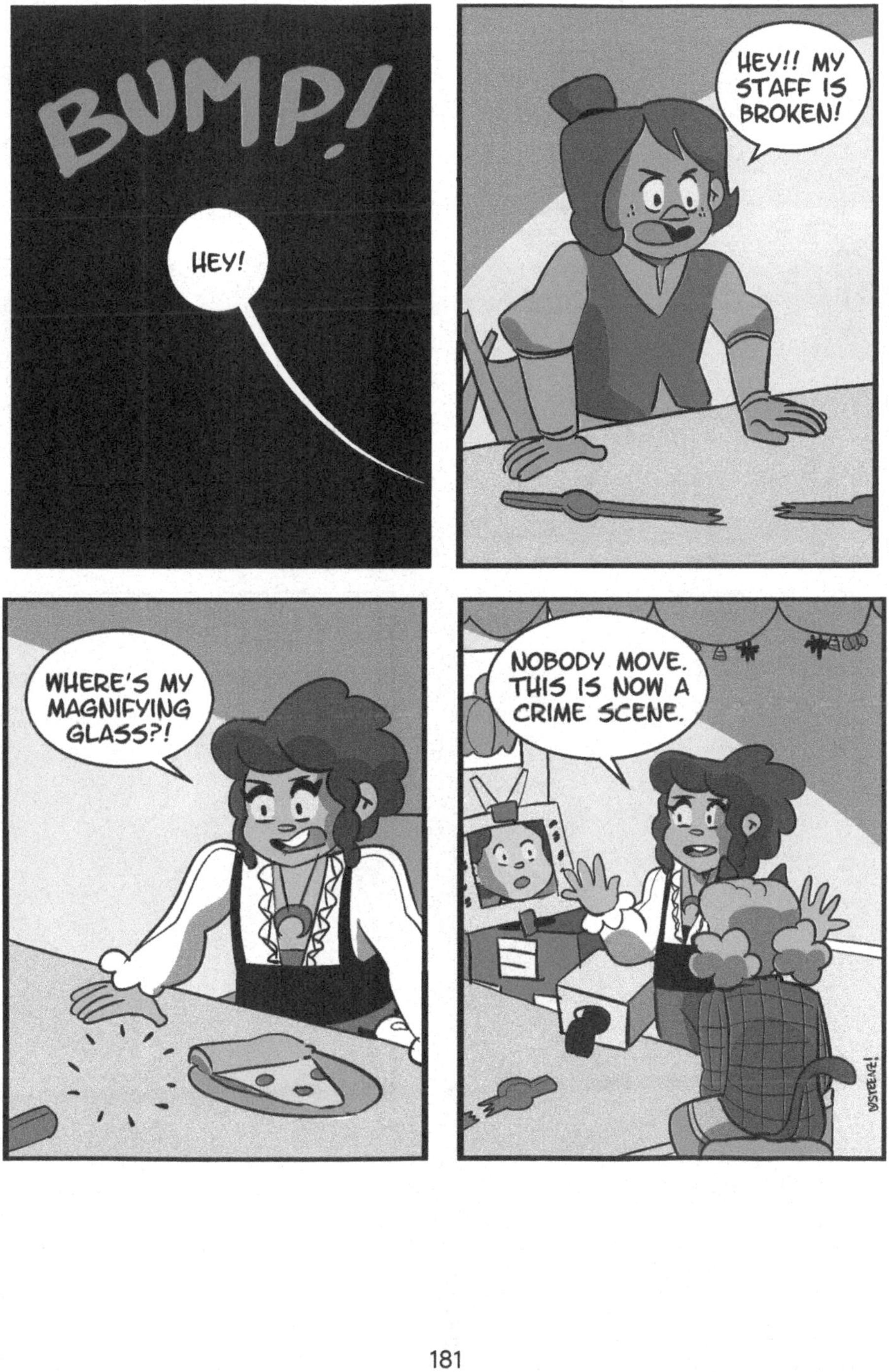
BUMP!
HEY!
HEY!! MY STAFF IS BROKEN!
WHERE'S MY MAGNIFYING GLASS?!
NOBODY MOVE. THIS IS NOW A CRIME SCENE.

IT WAS YOU! YOU WERE EYEING MY STAFF ALL NIGHT AND WANTED IT FOR YOURSELF.
ME?! I HAVE NO MOTIVE!
IT'S TRUE. CELESTE IS 13, AND AS FAR AS I KNOW, TEENAGERS HAVE VERY LITTLE MOTIVATION FOR ANYTHING.
WOW, THANKS.
LOVE YOU, SIS! HA..
VSTEENZ!

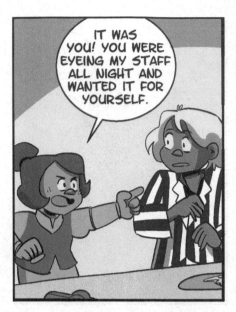

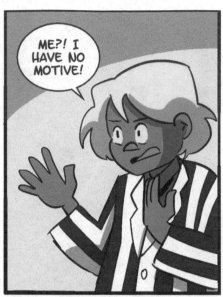

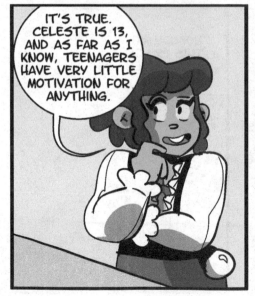

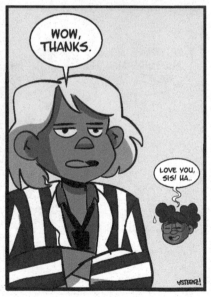

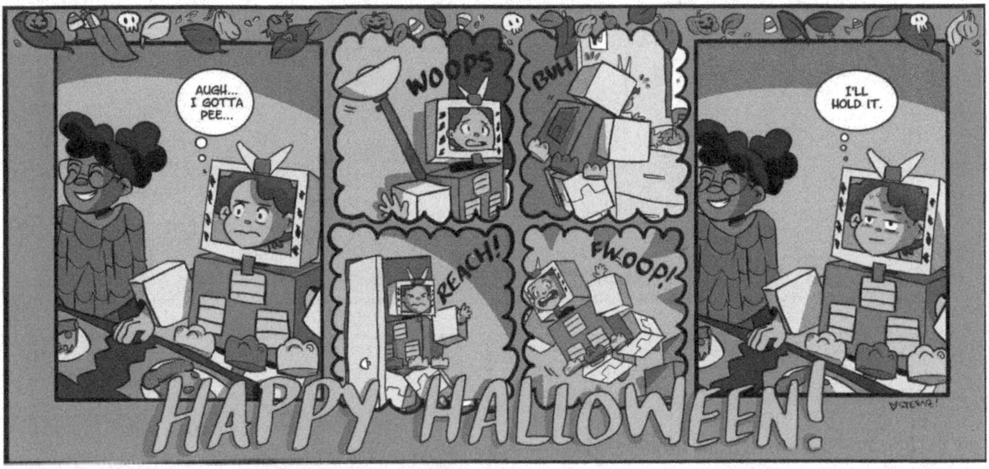
AUGH... I GOTTA PEE...
WOOPS!
BUH
REACH!
FWOOP!
I'LL HOLD IT.
HAPPY HALLOWEEN!

WHAT ABOUT DEAN? HE PROBABLY BROKE THE STAFF TRYING TO USE IT AS A LEG SCRATCHER!

I DON'T THINK SO. THE STAFF IS SO FAR AWAY FROM HIM, AND HE CAN BARELY MOVE IN HIS COSTUME.

DEAN IS BASICALLY USELESS RIGHT NOW.

WELL, HOLD ON. I'M NOT USELESS!

REACH!

YEAH, THERE'S JUST NO WAY.

♡STEENZ!

184

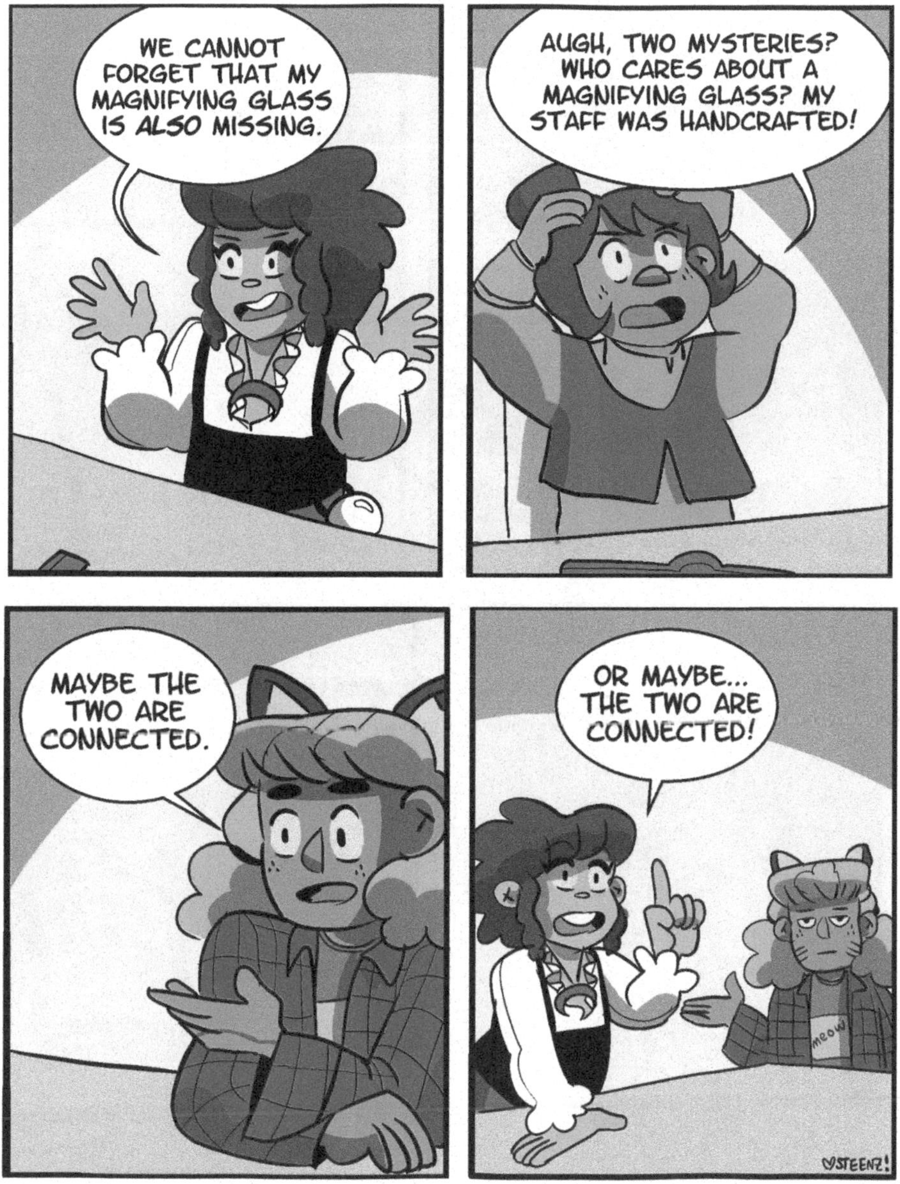
WE CANNOT FORGET THAT MY MAGNIFYING GLASS IS ALSO MISSING.
AUGH, TWO MYSTERIES? WHO CARES ABOUT A MAGNIFYING GLASS? MY STAFF WAS HANDCRAFTED!
MAYBE THE TWO ARE CONNECTED.
OR MAYBE... THE TWO ARE CONNECTED!
meow
STEENZ!

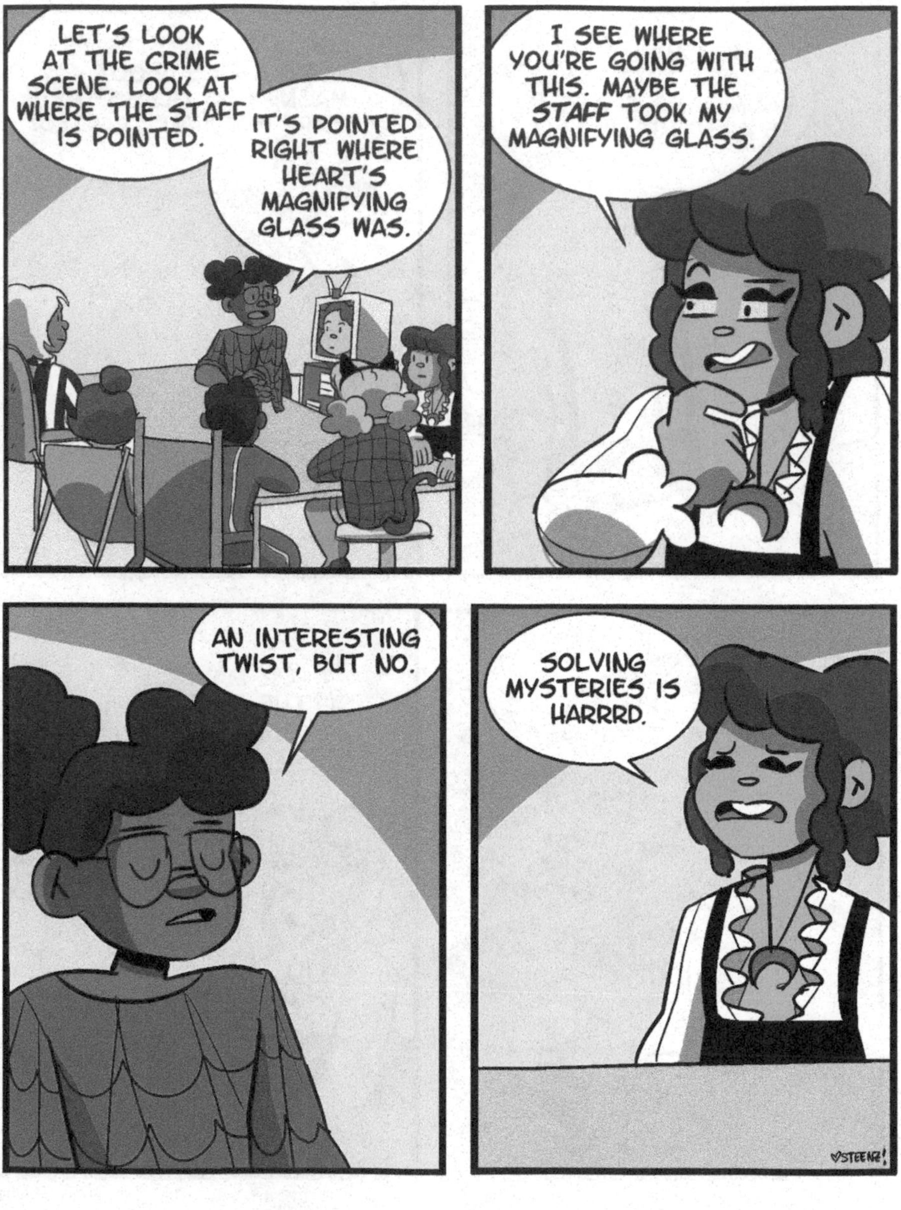
LET'S LOOK AT THE CRIME SCENE. LOOK AT WHERE THE STAFF IS POINTED.
IT'S POINTED RIGHT WHERE HEART'S MAGNIFYING GLASS WAS.
I SEE WHERE YOU'RE GOING WITH THIS. MAYBE THE STAFF TOOK MY MAGNIFYING GLASS.
AN INTERESTING TWIST, BUT NO.
SOLVING MYSTERIES IS HARRRD.
♡STEENZ!

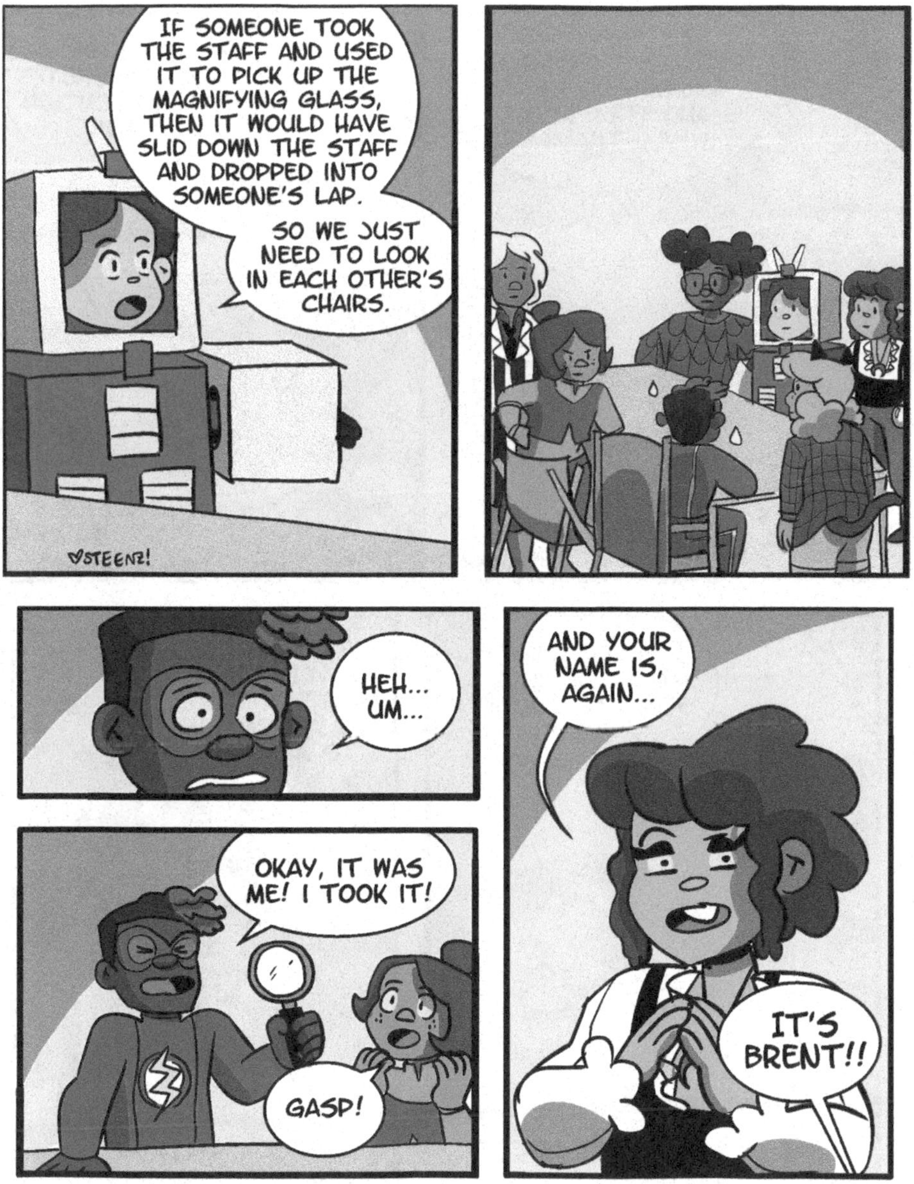
IF SOMEONE TOOK THE STAFF AND USED IT TO PICK UP THE MAGNIFYING GLASS, THEN IT WOULD HAVE SLID DOWN THE STAFF AND DROPPED INTO SOMEONE'S LAP.
SO WE JUST NEED TO LOOK IN EACH OTHER'S CHAIRS.
♡STEENZ!
HEH... UM...
OKAY, IT WAS ME! I TOOK IT!
GASP!
AND YOUR NAME IS, AGAIN...
IT'S BRENT!!

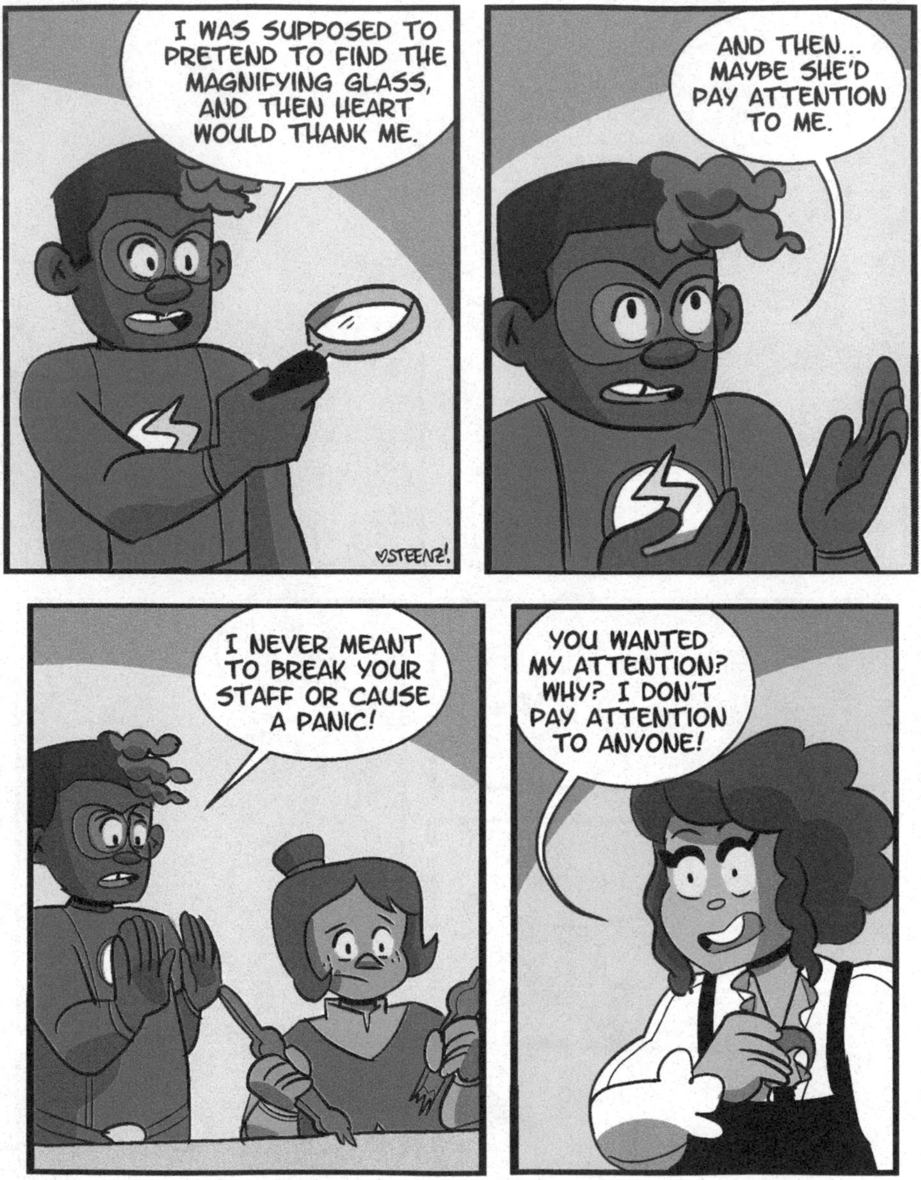
I WAS SUPPOSED TO PRETEND TO FIND THE MAGNIFYING GLASS, AND THEN HEART WOULD THANK ME.
♡STEENZ!
AND THEN... MAYBE SHE'D PAY ATTENTION TO ME.
I NEVER MEANT TO BREAK YOUR STAFF OR CAUSE A PANIC!
YOU WANTED MY ATTENTION? WHY? I DON'T PAY ATTENTION TO ANYONE!

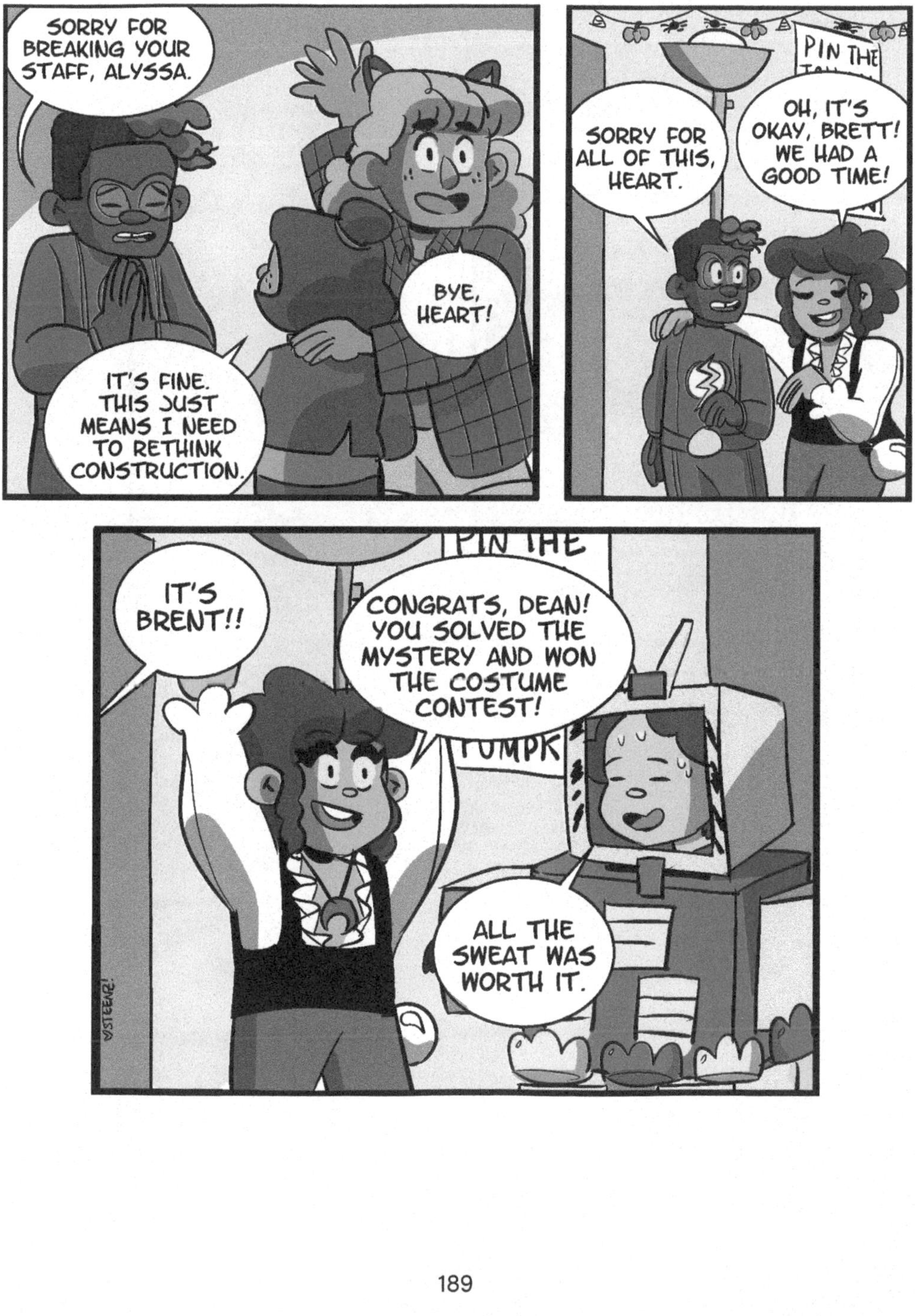
SORRY FOR BREAKING YOUR STAFF, ALYSSA.
BYE, HEART!
IT'S FINE. THIS JUST MEANS I NEED TO RETHINK CONSTRUCTION.
PIN THE
SORRY FOR ALL OF THIS, HEART.
OH, IT'S OKAY, BRETT! WE HAD A GOOD TIME!
PIN THE
IT'S BRENT!!
CONGRATS, DEAN! YOU SOLVED THE MYSTERY AND WON THE COSTUME CONTEST!
ALL THE SWEAT WAS WORTH IT.

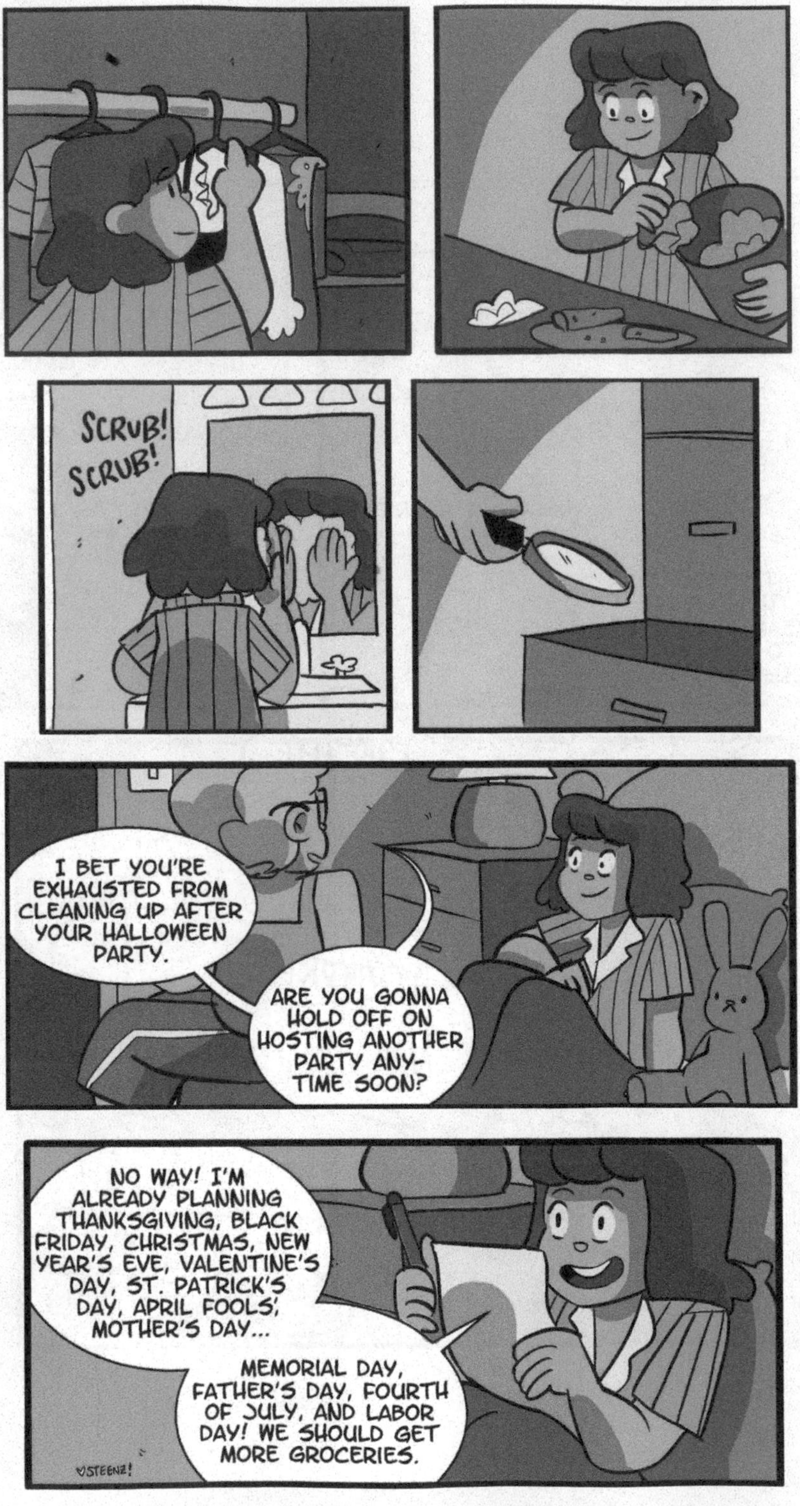
SCRUB!
SCRUB!
I BET YOU'RE EXHAUSTED FROM CLEANING UP AFTER YOUR HALLOWEEN PARTY.
ARE YOU GONNA HOLD OFF ON HOSTING ANOTHER PARTY ANY-TIME SOON?
NO WAY! I'M ALREADY PLANNING THANKSGIVING, BLACK FRIDAY, CHRISTMAS, NEW YEAR'S EVE, VALENTINE'S DAY, ST. PATRICK'S DAY, APRIL FOOLS', MOTHER'S DAY...
MEMORIAL DAY, FATHER'S DAY, FOURTH OF JULY, AND LABOR DAY! WE SHOULD GET MORE GROCERIES.
♡STEENZ!

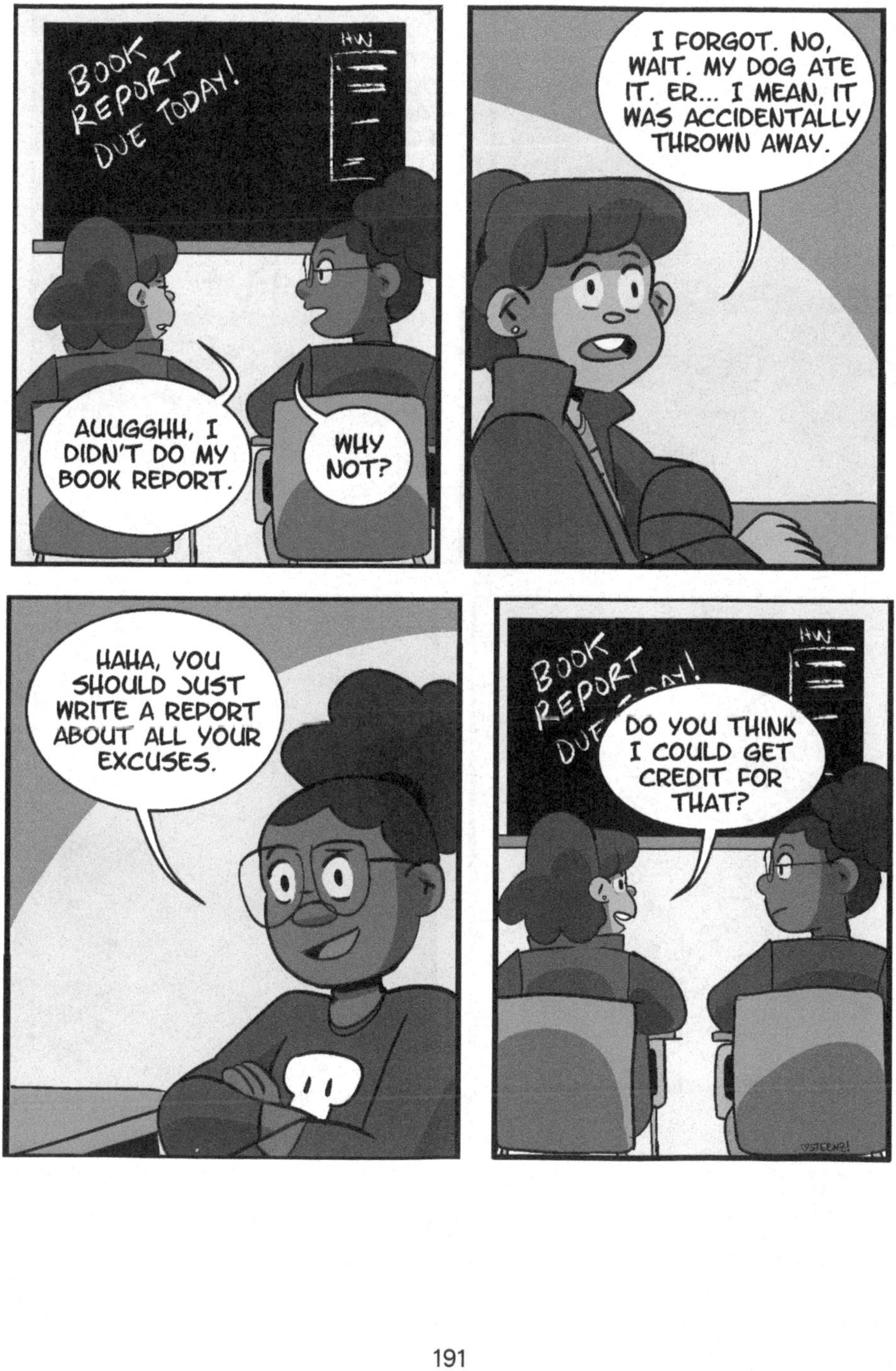
BOOK REPORT DUE TODAY!
HW
AUUGGHH, I DIDN'T DO MY BOOK REPORT.
WHY NOT?
I FORGOT. NO, WAIT. MY DOG ATE IT. ER... I MEAN, IT WAS ACCIDENTALLY THROWN AWAY.
HAHA, YOU SHOULD JUST WRITE A REPORT ABOUT ALL YOUR EXCUSES.
HW
DO YOU THINK I COULD GET CREDIT FOR THAT?

HEART, COME ON UP AND GIVE YOUR BOOK REPORT.
UUHH, CAN I NOT? I WANT TO SAVE MY VOICE FOR PLAY AUDITIONS.
YOU CAN EITHER COME UP AND GIVE YOUR REPORT OR YOU CAN GET DETENTION FOR MISSING, NOW, *TWO* REPORTS.
♡STEENZ!
HMM...
SO I GOT DETENTION.
D

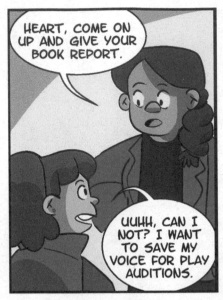

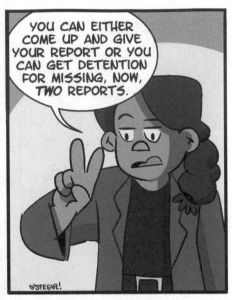

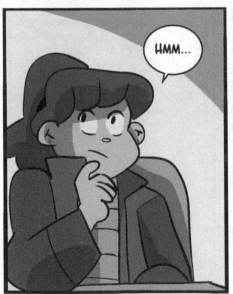

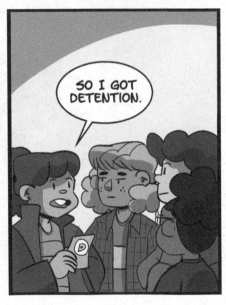

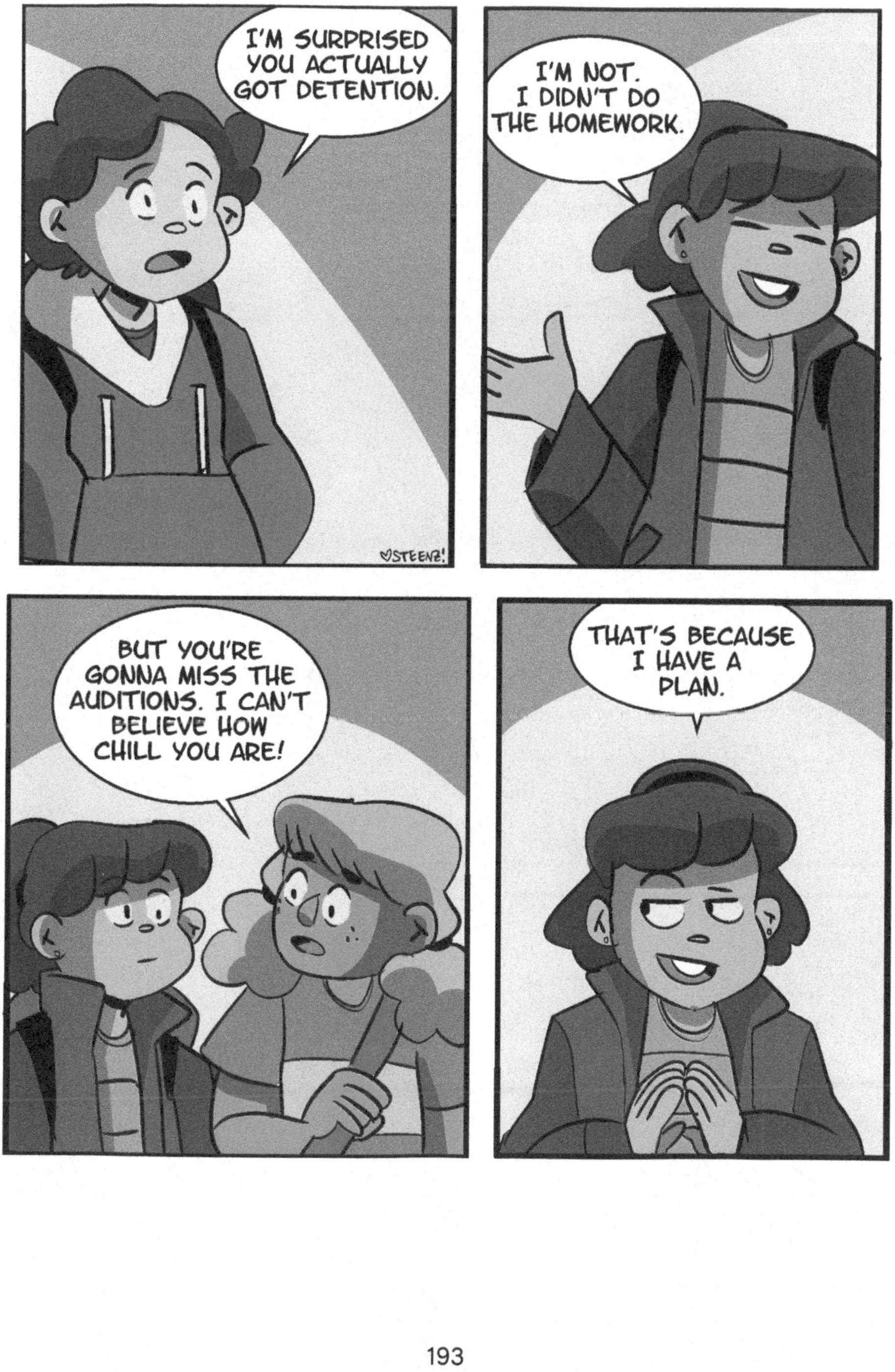
I'M SURPRISED YOU ACTUALLY GOT DETENTION.
♡STEENZ!
I'M NOT. I DIDN'T DO THE HOMEWORK.
BUT YOU'RE GONNA MISS THE AUDITIONS. I CAN'T BELIEVE HOW CHILL YOU ARE!
THAT'S BECAUSE I HAVE A PLAN.

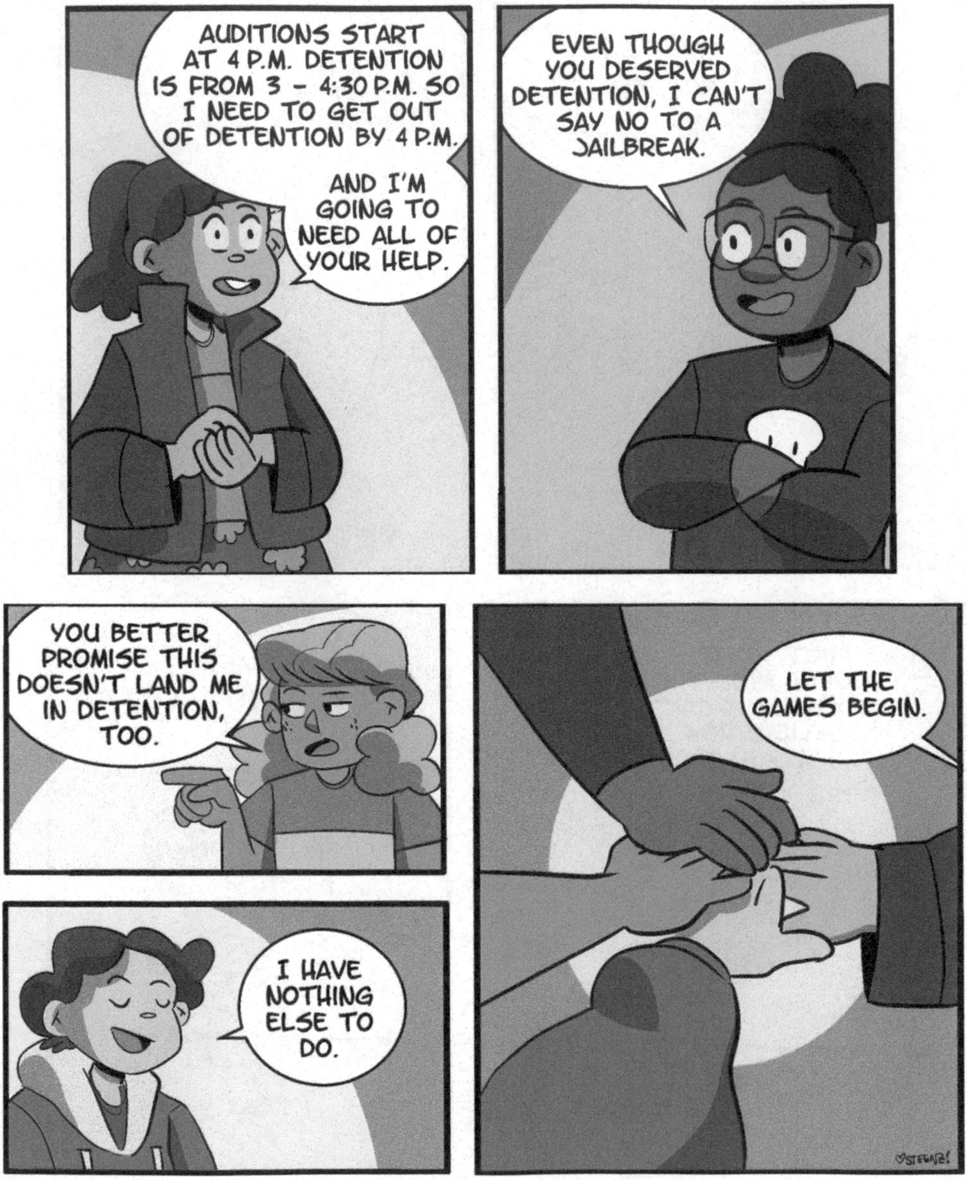
AUDITIONS START AT 4 P.M. DETENTION IS FROM 3 - 4:30 P.M. SO I NEED TO GET OUT OF DETENTION BY 4 P.M.
AND I'M GOING TO NEED ALL OF YOUR HELP.
EVEN THOUGH YOU DESERVED DETENTION, I CAN'T SAY NO TO A JAILBREAK.
YOU BETTER PROMISE THIS DOESN'T LAND ME IN DETENTION, TOO.
I HAVE NOTHING ELSE TO DO.
LET THE GAMES BEGIN.

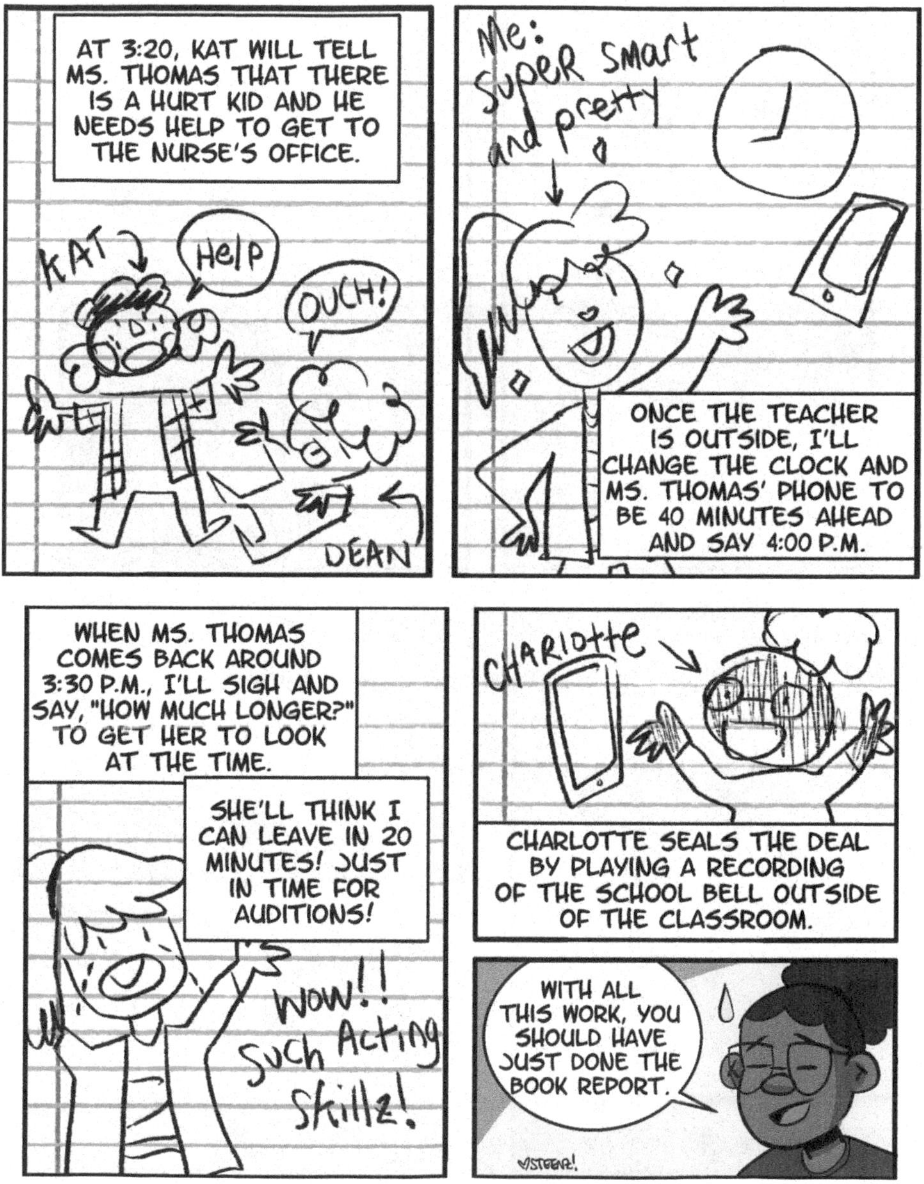
AT 3:20, KAT WILL TELL MS. THOMAS THAT THERE IS A HURT KID AND HE NEEDS HELP TO GET TO THE NURSE'S OFFICE.
KAT
Help
OUCH!
DEAN
Me: Super smart and pretty
ONCE THE TEACHER IS OUTSIDE, I'LL CHANGE THE CLOCK AND MS. THOMAS' PHONE TO BE 40 MINUTES AHEAD AND SAY 4:00 P.M.
WHEN MS. THOMAS COMES BACK AROUND 3:30 P.M., I'LL SIGH AND SAY, "HOW MUCH LONGER?" TO GET HER TO LOOK AT THE TIME.
SHE'LL THINK I CAN LEAVE IN 20 MINUTES! JUST IN TIME FOR AUDITIONS!
Wow!! Such Acting Skillz!
CHARLOTTE
CHARLOTTE SEALS THE DEAL BY PLAYING A RECORDING OF THE SCHOOL BELL OUTSIDE OF THE CLASSROOM.
WITH ALL THIS WORK, YOU SHOULD HAVE JUST DONE THE BOOK REPORT.

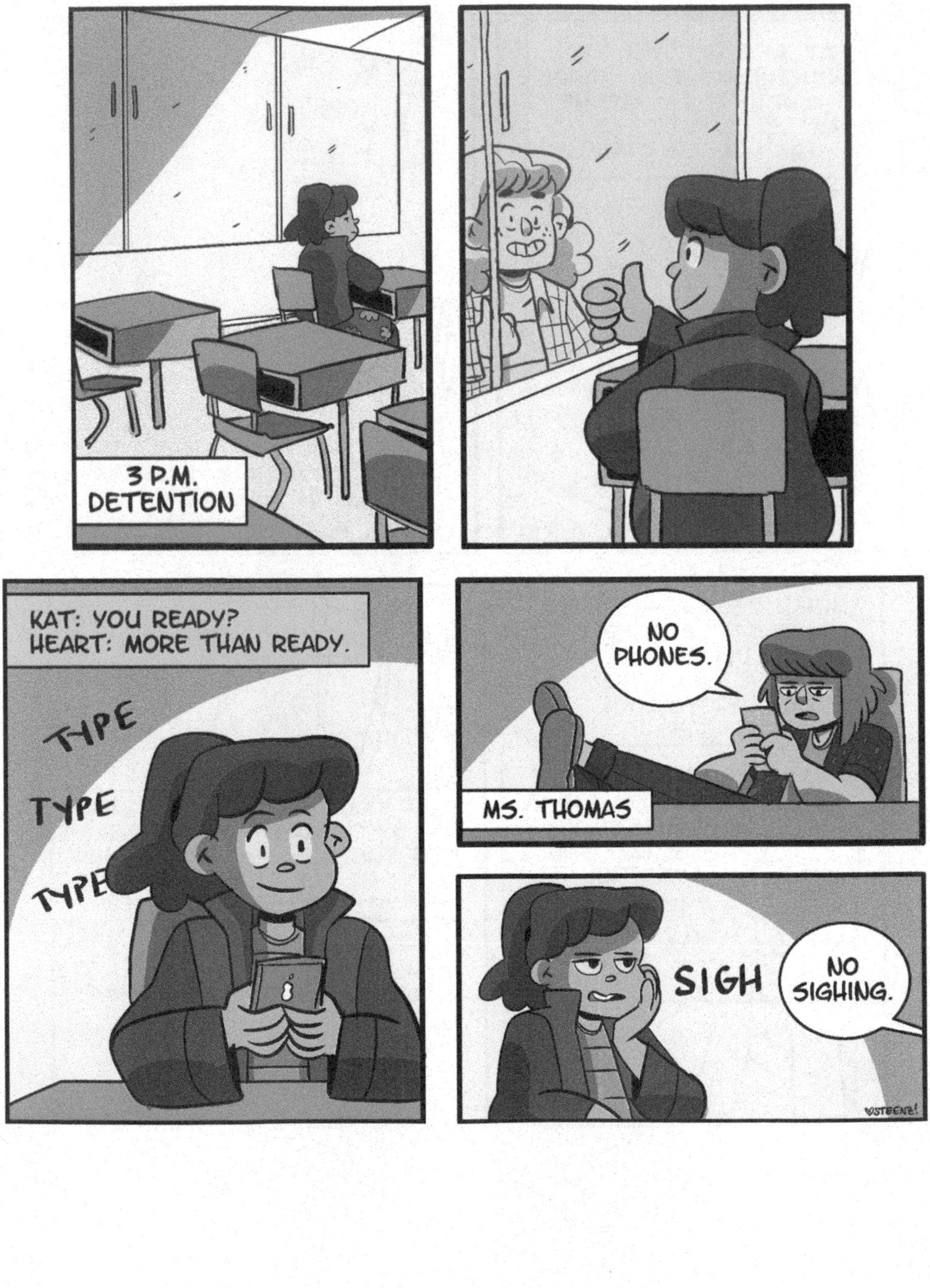
3 P.M.
DETENTION
KAT: YOU READY?
HEART: MORE THAN READY.
TYPE
TYPE
TYPE
NO PHONES.
MS. THOMAS
SIGH
NO SIGHING.
STEENZ!

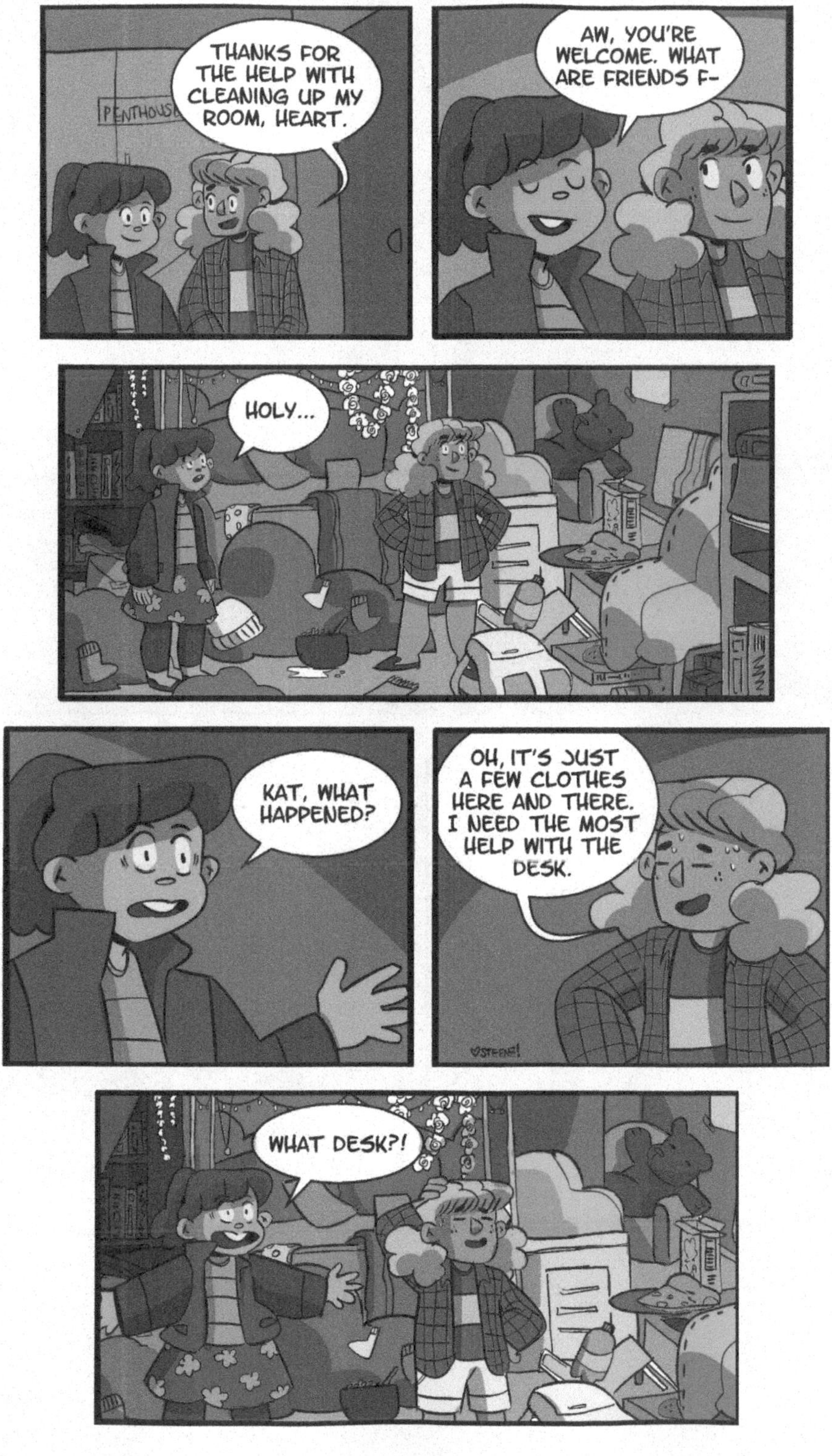
PENTHOUSE
THANKS FOR THE HELP WITH CLEANING UP MY ROOM, HEART.
AW, YOU'RE WELCOME. WHAT ARE FRIENDS F-
HOLY...
KAT, WHAT HAPPENED?
OH, IT'S JUST A FEW CLOTHES HERE AND THERE. I NEED THE MOST HELP WITH THE DESK.
WHAT DESK?!

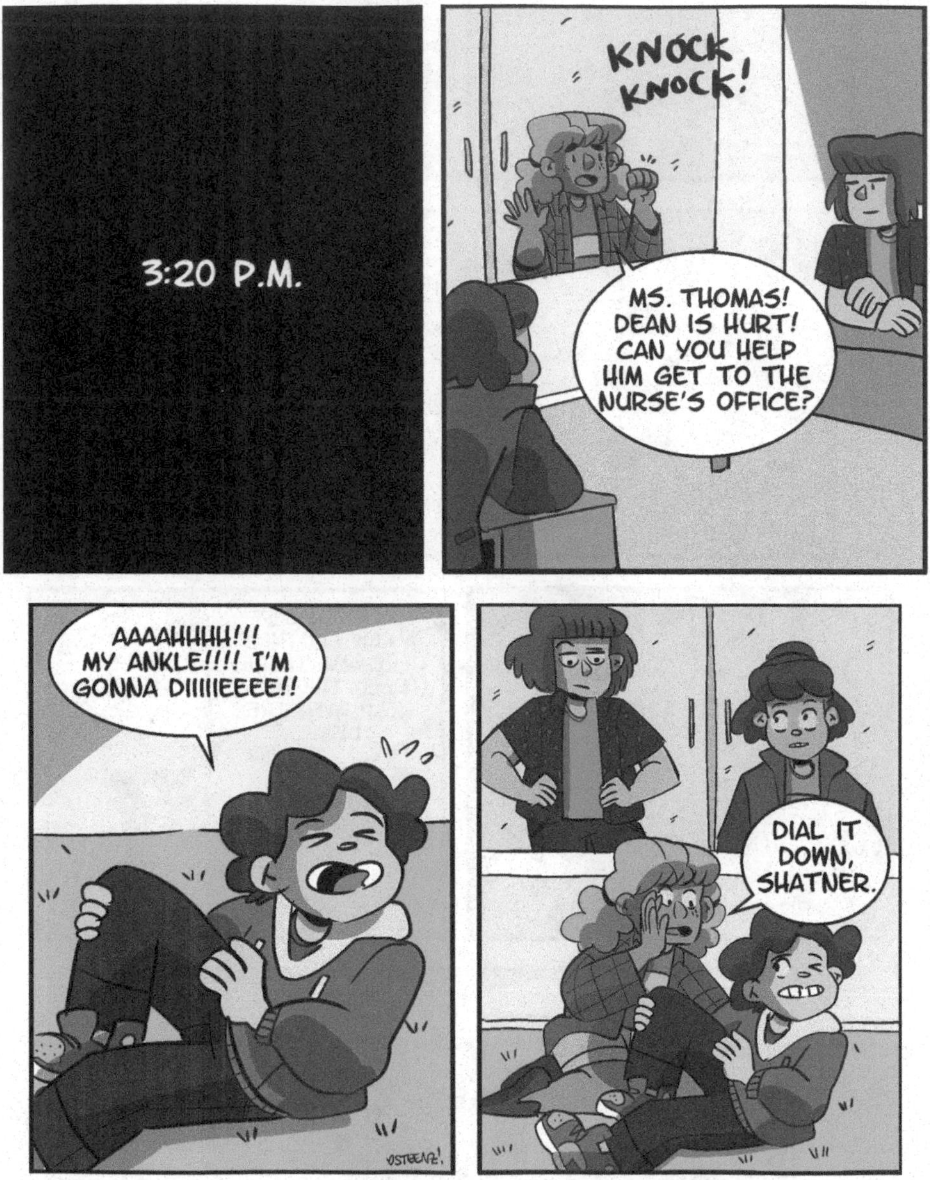
3:20 P.M.
KNOCK KNOCK!
MS. THOMAS! DEAN IS HURT! CAN YOU HELP HIM GET TO THE NURSE'S OFFICE?
AAAAHHHH!!! MY ANKLE!!!! I'M GONNA DIIIIIEEEE!!
DIAL IT DOWN, SHATNER.

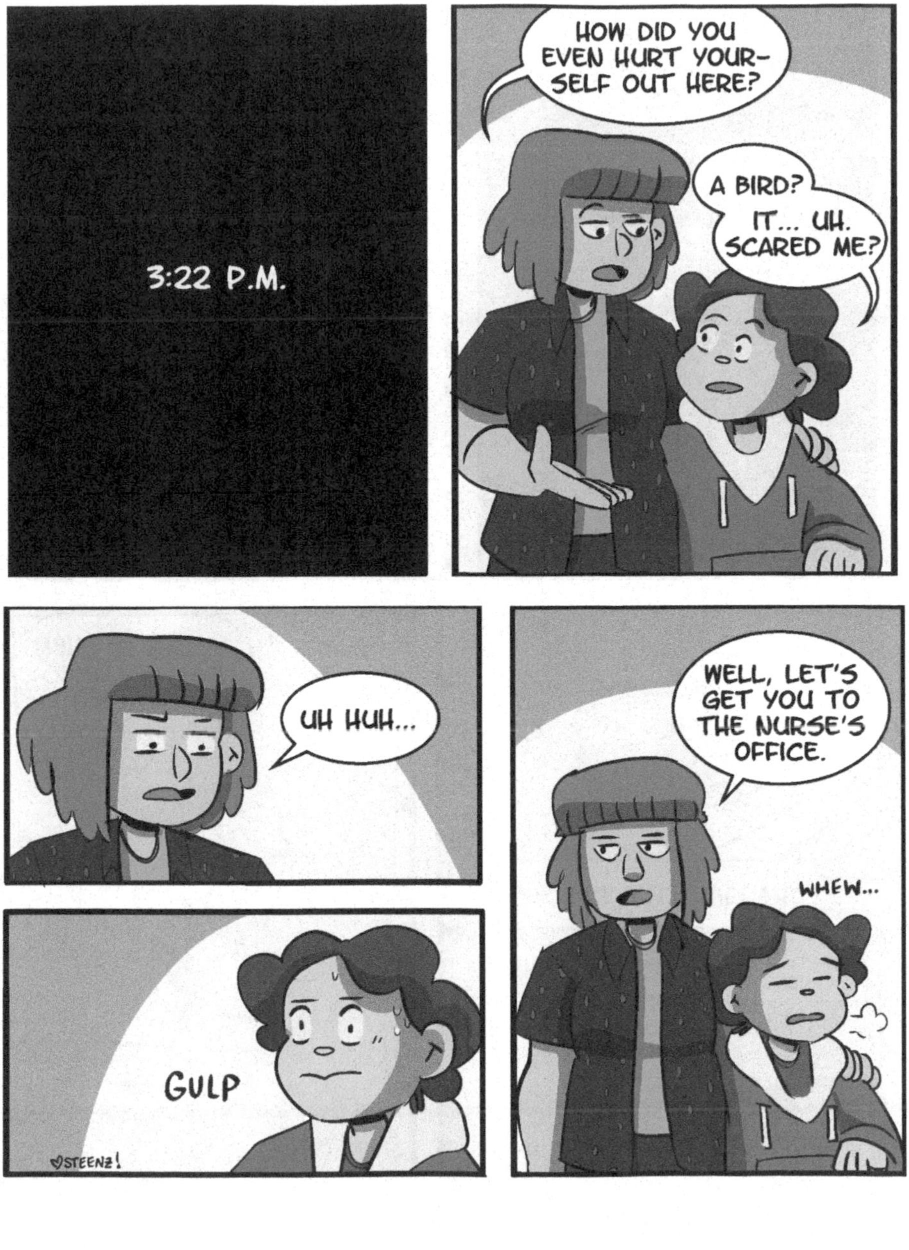
3:22 P.M.
HOW DID YOU EVEN HURT YOURSELF OUT HERE?
A BIRD?
IT... UH. SCARED ME?
UH HUH...
GULP
♡STEENZ!
WELL, LET'S GET YOU TO THE NURSE'S OFFICE.
WHEW...

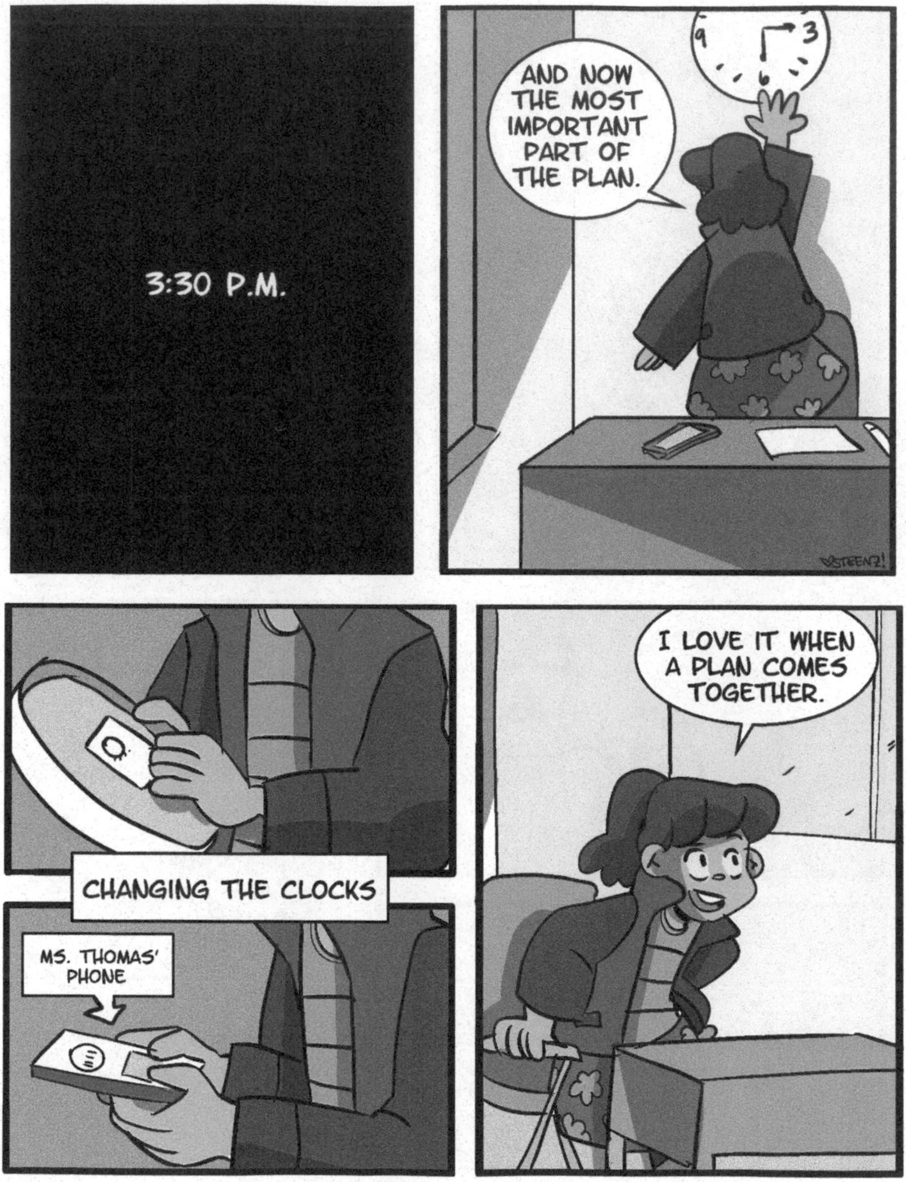
3:30 P.M.
AND NOW THE MOST IMPORTANT PART OF THE PLAN.
CHANGING THE CLOCKS
MS. THOMAS' PHONE
I LOVE IT WHEN A PLAN COMES TOGETHER.

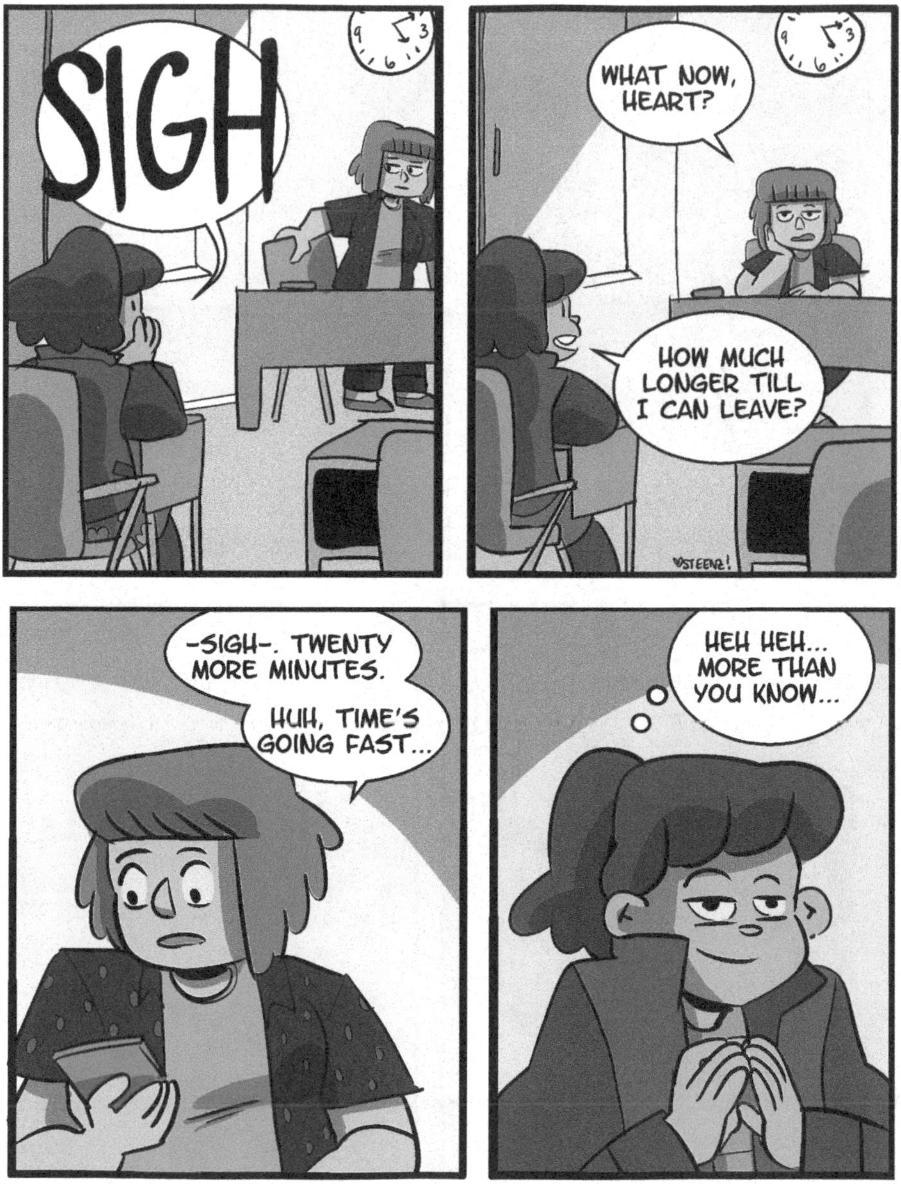
SIGH
WHAT NOW, HEART?
HOW MUCH LONGER TILL I CAN LEAVE?
©STEENZ!
-SIGH-. TWENTY MORE MINUTES.
HUH, TIME'S GOING FAST...
HEH HEH... MORE THAN YOU KNOW...

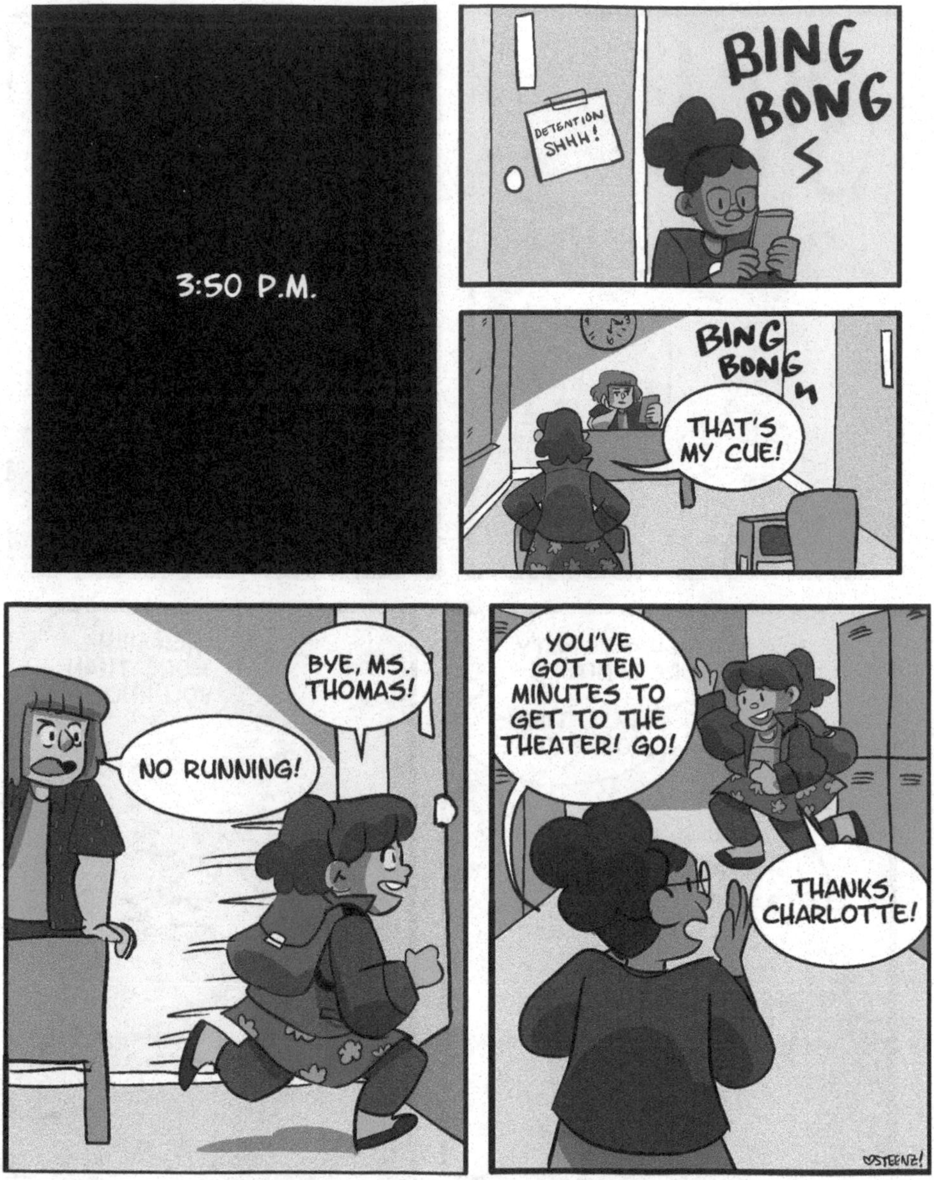
3:50 P.M.
DETENTION SHHH!
BING BONG
BING BONG
THAT'S MY CUE!
BYE, MS. THOMAS!
NO RUNNING!
YOU'VE GOT TEN MINUTES TO GET TO THE THEATER! GO!
THANKS, CHARLOTTE!
STEENZ!

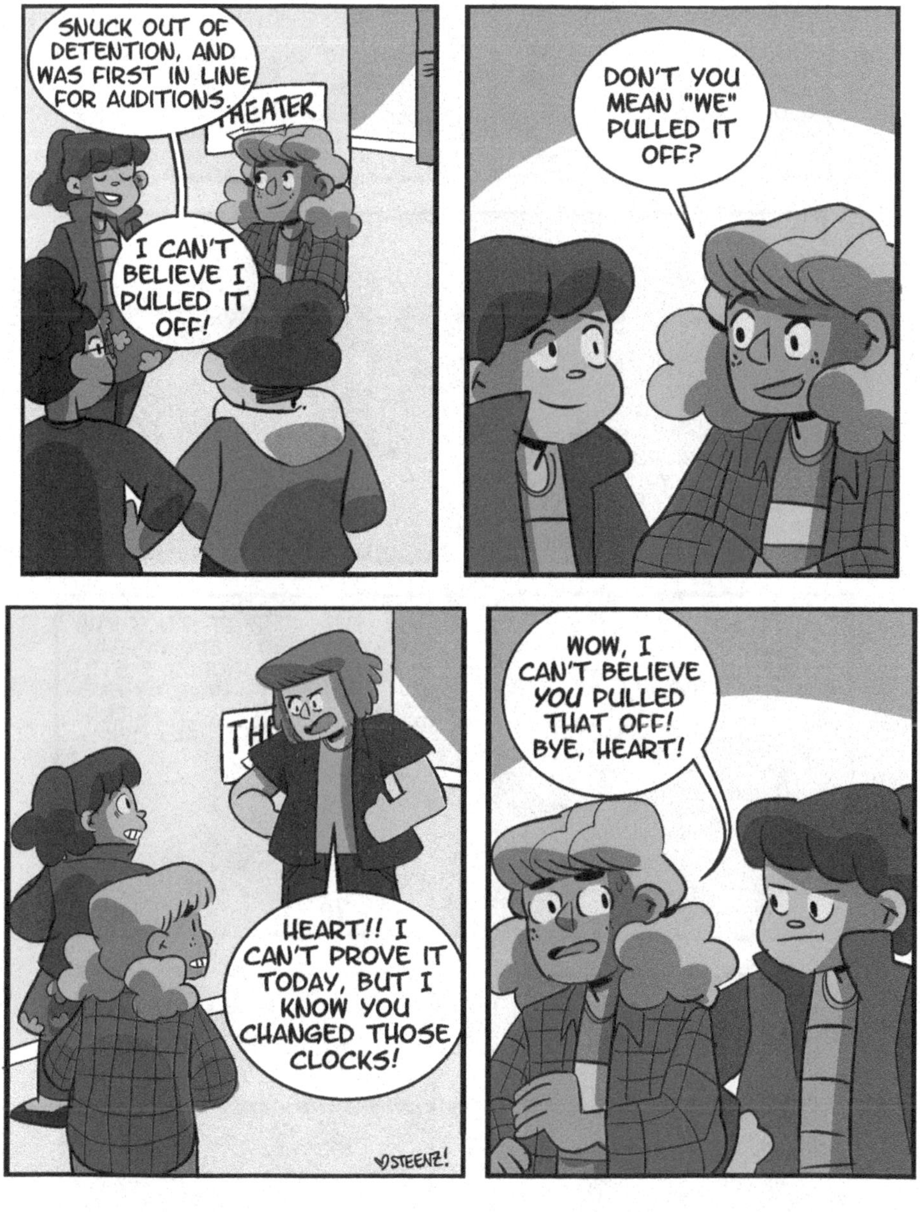
SNUCK OUT OF DETENTION, AND WAS FIRST IN LINE FOR AUDITIONS.
THEATER
I CAN'T BELIEVE I PULLED IT OFF!
DON'T YOU MEAN "WE" PULLED IT OFF?
HEART!! I CAN'T PROVE IT TODAY, BUT I KNOW YOU CHANGED THOSE CLOCKS!
STEENZ!
WOW, I CAN'T BELIEVE YOU PULLED THAT OFF! BYE, HEART!

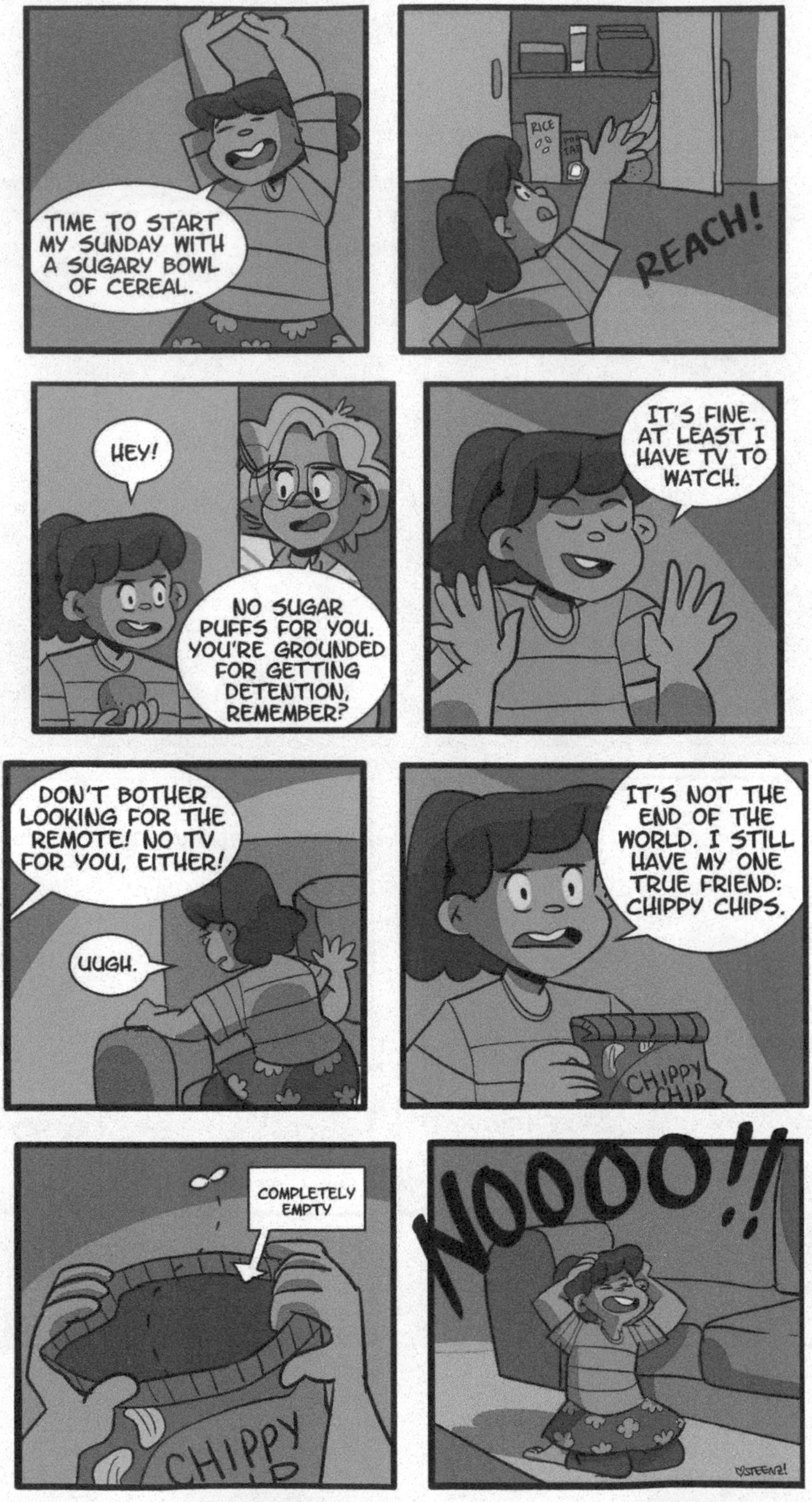

TIME TO START MY SUNDAY WITH A SUGARY BOWL OF CEREAL.
RICE
REACH!
HEY!
NO SUGAR PUFFS FOR YOU. YOU'RE GROUNDED FOR GETTING DETENTION, REMEMBER?
IT'S FINE. AT LEAST I HAVE TV TO WATCH.
DON'T BOTHER LOOKING FOR THE REMOTE! NO TV FOR YOU, EITHER!
UUGH.
IT'S NOT THE END OF THE WORLD. I STILL HAVE MY ONE TRUE FRIEND: CHIPPY CHIPS.
CHIPPY CHIP
COMPLETELY EMPTY
CHIPPY
NOOOO!!

Heart of the City is distributed internationally by Andrews McMeel Syndication.

Andrews McMeel Publishing
a division of Andrews McMeel Universal
1130 Walnut Street, Kansas City, Missouri 64106

www.andrewsmcmeel.com

22 23 24 25 26 SDB 10 9 8 7 6 5 4 3 2 1

ISBN: 978-1-5248-7159-8

Library of Congress Control Number: 2021946301

Made by:
King Yip (Dongguan) Printing & Packaging Factory Ltd.
Address and location of manufacturer:
Daning Administrative District, Humen Town
Dongguan Guangdong, China 523930
1st Printing—1/17/22

Look for these books!

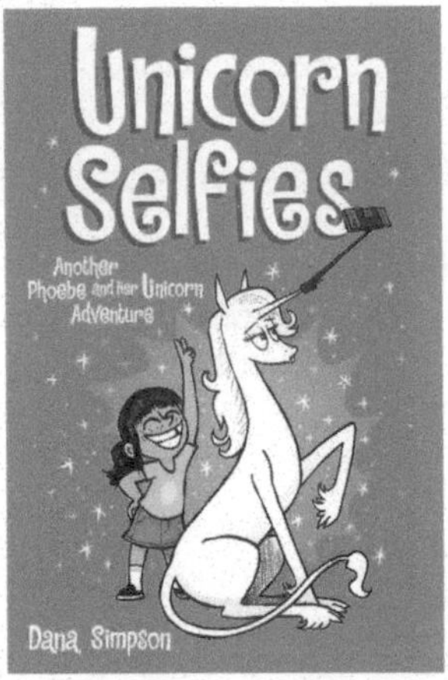
Unicorn Selfies
Another Phoebe and Her Unicorn Adventure
Dana Simpson

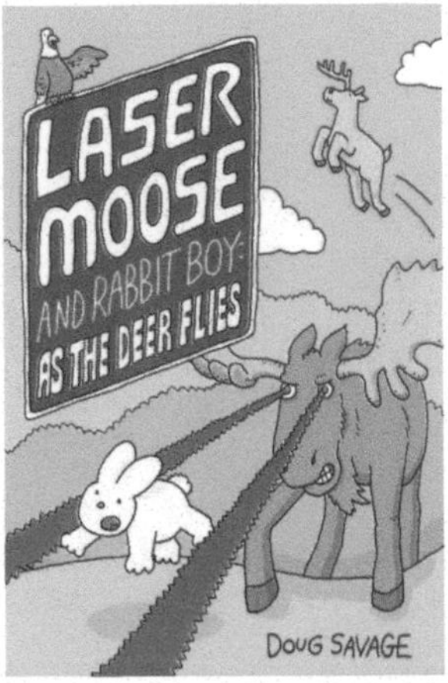
LASER MOOSE AND RABBIT BOY: AS THE DEER FLIES
DOUG SAVAGE

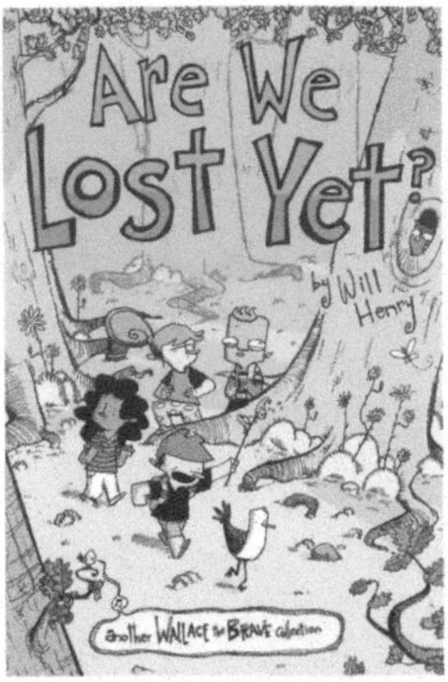
Are We Lost Yet?
by Will Henry
another WALLACE the BRAVE collection

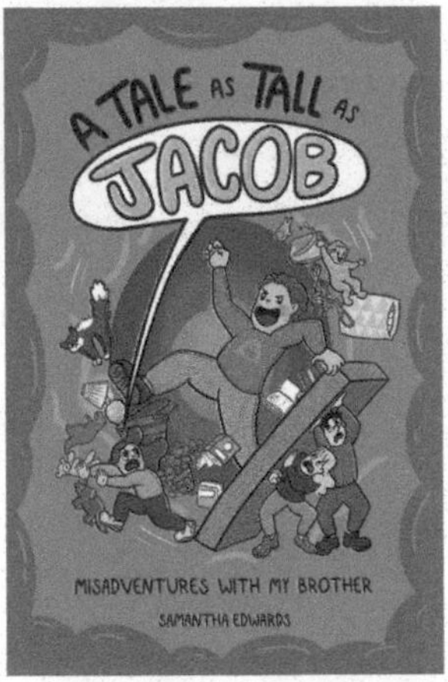
A TALE AS TALL AS JACOB
MISADVENTURES WITH MY BROTHER
SAMANTHA EDWARDS

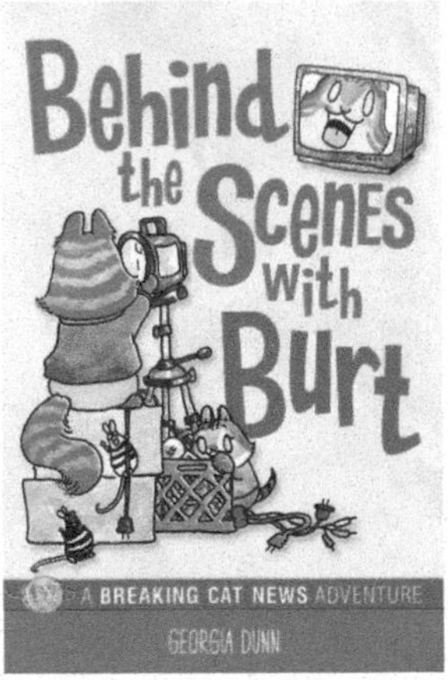
Behind the Scenes with Burt
A BREAKING CAT NEWS ADVENTURE
GEORGIA DUNN

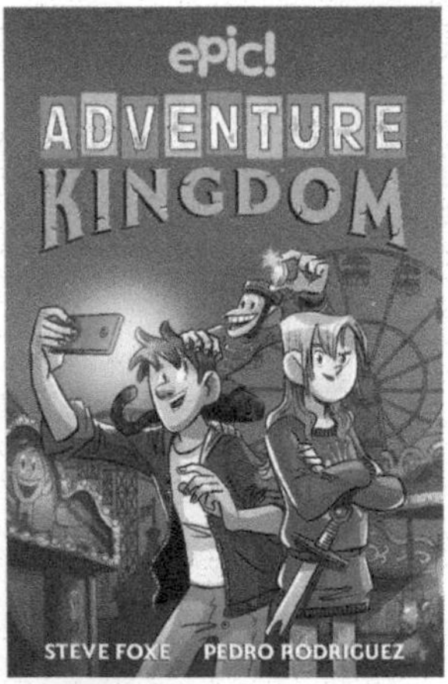
epic!
ADVENTURE KINGDOM
STEVE FOXE
PEDRO RODRIGUEZ

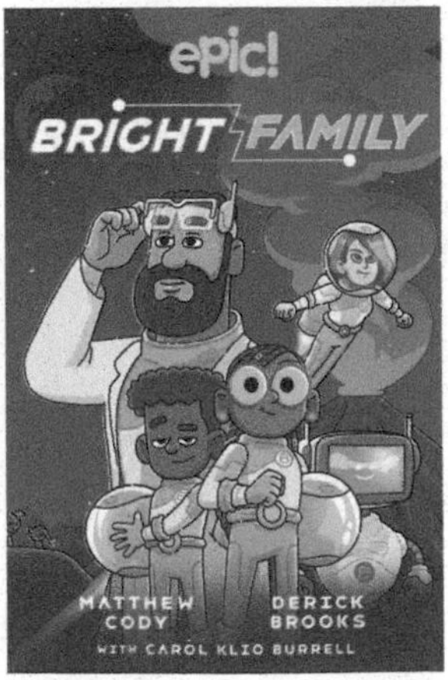
epic!
BRIGHT FAMILY
MATTHEW CODY
DERICK BROOKS
WITH CAROL KLIO BURRELL

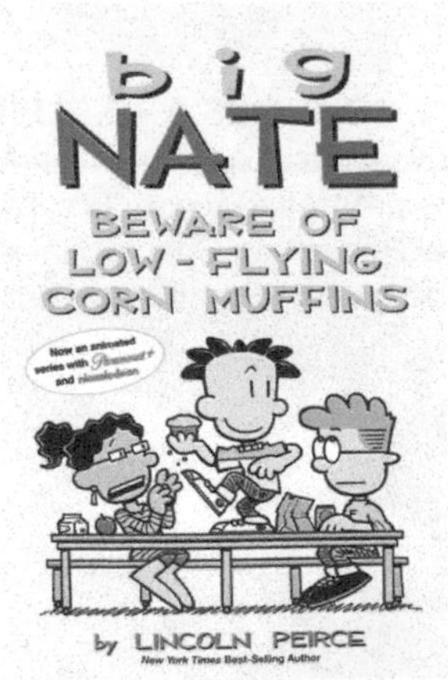
big NATE
BEWARE OF LOW-FLYING CORN MUFFINS
by LINCOLN PEIRCE
New York Times Best-Selling Author

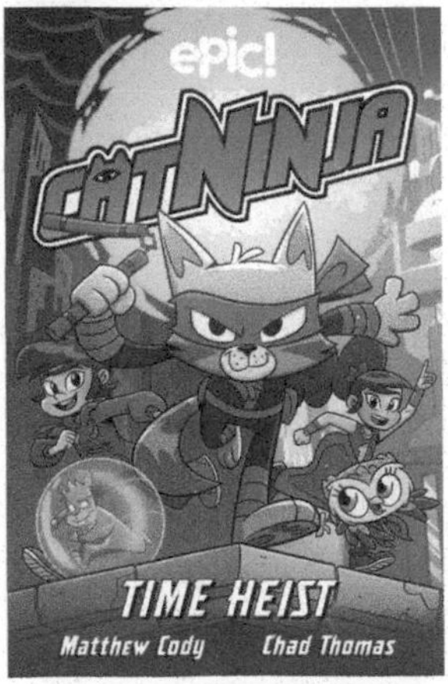
epic!
CATNINJA
TIME HEIST
Matthew Cody
Chad Thomas